The Edge of Justice

Anniversary Edition

a novel about the application

of

ethics and morality

by

Robert Luis Rabello

Dedicated to the glory of God,
who blesses me with every good gift,

and to my devoted wife, Benita Madaline

Robert Luis Rabello

Aldergrove, British Columbia
December 2001

Dramatis Personae

Dathan Herulus: Conscientious Azgar officer

Sergeant Aransen: Dathan's most trusted sergeant

Lieutenant Hicks: Dathan's right-hand officer

Lieutenant Rangell: Dathan's engineering officer

Legate Braegan: Dathan's commanding officer

Vice General Diabilos: Legate Braegan's commanding officer

Lord General Balinor: Commander, Azgar Northern Liberation Army

Brenna Velez: Daughter of Lord Lynden and Lady Alexina

Woodwind: Captain of Lord Lynden's personal guard

Garrick Ravenwood: Tamarian Junior Scout

Jan Bordmann: Garrick's best friend

Sergeant Streckert: Tamarian Defense Force

Colonel Brandt: Tamarian Defense Force

PFC Darrold Braun: Tamarian Defense Force

Colonel Brandt: Commander, Dead Hand Ridge, Tamarian Defense Force

Mrs. Mikkels: owner of an inn, located in Dieter, Tamaria

Heinz Neergard: Civil Defense Liaison in Dieter, Tamaria

Lynden and Alexina Velez: Wealthy Lithian refugees

Acacia, Cynthia and Camille: Lord Lynden and Lady Alexina's daughters

Tegene, son of Asabi: Commander of Lord Lynden's army; a close friend

Kimoni, Xola, and Jawara: sons of Tegene; friends of the Velez family

Sherman Mason: Lord Lynden's chief engineer

Alonso Meta: Mayor of Helena, a small town in Northeastern Kameron

Nemesio Fang: a Kamerese warlord

Illithia

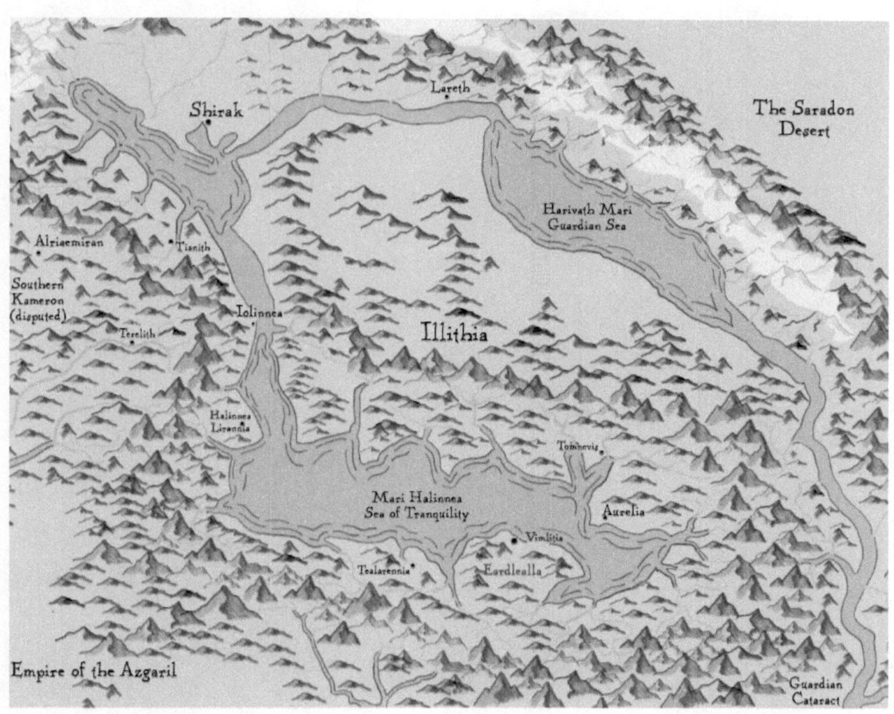

The Empire of the Azgaril

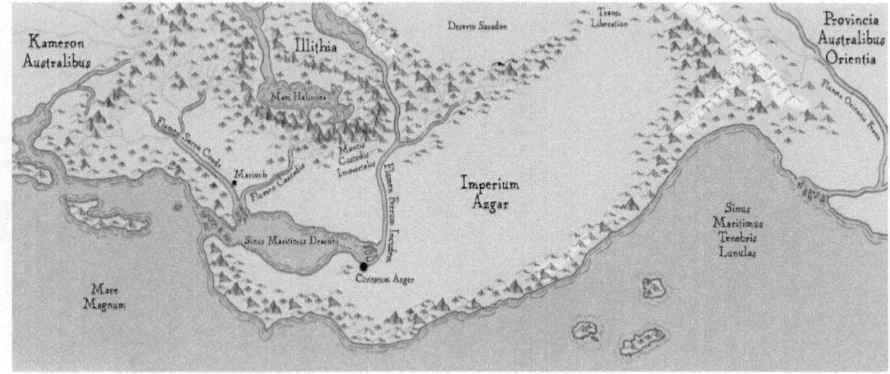

Tamaria and Northern Kameron

City of Fire

Clouds of bright red dust, mingled with hot, steamy smoke settled like a suffocating veil into my trench, coating my sweat-glistened arms with gritty powder. To my right, forty-five young men, many of whom had never fired a shot in anger, awaited nervously. Some coughed, others cursed, while a few prayed to obscure, small-town gods, or even the emperor himself. I didn't bother with prayers. I'd long ago given up on faith and forgotten how to pray.

The moment before me had haunted my dreams, occupying the free space of idle time, drifting through my existence like a lazy river in midsummer. I believed that my training and intellect could make a difference; that my destiny lay in changing the world, rather than ordering a mass of marginally insolent, bored recruits to carry out a shouting centurion's bidding.

We'd marched for weeks with little rest. Our journey began in the heat of the far south, gradually transforming into a miserable slog over rainforest-covered ridges. We swatted swarms of mosquitoes while living in a slimy, red muck that sucked the soles of our boots as we walked. Mud stained our fatigues and stuck to every speck of unprotected skin. Biting insects, interminable midsummer rain, heat, and high humidity sapped morale as we fought a retreating enemy. Now, with our objective in sight, we hoped this wretched campaign might soon meet its end.

Overhead, the shrieking of artillery shells faded as the proud battlements around the Lithian city of Shirak finally succumbed to our terrible pounding. A spectacular explosion showered the trembling ground with slivers of splintered stone. Through the haze I could see many wide breaches in the crumbling wall. A trumpet call rang out across the battlefield, followed by a tremendous roar as thousands of men's voices aspired in a unified war cry.

"Let's go! Let's go!" I screamed above the din, scrambling out of the sodden trench, racing toward the enemy with conviction driven by adrenaline. My legs pumped, my heart pounded, and my lungs burned from inhaling smoke; yet other, faster men more willing to die, surpassed me.

How the skinny vermin on the other side survived our shelling I'll never know, but they were still alive and waiting. Speeding silently through swirling fog flashed wickedly well-aimed arrows. Many brave men stumbled in mid-stride, screaming in torment as sharp ceramic-edged steel tore through their skin. I witnessed the slaughter of young men who would never again know a loving caress, the fine delight of friendship or the comfort of home. Most of our first wave fell face-first into the rain-drenched and shell-cratered ground. Fighting back unspoken terror I raced forward, hoping desperately that I would not be found among their number.

Before me loomed a shattered stone wall, its angular face designed to deflect catapult shots, battering rams and obsolete cannon balls. No proud stone could turn back our modern, high explosive shells. Its ruin, sealed from the order that brought our big guns forward, foreshadowed the demise of many nations that would fall into our hands, once we'd finished our work in this hell of heat and endless green. At that moment, however, I believed that this assault comprised the final act of a long and bloody drama.

I staggered toward shelter, coughing from the exertion and smoke, squatting down to recover near a shattered stone block. Sergeant Aransen, my favorite NCO, a veteran of many campaigns, began clustering enlisted troops into five-man squads, ordering bayonets fixed. Our advance, covered by an endless rain of gunfire from the trenches, stalled dangerously as we picked our way through a smoldering debris field.

Regaining my breath and evaluating the stiff resistance, I realized we might get pushed back if we didn't advance. "First squad," I shouted, "through the breach! Second squad, fire support on the left flank! Move! Now!"

Obediently my team responded. Within a single step, the point man dropped to the ground as an enemy arrow found its deadly mark. As he fell, another soldier stepped forward. The second group opened fire at the unseen sniper as I sent in the third and fourth, until our numbers overwhelmed opposition.

With our toehold established my unit and thousands more on our flanks, streamed through the broken walls like the tide of a rising flood, preceded by a rain of artillery, profanity, and bullets. The sight inspired my pride, but my confidence didn't long survive.

Beyond the shelling damage near its walls, Shirak looked unlike any city I'd ever seen – dense with trees, lacking much open space. As my eyes adjusted to the gloom, I realized that the Lithian savages lived in buildings crafted out of tight-fitting stones between thick, vine-covered trees. These custom-shaped structures perfectly fit the surrounding foliage. Graceful, gated archways led into manicured, private gardens, complete with obscene, ceramic fountains – evidence of how the immodest and lascivious Lithians enjoyed displaying nudity. Their stone walls mingled with living palisades of watered plants, extending two and three levels high into the trees.

Cautiously moving into the deep shadows of the multi-layered forest, we followed narrow, well-worn stone paths, bordered on both sides by ferns, mosses and other varieties of light-hating plants. Between the battle smoke and infernal gloom, I struggled to see where we were going. My compass spun crazily as I followed Lithian trails, slick with slime and rain that snaked through the city in a twisting, undulating maze of intersecting circles.

I'd formed my men into three units of fifteen soldiers, spaced apart by about twenty paces, with Sergeant Aransen up front controlling the first squad. I remained with the second group, leaving the third for Sergeant Laredimus – a tobacco chewer whose incessant spitting inspired my desire to keep him well behind me.

Confusion reigned in the twilight. Gunfire, gloom, the stench of loosened bowels and a sense of impending death, punctuated by the occasional whine of a stray artillery shell and the rumble of its subsequent explosion, isolated my senses from awareness of the larger battle lumbering around me. We plunged deeper into the alien city, losing contact with other squadrons.

The Lithians didn't attack us directly. Their armies no longer offered organized resistance, but instead, relied on ambush and stealth. Death arrived suddenly, silently and mysteriously as hidden snipers selected their targets, then slipped away into the darkness. We shot at shadows, sending concentrated volleys of lead in their general direction until I figured we'd driven off the threat.

Despite encountering many enemy casualties, the sniping intensified. Among the dead warrior bucks we also found Lithian cows, many dressed in gossamer silk and thin, transparent material, while others – perhaps older ones – littered the ground in more modest clothing. The ones we learned to fear were the *Black Widows* – cows dressed entirely in black. Their fearless, savage attacks with bows and swords sharp enough to cut through gun barrels dramatically raised the butcher's bill with every encounter. We cheered whenever we killed one of them.

The Lithians weren't alone in resisting us. We'd been told that traitorous Abelscinnians – big, dark-skinned people from the east – had joined their ranks. They fought with skill, using modern rifles, grenades and mortars, but they weren't as fanatical as the *Black Widows*.

Our battle, a taxing ritual of entering and investigating every building, flushing out snipers and evading traps, inspired increasing frustration as the enemy continually faded away from conflict. Their amorphous resistance steadily drained ammunition to the extent that I started limiting return fire to conserve bullets. By the time noon arrived I'd lost eight men, and the rest of my troops grew increasingly edgy.

We found trinkets, a few coins and alabaster or jade furniture, stepping over mangled corpses of the elderly, naked children mutilated by shrapnel, and anyone who dared oppose our entry. We couldn't use the more modern Abelscinnian guns because the ammo we carried wasn't compatible, but stripped the dead of their knives and swords as Lithian metallurgy surpassed our own in quality.

Roughly three hours into the battle a messenger arrived. He cursed profoundly that we'd been so hard to find, then breathlessly recited an order from my commander, demanding we push north to a certain plaza. Our century needed reinforcements in a hurry . . . .

Curiously, after passing on the orders to my sergeants, I noticed a lift in the men's spirits – enthusiasm spread with the anticipation of coordinated action. Finding this plaza, however, proved complex. We couldn't march there in a straight line. Deep gloom, the contradictory, deceptive battle sounds, my malfunctioning compass and an unfamiliar landscape confused everyone. We were soon lost, and I became impatient. I had not come here to fail.

Sergeant Laredimus, sensing my frustration, quietly suggested that we send a small scouting party ahead to map out the best approach, moving the main group only when we were certain that the chosen path did not backtrack. This sounded like a good idea. I picked my most reliable men, noting that their compasses weren't working either, but sent them off, hoping for success.

As our progress slowed my patience wore thin. Eventually, we arrived at a crossroads, a clearing where several paths intersected at odd angles. A fountain of jade and obsidian, carved indecently in naked male and female figures playing harps and woodwind instruments, lay at the center of this intersection. I paused to let the men refresh themselves while I tried to figure out where to go. I discreetly discussed the navigational problem with my sergeants, anxious to arrive where ordered, hoping to avoid more embarrassment.

Without warning, something very bright flashed around us, blinding our eyes in brilliant light. Female voices, speaking strange words, called fire out of thin air and directed it toward my soldiers, several of whom were completely engulfed in unquenchable flame.

"Hold your fire!" I screamed, trying to prevent the men from wasting ammunition, not understanding that the infernal Lithian magic had cooked off our ammunition packs and ignited loaded muskets spontaneously.

Over the din I heard more voices speaking the strange, musical language of the Lithians. The water in the fountain thickened and came alive. With great speed, it divided into multiple streams that gushed forward, each seeking a man's face, including mine.

It coiled around my flailing hands and wrapped around my neck when I turned my back – its force so powerful I could offer no effective resistance. My body slammed against the unyielding cobblestones. Water clung to my flesh, hammered in my ears, crawled into my mouth and nose, reaching down my throat like a malevolent serpent. I coughed, spat and rolled in agony, resisting death as I fought the urge to inhale. Nothing in my life had ever terrified me like this. Unable to breathe, blinded and defenseless, I faced the incredible prospect of drowning while laying on solid ground.

Just before I believed I would surely die, the water slithered back into the fountain. My heart pounded. I could hold my breath no longer, but when I gasped for air, my lungs functioned perfectly. I pushed myself upright, noting not even a drop of moisture on my skin, my uniform or the surrounding ground. Mysteriously, the fountain lay quiet once more.

Fear lingered in the eyes of every survivor.

Those of us who had not drowned endured the stench of cooked flesh and screaming as the magic fire continued burning. In an effort to save a friend, one man dunked his helmet into the fountain and tried to quench the fire, but the water simply recoiled and raced back from whence it came. When another tried to snuff out the flames with a blanket from his pack, he too, caught fire. It seemed that those destined to die in this place would die, while the rest of us watched, helplessly.

No new and clever leadership ideas came to mind. I felt like a complete failure. One by one, my burning soldiers succumbed to their fate. I watched them perish, knowing I could do nothing to save them. Their screams still echo in my memory . . . .

For want of a better idea I ordered all survivors fifteen paces away from the fountain, trying to mask my own panic by acting like I knew what I was doing. "Form up and count off!" I ordered, facing the water nervously. "Eyes on me!" I hoped that if the water erupted again, we would be wiser to have our backs to it.

Everyone felt unnerved by the fire, the fountain experience and the nauseating reek of burning bodies. A few men coughed, hacked, spit, retched and shivered, while others, glancing backward, grimaced. I worried they would blame me for getting lost and leading them here. Then, cursing profoundly, I added, "There's nothing you can do for them now."

That truth still haunts me.

Anxious to move onward, I sent the men across a creek and had Sergeant Aransen reassemble the seventeen survivors on its far bank before continuing on our way. I lingered to take up the trailing position, my eyes fixed upon a scene that inspired nightmares for months to come.

The rain resumed. My men fell into sullen silence, slogging along in wet boots that chafed their skin raw. I checked the compass again, wondering if other lieutenants performed with equal ineptitude, or whether my inability to inspire confidence indicated a personal problem. Thus far, my singular success consisted of leading men to pointless, painful deaths. The possibility that such a thing might happen under my command had never crossed my mind.

Sergeant Aransen waited for me. "Buck up, lieutenant," he warned, discretely. "You still have soldiers to lead. If they see you wringing your hands like an old woman, they'll start acting like old women too."

I bristled at the comment, but Aransen, a veteran of the coastal islands campaign, had survived some of the worst fighting any Azgar army had ever encountered, and I trusted him.

We never found the plaza. Almost two hours later, we couldn't even hear the battle anymore, and even the most dim-witted recruit realized that we'd become utterly lost. Hungry and footsore, we paused in an area dominated by large, empty villas surrounded by towering, moss-covered walls. Swarms of biting insects rose from their nesting puddles in welcome as we settled near the silent stones to eat cold rations and offer our blood to the bugs.

Just as I rose to move on again, one of the recruits approached me with an ornate dagger, its fishtail-patterned hilt adorned with turquoise and gold filigree. The beautiful weapon featured a hyper-sharp, ferro-ceramic blade. Curious, I inquired, "Where did you find this?"

"That house," he said, pointing to a gated structure behind him. "There's probably more stuff left. Backrin and Gehenoff went in further than I did."

I counted the men around me, only fifteen, and made a mental note to give these three a sound chewing out for wandering off, thinking the scolding would have to wait for another time. As I was mulling over my list of favored obscenities, I heard a stray shot and a distinctively male scream from inside the building. Some of the Lithians had guns, but this sounded like one of ours.

"Come with me," I ordered, signaling for the others to follow, pointing to where I wanted support squads to assemble. The troops followed my lead and I suddenly forgot about my confidence problem, plunging inside with my bayonet ready.

Private Backrin crouched at the base of a magnificent stone staircase that spiraled up to the next floor. He suffered obvious grief, clutching his right wrist, biting hard on his lower lip to avoid crying out again. I inspected the damage, and although little daylight penetrated the house, I could see that a very sharp blade had cut quite easily through his leather glove, slicing flesh to the extent that bone appeared beneath the exposed sinew and muscle.

"Get Sivestri up here!" I ordered, calling for our medic. The bleeding seemed serious, darkening the cowhide glove that Backrin could not bring himself to remove.

"What happened?" I inquired.

He wouldn't meet my gaze, trembling with shame. "We saw light, heard voices, and found a girl in there," he began. "She's dressed like a whore, and we thought . . . . Well, we didn't think she could fight."

"Lith cow!" I muttered, grateful that she wasn't a *Black Widow.* "Where's Gehenoff?"

"Upstairs," Backrin replied. "Be careful, lieutenant. She's got a bow and she's a damn good shot."

I arose to ascend the stairs but Sergeant Aransen put his hand on my shoulder, stopping me. He sent two privates up first. "We need you, sir," he warned.

Once the lead man reached the top step I saw him panic, raise his gun and fire a shot. Immediately, an arrow sank into the soft spot at the base of his neck. After his companion fired, another arrow followed rapidly, striking him in the same place. Horrified at their swift demise, I watched both men slump and tumble down the stairs, gasping grotesquely as their lives slipped away.

Blindly, a trio of nearby comrades opened fire on the second-floor railing in an ear-shattering fusillade that matched my personal rage with its fury. It had been stupid to do that, however, for as soon as they began reloading, she appeared at the rail and quickly picked off all three. I screamed at my men to take cover, huddled beneath a table and recited the most foul list of obscenities in the Azgar Vulgate for emphasis. To my surprise, she answered me!

"Leave now, and I'll spare your wretched life!" she threatened menacingly, in my own tongue.

I was astounded at her audacity. "Who are you to talk to me that way?" I'd never heard anyone speak to an Azgar officer in such an insolent tone of voice.

"I live here. Go away! Leave me alone!"

As our gun smoke dissipated I peeked above the table to check for myself. Gehenoff lay on the upper landing in a pool of his own blood, an arrow extending from the exact place at the base of his neck where his companions had been struck.

Illuminated by light from a window, dressed in a dark skirt and a tight, silky camisole, the Lith cow stood one step back from the top of the stairs. Strong, beautiful, and raven-haired with shining blue eyes, she was the first Lithian I'd ever seen alive. My heart raced with fear and desire as I lowered my gun and slowly inched forward.

She held a recurve bow ready. A pair of arrows, one nocked into her bowstring, the other just half a heartbeat from its mate, awaited flight in her right hand. She glared at me, slowly backing away, her every step echoed in trembling flesh that transfixed my gaze. Yet she allowed progress as if killing me would be like spitting on the floor.

The staircase opened into a room with windows made of mosaic-patterned green and yellow stained glass. Underfoot, ceramic tile clicked at my booted step. Eating couches with carved, stone legs lay arranged around a huge oval table hewn from a single slab of polished jade. A parquet-patterned bowl filled with fresh fruit graced the center of the table.

Dario deGaspar, a soldier from the town of Marioch, rose to my side with his gun upraised. The girl lifted her bow toward him and took aim. I motioned for him to lower his weapon, and as soon as he complied, the girl did the same, standing her ground. She said nothing further.

One by one, my ten surviving men gathered around me. I knew by the lust overflowing in their eyes what they intended to do once we'd subdued this lovely creature, and I can't deny that I wanted her also. Many might think she was asking for it, shamelessly wearing a camisole that left little to my imagination, but we'd seen many Lithian carcasses clad like this, and I figured she was just reflecting the indecent customs of her people.

Before the battle, however, my centurion had threatened every NCO and officer with unspecific retribution, should we allow what he called *improper relational encounters* with the Lithians to occur among our men. Sergeant Aransen knew as well as I did that in an isolated room, the impropriety would be impossible to police. Momentarily overcome with long-dormant desire and wanting my soldiers to be pleased, I called for a volunteer to disarm her.

An eager recruit stepped forward, inciting a ripple of smirks and lurid remarks from the other men. Seeing her smirk, however, I asked for my gun, just in case . . . .

The young woman remained motionless until the hapless soldier reached for her. In a blur, she crushed his private parts with a swift kick and slid to the right, launching an arrow that followed deGaspar's erupting gun barrel all the way up to his eye. As the volunteer crumpled to the floor in agony, she loosed another arrow that clanged against my helmet so hard it twisted my neck and slammed my head against the wall. My ears rang fiercely, but I maintained the presence of mind to withhold my shot.

Once deGaspar's musket went off, the rest let their rounds go, in spite of my pleading to the contrary. Smoke clouded the room, but the ensuing screams of dying soldiers made it clear to me that my men were trying to load their weapons in a confined area with a bloodthirsty Lith cow who hadn't been touched by a bullet.

As the air cleared, I saw that she'd squatted down with her left knee forward and right leg back, so low that her face was but a handbreadth from the floor. Every round we'd fired had arced harmlessly over her head, and now, with her lean legs tense as a tigress ready to pounce, she pushed her left arm forward again. The bowstring stretched. She had another arrow ready for me . . . .

That moment lasted longer than any other I can remember. Her gleaming, angry eyes never left mine, and I knew that she could have killed me before I had her in my sights. Suddenly, I realized that she was waiting for me to pull the trigger first.

I found myself unable to do it.

At that instant, the thought of holding this girl down and letting my men have their way with her repulsed me. Her respect for my life constrained my behavior and slowly, I turned my gun to the side and fired, well to her right.

She gave me a knowing look, slung the bow over her shoulder, then raced for an open window and gracefully swung herself outside. I followed a moment later but she'd slid down a drainage pipe and raced across the garden. My heart beat fast as I heard the light sound of her rapidly retreating footfalls pattering through the forest below.

Sergeant Aransen patted me on the shoulder. "Outwitted by a Lith-cow," he muttered. "I don't know how you're going to live that one down, lieutenant . . . ."

The deceit didn't come easy at first. With time, I've been able to lie about that scene as if I were really telling the truth. I suspect that my sergeant sensed the falsehood in my words, but he said nothing when I replied with incredulity, "I can't believe I missed!"

A thorough search of the house revealed nothing more than damaged, discarded tools, very heavy furniture and abandoned food. My depleted troops gathered our dead as we began to smell wood smoke. Cautiously, we ventured back into the street to get a better look. The tree canopy concealed the fire, but ash fluttered from a blackened sky like falling autumn leaves. An orange glow arose from an area to the right of our current position.

"Maybe we should keep moving," Aransen suggested.

I thought about that for a moment, but could only picture a hungry predator lurking along a fire line, waiting to pounce upon prey flushed out by the inferno.

"It may be another trap," I warned. "Let's double back and cross over an area that's already been burned. They won't expect us, and maybe we can sort our bearings."

Sergeant Aransen raised his brow, as this was technically a violation of orders. But the sergeant knew our losses had rendered us combat ineffective and didn't object.

In retrospect, that order proved to be the only independent decision I'd made all day. It was also the first of many choices that led to the demise of my career.

Heat intensified as we retreated. I noticed a wind picking up at my back and watched airborne debris funneling toward the flames. A howling soon assailed my ears, a sound like that of an angry wind or a deathwolf in the distance. Flakes of ash fluttered past. Wisps of steam rose from the damp ground, flushed away by a rushing tide of hot air.

The howling turned into a furious roar. A massive, flaming pillar writhed in ecstatic annihilation, consuming tons of ancient forest moment by moment. The fire danced and swayed in the growing wind, leaping through the tree canopy in an insatiable lust for destruction. Nothing remained in its wake but grey ash and hot embers.

This fire raged for eight days. When it finally burned out, no trace remained of Shirak, save for a huge plot of black blight amid the deep green forest. Although we had done our best to extinguish the blaze, it did not die until the flames consumed even the city walls. Then, mysteriously as it had begun, the fire halted.

Lord General Balinor, our high commander, withdrew from the desolation and turned the fury of our forces against every vestige of Lithian culture. We seized control of the surrounding lands and obliterated all traces of their society by killing every survivor we could find, tearing down their secret temples and burning their sacred writings. At the end of our genocidal spree, we believed that no Lithian remained alive on the eastern side of the mountains.

At the time, I rationalized our actions as moral, legal and justifiable. I believed my commanders were acting in the best interest of our nation. I believed that my destiny was linked to the success of our forces as we turned northward and began systematically subjugating the technically primitive peoples in our path, taking control over land and resources that had never belonged to us. I never thought twice about the people we displaced.

In retrospect, I've come to understand that I was wrong. Every story has two truths to tell, and it's only right for me to recount this one from both sides. I will write honestly about my experience and what my army put others through, for I have learned something vital about justice in the months and weeks following the day my army marched northward from the city of fire.

Junior Scout Garrick Ravenwood, Tamarian Defense Force;
Brenna Velez; Woodwind

Warrior's Soul

A cold, northwest wind blew down from the Tamarian highlands, sweeping through foothill canyons that lay at the western border of the vast Saradon plateau. A verdant grove of pine and cedar swayed, the breeze whispering through their branches. Ancient oak and sycamore bared lofty limbs to the late autumn sky, their fallen, yellow leaves swirling and dancing in the cobbled gardens of the Ice Dragon Inn. Snow patches lay in the shadows of the inn's grey stone walls, warning of the oncoming winter.

Junior Scout Garrick Ravenwood, dressed in a military uniform featuring a high tech, armored vest made of steel thread, ceramic plates and structural padding, sat on his bedroll, with his back to the wind. Methodically, the young man stripped and cleaned his seventy caliber rifle, making sure the bolt action mechanism for its six-round chamber slid smoothly after assembly.

It worked perfectly.

Turning his attention to its close-quarters function, the cadet took out his bayonet, shaving the blade with a whetstone to a satisfactory sharpness. Garrick paused only to shift the weapon, pull his heavy overcoat a bit closer, or brush away a stray lock of blonde hair that the wind tossed carelessly into his face.

Twenty-four other junior scouts, arrayed in a semicircle near the inn's outer gate, also readied their equipment. Sergeant Streckert posted a list on the announcement board that afternoon, detailing every item each recruit had to carry. He'd warned of serious consequences to those who did not follow its guidelines to the letter. Every cadet had to pack one change of warm clothing with extra socks, his bedroll, a canteen, personal hygiene kit, his weapon, armor and ammunition.

Traveling light meant traveling fast. This exercise, the final chapter of a six-month training course, would test the endurance and survival skills of each recruit on a two-night and two-day expedition into the wilderness near Tamaria's southern border. Some of the cadets would have packed a bigger bag, but none dared disobey an order. Good soldiers, they were told, followed orders to the death, and every one of them believed this.

In the southwest, the Daystar began falling behind the majestic ridge lines of the Angelgate Mountains. These towering, forbidding peaks remained forever shrouded in snow, and the melt from their heights cascaded to the lowlands with an awesome roar that echoed through the alpine valleys like thunder in a storm. The waxing wind from the northwest warned that this night would be cold enough to silence even the greatest of these.

Junior Scout Jan Bordmann glanced furtively at each of his comrades. Moving stealthily, he reached for a handful of dirty snow, carefully positioned himself into the blind spot behind his intended victim, and then hurled the snowball at his best friend.

Garrick felt something cold splatter against the back of his head. The young man swirled around just in time to catch Jan in the act of compressing more snow for his next round. Garrick dropped his bayonet and batted away the incoming snowball with a gloved hand.

"I'll fix you!" he threatened, scrambling to pursue his smaller, more agile friend around the courtyard. The Tamarian cadet scraped up a bit of snow on the run and flung a wild shot that missed his friend badly and struck someone else instead.

No junior scout could long resist the temptation to join the fray. Neglecting their sergeant's orders, exuberance replaced quiet concentration as twenty-five young men quickly created their own blizzard.

Garrick cornered Jan near a watchtower. Here, his size and stamina prevailed over his friend's stealth and agility, although Jan continued scoring direct hits at close range. Eventually the friends paused, out of breath, watching others continue the mischief they'd begun.

"The sergeant's gonna skin us alive for starting this," Jan remarked in a manner indicating he'd not thought seriously about the impending consequences.

"What do you mean us?" Garrick replied. "It was your snowball that got this going, and I'm not gonna take any heat for you!"

"Well, you're a great friend . . . ." sneered Jan, noting misbehavior from across the courtyard.

Freddy Olsen, another cadet, had begun stuffing snow into Jan's backpack. Witnessing the nefarious deed, Jan was not at all amused. Spouting curses that linked Freddy's family to many microscopic creatures maligned, Jan hustled over to chase Freddy off.

At that moment, Garrick experienced the uneasy sensation of being watched. He scanned every window and door frame, fearing the disapproving stare of Sergeant Streckert, but the drill master's stern face did not appear in any portal.

"You there!" a strong male voice called.

Startled, the cadet heard footsteps crunching in the snow from behind and turned, his heart racing fearfully, his grey eyes widened.

"Yes, you. Can you help me?"

The man spoke Southern Vulgate, the tongue of the Azgar, the most common language among nations in the west. Its cultural dominance and power of literary expression made it mandatory study in Tamarian classrooms. Yet with rumors of an Azgar army marching northward, Garrick felt nervous to hear their language spoken and secretly wished that his rifle lay within reach.

The stranger's sudden, nearly soundless appearance, coupled with his speech and confident demeanor, inspired suspicion. By virtue of his dress and accent, Garrick deduced he might be from Kameron, Tamaria's large and powerful ally, but couldn't be sure. The man approached fearlessly, his features deeply tanned, his expensive clothing spattered with dark stains. He wore a thin, armored vest of unusual design over a filmy silk shirt, with a finely-crafted, two-handed longsword at his left hip. Contrasting his wind-weathered, bearded face, pale blue eyes appraised the young Tamarian, then shifted quickly to scan the inn's windows and watchtowers. Laden with supplies a few yards downhill, a beautiful black gelding nosed the cold ground for grass.

"Sorry to bother you," said the stranger, rubbing his bare arms. "Have I arrived in Tamaria?"

Garrick, noting that the southerner's clothing stains looked suspiciously like blood, replied simply, "Yes."

"How can you stand this God-awful cold?" the man inquired, trying to ease the building tension. "My face hurts. In fact, it hurts to breathe! Can I find a room here before I freeze to death?"

A single word response could have answered the question, but Garrick felt mildly indignant at the disdainful remark. "If my land has so offended your god, then go back home!" the cadet countered, nationalistic bravado hiding his apprehension. "This is an army training compound and there's no room for you here. If you come in peace, you'll find lodging in a town about thirty minutes northward along that road." Garrick pointed to the trade route that ran north-south along the western edge of the Saradon, and fully expected the southerner to move on.

Reconsidering, since the man was armed and didn't flinch, he added: "If you're spoiling for a fight, you'd best leave now. There's nothing but defeat awaiting you here."

But the stranger merely scoffed. Overlooking Garrick's spiteful reply, the man reached into his shirt pocket and produced a small, thin, metallic box that glimmered prettily in the twilight.

Garrick stepped back. "What's this? I don't have time to waste on shiny foreign trinkets. Move along! Or better yet, go back to wherever you belong!"

The stranger, glancing at the continuing snow fight, almost turned to leave without another word, but reconsidered. His tone of voice changed into something very close to menacing as he continued. "I've come from Illithia my young friend, and I've traveled too far to tolerate bad manners. If I'd intended harm, I could hurt you, but that's not why I'm here."

In one smooth motion, the southerner unstrapped the magnificent, straight-edged blade from his hip. "Given your obvious youth, and the fact that we will soon be united in a common cause," the man stated, "I understand your insolence." He gently set his sword on the ground. "But to you and your people, I come peacefully."

Garrick remained suspicious, wary that he might be conversing with a spy. "You don't look very Lithian to me, and your language is uncommon around here."

A smile spread across the stranger's face. "It's no more my language than yours, but we're conversing, and for this blessing I thank Allfather!" The man stepped forward, raising his right hand in the universal gesture of peace. "Allow me to introduce myself. My name is Woodwind. I'm a captain in the service of Lynden Velez."

Garrick, trying to let go of his distrust, accepted the greeting. The stranger's hand felt strong, and its lingering vigor, synergized with the southerner's intimidating self-confidence, made the young Tamarian think it wiser to have this man as a friend than an adversary. "I've never heard of Lynden Velez," Garrick said at length.

Woodwind smiled. "That's a shame," he replied. "If you knew him, you would have no fear of me. He's a good man, but that's not important right now. I'm looking for a young woman – his eldest daughter – and I wonder if you might have seen her."

"I doubt it," said Garrick. "If this is your first visit to my country it's unlikely I've met anyone you know."

Woodwind shivered, hoping that he'd never again need to set foot in the north and tolerate such a bitter wind. "Trust me. Once you've set eyes on her, you'll not forget as long as you live." The southerner opened the shiny, metallic device. It fit neatly into his open hand. "This does her beauty no justice," he said, handing the apparatus to Garrick, "but it will give you a general idea."

The young soldier felt startled as a 3D hologram mysteriously arose from the trinket, revealing a young woman's lovely face. Her image stirred a deep longing in his soul. "No sir. I've never seen her before."

Woodwind's gaze dropped and the tone of his voice changed, as if he were speaking to himself rather than someone he'd just met. "She's around here somewhere. I just know it!" Memories flooded the traveler's mind, vanishing as he willed them and the smile she inspired away. "Her name is Brenna. She's twenty-seven, and while she's rather tall and strong for a Lithian, she looks no older than you. Brenna's quite shy and not inclined to trust a stranger, but you may hear word of her soon."

Garrick found the image captivating. As if responding to his will, the hologram enlarged and rotated, displaying her feminine form. While typically respectful and not inclined to stare, the young man held his breath as her shapely image slowly turned before his eyes. Waist-length hair flowed over her sculpted shoulders like a veil of modesty. "Any girl dressed like this would create quite a stir around here . . . ."

The implication didn't seem to bother Woodwind. "She's a maiden," he said. "Lithians display their beauty like this until they marry. But don't get the wrong idea. She can fight, she's smart, and is a very devout woman. Touch her inappropriately and you'll regret it."

Focusing on her face again, Garrick felt as if the hologram image whispered soothing words into his soul. He couldn't help feeling intense, physical attraction, but cultural deference to women guided his response. "I've read that Lithians are small and slight of build," he stated. "But this girl looks strong enough to hurt you if she set her mind to it."

"Brenna's paternal great grandfather was a man like you and me," the southerner continued, his explanation revealing the thinly-veiled truth that he really enjoyed talking about her. "But she retains many Lithian features. Her hair is long, so it covers her ears, but you see it in her eyes. They're dark as midnight during the day, but at night they shine like the twin moons . . . ." He thought of her fondly, then added, "They do that when she's angry, too."

Garrick's exposure to the Lithian people had been limited to anthropology books and crass talk. Since the prefix of the adjective, *Illithian*, sounded very much like the word for "sick" in the Tamarian language, he'd always heard Lithians referred to as *"sicklians,"* or *"sicklies."* Further, their lascivious reputation among his own people had nothing to do with superstitious talk of godliness, and poetic descriptions of eyes shining like the twin moons. Garrick couldn't help remarking in amusement, "Does she mix herbs, chant incantations and cast spells?"

"She's *not* a witch!" Woodwind snatched the device from the young man's hand. "Your ignorance is great and your tongue betrays it quickly!" The traveler's eyes narrowed, displaying a menacing demeanor that appeared with frightening suddenness. "Don't mock me, boy!"

"I'm sorry, sir. I meant no disrespect."

The stranger picked up his longsword and strapped it to his hip. "This is a serious matter," he said tersely. Then, as he observed remorse in the expression of the young man, his heart and tone softened again. "I could use your help, and I'd be in your debt if you'd do me a favor."

Garrick, who'd accepted the scolding without protest, hedged. "I'm leaving here soon. We're shutting down for the winter, but tell me what you need, and I'll do what I can."

Woodwind scanned the darkening ride lines to the west. "I'll ride north to the town you spoke of and stay there to search the area for three days before I move on. If you see or hear about the young woman in that time, will you send word for me at once?"

Garrick nodded.

"*Excellente!*," Woodwind replied. "I am pleased."

Without another word, the foreigner returned to his mount and trotted off into the northern shadows. Garrick watched the darkness overtake his fleeting form, then looked west, over the mountains, where the twin moons hovered just above the horizon as slender, barely visible crescents. Eyes like that would truly look strange!

Suddenly, the shrill shriek of the sergeant's whistle snapped Garrick out of his reverie.

"Fall in!" the sergeant bellowed.

Immediately, the junior scouts ceased their scuffling and scrambled to line up in order. Swiftly, they brushed themselves off, straightened their armor, then stared directly ahead while the sergeant lambasted the lot of them for their misbehavior.

"I have never seen such a pathetic collection of undisciplined, pit-brained, hairless no-wits in my entire military career! Who, may I ask, gave you the order to act like pant-wetting pansies tonight? Did I give that order?"

"No sergeant!" they chorused.

"Did some divine being appear to you and demand that you squander what precious little preparation time you have in prancing around like a pack of hyperactive, juvenile baboons in heat?"

"No sergeant!"

"Then what was this lobotomized display of simian depravity all about?"

Silently, Sergeant Streckert paced among the five rows of his class, resting his fierce-featured countenance upon every cadet. He stopped at Jan Bordmann and tersely asked, "Did you start this?"

"Yes sergeant! I started it!"

"Ravenwood! You were in on this too. Is that right?"

Garrick, trembling, replied. "Yes sergeant!"

"Very well," the sergeant continued. "Bordmann, Ravenwood, Vortlund and Olsen, fall out!"

The four cadets stepped to the front. Sergeant Streckert scowled as he scanned the other junior scouts, untouched, it seemed, by the cold afflicting his shivering class. Turning to the four cadets he'd singled out, the sergeant spoke in a low, threatening tone. "I want you hairless bipeds to sweep this courtyard. I don't want to see so much as a single snowflake left on the ground when you're done. You will do it now, and you will do it as if the great baboon in the sky was personally supervising every stroke your broom lays on this pavement! Is that clear?"

"Yes sergeant!" they replied.

"Now, the rest of you, who think so little of the high honor and responsibility of soldiering, you will remain at attention while your primate playmates preen the grounds you have defiled with your despicable display of dissipation. You will not move. You will not laugh. You will not talk. You will not scratch the itch in your behind. You will learn that wearing your uniform is a privilege, or you will not be deemed worthy of being seen in it!"

The sergeant stalked back into the inn without another word, leaving twenty cadets to ponder their predicament in the rapidly descending bitterness of oncoming night. The four who'd been singled out hustled to the back entrance of the inn's kitchen to find brooms for their duty outside. Once beyond the sergeant's earshot, Freddy Olson and Harold Vortlund raged against their companions for getting them into trouble.

"It's your fault, Bordmann!" complained Freddy. "I did nothing to deserve this!"

Jan, full of resentment, replied sarcastically, "Cramming my backpack full of snow is nothing?"

"Yeah, maybe. But you started it, Bordmann," said Harold with a shove. "If it wasn't for you, none of us would be here . . . . "

Garrick, who'd defended his little brother and sister for as long as he could remember, immediately stepped in front of Harold. "Back off!" he snapped. "You're no more innocent than a naked priest in a whorehouse!"

Harold's anger flared, inspiring an impulse to take a good swing at Garrick, whose size exceeded Harold's by a fair margin. Hoping to hurt and yet avoid a fight, Harold opted for an insult. "Farm boys!" he spat. "Go back to the dung heap where you came from!"

Unwilling to back down, Garrick glared at the smaller cadet, but let the affront go rather than raising the stakes. Deeply wounded by memories of a dysfunctional family, Garrick remained silent until the other cadet looked away.

The inn's kitchen, built along the south side of its main building, lay within a few strides of a twenty-foot stone wall encircling the complex. A quirk in the inn's layout allowed swirling wind to whisk between the outer wall and the kitchen's back entrance. Buffeted by the icy breeze, the cadets put their differences aside for the moment and huddled together for warmth.

Just then, Garrick heard a faint sound rising from the south. He peered into the gloom, but could see nothing unusual. Garrick nudged his friend Jan. "Hear that?"

"Hear what?" Jan replied.

"Shh . . . listen! There it is again! Did you hear it?"

An eerie call aspired above the rushing of the gelid windstorm, stirring fear into every beat of Garrick's young heart. The cry sounded a little closer with every passing moment, but he dared not speak of the foreboding he felt.

"Great and good spirits!" Jan wondered aloud, spooked by the sound. "What unholy thing is that?"

"Yeah, sounds like something evil," Garrick replied.

"Nah," sneered Harold. "It's probably just a wolf."

Freddy smirked, his mind forever focused on sex. "Or a tight witch on her wedding night!"

"Hmm . . . ." Garrick mused. "If that's so I'd hate to meet her husband."

***

In the wilderness several miles southwest of the inn, Brenna Velez watched the twin moons descending in the west. From her vantage point, high on a windswept foothill ridge line, her bright eyes could see an array of dark hues that painted the magnificent landscape deep into the indigo horizon. As a tetrachromat, sensitive to ultraviolet light, she would see very well tonight.

Once the moons dipped below the mountain ridge, a familiar, violet glow brought a hidden world of wonder to her sight. Every star blazed brilliantly in the cold air, arranged in patterns she'd recognized on the northern horizon from her treetop lookout at home, far away. Fluorescing interstellar gas and dust clouds, bright planets and far-flung galaxies, along with the ephemeral flash of meteoroids burning high overhead stirred awe in her heart.

From the ridge line, Brenna admired the natural fortress that made up the backbone of Tamaria. High mountains loomed to the west and northwest – a massive uplift creating the loftiest cordillera on the continent. Their perpetually snow-covered peaks glistened prettily in the purple light – steep, defiant and intimidating.

Ugogo Penda, the half Tamarian, half Abelscinnian third wife of Tegene – her *Amair's* lifelong friend – told stories about cruel giant kings once ruling from within them. Penda related tales of an ageless, immortal warrior queen named Tamar, who suddenly appeared to lead her people to freedom, shattering the giants' centuries-old reign. As a girl, this history fascinated Brenna, and for years after hearing these childhood tales, she'd secretly dreamed of seeing this mountainous nation, with its high regard of women – at least, according to Penda – for herself.

Now these ancient heights stood before her eyes. A waxing wind that grew steadily colder with nightfall blew into her weary face, swept through the fine, maiden blouse and pleated skirt she wore, teased through her hair and then raced stiffly out over the immense, semi-arid Saradon.

Although nearly nine hundred miles from home, Brenna walked in faith and in harmony with the lands she crossed. For over sixty days she'd averted large-scale battles, enemy patrols, predators and starvation. *Believing* that her survival hinged upon Allfather's care, Brenna thanked him for his providence in a whispered prayer.

Her faith inspired peace within her soul, a repose tempered in genuine fear. As Azgar legions who'd destroyed her home advanced, no nation had been able to stop them. Brenna didn't know whether she was in front of, or behind their northernmost line of control, so she pressed northward relentlessly. The young woman had good reason to fear, for the Azgar did not tolerate Lithians, and her family had been prominent among them.

Following the western ridges to her left, Brenna fled northward. Whenever possible, she avoided roads and traveled alone through desolate stretches of wilderness, subsisting on an extensive knowledge of edible plants, occasional hunting and a lot of fishing. The relentless exercise hardened her athletic body, but she'd lost weight.

Her exhausting flight also inspired fatigue. Under these extreme conditions, she'd survive on as little as two or three hours' rest just before dawn, a time when the deathwolves returned from their ravaging and the Azgar army still lay encamped.

Most active during the early evening, deathwolves served the enemy by spreading terror. They hunted in packs, killing any living thing unable to outwit or outrun them. Fearful and taking no chances, Brenna found a large creek before twilight fell and followed it upstream for nearly an hour before climbing to the ridge line, leaving a long gap in any trace of scent that might be detected by the deadly canine predators.

Brenna's youth and Lithian heritage endowed her with great stamina, but the cold water had cramped her legs, and the chilling wind sapped strength from her aching body. Longing for relief from unremitting danger, weary of constant travel and desperately needing warmth, she feared that she'd not long endure the bitter wind without finding shelter soon.

On a hilltop not more than half a mile to the south, a deathwolf raised its wicked voice to the setting moons. The howl of the beast sounded much like a woman's scream: high-pitched, powerfully intoned, but dreadfully long in duration. A second deathwolf called out, then another, and a fourth. The screeching voices of the gathering pack created overtones of an unholy chorus that crashed against one another, dissonant, twisted, and altogether horrible in her music-loving ears.

Terrified, Brenna scampered down a deer path that wound its way along the hillside. Deftly, she stepped over rocks, roots and slippery places, pausing only to renegotiate thirty foot leaps that a deer, not a half-breed Lithian woman, could easily make.

Although she'd never seen one up close, Brenna estimated the average size of a deathwolf from the pug marks they left behind, their speed from the length of their stride, and believed that a single wolf could bring her down without trouble. She'd often seen the remains of wild and domesticated animals, their viscera alone consumed, their mangled carcasses left to rot on the ground, and it stirred in her an anger altogether human.

She was, after all, more than a little human . . . .

To the west lay a parallel ridge line. Brenna threaded her way through thick brush, careful to move quietly, nervous that a nearby deathwolf might catch wind of her. But a whiff of wicked scent warned her to slow as she neared the crest of the westerly ridge. Her heart began to pound. Adrenaline pulsed through her body. Noiselessly, the young maiden crept through a juniper thicket that grew on the lee side of the hill and peered into a clearing. Her eyes widened . . . . Deathwolves!

There were eight of them.

The huge, hunchbacked, slavering creatures stood nearly five feet tall at the withers, roughly as high as Brenna's nose. A mane of thick, coarse fur extended from their necks down to the midpoint of their backs, while the rest of their bodies grew short, spiny hair. They varied in color from silvery-red to black, with eyes of yellow or scarlet. Snapping and snarling, they bared canine fangs as long as Brenna's little finger, flexing powerful claws rivaling those of a bear. Scariest of all, they spoke in guttural vulgate. Their talk overflowed with hate, profanity and expressed the full extent of their malicious ill-intent . . . .

One male, bigger than the others and more aggressive in his posture, reigned as their undisputed leader. The speech of this wolf roused the others into a blood-lusting frenzy. He paced among his pack, biting and cursing them, forcing each one to submit to his dominance and humiliating any who dared challenge him.

Suddenly, he stopped, as if told by some creature unseen that he was being watched. He raised his evil head to inspect the surrounding foliage, where he could see a mass of warmth, the outline of a trembling, blue-eyed maiden in the shadows.

"Lith cow!" he spat.

Brenna turned to run, and the chase began.

***

Methane lamps poured blue light into the Ice Dragon Inn's cobbled gardens. Working swiftly, dreading any further reprimand from Sergeant Streckert, Garrick and his comrades swept every bit of snow in the courtyard into neat piles near the old stone walls. This operation required twenty minutes.

Meanwhile, the sergeant reappeared, directing men to unload extra supplies they'd brought from a storeroom. These included dried food, first aid materials such as bandages, antiseptic, chemical warmers, a few pots, axes and other tools, and a box covered with canvas.

The sergeant pried this box open and produced a pair of chemical light sticks for each cadet. These were activated by twisting each end in opposite directions. As long as the outside temperature remained above -10 degrees, the reaction inside produced white light for several hours at a range of forty feet. Each cadet selected a partner by lot, with whom he would alternate in using the light sticks so that the supply would last two nights.

After this, the sergeant distributed the extra gear evenly among the cadets, gave final instructions for the exercise, and Garrick's junior scout class marched past the inn's sheltering gate and out into the darkness of a harsh, blustery night.

Far away the evil howling continued. Whatever fear it inspired within the young cadets went unmentioned, for they felt more afraid of appearing frightened in front of their peers than of the intangible threat that lay ahead. Their military training instilled a naive confidence in their combat ability, as they believed any foe could be defeated by cooperation and discipline.

Even Garrick, who hated to harm living things, succumbed to this influence. He wrestled with silent fear while marching southward in the autumn darkness, but the young man could not escape the influence of his culture, which glorified death in defense of the nation as honorable. He believed in freedom and would fight for his people's autonomy with all his strength, even if such liberty could only be bought in his own blood.

Many miles down the road, Sergeant Streckert called the column to a halt. Four corpses lay at the side of the path, near a towering oak tree. The sergeant inspected the carnage thoroughly before speaking.

"I want all of you to take a good look at this!" he shouted. "What we see here is evidence that one skilled warrior with a weapon can ruin your day." Sergeant Streckert proceeded to paint a plausible picture based on the evidence at the scene.

"Note, one set of horse tracks leading from the south, no doubt a lone traveler who looked like he might have some money. We see boot prints leading from behind the tree, but the surprise attack went wrong. These broken twigs lying around indicate that someone probably tried to jump on the horse from the branches above.

"There was at least one shot fired by the first victim. You can plainly see the powder burn on this old trapdoor musket." The sergeant held the weapon out for his cadets to examine. "He was probably cut down while the traveler was still in the saddle. Observe that there is only a single wound, high up on the throat of this body. It was a powerful, well-executed and lethal cut."

Sergeant Streckert picked up a musket barrel that had been cut clean through and held it aloft. "This came from a cross-body block. It might have been done from the back of the horse, but more likely, our swordsman hacked through this weapon while he was standing on the ground."

Garrick edged closer, his eyes widening in disbelief. What kind of sword could cut through a musket barrel?

"You can see that the body of this victim is missing its right hand, and that his finger guard shows a bloody slash mark from a swallow-cut where our horseman knocked the weapon away. Pay attention. There's just one thrust wound in the chest of this man. It looks like a very sharp sword did all this damage."

Garrick stared at the carnage, his mind filling with a queasy mixture of dread and morbid fascination. Dark stains drenched the ground where the fallen bodies lay, the pain of their demise still evident on unshaven faces. He'd grown up on a small farm and had seen death many times before, but this kind of killing seemed utterly ruthless. That's when he linked this scene to the stranger at the Ice Dragon's gate – the lone traveler with similarly-stained clothing and a very big sword . . . .

As Sergeant Streckert extolled the swordsman's combat virtues, Garrick's attention wandered. He remembered Woodwind's words, his intimidating manner, his penetrating stare and strength wisely tempered by restraint. Regretting his insolence, Garrick now wished he'd treated the southerner with greater courtesy.

The sergeant concluded with an object lesson. "I want every one of you to be like this. When you're in a fight, you don't cut your enemy any slack. You don't let him breathe, and you don't stop when he hits the ground. You go all the way. You take his life before he takes yours. Are you juvenile baboons gonna cry when we face the enemy?"

"No sergeant!" the cadets chorused.

"That's right lads. You kill them before they kill you. If they get you first, you've done nothing for your country!"

"Yes sergeant!"

Sergeant Streckert nodded approvingly and hoisted his backpack. "All right lads, move along!"

Garrick's gaze remained riveted on the black-uniformed bodies until Jan urged him onward. At length, Garrick whispered to his friend, "Trapdoor muskets."

"Yeah, I saw," Jan replied. "Small bores, too."

The two friends shared the thought as they exchanged a knowing glance. Tamaria, a small nation beset by conflict, stayed on the forefront of infantry technology by investing in excellent, bolt-action rifles, smokeless powder, center-firing cartridges, expensive rockets and top-tier artillery. Lavishly equipping her soldiers limited Tamaria's army to a modest, professional fighting force.

Furthermore, because of their history of conflict against giants, Tamarian rifles normally exceeded fifty caliber, and their ammunition carried a small explosive charge designed to penetrate plate armor. Small bore muskets did not provide enough stopping power to take down mountain giants.

Both cadets reached an obvious conclusion. Inexpensive trapdoor muskets came from somewhere far away. No native northerner wore lightweight clothing at this time of year, and no army either one of them knew wore black uniforms. This evidence suggested that elements of a foreign force had crossed the Tamarian border.

Rumors about advancing Azgar legions had been circulating for weeks, but no one believed a large army could make it to the frontier before winter arrived without marching its soldiers to death. "Do you think the sergeant didn't notice?" Jan inquired, disbelieving that his vaunted sergeant would miss such conspicuous clues.

Garrick shrugged. "I don't know, but I doubt it."

"I wonder why he didn't mention it," Jan mused, knowing his friend's mind. "We ain't ready for no invasion."

Garrick shook his head, listening to the crescendo of the windstorm, mingled with the steady crunching of leathered feet along the graveled road. The frigid fingers of the freezing wind crept beneath his clothing, grasping his body in its cold embrace. As the swelling storm stilled for a moment, he heard the chilling howls drawing closer and closer. Nervously, he pulled his overcoat tighter and held his rifle closely against his shoulder. The young man didn't want to be scared, he just couldn't help it.

***

Brenna ran faster than she had ever run before, fleeing north near the ridge line, followed closely by the pursuing wolf pack. She darted through openings that her eyes, and not those of the wolves, could easily see. Strong and athletic, her muscular body responded with a long, sustained burst of speed, her young heart quickening, her mind overwhelmed with fear. Steadily, she raced to the top of the ridge, and there – as she dashed across a stretch of open ground – the pack leader drew close enough to strike.

Abruptly, Brenna changed course. Swiftly and gracefully down the west-facing slope of the hillside she descended, leaping over the rocky bed of a south-flowing stream, and then briskly up the opposite side of the canyon she climbed.

Her lightning quick maneuver had been so sudden it took the leading wolves by surprise. None of them could duplicate the turn at top speed, which extended the Lithian woman's lead by several strides. The steep hillside, laden with fallen leaves, proved treacherous. Heavy deathwolves tumbled down the canyon at the ragged edge of control, their descent frequently and painfully slowed by contact with underbrush and hidden rock.

One of them lost its footing and began sliding in a leaf bed. The massive creature plowed into an oak tree with such force, Brenna heard its shoulder bones break as she dashed up the opposite bank. The beast yelped pitifully, limping in pain as it dropped out of the chase.

The deer paths crossed in many places. Brenna switched her trail at random, cutting sharp, sudden turns that led her adversaries and on winding, twisting, up and down, desperate race through the wild land. Cold wind combed the maiden's raven mantle, tossing her long black locks into a shimmering shadow that followed, whither her fleet footsteps fled.

Breathing hard now, the chill air began to hurt. Her ankles, stiff and sore from cold water, protested every turn. An occasional pang in her lean leg muscle warned that sprinting like this could not long be sustained, but the deathwolves drew nearer with every stride. For the first time since escaping from Shirak, Brenna worried that she might die.

And the singular desire of every deathwolf in pursuit was to be the one who killed her. Centuries of careful breeding had produced competitive temperaments, driving each creature to the extremes of its endurance in a chase. In addition to formidable strength and stamina, the evil creatures could see body heat from their prey as a red glow in the darkness. Once pursued by a pack like this, very few living creatures could escape them.

But on this night, the roaring wind howled in their ears, its cold breath numbed any scent they tried to follow, and its chill touch quickly faded warm images left behind by the fleeing feet of their prey. Only moments after her passage, no trace of Brenna remained.

Intelligent and experienced, the pack leader realized that he had to kill quickly and pressed the chase harder, bounding across the stream bed, past the oak grove that flourished at the bottom of the canyon, through the thorn brush and juniper, faithfully following the fading footfalls of the lithe, Lithian woman. He could see her warm body as she dashed along the deer path. Instinct urged him onward, faster, stretching his lengthy stride to close in for a fatal strike.

At that moment, a mighty gust of wind loosened a huge, dead sycamore tree near the top of the ridge. As if moved by an unseen hand, the ancient tree turned and tumbled sideways into the canyon, the sound of its crashing branches smothered by the screaming wind as it careened downhill.

The deathwolf could smell the maiden's sweat. He could sense her fear. The longer she eluded him, the more he hated her for it. Lunging forward, he nipped at her foot once, then twice; the second time drawing blood.

Something painful stabbed at Brenna's heel, she lost her balance, and tumbled uncontrollably downhill. "Help me!" she screamed. "Allfather, save me!"

The deathwolf remained hyper-focused, confronting his prize with bared teeth and malevolent intent. Pausing to savor the triumph over his prey, he heard a loud snap from behind. Invisible against the cold night sky, the derelict tree bounced high over a boulder, then slammed onto the deathwolf's head like the hammer of God's vengeance. Crushed against unyielding stone below, the ruthless predator let out a single, pained yelp.

Brenna slid into a deep layer of dead leaves in the arroyo. She suffered many bruises and scratches from her fall, watching in dread as the sycamore snuffed out the deathwolf's life before settling peacefully in the stream bed.

Terrified and overwhelmed by the desire to survive, she scrambled to her feet again. With her adrenaline up and her flight instincts screaming for action, the young woman pushed through her pain and raced onward as fast as her rapidly tiring legs would permit.

Approaching the scene, the six remaining wolves could not find Brenna's trail. A familiar scent led them to their leader's broken body, and once they'd each confirmed his death, a ritual fight for leadership began immediately.

Brenna fled northward on the far hillside for a long time. The landscape rose beneath her feet, its oak and sycamore yielding to groves of pine as the soil became sandier and less well-watered. She climbed over the ridge and descended into another canyon to escape the frigid force of the windstorm, where the air didn't feel as bitterly cold. A small stream still trickled south, its banks edged in ice. Brenna slackened her pace, her lungs heaving as she sensed the wolves had miraculously fallen behind. As she continued, the Lithian woman whispered a grateful prayer for her deliverance.

Soon, the wound in her left heel impeded progress to the point of a limping trot. A burning sensation slowly crept into the lean muscle of her lower left leg. Brenna slowed to a brisk walk, ignoring the cold. Every time her left heel touched the ground, pain twisted her step until she stopped to inspect the injury.

Her left boot had been torn just above the heel. Sticky gore spattered the leather, and bits of blood-drenched stocking trailed behind. Clumps of dirt and crushed bits of dead leaf clung to the strings, the boot, and open flesh.

Brenna breathed deeply to control the pain. She sat on the cold, wet ground and pulled on the boot to free her injured foot. In four afflictive moves it emerged. With her boot knife, she cut the unraveled stocking and plunged her bleeding foot into the frigid water. Cold numbed her toes. Slowly, the pain ebbed.

In the quiet of that moment, Brenna calmed her racing pulse in a heartfelt, whispered petition.

A few minutes later, she reached for her boot and examined it closely. Tooth marks marred its soft sole. Most of the heel piece had been bitten off, and the reinforced section protecting her heel tendon had been shredded beyond repair.

Her injured foot suffered a like fate. The back of her left heel had been bitten badly, leaving behind a bloody mass of torn tissue. Brenna cleaned the wound thoroughly, and dried it. With supplication on her tongue and power surging through her flesh, the Lithian woman bent her left leg to her lips and kissed the lesion. Unnatural warmth flowed into her injured heel, mystically repairing all the damage done by wicked teeth

Brenna strung her bow and set out an arrow, then paused to pray again.

Far downstream, over the ridge she'd recently climbed, the deathwolves resumed their effort to locate their fleeing quarry's trail. The new pack leader ordered his followers to fan out in a search for her scent. Instinct informed his hunting. Cursing the cold, he let out a frenzied, evil howl. The pack replied wickedly, hoping to frighten their prey into moving.

It worked. The morbid screaming renewed Brenna's fear. She arose and gently pushed her numb foot into the torn boot. Its heel piece flopped awkwardly as she walked, but the terror of being hunted motivated the Lithian woman into climbing up the canyon.

"Allfather, hear my cry," she prayed in desperation. "Please, God. Save my life that I may serve you!"

***

Sergeant Streckert led his junior scouts down the Saradon road for a long time before turning westward, into an island of foothills overlooking the Tualitin River, which formed Tamaria's southern border. Howling, freezing wind amplified the danger of hypothermia, and this, coupled with the combat scene he'd witnessed, gave the sergeant ample cause to worry for the safety of his cadets. He needed to get them sheltered soon.

Gerhardt Streckert did not speak of his concern. After witnessing the oak tree carnage, he'd changed his plans about camping on the Saradon and instead, marched his class toward a forested hill that commanded an outstanding view to the south. Protected on its northern flank by a steep ridge line, the potential campsite provided access to firewood, shelter from the brutal wind, and he hoped, safety from potential enemy attack.

The middle-aged noncom briefly outlined the traditional principles for selecting a campsite to his shivering class: its suitability for observation, how it might be defended and its access to critical survival resources, like a reliable water supply. He then selected a small party to climb a steep, east-facing slope and secure the hilltop before the main company joined them on the summit.

The sergeant assigned Garrick, Jan, Freddy and another cadet named Karl to this initial group. Agile Jan carried a coil of rope on his back and led the way. Struggling to find a stable path among the sharp rocks, he ambled steadily higher, occasionally loosening a minor rockslide that tumbled downhill and made the climb a miserable chore for his comrades who followed.

Garrick cursed under his breath, reasoning that inflicting misery had been the real motivation behind the sergeant's selection of this particular hill. Fingers frozen in the frigid night, his nose running, cheeks and toes utterly numb, Garrick struggled behind his friend Jan, followed by Freddy and Karl.

The unrelenting gale bustled through the bristle pine at the crest of the hill, breaking branches and bending boughs, showering the summit steadily with dry seed cones and conifer needles. Jan secured his rope to a stout tree, then flung the remainder of its length downhill.

Garrick beamed his light stick around a clearing just beyond a thin stand of pines, searching nervously for any sign that might betray an unfriendly presence. He could have sworn he heard the sound of metal striking metal.

Freddy had his back turned, and Karl was telling a lurid story to Jan about a certain village girl. The conversation ended abruptly with a gunshot.

Garrick heard a whistling sound and dove for the dirt. "Get down!" he screamed, tossing his light stick into the clearing. "Ambush! Ambush!"

A bullet slammed into Freddy's back, directly between his shoulder blades. The force of the blow knocked him to the ground, where he discovered, to his dismay, that he couldn't breathe. Panic-stricken, the cadet clawed at Karl for help, but his terror-stricken friend wouldn't move.

In the shelter of shadows behind trees on the north side of the clearing, a furtive footfall caught Garrick's frightened eye. Suddenly, he saw many more of them . . . .

Jan had a better view and began counting feet. "I'd guess ten or less," he rasped.

Garrick, acting as team leader, brought his rifle around. "Get behind a tree. I'll cover you." He didn't admit that his cold hands were shaking badly. All movement and stray sound ceased as the enemy waited.

Jan Bordmann crouched behind a tree and leveled his weapon, motioning for his friend to find cover to the left. Garrick crawled toward a thick bristle pine, slithered behind it, then knelt and peeked around the trunk. He watched a shadowy pair of figures alternating a stealthy advance through the woods. "They're a'coming!"

"Say when," Jan replied. "I'll go right. You go left."

Garrick nodded, wincing as he heard Freddy cough repeatedly. "Karl, get over here!" he ordered.

Somewhat reluctantly, the other cadet obeyed, his movement drawing a pair of shots from across the hill. Both Garrick and Jan fired, even though neither had a clear target. But this had a suppressive effect, momentarily forcing the enemy down. Their brittle, ceramic bullets shattered in the branches of a bristle pine some fifty paces distant, showering the immediate area with sharp, porcelain shrapnel. A male voice cursed in the darkness.

A volley of well-aimed musket rounds shot back in response, forcing Garrick and his friend to duck for cover. The clinking of trapdoor mechanisms filtered through the bending branches as the shooting paused.

Freddy, whom his companions were certain was dying, turned northward and fired five of his six rounds, screaming curses with angry vindictive. While the bullets raced toward nothing in particular, Garrick saw two men appear in front of the tree line. As the cadet aimed to fire another round, one opponent dropped to his knee and leveled his musket right at Garrick. A bullet splintered a fist-sized piece of bark from Garrick's shielding tree just as his own shot sailed high and wide to the left. The second man raised his gun and began to squeeze his trigger.

Jan fired, but he hadn't lined the target up in his sights and succeeded only in raising a cloud of dust. However, his bad shooting forced the enemy soldier to discharge his weapon prematurely.

Stricken by panic, Jan shouted, "Sergeant! We need help! They're gonna kill us!"

Sergeant Streckert urged his cadets onward. "Move! Up the hill! Double time, boys!"

An ambush of this kind might have quickly turned into a rout, but six months of intensive drill provided a rowdy group of young men with the skills necessary to survive such an encounter. As long as they followed their training and kept their heads cool, they had a chance of living to see another day. In spite of this, their pre-combat bravado vanished as the teenaged boys faced a real threat for the first time.

Garrick noticed that after firing a single shot, the enemy troops had to pull back on their rifle hammers until they clicked three times, lift the trapdoor breech loading mechanism to eject spent shell casings, insert a replacement bullet, close the trapdoor, then aim and fire their weapons. This process took several seconds, during which time the enemy had to pay attention to their guns, rather than focusing on their targets. Tamarian bolt action rifles loaded faster, using a munitions magazine, and the Tamarian cadets could keep their eyes on the enemy while chambering new rounds.

It didn't seem like much of an advantage at the time, but it gave Garrick enough of an edge to overcome the racing of his heart and inspire courage to stand his ground. He reached for his spare magazine, setting it down near his left knee. Ahead, two lines of men stepped out from behind the trees. The first group crouched to fire.

Karl – who'd moved farther to Garrick's left – shouted, "What do we do?"

Garrick saw sheer terror in Karl's expression, and strangely, it calmed him. "Fix bayonets!"

Attaching bayonets to rifles took only moments, after which, Garrick commanded, "Fire on that first line!"

Tamarian bullets covered the gap between opposing forces in the blink of an eye. Two impacts tore into enemy soldiers, spewing hot shards of baked enamel through armor and exposed flesh. A chorus of trapdoor carbine rounds sang through the cold air in response, screaming over the Saradon to drop harmlessly into rocky soil.

"Second line!" Garrick shouted, working the bolt of his rifle to engage another round.

Again, the two cadets fired in concert. This time, Jan joined the fray a moment later, and one enemy soldier took the full force of all three shots in his upper body. The impact killed him instantly and drove his lifeless form into a tree.

Garrick struggled to find and exchange his spare magazine. Being nervous and wearing gloves complicated the task. During these idle moments, the surviving enemy loaded their rifles and regrouped to attack again.

A flurry of shots rang out, two of which found their mark in Garrick's chest. The sharp blows hurt like fury! Garrick felt like he'd been hit with a sledgehammer. His feet skidded out from beneath him. The young man landed hard on his back, unable to draw breath or move. To his horror, the enemy soldiers charged forward, yelling a war cry, with their bayonets gleaming in the chemical light.

***

Brenna crept quietly along a path that wound through clumps of ragweed and honey locust. Juniper shrubs screened her from sight as she climbed the east-facing escarpment of the narrow canyon again. Her pulse quickened with every sickening screech uttered by the rapidly approaching deathwolf pack, but she could not increase the tempo of her ascent without losing balance and risking a fall.

The warmth she'd felt in her left foot faded but so had pain from the deathwolf bite. Brenna couldn't explain how a kiss of faith enabled her to heal injuries, but grateful to Allfather, she accepted this mysterious power without question. Now, holding the high ground, if the deathwolves came into range she could defend herself with her bow.

Strong wind and plummeting temperatures numbed her fingers, nose, ear tips and toes. While she'd never experienced frostbite or hypothermia – having lived in a warm climate all her life – the educated woman understood that she needed to build a fire before the cold killed her.

Weary Brenna also needed rest, but tenacious deathwolves weren't likely to give up the chase. Finding a place to hide might work, if she could protect her back and build a big enough fire to keep the evil creatures at bay. Frustrated and afraid, she prayed in a whisper and listened for a reply.

The northwest wind howled without respite. This mass of moving air served as both an ally and an enemy, as its icy breath not only chilled her footprints but also numbed the noses of the wolves in pursuit, robbing both predator and prey of warmth. And while the cold current created a myriad of moving sounds as it swept swiftly across the landscape, every turning leaf, every sighing pine and falling seed cone that muffled her passage also covered the telltale patter of advancing predator feet.

She heard no answer in the wind.

Brenna climbed toward an overhanging rock, high above the area where she had dressed her wound in the water below. Arriving there, she watched the deathwolves appear, circling around the place where she'd rested only minutes before, searching in vain for a lead on her trail. Had she been more confident in her safety, and had she felt warm, the young woman would have found the scene amusing. The deathwolves had lost her . . . .

Then, faint sounds caught her ear, and a flash of light found her eye. She could see a natural break in the pattern of hills from her vantage point, looking north. A river ran rapidly to her left, carving a steep canyon through a mountain pass many miles to the west. Below her, however, it looked shallow enough to ford. The light came from a hilltop overlooking the same river on its northern shore. At a walking pace, she believed she could make it there in about an hour.

"Thank-you for hearing me," she prayed, knowing the Azgar had no magic light. The radiance on the next hill had to be local, and if Tamarian, would likely be friendly. At least, that's what *Ugogo* Penda's stories promised . . . .

Climbing down through a sheltered fold along the northeast slope proved a tiresome and slippery task. Once beyond the relative shelter of the ridge, the malevolent might of the maelstrom made its awesome power an intimate and cold companion. Brenna felt weak. Her steps faltered, and several times, she wanted to fall down and die. The shrieking wind swept across the wild land like a cold broom of destruction, sapping life from all who dared to face its frozen ferocity. She could not easily explain the force that compelled her steps, as that inner strength developed from years of living in faith that must be lived to be understood. Pressing onward, she plunged into the shallow water.

This late in the season, the Tualitin River ran only several inches deep in most places. Brenna braved the icy stream, shocked at the strength of its flow. A great gust of wind pushed the maiden into a deeper channel cut by the current, and she gasped as cold water swept over her shoulders. Instantly weakened by the sudden loss of body heat, Brenna willfully dragged herself across the river and collapsed – shivering uncontrollably – on its northern bank, having finally arrived in the Republic of Tamaria.

***

Jan Bordmann raced ahead to protect his friend. The cadet shoved his bayonet-tipped rifle forward with a mighty grunt. "Die, foreign scum!" he shouted.

Surprised that a mere boy with an acne-scarred face would dare attack so boldly, the Azgar soldier hesitated for a fatal moment before turning to honor the threat. Though slight-of-build, Jan's aggression overpowered his enemy's feeble defense and he drove the foreigner into the ground. Thus, in the first hand-to-hand fight between the Azgar Northern Liberation Army and Tamaria's Defense Force, a teenaged soldier candidate from the northern hill country savagely killed a stranger from a distant southern coast.

Karl charged ahead on Garrick's left. Larger and stronger than Jan, Karl's weight, multiplied by his forward momentum, drove a doomed invader back on his heels. Overwhelmed by powerful, repeated thrusting, the foreigner fell, his blood cooling and congealing as it spread across the frozen ground.

Close combat proved to be an intense and brutal business. Fortunately for Garrick, the Junior Scouts learned well from their training and had become quite proficient at the ruthless act of taking life. Their quick, instinctive action prevented any further attack upon him, and as the moments passed, his ability to breathe and move returned. Though Garrick felt sore and badly bruised, tough armor prevented the direct hits he'd suffered from killing him.

Freddy Olsen, recovering from being hit in the back, refreshed his magazine as three more cadets arrived. In near unison, their large-bore rifles erupted, and the devastating effect of their close-range fire quickly turned the tide of battle.

Each explosive Tamarian bullet punched fist-sized holes through Azgar armor, savagely obliterating flesh. Two enemy soldiers shuddered, their torsos torn open like ripe fruit. Experiencing point-blank firepower, the surviving enemy infantry executed a tactical retreat into the trees. From the woods, they used darkness as cover and selected their targets carefully.

Their firing tactics changed as well. Realizing that Tamarian armor stopped their bullets, the battle-hardened Azgar scouts aimed for knees and faces. This altered the battle dynamic immediately.

Karl screamed. Searing pain ravaged his right leg, forcing him to drop his rifle and fall, clutching his bleeding thigh. Another cadet took a bullet full in the face, while the companion to his left fell victim to a glancing blow that tore his steel helmet from his head.

Sergeant Streckert pulled himself to the top of the hill and spat a stream of vulgarity virulent enough to embarrass a slum-district madam. "Pour it on, boys!" he yelled. "Attack! Keep firing and don't let 'em reload!"

Garrick watched Karl's agony in sheer horror. As his comrades fell, the young soldier nervously jammed his spare magazine into his rifle. The tree line that sheltered the enemy seemed a long way off, but he began crawling forward, acting as his training had taught him, rather than yielding to the intense urge to run away.

Jan and Freddy dropped down to follow. The Tamarians returned fire when bright flashes illuminated the dark, smoky forest ahead, but their shooting found no mark among the enemy.

Sergeant Streckert formed two squads of eight junior scouts, ordering each to advance on either flank in a spread V formation. Crouching down, steadily and methodically firing, the sergeant kept pressure on the invaders, allowing his leading troops to reach the tree line.

Jan arrived near Garrick's right side as Freddy paused behind a skiff of snow to refresh a magazine with his third set of ammunition. The two friends knew they should continue advancing, but neither felt certain of how to do so without dying in the process.

"Open a light stick and toss it in," Garrick ordered.

Jan wriggled out of his backpack, removed two chemical lights, activated one and hurled it mightily into the trees. The light stick flipped end-over-end, hit several low-hanging branches and fell in front of a tree trunk less than ten feet ahead.

But the tactic worked. With the familiar routine of training taking over, Garrick brought his rifle around, lined up an enemy soldier in his sights and carefully squeezed his trigger. The cadet worked his bolt action and quickly hit another invader in rapid succession.

The enemy retreated again, returning fire while falling back. By now, however, many more Tamarian rifles responded. The air thickened with blue smoke and bullets. Overwhelmed by the sheer volume of ordnance directed against them, the Azgar soldiers turned to flee.

Sensing victory, the leading Tamarian flank troops dove into the woods, their shouts mingled with an occasional gunshot and cry of pain. Jan dashed forward to retrieve his light stick, then joined in the chase.

Garrick, feeling drained, rose to his haunches as the firing stopped. He examined the spot on his chest where he'd been struck by Azgar rounds, noticing that the lead projectiles had splattered on impact, unable to penetrate his tough armor. Although the outer layers of fiber had been singed, cross-woven steel thread, ceramic plates and a thick under pad had spread the shock over an area roughly ten times the diameter of the enemy's forty caliber bullets. Garrick would be left with a pair of nasty bruises, but little else.

Twenty-yards into the woods, however, three shots resounded over the Saradon, followed by two agonized screams. The Azgar remained dangerous and had not yet finished killing Tamarians.

***

Brenna felt the ground growing warm around her. A pleasant feeling tingled in her fingers and toes. She imagined herself beneath the towering tree canopy at home, watching warm daylight filter down through leaves a thousand shades of green. Her mother, whom Brenna called *Umma* with reverent respect, hummed a hymn in the kitchen as she painted a portrait of her servant preparing a spicy, heart-of-palm pie. Camille, the youngest of her three sisters, danced a spirited step with her cousins in the courtyard as Acacia, their lovely, dark-eyed sibling, played a lively tune on her lute. Their *Amair*, a devoted father, and Cynthia matched wits in a board game, while Jawara, son of Tegene – of the Abelscinnian family who lived in the Velez villa – discussed strategy with his brother, Kimoni.

Close by lingered her friend, Woodwind. The Kamerese warrior exchanged stories and laughter with his dark-skinned companions, many of whom Brenna had known all her life and regarded with deep affection. Other members of Tegene's huge clan strolled through the gardens, admiring *Umma's* paintings while small children from both families scampered through grounds in a lively game of tag.

The Lithian woman would have perished on the northern bank of the Tualitin had it not been for an inexplicable event. Her pleasant dream filled with unapproachable light, and the very wind that sought her life soothed words of comfort into her soul. "Awaken, little one. I am with you."

A gunshot startled Brenna from her slumber. Gone were the green leaves and the melodious tones of Acacia's lute. Instead, the merciless wind howled from the far northwest, tugging at her tangled raven tresses in its terrifying fury. She came to her senses, remembering that she felt dangerously cold and alone in a vast, empty land.

Summoning a deep strength from within her soul, Brenna staggered to her feet and willed the fabric of her blouse and skirt to shed water, which evaporated, froze and fell to the ground like snow. She stumbled northward, shivering, crossing her arms to preserve warmth while her strong legs cramped under the strain of her own weight. Brenna's soul cried for shelter and sleep as she resolutely headed for the hill that loomed high against the silver-swathed canopy of darkness overhead.

Alluvial fans curtained the foundation of the foothill, masking its ancient core of igneous rock in deep debris drifts. She found no easy approaches to its flanks, but as Brenna moved to the eastern side, seeking shelter from the wind, her eyes discerned a slender shape swaying gently in the backwash of the windstorm. What a blessing!

She climbed wearily, finding a new and sturdy rope that looked like it had been attached somewhere at the summit, where she'd seen the light. However, her fingers felt so cold, she could neither feel nor apply the appropriate grip. Brenna had climbed quite a distance when the loose rock beneath her feet gave way and she fell, sliding downhill until she tumbled onto a ledge, several feet beneath the dangling rope.

With nearly no strength left, her stamina totally taxed and her will depleted, she screamed in desperate frustration, "Help me!"

***

Sergeant Streckert ordered twelve junior scouts to form up into three squads, each with a designated leader. He instructed these cadets to move into the woods and clear the hilltop of any remaining enemy soldiers, holding no quarter for any invader they found. "Be sharp!" he warned. "Remember, your friends are out there. Don't fire in the trees without a positive I.D. on your target."

Combat shock, and its accompanying adrenaline rush, faded quickly as the young men who remained at the clearing assessed the aftermath of their first battle. A few cadets felt elated as they collected firewood, set up camp and began caring for their injured comrades. Garrick, however, struggled to calm a vivid awareness of how near he'd come to death. Suppressing an urge vomit, the young Tamarian looked away as Sergeant Streckert completed the grim task of bayoneting wounded enemy soldiers.

After recovering all casualties, the sergeant recorded seven Azgar soldiers killed, three slain Tamarians and another four who'd been wounded, one of them seriously. After inhaling aromatic morphine to dull pain, each injured Tamarian received aid from his comrades, who cleaned and bandaged wounds in harmony with their training.

Sergeant Streckert turned his attention to the lifeless cadets, shaking his head in deep thought, but saying nothing while he covered their bodies with blankets taken from their backpacks. "Ravenwood," the sergeant called, noting that Garrick was crouching idly near a tree. "Go get that rope. We don't need any more surprises like this."

Garrick obeyed, retrieving his light stick. As he approached the bristle pine where Jan had secured the rope, he noticed sudden tension on the line. Chambering a round in his rifle, the young soldier prepared for action. However, the tension on the rope suddenly slackened, and he heard a scream that sounded very different in quality to the screeching that had quickened his pulse at dusk.

Creeping forward and peering over the edge, Garrick shone his light stick downhill, revealing the debris fan where he had begun his ascent. There stood the woman whose image had captivated his attention in the hologram. Seeing him she sat, drawing her knees tight against her body, shivering as her bright eyes met and lingered on his.

"Jan!" he called over his shoulder. "Get over here! I need help!"

Garrick's friend approached quickly, a puzzled expression on his face. "What for?"

"Cover me," Garrick replied, setting his weapon down. "There's someone down there."

Jan expressed incredulity. "Are you crazy? Just pull up the rope. There may be more enemy running 'round."

"Not this one. I know who she is." Garrick took hold of the rope with his gloved hands and began working his way backwards, down the slope.

"She?" Jan worried about him, continuing to protest. "What if she's the bait to some kind of trap?" he inquired.

"I don't think so," Garrick responded confidently. "Besides, we can't leave her down there. It's too cold!" He descended carefully to avoid sending rocks downhill.

Jan held Garrick's light stick. When he saw the maiden stand and pull a blade out of her boot, he lined her up in his gun sights, but she looked so small and so lovely, he lowered the weapon and stared at her as if smitten.

As Garrick arrived at the end of the rope, he turned and held out his hands. "It's okay," he soothed in Tamarian. "I won't hurt you."

She heard concern in his expression and lowered her dagger, but stood her ground, shivering. His gentle tone and manner inspired trust, but she didn't understand him.

Noting this, Garrick hoped the woman knew vulgate. "You must be very cold," he said in a reassuring tone.

She nodded, backing away.

"Please, let me help." Wishing he could remember her name, Garrick removed his greatcoat and offered it to her.

Brenna had always feared meeting strangers. She knew a few Tamarian words that *Ugogo* Penda had taught her, but this young man spoke vulgate fluently, albeit in an odd, thick accent. When Brenna bent to sheath her weapon, she noticed that he turned his head away.

The cadet returned his gaze to her as she stood. "My name is Garrick."

Trembling, mostly from the cold, but also because she found the boy very handsome, Brenna appreciated how he did not let his eyes wander. His self-control favorably impressed her in a moment of vulnerability. "I'm Brenna from Illithia," she replied. "Is this Tamaria?"

He nodded, slipping his greatcoat over her shoulders. The garment felt wonderfully warm on her cold body.

"If you're feeling strong enough to hold on, climb onto my back and I'll carry you up."

Brenna needed shelter, but feared meeting strangers, especially since she knew so little of their language. "Are there more of you up there?" she asked fearfully.

The blonde-haired soldier shrugged. "Only one of me, but about twenty cadets my age, plus my sergeant."

She didn't like the sound of that at all. "Can you bring me a blanket? I'm cold, but I can take care of myself."

He shook his head. "You need warm clothes and a long sit by the fire. I can't leave you down here, you'll freeze to death. But if you come with me, I'll look after you."

Reticent Brenna found the young man's gentleness and courtesy disarming enough to trust him. She climbed onto his warm, strong back, resting her head on his left shoulder as he struggled to scale the steep and slippery slope. In his company she felt safe for the first time in weeks, even as he ascended toward a menagerie of strange-sounding voices and bright lights.

Sergeant Streckert, appraising the woman's condition, ordered his cadets to keep their distance. To Garrick he said, "Get her to a fire. Give her a chemical warmer and a blanket."

The petite maiden slipped from Garrick's back, too weak to protest as he maneuvered her into the camp. He dug through his pack, offering a torso heating bag, which he explained how to wear and activate. Her skin, tinged a bit blue, felt cold to his touch. Fearing that she might already be suffering frostbite, he handled her gently.

Garrick also noticed that her bright eyes darkened in the firelight. Despite her muscularity and the weapons she carried, the young woman looked frightened. Anyone who'd survived such a long journey had to be clever and skilled, yet her small size and precarious condition stirred his pity. In an oddly innocent way, she made no move to conceal her features as she took off his coat to strap on and activate the torso warmer. He looked away until she'd wrapped herself in a thermal blanket and sat down by the fire.

Still shivering, Brenna wavered between appreciation for Garrick's care and fear of the others, whose initial staring and whispering unnerved her. After suffering in the bitter cold, even the tiny fire in a tin can burner felt very hot. Discomfort with strangers stirred the temptation to escape as soon as she felt better, but Brenna appreciated the kindly manner of this gentle soldier she'd just met. Discerning his endearing, vulnerable, and self-disciplined character, she chose to linger in his company.

The older man draped another blanket around her shoulders and tried to pull off her boots. Brenna objected stridently. He spoke to her, but she didn't understand.

"The sergeant says you need to put on wool socks," Garrick explained. "But first, I'll give you chemical warmers to put around your feet. They'll prevent frostbite. Sarge says you might lose your toes if you don't follow his advice."

Brenna complied, hiding her torn boot from scrutiny. The foot warmer – a thin sock containing the same reactive compound as the body warmer – provided blissful relief from the cold. Garrick carefully slipped them over her feet, followed by a large pair of woolen socks. His genial manner eased her anxiety, and for the first time, the Lithian woman gazed appreciatively into his grey eyes and smiled.

Sergeant Streckert questioned his returning junior scouts about their contact with the enemy. Harold Vortlund reported that at least two had escaped on horseback. Several pack animals had been tied up a few dozen yards away, and upon arrival, the Azgar soldiers mounted up and fled north, leading the other horses. The Tamarians did not pursue. Harold testified that all approaches to the campsite had been thoroughly checked and felt certain that the hilltop was now secure.

"Set up a perimeter guard and cast lots for the night watch," the sergeant ordered. "Do the same for taking care of the wounded. Anyone not on duty should sleep. It'll be a long night and I don't want anyone dozing off on watch." Turning to Garrick he said, "Get that girl a bedroll."

Several junior scouts joked lewdly at his expense, encouraging Garrick to share his own bed with the foreign woman. Blissfully unaware of their intent, Brenna continued smiling at her handsome acquaintance, her behavior inadvertently encouraging their teasing.

Two hours later, when Garrick's turn to stand watch arrived, another cadet tried to join her, but Brenna pushed the boy away with her foot and huddled by the little gasifying stove alone. Comments made in response to her rejection went mercifully untranslated, and no one bothered her afterward. The Lithian woman prayed as she fed the stove from a collection of sticks gathered by the young men earlier that evening. Despite the wind, the device produced a lot of heat with very little smoke.

Brenna watched Garrick pacing back and forth, performing his task with sober resolve. She drank hot tea that the older man offered, then snuggled into the sleeping bag, gradually feeling warm again. Brenna found her heart pounding whenever the young soldier looked her way. At the sound of a deathwolf's howl, he tensed and turned nervously toward the south, listening to the wicked winter wind rushing through the trees.

Garrick stayed on the perimeter of the camp, using a chemical warmer to endure the harsh cold. He passed near the fire every few minutes, glancing at his pretty companion for a moment before scanning the trees again.

Though she wished otherwise, he never lingered while on watch. Garrick yawned, joking about how she might be better at keeping alert, but he remained vigilant until his duty expired. Two hours later by lunar reckoning, when another cadet arose to take his place, Garrick crawled into his bedroll near Brenna, finding her still awake, waiting.

They talked in whispers for a long time. She spoke about her family and the people she loved. He told her everything she wanted to know about his nation, its ideals and his desire to be a good soldier. They shared their hopes and dreams – she of Allfather's goodness, and he of human kindness – finding their paths of thought crossing in many places before exhaustion overtook him. Garrick drifted to sleep with the sound of her voice on his mind.

Brenna, feeling stronger, inched closer when she noticed his slumber deepen. She smirked at the way he kept his rifle tucked under his left arm, as if ready to spring into action at a moment's notice. Then shyly, tentatively, the Lithian woman touched the cadet's hand with her own. "You have a warrior's soul," she mused.

And she was right.

Destiny

I stirred from sleep feeling exhausted, as though I'd only shut my eyes minutes before. Thin blankets failed to keep me warm, and I'd spent most of the night shivering, pursuing slumber like a hunter stalking a creature more clever than himself. Under a clear, autumn sky, cold air swept across the steppe, pounding into my tent until the water in my washbasin condensed into a useless lump of ice. I cursed but considered myself more fortunate than the men camped outside, without shelter. At the very least, my canvas tent slightly slowed the thrice-damned wind.

Our camp normally stirred at daybreak. On this morning, however, I heard nothing more than the infernal gale howling from the northwest, tugging at tent stakes, casting the flotsam from nearby hills noisily into the camp. It rippled wickedly past our proud battle banners on its way to a distant, unknown destination.

The moment I stepped outside my tent, the full, naked fury of the freezing storm forced me to bow my head and shield my face in subservience. The rushing torrent sapped moisture from my eyes, cutting through my centurion's uniform, chilling my face and body to its core. I felt instantly colder than I'd ever imagined I could be. Eastward, the Daystar limped into the heavens, feeble in its power to warm this bitter, godforsaken land.

Sergeant Aransen, embracing his own body for warmth, joined me. "The news isn't good," he began, shouting over the shrieking, frozen wind.

I had learned since my promotion that first-thing-in-the-morning news was seldom good, so I wasn't surprised. "Tell me."

"We have about two dozen cases of frostbite in the unit. Some of the men can't even stand. Between me and Sergeant Vitus, we lost five who froze to death last night."

I felt my heart sink at his report. Our situation deteriorated further with every mile north we marched. Our misery magnified with every moment approaching the onset of winter. "Let's get something to eat. I hate hearing bad news on an empty stomach."

Our breakfast consisted of teeth-shattering bread and hard cheese. The beleaguered mess commander complained that not only was it too windy to light fires for cooking, but that all our water had frozen during the night. The storage kegs burst open, so we had no water available and no way of collecting any more.

Problems related to the weather had moved far beyond the normal wretchedness I expected my soldiers to endure. As the summer campaign extended, someone in the senior officer's corps should have foreseen the need for warm clothing and hot food. Wasn't that reasonable? Yet with every passing day I felt an increasing sense of powerlessness, watching my men shiver in their fatigues, listening to their bickering while we waited in a long line for frozen rations.

Biting back my frustration, I remained outwardly calm. "Make sure Sivestri has whatever he needs to get those frostbite cases on their feet again. I'll need a list of the dead men's names for family letters. Anything else?"

Aransen nodded. "Scuttlebutt has it that one of our scout units ran into a barbarian mob last night. They were badly outnumbered and suffered heavy casualties. Apparently, the locals have decent guns. I also heard their body armor is bulletproof."

Although the story sounded ridiculous, Aransen's expression remained dead serious. "That sounds like something laying about the barnyard," I muttered. "Look around. There's no advanced civilization up here."

Aransen shrugged. "I couldn't tell you either way, sir, but I thought you should know."

I attended an officer's meeting after breakfast. Our forces, while equipped with updated versions of older weapons, benefitted from a modern organization system that configured various combat disciplines into Combined Arms Units. Each of these self-contained groups assembled in large tents with central fire pits. Holes in the tent roofs should have provided an outlet for smoke, but the wind made these ineffective. Thus, we endured a choking, eye-stinging session with Lord Balinor and his cadre of vice-generals. At least the air felt warmer inside.

In deference to historical religious observances, we followed a rigid routine. A priest examined the victuals of a freshly slaughtered animal to determine whether our actions offended any of the hundred-odd deities in the ancient pantheon. Although few of us believed in this kind of thing anymore, no one ever complained.

Standing with both arms raised as if swearing an oath, a fiery-eyed priest lead us in adoration of the emperor, whose exalted name was to be glorified above all others. It seemed silly that we made grandiose efforts to appease gods who were actually less important to us than our supreme leader, but I hadn't broached the subject with those learned in spiritual affairs because we weren't supposed to question priestly authority. Liturgy seemed an end in and of itself to them.

Personally, I found these worship services amusing. While I never laughed out loud, with all the suffering my men endured I appreciated having something to smile about. While the rest of us stifled coughing fits during the invocation, the row of black-robed priests standing on the dias remained sublime in their ecstatic utterances. They seemed impervious to the smoke pressing down from above, a hint, perhaps, that the Place of Burning threatened against infidels was friendly to, and perhaps frequented by, their own kind.

Next, a staff centurion read through unit troop strengths, compiled by sergeants before breakfast while many of us were still asleep. The centurion announced we'd suffered attrition and desertions, a fact that he attributed to the cold. Requisition officers were duly informed of the need for warm clothing and heavier blankets.

I shook my head, in disbelief, shame, and anger. The senior officers had promised that our campaign would end once we'd subjugated Shirak and gained control over its surrounding resources. We'd begun a long push northward because of genuine and perceived hostility from petty kingdoms, primitive tribes and small clans whose armed alliances quickly succumbed to our cavalry, infantry and artillery. One after another they'd fallen, yet ongoing calls for the subjugation of new threats continued until we found ourselves standing on this frozen wasteland, over a thousand miles from home. We didn't have heavy blankets because no one had seen the need to bring any along.

Our logisticians were now supposed to provide material unforeseen when the campaign began, as if merely being told to give the men warmer clothes would enable them to conjure winter vestments out of thin air. Our supply train, at this point well over a thousand miles long, made it unlikely that we'd get our blankets any time soon.

My cynicism grew out of a pattern I'd seen repeated many times. Complex, intricately machined weapons worked best in hot, low-humidity climates. The breech loading kits for our trapdoor carbines did not tolerate dirt or moisture very well, and the big guns required constant maintenance because of similar breech problems, rifle wear or elevation system failure. As spare parts became scarce, our engineers fabricated and machined replacements in portable smith shops. Artillery units suffered chronic supply deficiencies, forcing their commanders to conserve ammunition on fire-support missions.

We'd succeeded because we'd outclassed our enemies. Our destiny, it seemed, involved conquering every inch of land in sight, so long as it was poorly defended and blessed with material resources.

After this, a commander from the eastern province of Abelscinnia, an outrageously tall man with very dark skin and a curious accent, explained the need for a northern headquarters. He told us that influential senators back home were demanding justification for our operations, and in order to establish a lawful presence among the northern nations, we needed a legitimate claim to territory.

Fortunately, our embassy had been contacted by the heir of a former king – a giant whose easily-forgotten name I could not pronounce – in the hope that we would be able to assist him in regaining control of the area captured by local barbarian tribes. The town of Burning Tree, now an important industrial port, had long ago been his father's regional capital.

Conquering this city and holding it against the enemy would give us access to the raw materials of the far north. Further, we would stand in history as the brilliant army that finally isolated the Kingdom of Kameron, an ancient and powerful rival on our western border. Since the giant king's contact had come through diplomatic channels, only a two-thirds majority vote in the senate could override the emperor's executive order for Lord Balinor to take the city. This outcome was unlikely, no matter how unpopular his policy.

Cynically, I wondered how much of this plan glorified the emperor, and how much served to consolidate Lord Balinor's power, while securing access to new resources on behalf of his wealthy, influential, industrialist friends at home in Marioch. They'd financed this campaign in the hope that conquering new land would prove profitable for their businesses.

Our first task involved establishing a permanent military presence. Scouting reports described small fire keeps scattered through the hills to our northwest that likely housed no more than a few hundred soldiers each. Almost directly north of our position lay an island of foothills, behind which we could camp to get out of the accursed wind. Fruit orchards in the hills to the west could provide firewood, and we would compel a small population of locals to relinquish stored food to sustain us during the winter months. A four-day march to the northwest of this region would bring us to Burning Tree, after we'd passed though a heavily populated valley bristling with defenses.

The giants, who had provided us with additional intelligence, expressed a healthy respect for barbarian firepower. They warned us about excellent rifles, repeating cannon, artillery and rockets that carried explosive shells over vast distances. Their report stated that local soldiers were well-trained and tough, supported by flying machines, underground tunnels and steam trains, all of which I'd dismissed as fantasy. Weren't these primitive people?

Our meeting concluded with unit assignment sessions. Every field commander and his subordinate officers met with their respective vice-generals. In theory, every legion could operate as a self-contained army, complete with infantry, cavalry, artillery, medical and supply units. In actual practice, however, these arrangements were never so tidy.

My unit drew the luxury of standing near the fire. After indulging in this for a few minutes I felt warmer than I'd been in recent memory, and fortunately for me, the hot smoke spiraled upward, away from my eyes and out of my lungs. The pall of pollution cooled at the top of the tent and settled along its cold, canvas sides where less lucky officers huddled, hacked, and cast longing glances toward the billowing tent flaps.

Our commander, Vice-General Diabilos, wasted no time in outlining his plan. He said we needed to secure a command center. Since the barbarians had an army in the area, we could ill-afford to leave our highest-ranking officers camped in the open where they'd be exposed to enemy action. The vice-general mulled over our scouting reports and selected an old inn that he believed would serve well for such a purpose. The lot fell on my century to wrest control of the compound from the locals. I had only three days to plan and carry out the attack.

Characteristically, the senior officers needed a building for shelter, rather than a lowly bivouac on the cold ground with the rest of us. As I listened, I knew my men would curse and complain that special treatment for the senior officers violated the egalitarian principles of citizenship we'd been fighting to spread among the uncivilized. Sighing in impotent resignation, I figured we'd suffer many more desertions and deaths from freezing before this campaign came to its bitter, exhausted end.

After the meeting dismissed, I heard one soldier shouting to another that only a few deathwolves had returned from their rampage last night. In truth, I felt inwardly amazed that anything alive could survive without shelter through an entire night on the high-altitude steppe at this latitude. Deathwolves did not have the heavy fur coats of their smaller, wild cousins. I worried that if such fearsome creatures could not last when exposed to this cold, it didn't bode well for the rest of us.

Back at my tent, I swaddled my body in three layers of clothing. I'd have put on more if I'd had more to wear. Although a senior officer might disapprove of my ridiculous appearance, as long as I had to brave the bitter weather, I wanted to feel as warm as possible. When Sergeant Aransen reported, I told him to make certain that the men we'd take north today were similarly attired.

As soon as Aransen stepped outside I could have sworn I'd heard him laugh. But when he returned, about ten minutes later, he and the eight soldiers in his company looked no less ludicrous than I. No one in my scouting party expressed dismay concerning his appearance, but as we went to the quartermaster for horses, I sensed that each man shared my desire to vanish before too many eyes caught sight of us.

We settled into a steady march, our faces bowed and eyes squinting, walking beside our steeds to stay out of the relentless wind. Primordial fear of the gusting breeze made our horses nervous and difficult to control, especially from the ground. They needed water too. I wondered how much of their skittishness resulted from thirst.

At this latitude, the sheer immensity of the Saradon inspired awe. Its extreme horizontality, its utter lack of terrain features and any sign of life wearied my eyes with monotony in minutes. Pure sky, an intense blue made hard by the bitter cold, rose from three horizons, its bleakness broken only by the glacier-crowned ridges stabbing into its indigo domain some distance west. What a worthless place! Why were we starting a war over it on behalf of the giants?

I wanted to go home. I wanted to be warm. I wanted to eat a decent meal, too . . . .

We moved north at about 90 paces per minute, following a minor trade route that skirted the western fringe of the Saradon. Silently, we marched through a sea of tall, swaying prairie grass that rippled in random, golden ranks, bowing subserviently to the breeze. Hours later, we closed in on an outcropping of steep, tree-covered hills, and finding much less wind on its eastern flanks, stopped to rest our weary horses. There, beneath an oak tree, we found the remains of a scouting party.

"Looks like an ambush," Aransen remarked. "Maybe someone jumped them from the tall grass."

The bodies lay stiff, their flesh and faces blue. A long line of boot prints obliterated all clues that might have shown how the butchering began and ended. Clearly, however, blades, rather than bullets, had been responsible for the carnage. Given our recent intelligence assessment, that detail seemed enigmatic to me.

As a precaution, I ordered loaded rifles in case any trouble headed our way. I said nothing though, my senses numbed by the cold and my spirit dulled by the solemn duty to follow pointless orders. Carefully avoiding the road, we continued north.

About two hours later, the hills hooked eastward for several miles. On a low rise overlooking the steppe an old stone inn stood guard. Encircled by an ancient, lichen-encrusted wall of bleached granite blocks nearly twenty feet in height, the site looked more like an ancient temple than a place of lodging.

Above its gate a sign swayed in the wind. Written in four languages, one of them the common form of ours, it read, "The Ice Dragon Inn, established 2377." That meant the building had been standing for over 900 years.

From a distance of about 300 yards, I saw my first barbarian soldier. Peering through a field lens, I could see a male figure in mottled brown fatigues who didn't look old enough to shave. "A virgin with a long rifle!" I smirked, mentally questioning the courage of any giant who'd be afraid of a mere boy like this.

Another soldier approached as I watched. Absorbing as much detail as possible, I noticed no obvious armor, but their clothing looked quite bulky and seemed to restrict movement somewhat. Whether they wore some kind of armored vest or just many layers of winter clothing couldn't be ascertained from my position, but they didn't appear to be bothered by the cold. I wished I could have said the same for myself.

"Let's move up a hill to get a better view of the compound," I said, weary from walking, but already imagining how I might lead an attack on this place.

The complex contained four buildings. Two of these, probably living quarters, were tall and dotted with windows. Another structure, this one low to the ground with few windows, had a capped stack on its roof and at least five doors, with a maze of pipe extending from its southern wall directly into the ground. The fourth appeared to be a large livery, located ten yards west of the small building with its tangle of pipes, behind which lay a swine pen. A strange-looking, circular-shaped tank with a low, domed roof had been built to the south of the pig sty. Some kind of pipe rose from the ground and turned into the top of it, but I had no clue of its function.

Along the perimeter of the complex lay an extensive garden of trimmed shrubbery and hand-groomed hardwood forest. Late autumn wind had swept nearly all the leaves from the trees, giving gunners an unobstructed view over the walls at this height – perfect for eight-pound mortars.

It would be a shame, I thought, to damage the main buildings. Majestic and old, built with flying buttresses, towering, steep-pitched roofs and stained-glass windows more reminiscent of a cathedral than a traveler's tavern, the living quarters must have been some long-dead architect's finest work.

Further, I noted that several paths, paved in grey cobblestones and swept clean by diligent hands, meandered through lovingly tended gardens. Arranged throughout the courtyard were devices that looked like lamps, but they didn't resemble the oil burners I remembered from home. For a moment I pondered the possibility that this civilization aspired to a higher level of technical expertise than I'd initially believed, but I quickly dismissed the thought.

On a fifty-foot tower near the back wall a multi bladed aeropump spun rapidly in the wind, no doubt lifting water from a well deep beneath the frozen soil. While I was pleased to see a secure water supply, I wondered how the barbarians prevented it from freezing.

Further observations fueled additional speculation. A steady, bluish *glow* radiated from several north-facing windows on the back side of one building. Given the season and the hour of day, these rooms had to be illuminated from the inside, and I knew of no lamp that emitted blue light. Also, an exhaust stack on the small building remained smokeless during my examination. I saw no soot on its weather cap, either. How did they keep the buildings warm in such a cold climate?

I ordered a preliminary artillery survey from two key hilltop positions located north and west of the inn, then discussed lines of infantry attack with Sergeant Aransen. We'd have to bring in a lot of munitions and manpower for this operation, so we mapped supply routes that could not be directly observed or attacked from the inn itself. Then, we planned a staging area, sufficiently distant to ensure surprise during our advance on the compound.

Before leaving, I ordered Aransen to remain behind with four men. "Watch everything that comes in and goes out," I told him. "Give me an indication of how many soldiers are quartered there and what kinds of weapons they have. I'll expect your report by noon tomorrow."

"I'll get right on it, sir," he replied, apparently pleased that I had turned out to be a half-decent officer after all.

If I rode back to camp and set to work right away, it was possible that we might take the inn within two days. Although that timetable made my schedule very tight, it fit into the senior officers' outline and I felt confident that my soldiers would work as hard as necessary to turn my attack plan into reality.

A bold and successful territorial seizure would certainly boost their waning morale after twenty-four days of hard marching through the deepening cold. Fresh food and warm clothes would surely lift spirits long wearied by misery and monotony.

I hoped that our strike to secure this place as a headquarters would serve to fulfill many of our needs, but I didn't understand until later just how my plans for the Ice Dragon Inn would affect the loyalty I felt for my nation and utterly, irrevocably change my destiny.

Junior Scout Garrick Ravenwood, Tamarian Defense Force;
Brenna Velez; Woodwind

Serenade

Braving the bitter cold before dawn, Brenna slipped out of her warm bedroll and glanced furtively around the camp where her newly found friend and his companions lay sleeping. She noticed a neat stack of heavy clothing at her feet, consisting of a sweater, fur leggings, a thick, hooded overcoat and a large pair of leather gloves. Hurriedly, the young woman slipped into the garments, aware that they had once belonged to some dead Tamarian cadet, but too cold for a response more meditative than gratitude.

Anxious to avoid being seen, Brenna tiptoed past the sleeping Junior Scout on watch. The temptation to slip away unnoticed nagged from deep in her soul, but the distasteful thought of continuing her long, lonely trek mingled with a pang of conscience and made her pause. Turning back toward the camp, Brenna glimpsed a bloodstained bandage wrapped around a delirious, slumbering cadet's right leg. She let out a sigh and trudged over to where he lay.

Someone had applied a tourniquet to control bleeding from what looked like a gunshot wound, but had not loosened it afterward. Brenna noticed discoloration and swelling of the cadet's flesh. She frowned, removing the bandage to examine the damage, but drainage from the puncture had freeze-dried during the night, causing a crust of pus to stick to the bandage. As she pulled it apart, he flinched and began to waken.

"Sleep," she commanded gently, *believing* he would.

The cadet settled back into his dreams, allowing her to continue undisturbed. She pulled out her boot knife, cut off the tourniquet, worked on the injury with healing kisses, then gently pressed on his leg to restore circulation. Brenna prayed for him before moving on to the next cadet.

Rugged body armor prevented many serious injuries, and the cadets' canteens were so well insulated, water inside them hadn't frozen. Brenna performed her ministrations on cuts, sprains and scratches that restored easily. The Lithian woman spent several minutes methodically washing and healing wounds, so absorbed in her task that fear slowly melted from her mind altogether.

Near one of the smoldering camp stoves she found a cadet with a head injury. Several broken ampules lay scattered about, the contents of which smelled fruity, like methoxyflurane. Brenna frowned, knowing that opiates suppress the cardiovascular system. If he'd lost a lot of blood he'd be in trouble. But when she checked his pulse she found his heart beating strong and steadily.

When she unwrapped the injury, it looked awful. A razor would have been useful in shaving away the boy's blood-matted hair, but since she didn't have one, Brenna held her blade over the hot coals, rinsed its crystalline edge with canteen water, then very gently feathered back the young man's hair line. She washed away all traces of dirt and blood from the wound, worried that the glancing blow from a bullet might have damaged this cadet's skull.

"Sleep in Allfather's hands," she whispered, kissing her forefinger as supernatural power flowed through her flesh to heal the soldier's injury. Satisfied, she turned her face into the force of the freezing windstorm, seeking a sheltered place below the camp for her morning prayer.

The young woman climbed into a ravine to the west, emptied her bladder where she could not be seen, then hiked back up to a circle of black oak and juvenile bristle pine that formed a hidden sanctum. Beneath the naked oak branches lay a thin carpet of sparkling snow, untrodden by the foot of neither man nor beast. Having never before seen snow up close, its glare forced Brenna to shield her eyes and squint.

Luminescent in the purple light only Lithian eyes could see, the frozen veil glistened like a bright aurora borealis. Scattered across its gleaming surface, random patterns of dark shapes and lines crisscrossed where the radiant snow lay speckled with fallen oak and cottonwood leaves, and slender needles of bristle and ponderosa pine.

Turning away from the brilliant scene, hearing nothing more than the surging sound of restless wind within the trees, the Lithian woman carefully balanced her bow against the rugged trunk of an old cottonwood, kneeling amid the icy blanket to pray.

She began every morning this way. But now, tired of running and afraid that she could never again return home, Brenna grew increasingly desperate. Lacking the love and companionship of her family, she felt vulnerable in this cold, windy land. "I didn't want to marry," she lamented, "so I shut down *Umma's* portal and fled north. I'd promised *Amair* I'd comply with whatever he asked me to do, though I knew in my heart I would not."

Brenna paused, remembering reckless words while thinking of things that should have been said. Pondering personal motives, she knew that what she'd rationalized as a split-second decision at the last, critical moment had in fact been long premeditated. The young woman gazed into the dark heavens, marveling at the breathtaking beauty of the early morning stars, only to shut her misty eyes. Defiance, not fate, had set her on the path leading to this foreign land.

Brenna valued the freedom to choose, but exercising that privilege at the expense of honesty – especially toward her parents – had been a compromise that was likely causing her beloved family much grief at this moment. While she had a right to disagree with her *Amair's* plans, as Lithian culture permitted, the devout woman should not have behaved dishonorably toward him.

This issue stained the fabric of her soul. Despite her intelligence and outstanding physical condition, she could not dictate the outcome of her choices and resolve every detail to her own satisfaction. When she meditated on this, in light of the previous evening's events, she realized that her profoundly fragile life depended on Allfather's magnanimous grace. Brenna needed his protection and sustenance, and because she wielded Allfather's healing power, she felt obligated to reflect his integrity.

This contrarian part of her nature always contended against the ideal relationship with God that she aspired to achieve. Years ago, she had learned to accept the reality of this conflict, the doubt it wrought, and the difficulty brought about by believing in ideas that could not be seen, heard, nor touched when existential matters muddled her mind. Seen through the perfect lens of hindsight, Brenna wished she had applied the principles of love and honesty to a higher degree and depended less on her own wisdom, as she had so regrettably done in the recent past.

And so, the Lithian woman poured out her heart. She asked for mercy and forgiveness, *believing* that loving, compassionate Allfather would listen to her plea, continue preserving her life while protecting her loved ones from harm. "Give me courage to live with consequences I can't choose," she prayed. "Lavish on me the wisdom to speak and act with integrity that reflects your character as I move among the people of the High Land."

The chill of the windy morning constrained her concentration. Brenna shivered in the snow, her eyelashes frozen shut, distracted by a desire to return to a warm place near the fire. She recited a list of things for which she felt grateful, including the attractive soldier she'd met the night before, and concluded her petition nearly twenty minutes after embarking upon it, with a litany of praise and exultation.

After this Brenna felt strong in spirit again, ready to greet the new day with a smile. Humming a favorite hymn, she rubbed her eyes until the lids unstuck, watching in awe as the scenery about her undertook its daily metamorphosis. The soft, phosphorescent, ultraviolet colors of night yielded gradually to longer, brighter wavelengths that heralded the imminent rising of the Daystar. White light soon overpowered the bluish, nocturnal glow that had so drawn the Lithian woman to this place. Within minutes, the human spectrum of colors became visible to the indigo-eyed maiden.

But the freezing wind belied the promise of warmth borne by the ascending star. Brenna picked up her bow and scurried uphill with fleet-footed grace, pausing to catch her breath before returning to the camp.

***

"I'm telling you, he's a spy!"

Heinz Neergard, the local militia chairman for Dieter, a small town on the Tamarian frontier, had only two weeks of tenure left at this position and longed for it to end. His job involved coordinating the town's response to potential threats against its citizens and property. As daylight hours shortened and autumn drew to a close, the level of paranoia in this sleepy, agricultural hamlet had risen dramatically. More often than he cared to remember, some concerned citizen had pounded on his door at daybreak with news that couldn't wait until after breakfast.

Standing unshaven in his nightclothes and bare feet, growing colder in direct proportion to the time he spent with his front door open, the tall, gray-haired gentleman listened patiently to the frantic tale of Winnie Mikkels, the elderly proprietress of a bed and breakfast establishment on the south end of town.

"He came in last night after dark. Franz would never have let him in the door because he looked an absolute mess, but he was cold, and I felt sorry for him. Then I got to thinking straight," the old woman explained, gesticulating pointedly as if her skinny, vein and sinew shrouded hands could paint a picture where words failed. "He's got this huge sword and looks around at everything like he wanted to steal it all. Spoke the vulgate, he did, then gives me this worthless foreign coin for his room!"

The old woman produced a heavy golden disc from a pocket in her musty, moth-eaten, knee-length coat, waving it in the kindly man's face. He backed away from her wrinkled, liver-spot covered hand, which, despite the cold, reeked of menthol.

"Is it real?" Heinz queried.

"Well, the old dwarf says so, but his eyes aren't so good anymore and I'm not sure he's not in cahoots with them anyway."

The old dwarf was a goldsmith who'd been stricken by a congenital spinal condition that left him deformed. His name was Alfie, he had a reputation for honesty, and while Heinz recognized the old woman's prejudice, he didn't comment on it. "If the dwarf says it's good, then it's good," the shivering man replied. "If it will set your mind at ease, my boy and I will stop in and see this man after breakfast."

"You'd better hurry," she warned, sensing that he wasn't taking her as seriously as she thought he should. "If he leaves before you get there, I'll hold you responsible!"

Heinz smiled, sensing an opening. "Why don't you delay him until we arrive? Give him an extra-large breakfast and draw him a hot bath. If you treat him well, he won't suspect you've spoken to me this morning."

Mrs. Mikkels' thick glasses nearly bounced off her face as she nodded. "You know, that's exactly what I'll do. He won't suspect. No sir! We'll stop these foreigners yet!"

"Thank-you for stopping by," Heinz called, closing the door with relief tempered only by the grim realization that he'd have to see and smell her again after breakfast.

Rheanne, his ebullient, sixteen-year-old daughter, bounded out of her room. Like her mother, Rheanne always overflowed with energy in the early morning. "*Vati*, what was that all about?"

Heinz drew his arm around the girl and kissed her forehead affectionately. "Mrs. Mikkels has another spy," he replied. "Tell Wolfie to get up and eat. We have to pay a visit to her guest and save the Republic from tyranny."

Rheanne skipped over to her brother's room, opened the door, and shouted, "Get out of bed lazy bones! *Mutti's* been at work in the kitchen since daybreak and *Vati* mistakenly thinks he needs your good-for-nothing help defending the country against un-bathed, lice-infested foreign spies, of which you, by virtue of extreme laziness, are probably in treasonous collaboration!"

The girl quickly pulled shut the door to avoid being hit by a trashy novel hurled from the bed. "He's coming, *Vati*," she said with a smile.

***

Woodwind awakened before dawn. Although not normally inclined to stir at such an hour, the combination of cold air seeping through poorly sealed window frames, incessantly rattling glass and the rasping rake of tree limbs against his room's outer wall prevented needed sleep.

Like Brenna, Woodwind believed in Allfather, but with far less fervency. He rarely spent more than a few moments in formal meditation. Days passed between his prayers, but his conscience remained clear, believing that integrity of mind and sound, moral conduct evidenced Allfather's continuing influence.

Woodwind remained a servant by his own choice. His master, Lord Velez, treated him like a son, paying for his martial training and formal education in life sciences. Lithian scriptures stated that Allfather endowed every intelligent race with a mandate to preserve and manage his creation for the benefit of living things. Applying his pragmatic insight to this spiritual paradigm convinced Woodwind that exploiting resources for profit as the Azgar often did – especially at the expense of the poor and the weak – opened the floodgates for many kinds of evil.

Woodwind loved nature, and though his heart grieved at its destruction, he often made observations that softened this pain with humor. "We're born between organs of excrement," he'd say. "Is no wonder our behavior stinks!"

Brenna did not find his talk amusing in the slightest, he realized, but she acted altogether too serious and would benefit from a good distraction. Woodwind longed to be her companion, but they'd grown up together and she would have nothing to do with that idea. Thus, he settled for friendship, though secretly, he longed to fill her life and sate her strong desire with passion.

Their stormy relationship inspired whispering and rumor. Many people didn't understand why Brenna – who'd struggled to find a partner who wasn't put off by her talent, intelligence and strength, or whose interest lay only in her shapely form – refused to commit herself to him.

Woodwind set aside all emotional and physical frustration for her sake without overt complaint. He understood that every experience had a deep, spiritual significance to her. Brenna read the Lithian scriptures voraciously, always striving to apply principles of moral conduct to her own behavior. She harmonized her attitude with Allfather's will, expecting divine influence over the most personal aspects of her life. Woodwind knew he could never aspire to the intensity she sustained in that domain.

He'd been thinking about her and found himself in prayer, quite by accident. "I've exhausted every option. I'm afraid I'll never find her, never see her lovely face, never hear the music of her voice again. I am lost as long as she is lost, and I can't protect her when she's not in my company. Please keep her safe."

Unaccustomed to long, prayerful discourses, his request trailed off into a path of more practical thoughts, as it usually did. In moments of self-reflection, Woodwind habitually blamed his lack of spiritual discipline for Brenna's disinterest. He could discern no other reasonable explanation for her rejection of his devotion.

Then he felt foolish for his personal, emotional outburst. *If anyone can survive out there, it's Brenna. She can outrun a horse, no one can match her with a bow, and Allfather always takes care of her. Why am I worried? Why do I fear for her? Where does this loss I feel originate?* This silent reasoning wrought comfort, and as the minutes passed, he sensed Allfather's spirit assuring that Brenna remained alive. Soon, his fear for her safety faded like a forgotten dream.

Woodwind's reverie ended, interrupted by the steady, clomping of shoed feet on the wooden stair beyond his room. The sound of running water followed for several minutes, then suddenly stopped. Footsteps shuffled toward his room. Knocking, for a reason the southerner did not understand, the old woman remained behind the door and announced, "Your morning bath is ready, sir!"

Woodwind opened the door. The elderly proprietress smiled. Her manner seemed strangely pleasant, in sharp contrast with the abrupt, almost rude reception he'd received the previous evening. Of the two Tamarians he'd met thus far, she had regarded him with greater suspicion, making him wonder if another foreigner had come under her roof the night before and wet the bed . . . .

Perhaps the Kamerese kroner he'd given her brought out better manners, though she'd taken it reluctantly. The sudden change in her behavior inspired Woodwind's worry that matters were amiss and his life was in danger.

"Thank-you. I appreciate the trouble you've gone to for me this morning," Woodwind replied. "But it would be a waste of your hot water for me to wash up if I have to return to my dirty clothing."

The old woman pushed past him, her arms laden with clean linen for the bed and a fresh towel. "The best you can do with that ratty outfit is throw it in the fire! You smell like a billy goat with the pox!"

Woodwind accepted the insult without protest. "Isn't it a bit cold to go running about naked?" he replied, hoping the woman might find that remark funny, then uncertain how to respond when she didn't.

Stripping the sheets from Woodwind's bed, she muttered something about how much work she had to do before breakfast. "My youngest son was a big man like you," she said. "Take anything of his you like."

Woodwind appreciated charity but disapproved of people who sought advantage from other's generosity, and certainly didn't consider himself needy. Although the old woman kept a fairly nice place, her apparel suggested that frugality sustained her lifestyle. "I'll gladly pay for warm clothing," he offered politely.

"Take it all! He ain't needing a thing no more," she scowled. The silence that followed felt protracted and socially unnerving. Several awkward moments later, Woodwind noticed tears in the old woman's eyes. She turned her back to him and began sobbing, mumbling in the consonantal gibberish of the Tamarian language.

Uncertain of the reason behind yet another change in demeanor, Woodwind hedged. Yet when he asked why she'd become upset, the matron raged like a pent-up flood.

"If it ain't the giants coming to take what we got, then it's you foreigners! It's always war after war. The army needs our children. They fight, they die, but that's never enough because the killing never stops! I lost my husband, my daughter and both my boys fighting foreigners like you!" She threw a wadded-up pillowcase at Woodwind for emphasis, missing him badly.

"I'm truly sorry for your loss," he responded. "I didn't come here to fight anyone, most certainly not the people who have shown me kindness and hospitality." The southerner retrieved the pillowcase and began folding it.

"Go take your bath!" she commanded. "Let an old woman cry in peace! I'll set a change of clothes outside the doorway for you."

Woodwind obeyed, a little bit puzzled why she would leave the promised clothing on the other side of the door. Reflecting the influence of a Lithian upbringing, unmarried Woodwind had no sense of modesty and didn't realize the extent to which Tamarians abhorred nudity of any kind. This misunderstanding inspired even more worry for his personal safety. Woodwind reached for his blade but left his armor behind. The woman didn't seem to notice, and he slipped out of the room without another word.

***

Ghosts from days gone by mingled with terror from the previous evening. Fear invaded Garrick's final dream, sometime in the early morning hours. After he'd fought and killed his first enemy soldier, Garrick's adversary regained his feet and pressed the battle further. No combat skill countered the enemy advance, and no weapon stopped him. Garrick called for help, yet he stood alone among dead comrades whose skulls had been blown apart by Azgar bullets, and whose intestines shone wetly in the light.

Having no recourse he tried to run, but found that his legs completely betrayed him. A sensation of lightness, of floating higher by leaping, allowed him to escape. Garrick watched the ground grow distant as the terror of falling gripped his belly. From within the clouds, he heard his father's drunken voice slurring obscenities, along with the whimper of his sobbing mother as she cowered from her husband's explosive rage.

"Kira!" he cried out, fearing for the safety of his younger siblings. "Algernon!"

Then Garrick fell from the sky fast and hard. As the grass-carpeted Saradon rose to meet him, the young Tamarian lurched awake.

Cold morning air embraced him. Panting and trembling as terror raced through his veins, Garrick experienced momentary disorientation that heightened his apprehension. Sharp daylight assailed Garrick's vision as he surveyed an unfamiliar scene. Several seconds later, as events remembered from the night before fell into place, the young man regained control over his racing heart.

His blonde-haired companions huddled around their fires, sleeping peacefully. Yet something felt odd, out of place. Even the wounded seemed comfortable in their slumber. Where had their bandages gone?

Andreas Pflieger heated water for tea as Sergeant Streckert returned from the trees on the eastern edge of the hill, tightening his belt. When he saw that Garrick was awake, he queried, "Ravenwood, last night the way you cozied up with that foreign girl seemed a bit too friendly for my comfort. How do you know each other?"

"It's not what you're thinking, sergeant," Garrick replied, glancing around, wondering where she had gone. "A traveler showed me her image in a locket yesterday afternoon and I recognized her face. The two of us had never met before last night."

The sergeant began nudging sleeping cadets with his boot, not quite as gently as each would have liked. "What do you know about this traveler?" the sergeant queried. "Tell me everything."

Garrick repeated the incident, including his idea that the demise of Azgar soldiers at the oak tree had been Woodwind's work. "It's where the evidence leads," he said.

Sergeant Streckert stalked closer with his arms akimbo, glaring at Garrick in such a way that the cadet felt certain he'd done something else wrong. "Why didn't you tell me about this earlier?"

"You were mad at me because of the snowball fight, and I didn't want any more trouble," the young man stammered, a little bit fearfully. "I knew we'd be out here for two days, so I didn't expect to actually meet her. The man told me she was shy, and truthfully, I didn't really believe his wild story, anyway."

The middle-aged man tightened his lips, shook his head and looked into the pale heavens. He thought for a moment before returning his hawk-eyed gaze to the cadet. "As soon as we return, get up to Dieter and find that swordsman," the sergeant ordered. "Take the girl with you as a gesture of goodwill, and bring them back to the inn."

"I mean no disrespect, sergeant," Garrick replied, "but you saw what he did to those Azgar soldiers. If he decides to run off with the Lithian woman, I won't be able to stop him. Besides, how do we know he's not a bounty hunter hired to track her down?"

Remembering the carnage he'd seen at the oak tree last evening, the sergeant didn't think so. "Ask her about him and see what she says. I don't think your swordsman is going anywhere. He's out of his mind trying to track down a half-naked *sicklian* girl through the countryside. Yet if he's stayed ahead of the Azgar this long, I think his brand of lunacy might benefit us.

"Winter's coming, an army's in the way, and he has nowhere else to go. You tell him we'll protect both him and the girl, and I'm sure he'll cooperate."

Garrick let his sergeant's words sink in before responding, feeling disbelief, excitement and tension, all at the same time, as the sergeant had actually ordered him to spend more time in Brenna's company. That fact made his heart pound, even if she did belong to someone else. Conversely, his sense of duty compelled a response that focused on the safety of his people. "And what if the Azgar invade before I return?" he inquired.

"Then take them both up to Burning Tree. At the regional army headquarters, tell General Ziegler everything you know about what happened here. We won't get a resupply train until next month, and if we face a large-scale invasion, we're going to need help in a hurry."

Garrick promised he would follow the orders.

"Don't waste any time," the sergeant warned.

***

The old woman had shown Woodwind the washroom after he'd paid his money the night before, but any curiosity about its features had been overcome by fatigue at that time. When she discussed indoor, running water Woodwind didn't consider her statement strange, for households in Shirak also featured plumbing and multrum septic systems. Any moderately advanced civilization could boast of such amenities.

Yet as he pushed open the door, Woodwind walked into wonderland. In the center of a white-tiled, windowless room stood a porcelain tub filled to three-quarters of its depth with steaming water. A spout and shiny steel levers extended above its lip on one end, with words he could not read inscribed in the metal.

Woodwind shut the door, not out of modesty, but rather, out of concern for his personal safety. He clicked the lock into position, then turned to examine other fascinating features of Tamarian technology.

A gilded mirror on the east-facing wall reflected light from four white, porcelain lamps firmly anchored to the tile floor. Just above eye-level, glass enclosures that felt dangerously warm surrounded a pair of glowing metal crosses with many holes bored through them. A blue flame danced above the metal, swirling in beautiful, random motions. A knob, located about half-way up the lamp stem, could be turned to adjust the quantity of gas being burned, and subsequently, the level of light given off by the burner. Above the glass enclosure, a thin pipe, also hot to Woodwind's fingers, extended through the tiled ceiling.

A smooth, white quartz pedestal basin rose from the floor beneath the mirror. It also sported a spout and a pair of levers. Woodwind turned them, and as expected, water flowed out. One of the levers controlled cold water, and to his astonishment, hot water gushed from the other. The old woman had said nothing about hot running water.

"Clever people!" he mused, realizing that the tub must have been filled from its similar arrangement. Woodwind found, to his delight, that he could adjust the temperature of his bath by adding either hot or cold, so he fiddled with the levers until satisfied that the bath temperature suited his comfort. And thus, warm water soothed every ache in Woodwind's weary body. After scrubbing himself with soap he reclined in the tub and, feeling relaxed and content, drifted into a shallow sleep.

Suddenly, he heard heavy footfalls on the stairs and an angry-sounding male voice. Awakening from his nap, Woodwind nearly leaped out of the tub, and in doing so, slipped on the slick tile and landed unceremoniously in a wet heap on the hard floor. That hurt!

Certain that he'd be bruised for the rest of what promised to be a brief life, the Kamerese swordsman retrieved his weapon and retreated to the wall next to the door. His left elbow throbbed from its contact with the floor, but he did not curse.

The woman's voice came from somewhere down the hall, followed by more footsteps, each one getting closer. He could tell from the sound that there was probably only one person moving toward him on the other side of the wall. The doorknob rattled noisily, but its lock held. Woodwind pressed his back against the washroom wall, directly to the left of the door, holding his sword at the ready. He clicked open the latch just before the man on the other side hit the portal with his shoulder.

The door flew open, and right behind it, a light-haired young man charged in wielding an old revolver pistol. Woodwind gave him a hard shove on the back of the neck as he passed, forcing the aggressor to stumble on the slippery tile and slide face-first toward the tub.

Bracing for what promised to be a knee-shattering encounter with unyielding enamel; the boy dropped his weapon into the water and tried, unsuccessfully, to avoid tumbling in. A tremendous splash displaced most of the bath water, giving Woodwind a moment to check down the hall. Seeing no one, he slammed the door shut, then turned his attention toward the youth in the tub.

An expression of sheer terror filled the teenager's eyes as he turned and stared into the shimmering point of Woodwind's weapon, held with a steady hand only inches from his face. The southerner pressed closer, and the boy began to babble in his own tongue.

"Enough of your whimpering!" Woodwind ordered in vulgate, with uncharacteristic brusqueness.

"Please don't hurt me," the younger man stammered. "It was my father's idea to come here."

No sooner had the words left his lips, than the proprietress appeared in the doorway. She took one look at Woodwind's naked backside and let out a scream worthy of a woman many years younger than herself. "No killing!" she cried. "Please, no killing!"

"It's okay," Woodwind reassured. "I won't hurt him."

When this tactic didn't work, the southerner ordered the young Tamarian out of the tub and over to the mirror. "Don't even flinch!" he warned. After retrieving the boy's soaked and useless pistol, he placed the gun onto the tile and slid it across the floor toward the far wall. Then, gently putting his own weapon down, he shamelessly and with innocent intent, held out his hands to the woman. "See?"

An older man, utterly out of breath, arrived on the scene at that moment. He turned the woman around and said something soothing to her, then looked at Woodwind. "For all that is good and holy!" he exclaimed between breaths. "Get some clothes on!" Then to the boy, he said in a despairing tone, "And you, son, how disgraceful that you don't listen to your *Vati*! Look at you!"

The boy began to argue in the Tamarian language, but withered under his father's scorn. Overruled and ordered out of the bathroom, he complied meekly.

Woodwind found a towel with which to gird himself, all the while enduring the harangue of the proprietress, who knew that "foreigners couldn't be trusted."

Heinz Neergard handled the situation graciously. After he'd calmed the matron's frantic vituperation, he sent his son downstairs to dry off by the fire and suggested that Woodwind dress to avoid further offending the modest sensibilities of his Tamarian town folk.

After Woodwind clothed himself in the garments left near the bathroom entrance, he opened the door and found the old man leaning against the rail. "I suppose I'm in trouble now," Woodwind stated in resignation.

Heinz shrugged. "Mrs. Mikkels wants you charged as a spy. That's her right, and it's my civic duty to arrest you."

"I am not a spy. How can I answer these charges?"

"You will need to explain your business here in the north to the local army commander," Heinz replied. "Everyone is whispering about a southern army on the march, which is why I must act. Since spies are the army's jurisdiction, I can't say for certain how the process works, but I believe you'll find Colonel Brandt a fair man."

"How soon could this colonel talk to me?" asked Woodwind, worried about forever losing Brenna's trail while imagining that he'd waste away in some dreary dungeon for the rest of his days.

"I don't know. I will explain that you spared my son's life when you had the power to kill him. We value our young folk here in the High Land."

"And if I resist arrest?"

The old man's eyes twinkled, and a broad smile crept across his face. "You are free to do that, of course, but I recommend that you come along willingly. Hostility only deepens suspicion, and foreigners are generally not well regarded in my country."

Woodwind sighed, disappointedly. "I see." Without another word, he handed his prized longsword to the elder gentleman, hilt first, then followed him downstairs. In the entrance doorway stood two military policemen, identifiable in their black boots, berets, gloves and tan fatigues. They wore the same, bulky armor Woodwind had seen on the young cadet back at the Ice Dragon Inn, but they carried small caliber carbines and sidearms.

Heinz spoke to one of the men at length, outlining the circumstances of Woodwind's detainment. With apparent understanding reached, Heinz handed over the longsword that had been Woodwind's most cherished possession for many years.

"I hear you have a horse," the senior policeman said as he led the way to a pair of mules waiting outside. He spoke in the heavily-accented vulgate Woodwind had come to expect from the natives in this cold land.

"Yes," he replied. "I left my gelding at the livery down the road."

"Let's get it. We've got a long ride ahead. It's cold, and the days are short."

Once Woodwind retrieved his horse, the three men rode northwest, with the teeth of a gradually strengthening wind gnawing at them from the front flank the entire way. They had not been on the road more than five minutes before Woodwind felt utterly cold all over again. He suspected, rather cynically, that if he didn't freeze to death before he actually arrived at his destination, then nothing would ever be able to kill him.

***

Before Brenna returned to the camp, she gathered courage for several minutes while watching the young cadets through the trees. They hassled and harassed each other while preparing food, packing up their camp, cleaning their weapons and performing duties intended to keep them too busy for all-out hostility. The unattractive, middle-aged man in charge circulated among them, bringing minor conflicts to a halt, and making sure they continued to do as they were told. His language lacked words with more than two syllables, and he spoke to them in sentences no more than three words in length. The sergeant treated them like animals, she thought.

Brenna's heart fluttered. Her breathing rate increased as she faced the prospect of confronting so many unknown people. The young woman struggled against the urge to run away without being seen again.

What would she say if one of the braggarts started talking to her? The fear of engaging in conversation with a stranger inspired anxiety, yet courage vanquished her apprehension when her eyes found Garrick.

The Tamarian cadet worked alone, chopping then splitting dead fall. He'd peeled off his armor, revealing thick forearms and a shirt slightly damp with sweat. Broad shoulders moved with muscular grace whenever he swung the axe, flexing rhythmically in lean, youthful vigor.

Although not yet fully grown, his powerfully-built body showed the hardening influence of manual labor in his father's orchard, where pruning, chopping wood and fruit-picking, combined with shoveling snow in winter and a healthy diet, produced a fit physique that Brenna found irresistible. She caught her breath, staring at him.

But the root of her attraction reached deeper than the visceral impact of his masculine strength and handsome features. The other young men engaged in relentless swagger, where calm-voiced and serious-minded Garrick avoided their nonsense. His self-discipline inspired Brenna's confidence. Remembering the brute insensitivity and need for domination typical of other men she'd known, Brenna found his demeanor refreshing. A novel yearning for his company filled her soul, an innocent desire rising from a source she couldn't quite identify, and whose influence she didn't know how to handle.

As if sensing her presence, the Tamarian cadet turned in Brenna's direction, blushing like an embarrassed schoolboy. He smiled and pretended that it didn't matter that he'd suddenly become the subject of her attention.

She wondered why this group of new combat veterans were all so young, not knowing that they were about to enter a two-year national service mandate. Every cadet would be eligible for the Tamarian Defense Force after completing this exercise.

Hesitantly, the Lithian maiden stepped toward Garrick, trying not to be noticed. Yet she felt the weight of many eyes on her shoulders as she appeared from the trees, their reflexive response to a potential threat melding into either appreciation, or desire, as she approached.

Garrick paused to watch her with a quickened heart. A compelling force beyond her beauty, one he couldn't explain, drew his soul to hers. Grime, chapped lips and a wind-burned face did not detract from her attractiveness. The windstorm seemed less bitter as it billowed through her lustrous tresses, black as a moonless, midwinter night. Although dressed in an ungainly assortment of impossibly large clothes that mantled her form – the details of which had been so breathtakingly visible the night before – that didn't matter. Her voice had soothed him. Her words had moved him. Her mind inspired him. In truth, he would have wanted her even if he'd been blind.

"Can I help you?" she inquired.

Garrick's face flushed hot under the fire of her attention, but at the same time, he felt grateful that she was talking to him instead of someone else. "I'm almost done, but I'd be happy with your company," he replied, wondering how he was going to broach the subject of the Kamerese swordsman and Sergeant Streckert's orders.

The Lithian woman sat on a nearby stump, wishing to engage in conversation, but finding no words to express her cluttered thinking. Moments later, a flurry of frenzied discussion caught her attention. The cadet who'd had the leg wound examined his injury. His friends crowded around in astonishment, their bewildered faces alive with a blend of wonder and terror.

Garrick heard, "It had to be her! I swear she's a witch!" and paused to observe the commotion. A dangerous brew of ignorance and confusion reigned in their excited voices. What had Brenna done to deserve that accusation?

Another Junior Scout stripped off his combat blouse, discovering that he didn't have a scar from what had been a nasty laceration. Every injured cadet experienced this inexplicable phenomenon. Even Klaus Erickson, who'd suffered a head wound everyone thought would be fatal, was sitting up, asking for tea as if he'd not been hurt. But their discarded, blood-stained bandages, their damaged clothing and vivid memories told a very different tale.

Garrick read apprehension in Brenna's expression. She glanced quickly from face to face, and stood, backing away from the stump and all the attention directed her way. His was the last pair of eyes she sought, and in a single glance, she communicated more about her feelings than she had done with all her words thus far.

"Don't you worry," he reassured in a calm voice. "No one's going to hurt you."

Sergeant Streckert struggled to sort fact from fantasy. He too, noticed the maiden's anxiety and ordered his cadets to calm down and keep their distance. The sergeant approached and spoke in the gentlest tone Garrick had ever heard from the man's lips. "Did you attend to their injuries this morning?" he inquired.

Brenna retreated until her back met Garrick's upheld hand. He rested his fingers lightly on her shoulder, the sensation of which sent a shiver up her spine. She turned to listen to his translation, as Sergeant Streckert didn't speak vulgate.

"Yes," she admitted. "I arose early and prayed over their wounds while everyone else was still asleep."

The skeptical sergeant replied, "You *prayed?* They have all improved remarkably. How can this be?"

Brenna *believed* she acted as the vessel for Allfather's favor. Knowing she couldn't claim credit for the healing power she wielded, the young woman couldn't think of a way to explain this to the Tamarian sergeant.

"Allfather does his work through the faith of his *believers*," she said, worried that she might be accused of channeling demons, or some other ignorant nonsense.

Her cryptic expression puzzled the Tamarians for very different reasons. Gerhardt Streckert believed that natural forces remained under the control of deity-like spirits, each with its own sphere of influence, whereas Garrick maintained that the spirit realm did not actually exist. Thus, the sergeant assumed she referred to a healing spirit, while Garrick concluded that the young woman was trying to describe a natural phenomenon in words she thought the sergeant would understand.

Although he didn't scoff, Garrick didn't accept the idea of spiritual manifestations in the material realm. He believed in a natural order of the universe that did not personify forces, as faith in magic, spirits and gods could not be supported by verifiable facts. Had he been alone with her, he might have asked how an idea – a semantic label, a conceptual abstraction – could directly impact matter, but in the presence of Sergeant Streckert, he restricted himself to translating.

"Forgive my nescience," the sergeant said graciously. Whatever power this girl had, she'd clearly used it to help, not harm. "Perhaps there is much we can learn from you."

Hearing this translated, the young woman felt relieved. Garrick experienced a small, irrational sting of rejection when she did this, suddenly aware that the way she treated him mattered more than he cared to admit.

He'd never heard his sergeant talk in such a polite manner, didn't know the old man had a word like *nescience* in his vocabulary, and realized with painful clarity that even though she looked like a teenager, Brenna might be closer to the sergeant's age than she was to his. *Doesn't she belong to Woodwind? Why is she smiling at my sergeant, and why has she been paying so much attention to me?*

The breakfast call interrupted Garrick's insecure thinking. When Sergeant Streckert invited Brenna to eat, she turned her gaze back to Garrick and his heart pounded for a different reason. They languished in a gaze of obvious, mutual attraction. He'd noticed the mysterious way her pupils changed in response to different light. Whereas last evening they had been bright as a glacial lake at noon, dimming in the glow of firelight, now they appeared dark as the twilight sky. He had never seen a pair of eyes as pretty, nor lips as shapely and alluring as hers. Garrick felt compelled to draw near and kiss them, but he did not.

Brenna had seen the same expression of longing in Woodwind's face many times before. This young man, however, inspired a very different reaction within her. She felt warm inside. A shiver raced down her spine and tingled through her fingertips. She wanted to hold him, to be held by him, but this attraction had developed faster than her mind could rationalize and she felt afraid of losing control. The Lithian woman held her tongue, stifling hasty words that might later require an unpleasant retraction.

And thus, their hearts beat a little faster than before, testifying to unspoken longing. Without another word exchanged between them, they walked toward the breakfast line, making no move to move closer. The Tamarian cadet and the Lithian refugee ate in profound silence, with only the northwest wind to serenade the start of deep affection stirring between them.

Junior Scout Garrick Ravenwood, Tamarian Defense Force;
Brenna Velez, Woodwind

A Song of Victory

Nestled among massive granite boulders, high upon the barren height of a windswept hill called Dead Hand Ridge, a stout Tamarian firebase stood guard over the valley floor. Invisible from below, with an overgrown and unmarked trail winding up to its gate, only local residents and army personnel knew its exact location.

Hidden among hills and clustered around strategic passes accessing Tamaria's heartland, structures like this one provided defense for a thinly populated frontier. Each firebase shared a common plan: a sprawling, polyhedronal shape with thick, iron-reinforced concrete walls, measuring three hundred feet across on its first level, crowned by three additional odd-shaped floors. Several outposts and connecting conduits completed the design. The base, covered with native material, preserved the ridge line's natural contour, making these fortifications difficult to detect without coming very close.

Spaced within several thousand yards of each other, every shell keep lay within range of at least two other bases, so that the heaviest Tamarian rockets could be fired in defensive support of any one of them. In the event of an overwhelming assault, each base contained provision for quick evacuation through an underground rail network that also served as a resupply and transport system.

Soldiers and material, moved rapidly from one base to the next, allowed the Tamarian Defense Force to strike unpredictably from the flank or rear of an enemy. Any shell keep in danger of being overrun could be sealed to prevent entrance into the tunnel array, then attacked from within when the enemy was least expecting such action. In fact, however, not a single firebase had ever been successfully conquered in the nation's history.

A shout went up from one of the soldiers on watch, hidden among a series of firing ports built into the concrete at oblique angles. Three riders, two of whom were military policemen, approached from the northeast. A small, green flare arced into the windy sky, high above the open center of the base.

Woodwind – uncomfortable in his itchy, ill-fitting attire, hungry and bleary-eyed from lack of sleep – sat slumped in his saddle, following the lead of a black-bereted, junior military policeman. Woodwind's horse struggled uphill, following the lead policeman's mule. A few strides behind, the policeman's senior partner maintained a watchful eye on the flanks of Shadow – Woodwind's ebon gelding – to ensure that his prisoner did not suddenly decide to deviate from their course.

But the weary traveler thought nothing of escape. His innocense and faith in Allfather's providence, made him quietly compliant with whatever reasonable request these Tamarians made of him. Besides, he'd become curious about the firebase after first seeing it. Having never before encountered a fort of such unusual design, Woodwind wanted to have a closer look.

Even so, as he shivered in his saddle, the southerner longed for a good smoke to warm his insides. In thinking this he again remembered Brenna, who had asserted more than once that this particular habit – a most disgusting one in her view – had been acquired in response to Woodwind being deprived of his mother's breast as an infant. "It gives you something warm to stick in your mouth," she would say in jest. The memory of her inspired a smile, as it usually did. He missed her.

He wondered what she might be doing at that moment, and hoped she was okay. Had she slept well? Had she eaten? Had she found shelter to keep warm? Did she miss him as much as he missed her? Woodwind hoped so.

All across the landscape the windstorm shrieked, howling through stately conifers, stripping away the remaining leaves from ancient oaks with unceasing fury. As his horse ascended the narrow, leaf-littered, twig-strewn track, Woodwind felt grateful that the cold kept him alert, for while he needed sleep, a sense of perilous uncertainty required vigilance on his part. Rest would come, he assured himself, but whether in cozy bed or cold grave he could not be certain.

The stark, hilltop fortress embraced the gelid ground. Its brooding, angular walls appeared even uglier as the riders approached. Black and orange stains from runoff and rust mingled with many bullet holes that marred its surface. Newer, whiter patches of concrete covered major battle scars from conflicts fought many years earlier.

Once the road turned left for its final approach, Woodwind encountered an almost unbearable blast of unhindered wind. No longer protected by the bulk of the hill itself, the last few hundred yards of trail lacked trees and covering shrubs, allowing the unbridled breeze to rush swiftly through a lush stand of knee-high grasses in uninhibited fury. Waves of wind rippled across a swaying sea of wild grain, their dry stalks clothed in golden glory by the waxing light of the distant Daystar.

This foothill summit offered an unobstructed field of fire. Every approach angle faced at least two machine cannon, swivel-mounted rocket launchers and several individual firing ports enclosed in steel or concrete. The odd angularity of its perimeter created overlapping kill zones, where multiple gun emplacements from different walls and levels could concentrate a rain of death upon any advancing troops.

Woodwind concluded that attacking this place would be costly without a great deal of heavy artillery. That was, however, one element the Azgar deployed in abundance.

Observing the pitch of these Tamarian battlements, Woodwind concluded that they would deflect, rather than directly absorb, the impact of most artillery. Mortar shells, with their higher angle of attack, would be more effective, but only if they were capable of penetrating what looked like massive concrete walls. Although this base would likely withstand a terrible pounding, Woodwind remembered the terror of heavy Azgar guns and whispered a silent prayer for all the soldiers who would soon be – without doubt – defending against them.

Standing at the end of the approaching road where a wide band of gravel encircled the outer wall, a narrow arch of weathered limestone held its aquiline arms against the bitter sky. Its nameless architect had etched an aphorism on its eroding face more than 200 years earlier. A translation of the Tamarian words in Southern Vulgate, which Woodwind knew how to read, followed beneath. The inscription read, "Peace to all who come in peace, but death to those who destroy!"

Just before passing under the crumbling semi-circle, the leading Tamarian escort dismounted, as did his partner. The men urged Woodwind to do the same, as the keystone had been set at a symbolic height of seven feet. This was too short for the average giant to walk under without stooping, and also too limited a clearance for a man on horseback. But Woodwind soon learned about a more practical reason.

"You'll have to lead your horse down the ramp," the leading police officer stated. "And be careful. It's slick with ice and steeper than it looks. Take small steps."

Woodwind obeyed, leading Shadow by the bridle. A slippery flagstone path began directly beneath the arch, descending through the shadows toward a fortified gate. Recalling his earlier encounter with the bathroom floor, Woodwind carefully made his way downhill.

The redoubt's main entrance amalgamated features unique to the Tamarian fire keeps with more traditional, if considerably updated, defenses. These included a sunken barbican that held a pair of heavy iron doors, an outer curtain wall with embrasured inner walls, along with many steel encased firing ports set into steeply angled bulkheads. Its narrow, angular ramp prevented traditional siege engines from nearing the barbican and exposed any would-be attackers to a murderous, even predatory, approach.

To Woodwind's surprise, this structure flaunted form along with function, for in Tamaria, the art of architecture permeated nearly every building. This shell keep, and the others of its kind, reflected a tradition of beautiful buildings found everywhere in the High Land. He'd have never known this by judging on what he'd seen at a distance.

Close inspection revealed the ethic in startling clarity. Cast into austere concrete on the walls at its entrance Woodwind saw lovely figures representing the feminine incarnations of liberty and justice, themes endeared to the heart of every Tamarian. The art unsettled the southerner, whose religion prohibited the worship of images and icons, but he said nothing.

Upon a set of iron double doors, held in place by huge, well-oiled hydraulic hinges, he saw twelve different scenes cast into the metal. Strangely, none were of a military nature. The reliefs dealt with themes of civil government, the administration of justice and progressive agriculture, or portrayed pastoral landscapes and natural wonders like high waterfalls and mountains.

When Woodwind asked about the motive behind such depictions, his escorts met the query with a pair of puzzled expressions. They considered renderings of this nature commonplace and hadn't given it much thought.

"There's no art where you come from?" the junior policemen asked.

Soundlessly, the massive pair of black doors swung open and four bored soldiers approached from behind the iron gate. Three of these men led the animals up a broad, straw-covered passageway that ascended into the light of an open courtyard at the center of the base, while the military policemen chatted briefly in Tamarian with the duty officer.

Woodwind watched for some indication of his disposition, but noted only a brief, somewhat disdainful glance that seemed to exemplify the officer's low opinion of all things foreign. That didn't bode well.

"Come with me," said the senior policeman at length, walking down the corridor without looking back.

As Woodwind followed, he heard another Tamarian soldier spit on the tiled floor. Some apparently rude remark followed, inspiring laughter and additional commentary. The southerner didn't appreciate this disrespectful treatment, but when resentment surfaced in Woodwind's mind, he dismissed the fantasy it would have inspired in a man of less self-control.

The fire keep's indoor temperature felt moderate, using the same technological prowess that lighted what seemed like an endless maze of passages intersecting at oblique angles. Scrubbed scrupulously clean, the glistening floor reflected the characteristically bluish glow of methane lamps, different only in design to those Woodwind had studied in the bathroom earlier that morning by a wire cage, which cast shadows on the wall behind each fixture.

Soldiers in fatigues and berets marched purposefully toward destinations unknown, most paying only fleeting, cursory attention to the tall, bearded southerner who trudged behind his escort. The halls echoed with the consonantal chatter of men, and even a few women – to Woodwind's surprise – as well as the curious clicking of hobnail boots on the smooth tile underfoot.

Finally, a series of steel doors lay at the end of the corridor. As soon as the policeman opened one of them, Woodwind felt assaulted by a mildewy odor that diminished his heretofore developed respect for Tamarian cleanliness. The room behind the door, both windowless and bleak, contained only a sliver of cold light descending from a shaft high above.

"It's in here for now," the policeman said, somewhat apologetically. "We'll send down some lunch. As soon as the colonel has an opening, we'll get you up to see him."

Woodwind's unease deepened as he entered the stale environs of the cool, concrete room. "When will that be?" he queried, grasping at any hope that might be offered him.

But the policeman extended no reassurance. "Couldn't tell you. Rumor has it an army's on its way, and somebody thinks you're a spy. We don't take kindly to foreigners snooping around, but I promise you won't starve down here." Without another word, the policeman shut and locked the steel door.

As the footfalls faded down the hall from whence they'd come, Woodwind felt alone and afraid.

***

Windstorms occurred frequently in Tamaria's southeastern quarter. Their prevailing direction could be reckoned at a glance in places where tree branches survived only on one side of the trunk. Many thick-stemmed species grew so disfiguredly, they appeared ready to topple at the slightest provocation.

This microclimate existed because of an extensive glacier to the northwest of a verdant, lake-filled valley called *Broken Wing.* Most of the people who lived in this region had settled there, including Garrick's parents, who worked a small orchard high above the stormy waters.

Descending air, cooled by its contact with a thick blanket of ice and snow, funneled through a glacially-gouged trough between a pair of high mountain ranges in order to replace thermal convection currents rising over the hotter Saradon. This created powerful winds that shrieked across the steppe with impressive ferocity, waxing stronger as the Daystar climbed into the sky. Although adiabatic compression heated the frigid air in its descent, the difference in elevation between the glacier and the Saradon warmed the wind insignificantly from a human's view.

Sergeant Streckert knew from experience that conditions of this kind created severe windstorms, which imperiled the lives of his cadets. Further, their unexpected encounter with Azgar troops the previous night inspired grave concern.

The sergeant considered two options. In the first, he could send a reliable cadet back to the inn with a warning message that would be relayed to the appropriate military command authorities in a day or so, allowing him and his young troops to remain in the field and gather intelligence.

But this exposed his Junior Scouts to unnecessary risk from both the enemy and the weather. These young men were not adults yet. Even though they'd fought well against a surprised and outnumbered foe, the sergeant had long ago grown out of their naive bravado. He thought it wiser to refrain from fighting until Tamarian forces assessed the full extent of the enemy's strengths and weaknesses. Knowing when to fight and when to retreat kept soldiers alive, and the Republic of Tamaria needed everyone she could muster.

The second option involved returning to the inn immediately, arriving by mid-afternoon. This left the location of Azgar forces unknown, possibly exposing frontier units to surprise attack. Before making his choice, the sergeant asked what Brenna knew about the enemy.

"I'm afraid I can't say much," she began, her eyes reluctant to meet his, her voice so obscured by reticence that it was barely audible above the wind. "My *Amair* and his army fought them. He said the Azgar had more soldiers than there were people living in Shirak, and could quickly call up many more. I've known them to march as far as thirty miles in a single day, with cavalry scouting the way. If I'm ahead of them, they're close behind."

"What about their weapons?" the sergeant asked. "We've seen trapdoor muskets and bayonets. What can you tell me about their artillery?"

Hearing Garrick's translation, Brenna's eyes grew wide and sadness washed across her face. "Their muskets may be old, but what they lack in quality, they make up for in quantity. They have many thousands of them.

"And their artillery is terrible. I've seen shells fall like rain in a thunderstorm. My city had been verdant with life before they arrived. By the time I fled it was already a smoldering ruin. You have to stop them. If you don't, they'll destroy your land and enslave your people."

Sergeant Streckert scowled as he addressed Garrick, reiterating his earlier order. "Find her friend, and find him fast." With that, the sergeant turned on his heels and shouted at his cadets, several of whom had gathered around to hear what the pretty foreign maiden had to say.

"Will you please tell me what he told you?" Brenna inquired, meekly. "Am I free to go?"

Garrick dreaded telling her the truth. He had to relate the story about Woodwind eventually, but he'd wanted to put it off until their relationship had become better established. Although tempted to lie in order to buy time, he knew from experience that any advantage gained from being dishonest would not endure. Garrick's integrity prevailed over the expedient. He told Brenna every detail of his chance encounter with Woodwind the day before.

"He spoke highly of you," Garrick explained, "showed me your likeness in a hologram, and made me promise that I would notify him if I learned anything about your whereabouts. I gave him my word. As long as you're not threatened by him, I'm compelled to honor my promise." He watched carefully to gauge her reaction, secretly hoping that it might not be favorable.

Brenna didn't know what to say. She stared out over the windswept landscape and in complete shock, whispered "Merciful God," in her own tongue, while fighting back a flood of pent-up emotion that brimmed in her eyes. Woodwind had come all this way to find her, and of all people she could have met, this particular cadet had spoken to him. Was that not evidence of Allfather's favor?

Her thoughts drifted toward her loving friend, whose longing for lifelong companionship he'd uttered only once, on a starlit evening when the Great Eye Nebula – the ghost of a dead star that rose during the spring and lingered into late summer – graced the night sky. That memory seemed long ago now.

Presently, however, she became aware of how near the young Tamarian's body was to hers, and his proximity drew her out of her reverie. She gazed at him. Garrick's behavior toward her remained above reproach and far more respectful than she'd ever known from young men in the past. Someone of lesser principle might have tried to take advantage of her weakness, yet he'd proven himself trustworthy. He was intelligent and articulate. In the bright light of morning she found him both beautiful and strong. Uncontrollably, Brenna's heart began pounding . . . .

The Lithian woman stepped back, afraid she would lose control, unaware of the sting she inspired in Garrick's heart by doing so. She looked at the ground to avoid looking at him again, drawing a pattern in the dirt with her right toe.

Garrick shielded his eyes from the wind, pretending rather ineffectively that he wasn't bothered by her withdrawal. "And so my sergeant," he continued, "wants me to bring your friend back to the inn for questioning."

Brenna, her gaze still averted, responded dispassionately. "I know he'll want to help you."

"Woodwind said he was the captain of your father's personal guard. Is that true?"

"Yes," she replied. "He is also my best friend."

Garrick turned away, a Tamarian curse retreating from his lips. *She really is a rich girl. And worse, she belongs to a mercenary!* Covering his disappointment poorly he stated, "Then I'll arrange for you to be reunited."

Acting out of sheer self-preservation, Garrick judged her actions, words and appearance incorrectly, and the shift in his attitude toward her – while well-intended – inspired confusion in the Lithian maiden's heart. She didn't understand why he'd suddenly grown brusque, and felt hurt that he'd begun treating her this way. Then, as quickly as the conversation had begun, it ended, and the two did not speak again for hours.

Jan Bordmann, who'd been discretely watching from a distance, sensed a change in Garrick's expression and approached his friend with concern after Brenna turned away. "Girl trouble?" he inquired.

Garrick nodded. "Yeah. My rotten luck," he responded, trying to stifle envy. "I should have known she'd never be interested in someone like me."

Jan glanced over his shoulder. "Uh . . . that ain't what I'm seeing. I think she likes you. Is she married?"

"I don't know. She's got some other guy."

"Well if she ain't married, I wouldn't let the boyfriend trouble me none if I was you."

Garrick straightened, looking directly into his friend's eyes. "I'd really rather not talk about it," he warned.

Jan backed away from the subject, knowing that Garrick had no patience with anyone who did not respect his privacy. Whenever his comrades talked about their families, Garrick stayed quiet. If questioned directly, he spoke in generalities. His parents lived on a small farm above Deception Creek, and he had a younger sister and brother who were fraternal twins.

He didn't engage in lurid talk about the local girls either. Garrick expressed disgust whenever anyone openly talked about the unveiled physical attributes of a young woman, and personally refused to do so. Harold had once teased him about this – questioning Garrick's sexuality – but the husky farm kid from Deception Creek quickly ended that nonsense with a single, left-handed blow to Harold's face. Sergeant Streckert gave Garrick a serious chewing out and put him on dung patrol for a month, but no one dared challenge him after that incident.

Wishing to avoid conflict, Jan shifted the conversation to the previous evening's battle. Quiet words replaced the swagger recklessly expressed before their shared combat experience. As other cadets joined in with their own stories, a bond grew between them.

Sergeant Streckert organized his troop near the summit's edge. From this vantage point the landscape appeared vast, primeval, untouched by human hands and impervious to the destructive fist of international conflict. A brilliantly-hued autumnal blanket of swaying grasses stretched endlessly, it seemed, into the eastern horizon. The Saradon and nearby hills looked as they had since the great glaciers retreated thousands of years earlier.

When the sergeant addressed the cadets, he spoke to them about honor and duty, warning each one to carefully consider the danger their nation faced. "Find the man inside you," he encouraged. "Your country needs your courage now. It's time to leave boyhood behind."

The impact of the previous night's battle, the sergeant's rousing speech, and the moment of reflection wrought a profound change. Sobriety replaced lost innocence as the young Tamarians climbed down the hill. No one complained. No one goofed off. Combat forged them into a team that marched like veteran soldiers.

Upon their arrival at the oak tree, Sergeant Streckert called the column to a halt. The bodies that had lain there the night before had vanished, apparently dragged into the tall grass and buried. Several sets of fresh horse tracks hinted that a party of Azgar had recently occupied the area. Who else would bother to bury enemy bodies in rock hard ground? The proximity of this position to the grounds of the ill-defended inn troubled him. He ordered the cadets to march in battle defile – three abreast with loaded rifles at the ready – pointed into the tall-grass prairie on either side of the road.

Brenna walked between Garrick and his friend, a slim, brown-haired, brown-eyed kid with a mild case of acne, near the head of the marching column. The two cadets carried on a conversation as if she wasn't even there, which would have been fine if she had not felt badly about Garrick's sudden change in attitude toward her.

That's when she noticed other eyes lingering on her. That's when she heard whispers that ceased when she turned her head. Some of the boys looked fearful, others intrigued, while a few stared in a predatory way that amplified her longing for the safety of Garrick's attention.

Two tense hours passed uneventfully. An old stone wall, situated on an incline to the west of the Saradon road, encircled a compound of magnificent buildings whose slender, arched windows reflected many colors in the strong daylight. The cadets dared not display overt emotion as they marched, but a collective sense of relief swelled among them after they passed under the gate.

A tangled mass of limbs arising from dark, deeply textured oak trunks drew Brenna's eye. She noticed carefully trimmed juniper hedges and planting beds covered in deep blankets of fallen leaves. The Lithian woman listened to a pair of scrub jays screeching in the trees, and watched as one flew up to a rain gutter five floors above the cobbled courtyard. She'd not seen a place as lovely since fleeing from Shirak.

The inn conveyed an aura of old comfort inside the shelter its walls, as if, within its stone embrace, safety from the crescendoing storm might be found for awhile. Savory scents wafted from an unseen kitchen, wistfully reminding Brenna of home, where diligent servants filled *Umma's* oven with the wonderful aromas of baking bread, spicy dinners and, occasionally, sweet treats.

The cadets entered a large, rectangular building, whose slate roof reached for the ground through a series of flying buttresses. Garrick put his hand on Brenna's arm to get her attention, but was interrupted by the sergeant. The man said something the woman didn't understand, and in response, the handsome cadet gave her a helpless glance, then ascended a mahogany staircase with his increasingly boisterous comrades.

As her eyes wandered around the building's interior, Brenna saw boxes and supplies stacked near the walls. Adult soldiers and cadets in long lines carried material down the stairs and hallways in preparation for their imminent winter evacuation.

She also noticed a pipe organ at the far end of the main hall and secretly dreamed of playing it. Her slender fingers twittered unconsciously, as if dancing across its keys in practiced patterns long since committed to memory. She'd not played an organ in months, and though she longed to fill the rafters with magnificent sound, Brenna felt too shy to inquire about the instrument.

A tall, blonde-haired woman appeared from behind a desk in the main hall as the young men retreated. She spoke briefly to the sergeant, glanced at Brenna, nodded, then approached as the sergeant turned away.

The woman introduced herself as Warrant Officer Rand. "Come with me," she said in a voice that carried the husky quality of Woodwind's after he'd been sucking on that filthy pipe. "I'll get you geared up for the weather."

Brenna followed her escort and entered the women's quarters, where the female soldier offered her a warm shower. The tall woman appraised the petite foreigner with raised brows, surprised – as Brenna shamelessly undressed – that this obviously mature woman lacked body hair. Leaving a towel behind, the warrant officer returned a few minutes later, carrying a stack of winter clothes intended for use by female soldiers off-duty and off-post.

After her shower, Brenna examined the many garment layers with a wrinkled brow. "Am I supposed to wear all of this at the same time?" she asked.

The Warrant Officer nodded and patiently explained how to dress in layers for the cold. In doing this she extended social grace that foreign-born Brenna wouldn't have received from most of the women deployed here.

"Please don't think you owe us anything," the Tamarian woman stated. "Sergeant Streckert told me you saved the lives of three cadets this morning. Think of this cold weather kit as our way of showing thanks to you."

As Brenna rolled her skirt and leggings into a backpack, the warrant officer noted her torn boot, which appeared to have been bitten by something very large. "Well, that won't do. You'll lose your foot to frostbite in those. Tell me your size and I'll get you another pair."

Garrick waited at the main desk. He'd also taken a shower and changed into a fresh set of autumn-colored fatigues, clean boots, mittens, a scarf and overcoat.

He toyed with a note he'd folded up in his right hand, smiled briefly when Brenna's bright eyes met his, but the expression faded as soon as she turned to thank the warrant officer at her side. Garrick felt a shiver race up his spine. Brenna looked stunning in her new outfit. He glanced at her womanly form and quickly turned his eyes away, but blushing cheeks betrayed his attraction to her.

Warrant Officer Rand noticed the Lithian woman's apparent, reciprocal interest. She smiled and winked at Garrick before returning to her duties.

"Are you ready?" the young soldier asked.

She nodded, glad to hear his voice again, wondering why he suddenly seemed so unsure of himself. "The place where we're going, is it far?"

"No," he replied, finding her attention a relief. "But we don't have time to walk. Have you ever ridden a mule?"

Brenna shook her head. "Only horses. I've heard mules are aggressive and hard to train."

"Maybe so, but mules don't spook as easily. They're also sure-footed and not afraid of heights." Garrick led her outside, walking briskly toward the livery, noting – despite her small size – that she had no trouble keeping up.

Brenna waited as he vanished into the dark stable. She felt a little uncomfortable when he reappeared leading a single animal with a back blanket and no saddle, irrationally worried that he might take advantage of close proximity in a way that she was not yet ready to handle.

Garrick interpreted her uncertain posture and facial expression as disgust. Worried that she wouldn't want to be close to him, the cadet shuffled his feet nervously. "The quartermaster told me that one will have to do. You can ride. I'll jog alongside."

Knowing she could outrun both him and the mule, Brenna shook her head. "It's okay," she replied with a shy smile. "I'll trust you as long as you respect me."

Garrick's heart raced. He felt weak inside. "Let me help you up," he offered.

Despite his civil intentions, Brenna didn't like being patronized. "I'm neither fragile, nor an invalid," she warned. Almost effortlessly, she grabbed the mule's mane and in a gracile, leaping motion, swung her leg over its back.

Impressed with how easy she'd made that look, he nervously pulled himself up and sat behind her. In silence, the two rode past the inn's proud gate and turned northward along the windswept Saradon road.

Tension rose as she worried he'd let his hands wander to her breasts once they were alone. Other men she'd known could barely wait for an opportunity like this, but Garrick constrained his obvious desire. Favorably impressed with his self-control, the young woman savored the passing moments in silence, content in his presence, and grateful for his well-disciplined conduct.

As they settled into the steady rhythm of the mule's stride, Brenna leaned into Garrick's chest and shoulders, turned her head to look at him and broke the silence. "Are you upset at me?" she inquired.

"No, not at all," he replied. "Why do you ask?

The Lithian woman sensed that he wasn't speaking truthfully, but given his otherwise excellent conduct, she felt sufficiently confident in his integrity to broach her concern about their sudden communication breakdown. "I ask because you're acting like I've done something wrong, yet I can't recall saying or doing anything offensive. You were really nice to me at first, but your conduct became aloof and disinterested after breakfast. Am I at fault here, or is something else going on?"

While Garrick feared her rejection, he found the young woman so benevolent, so alluring, he took a risk. "You're beautiful and I can't stop thinking about you. I see your image in my mind whenever I shut my eyes."

An expression of sadness and disappointment crossed her wind-burned face. Brenna felt confident in her beauty, but she wanted him to appreciate more than her pretty face and feminine form. "So, your interest in me is purely physical?"

He, seeing the change in her countenance and correctly interpreting what it meant, summoned his eloquence. "No, not entirely," he began. "It's a lot more nuanced than that. While I can't deny that your appearance intrigues me, the more time I spend in your company, the more fascinating I find you.

"From the moment we met, you've been consistently courteous. You've treated me as an equal, even though I'm a nobody and you come from a family rich enough to raise its own army. There's never conceit in your voice when you speak. Everything I've seen you do is steeped in kindness. That alone sets you apart as a good woman, but you're also refreshingly smart, well-read and the way you look at the world reflects nobility of character. I've known enough people to understand that these qualities are uncommon."

Brenna felt better about his explanation, but it didn't answer her initial question satisfactorily. "Then why did you become so short with me this morning? What did I do?"

"You've done nothing," he replied a little bit sadly, hoping she wouldn't pounce on his vulnerability. "It's just that you belong to someone else, and I shouldn't want you like I do. It's not right for me to feel this way. I wish I'd never touched you because now I know what it's like and no one else will ever do." Once he'd spoken this sensitive thing, his soul winced for the hurt that had always come when he'd uttered something vulnerable in the past.

Brenna sat up, completely unaware that her actions reinforced Garrick's worst expectations, nearly causing him to retreat from her and the conversation altogether. "Who told you I'd been promised to someone else?" she queried.

"It's not important," the young man muttered.

"It *is* important. You don't know the whole story."

"What else is there to know?" he asked. "Woodwind came all the way up here looking for you, and the moment I mentioned his name, you backed away from me and got all misty-eyed. It's my honor as a gentleman to respect your love for him."

Brenna laughed spontaneously, prompting the mule to speed up as her heels dug into its side. "I love Woodwind like a brother," she replied. "He's been my friend since we were both children, but I don't belong to him any more than I belong to you, or anyone else for that matter . . . ."

Garrick let her words wash over his soul, his heart racing with hope, his tongue held, lest he spoil the moment. Quelling another nervous rush, the young man took in a deep breath and again chose his words carefully. "If you two ain't courting, then why'd he wander all the way up here looking for you?"

Brenna began a lengthy account, explaining how her people endured a long conflict with the Azgar concerning silviculture and land ownership. Over the centuries, the Azgar had turned their own forests into deserts and had begun falling trees in the Valley of Shirak to fuel their steam-powered industries. War broke out when an alliance of Lithian armies marched to end the cutting.

But the real reason for the invasion, according to Brenna, involved religious apathy and a corrupt priesthood that abandoned true worship for the idolatry of material possessions, resulting in declining concern for the needy. She claimed that Allfather withdrew his protection, allowing the evil of the Lithian people to bear its fruit.

Brenna's father – though an effective commander with his own army – couldn't stop the Azgar legions from pushing into Illithia. His outnumbered forces, allied with many other warlords, began a long, humiliating retreat.

By midsummer, Lord Velez concluded that he'd lost the Lithian cause. Hoping to save his family, he struck a deal with a Kamerese warlord named Nemesio Fang, who owned property over the mountains, far to the west.

According to Brenna, Lord Fang forced her father into a bad contract that exchanged *her* in marriage for a large tract of fertile land where her family could resettle.

"*Amair* didn't understand the laws of Kameron," she said. "He would never give me away like a slave. *Umma* didn't want to leave me behind, but I convinced her that I should stay to make sure everyone else got out. I'd been guarding the portals with my bow when the enemy trapped me during their attack. By Allfather's grace, I escaped when the city caught fire.

"I knew what their soldiers would do if they caught me. I'd seen how they abused other women. The easiest escape lay to the north, and I thought the Azgar would stop after destroying Illithia. But they invaded every nation's territory that I entered and kept marching north. I had to keep going in order to stay ahead. I thought I'd find safety here, but I didn't realize how cold it is in the High Land. If I hadn't met you, I'm sure I'd have frozen to death."

Garrick listened with a growing sense of relief. Brenna was not only uncommitted, she hadn't subjected his feelings to ridicule, either. The latter fact deepened his already favorable impression, but at the moment, her softness, nearness and warmth proved more influential. While he didn't agree with her fanciful, spiritual explanation for the aggressive Azgar expansion, that seemed inconsequential compared to her visceral impact.

Dieter, the tiny town at the fringe of Tamaria's southeastern frontier, arose from among the golden grasses like an island of civilization amid a nearly treeless ocean of empty, almost-arid, flat land. This farming settlement had never supported a population larger than it did currently.

Most of its buildings – pine-framed pole structures – huddled close to the ground, partially or completely covered in sod to protect against the winter cold and prevailing wind. The necessity of this construction became obvious as soon as Garrick and Brenna moved beyond the shadow of hills west of the Ice Dragon Inn, where the tremendous ferocity of rushing air blasted their backs with a brutality Brenna had never experienced before. Even in her new attire she found it necessary, or at least desirable, to snuggle a bit closer to her Tamarian friend for warmth. Garrick felt pleased by the close contact, but remained silent, afraid that spoken words would ruin the moment and drain away the happiness filling his heart.

An empty street greeted them. No one braved the cold in welcome, save for an orange cat that scurried for shelter behind an oak barrel as their mule strode past a cluttered alley. A few faces appeared in windows, mostly small children whose curiosity faded as the travelers moved out of sight. The rest of the villagers sought sanctuary from the storm behind their insulated walls. Garrick and Brenna dismounted in front of Dieter's only inn, tied up the mule and walked into the establishment. No sooner had they closed the door, however, when an elderly woman appeared and yelled at them to leave.

"What kind of wicked creature are you bringing in here?" she cried, her arms flailing wildly. "Take that slanty-eyed, slut foreigner back where she came from and close the door behind you!"

Garrick, stunned by her overt bigotry, didn't know what to do. He wanted to protect Brenna, but couldn't think of anything clever to say. Knowing that attitudes like this were common in Tamaria, he tried speaking calmly in the hope of reasoning with the woman. She didn't care, so he grabbed her by the shoulders, gave her a powerful shake and in a stern tone of voice said, "Now you listen here!"

Terror silenced the matron for the moment, as Garrick was very strong and she feared, quite irrationally, for her life. Once she stopped talking, he let her go and explained the reason for his visit as gently as possible.

His ensuing description of Woodwind agitated her greatly, and she ran out of the room venting curses. As Garrick tried to interpret the problem to Brenna, the old woman reappeared with a broom, which she wielded recklessly against the young couple in her foyer.

"They arrested that louse this morning!" she screamed, "which is what they ought to do with all these foreigners! Get that harlot out of here, I say! Get her out!"

Brenna retreated, protecting her face from the old woman's attack. "Let's just go," she pleaded, tugging at his sleeve, protecting her face with her free hand. "We'll find him on our own."

He, however, resented being attacked. Garrick tore the broom out of the woman's hands, pressed it against his left knee and snapped its handle. With an authority neither female expected of him, the young soldier flung the door open and tossed the broken pieces into the street. When the wind slammed the portal shut, Garrick had the old woman's undivided attention. Anger swelled in his voice. "We're not leaving until you settle down and tell us where he was taken. I have a good mind to report you to my commanding officer for obstructing orders."

The old woman's eyes clouded over. She began to weep, muttering unintelligible phrases between loud sobs, her whole body shaking as if mourning the loss of a cherished heirloom.

Brenna, whose high regard for Garrick diminished after witnessing his handling of the matter, didn't disguise the disdain in her voice. "That was intelligent," she said, her sarcasm further wounding his self-esteem. "Breaking her broom really mollified the old woman, didn't it?"

Surprisingly, Garrick accepted the rebuke without protest. He looked Brenna right in the eye, where his true feelings were unveiled in an expression of remorse that lingered on his face. "You're right. I handled that badly."

As the young man turned his attention back toward the old woman, Brenna's disgust cooled and she watched him with a renewing sense of appreciation. He was the first fully human male she'd ever known who showed the courage to admit that he'd made a mistake.

Garrick, feeling certain that Brenna would never be nice to him again, kept his attention focused on the sobbing innkeeper. "Forgive me, ma'am," he soothed. "I was impatient; it was wrong of me to wreck your broom, and I'll make it right. But I need you to understand that this is a serious matter." Then, seeing that she was also reasserting control, the cadet explained his encounter with the Azgar and how he felt Woodwind could help the Tamarian army.

Still, the woman remained suspicious. "What could you possibly learn from a good-for-nothing, flea-infested street dog like him? Why, I dare say he'd only teach you worse manners than you already have!" She glowered at Brenna, unwilling to provide any real information.

At this point, the Lithian woman realized that Garrick was getting nowhere. After uttering a short, silent prayer, Brenna interrupted the conversation, *believing* that Allfather would intervene on her behalf.

"Tell me the truth," she commanded in vulgate. "Where was the southern man taken this morning?"

Mrs. Mikkels stopped in mid-sentence, as if shocked back into mental clarity by the abrupt switch in languages. "The military police said something about Dead Hand Ridge, but I don't remember anything more."

Brenna turned to Garrick. "Do you know that place?"

Astonished, the young man nodded.

"Well," she replied. "What are we waiting for?"

Garrick thanked the old woman for her cooperation, then held the door for Brenna, who nearly snarled at these ostensibly polite, yet nonetheless condescending habits of his. Turning his back to the merciless wind, he inquired, "How did you do that?"

Brenna, still miffed at him for bullying the old woman, would not explain. "You wouldn't understand," she responded. "Let's go. I'm cold already."

***

Long hours of cold boredom inspired Woodwind to entertain himself with geometry. Since the Tamarians hadn't checked him for hidden weapons they had not confiscated his boot knife. He used the hyper-sharp blade to scratch the concrete where a shaft of daylight from a south-facing skylight inched across its rugged surface.

After an hour or two of this, he took off his belt, held it parallel to the floor and bored a conical depression in the wall at its end. Then, he drew an arc connecting all the scratches, extending it into a circle. Selecting a point on its outside edge, he drew another circle, then another on the opposite side. Connecting diagonal points across the diameter of his creation created new points at equal distances from which to draw additional circles. Once six of these were complete, he had created a twelve-hour clock.

Bisecting these wedges into half-hour, and then quarter hour segments allowed him to keep track of how long he remained locked up in solitary confinement.

The time piece was useless at night, but it provided enough diversion for Woodwind to endure his isolation. In addition to his chronic worry about Brenna and imagined conversations with real people who were not present, something else began to distract his attention by late in the second day of his captivity.

By this time, the skylight high above rattled intensely against strong surges of howling wind. Worried that it might fall, the southerner became fixated on its staccato trembling and didn't hear the clicking of footsteps in the hall outside. The sound of a key sliding into the lock startled him, and he realized, a bit late, that he hadn't returned the boot knife to its sheath. Reacting in partial panic, he jabbed the weapon into his right boot in order to conceal it, but missed his mark and cut his flesh on its sharp, crystalline edge.

A single Tamarian soldier, clad in fatigues and a brown beret, appeared from behind the door. "Master Woodwind?" he called. "You've been summoned."

The southerner left his cell with relief tempered by the discomfort from the cut on his right ankle. Trying hard not to limp, Woodwind walked behind his escort, up a spiraling stairwell that seemed strangely devoid of humanity. One floor from the top, they entered another hallway, this one paneled in red cedar and carpeted by a strip of worn rug, covered in faded mosaic patterns now blended together from the friction of many feet. The walls, though lacquered and polished, scented the air with the earthy, aromatic fragrance of a craftsman's workshop.

At length, Woodwind's escort stopped at a door and let his charge into a small room with a narrow, north-facing window. There, Woodwind recognized the Tamarian scout he'd met at the Ice Dragon Inn, and his heart skipped a beat when he realized who was sitting next to him . . . .

"Brenna!" he exclaimed, half-disbelieving his eyes, yet grateful to rest them on her lovely face again.

She smiled and rushed toward him with open arms, leaping into his embrace. She kissed him three times, the third time on the lips, then held him in a lingering embrace. Woodwind felt the familiar softness of her breast against his body and whispered thanks to Allfather for helping him find her, safe and sound.

Garrick watched the reunion in silence, trying hard to restrain surging jealousy. He seethed silently when Brenna kissed the Kamerese swordsman, looking away to conceal his disappointment. Had she been disingenuous about her relationship with this man?

However, Brenna and Woodwind did not remain long in each other's arms. After expressing her gratitude, Brenna moved away and a palpable tension emerged.

Woodwind approached the narrow window where Garrick stood, joining the young Tamarian in admiring the stormy scenery outside. "I must thank you," the southerner said. "You were a great help."

Brenna moved between them, but when Garrick backed off, unsure of his standing with her, she moved closer and took his hand in hers. Garrick felt a shiver run up his spine. Hand-holding violated conduct regulations, but he didn't let go. "I gave my word. My word is my honor," he replied. "But now I have to ask you to return the favor."

Woodwind glanced at Brenna, then at Garrick, recognizing the chemistry brewing between the two of them. Hesitantly, he asked, "What is it you'd like from me?"

The young Tamarian related his encounter with Azgar troops on the hilltop. After this, he explained his nation's need for intelligence about the enemy and the hope that Woodwind would be willing to assist. "My sergeant sent me to find you for this reason. Colonel Brandt directed your release after he read the orders my sergeant gave me. The colonel wants your help. That's why you're here."

"Does your colonel know why I was being detained?" Woodwind asked.

"I don't know," Garrick replied with a shrug. "I don't need to know."

Woodwind scowled. "It may cast some doubt on my credibility, and I'm under orders to return with the young lady as soon as I've found her."

Brenna interrupted. "You may return, but you will do so without me."

The two of them began arguing in the Lithian language, a tongue apparently devoid of consonant sounds to Garrick's ears, as much as Tamarian lacked vowels to hers. Garrick, who'd already experienced Brenna's willful personality, listened to her spar with Woodwind – who towered over her – in a manner so assertive, it seemed incredible that this woman could be afraid of anyone she'd never met before. Their argument ended abruptly when Woodwind could not endure the pain stabbing at his ankle any further.

"Will you stop fighting me?" he complained. "I've come to help, not hurt you! Besides, I cut myself a few minutes ago and I can't think straight enough to contend with you while I'm in pain!"

Brenna responded with a curt comment about his inability to think under any circumstances, but agreed to examine the wound. She pressed firmly on the area to stop the flow of blood, then bowed her head over the cut and kissed it.

Garrick, who knew something of asepsis from his training, shuddered. He'd seen the end result of her healing skill, but had never witnessed her procedure and watched with widened eyes and held breath. He suspected that her technique would spread – rather than stop – infection, yet wisely kept his counsel to himself.

At that moment the colonel's secretary, a thin warrant officer who looked ill-fed in his oversized uniform, entered from the next room. He paused, puzzled, watching until the long-haired foreign woman arose from her kneeling position.

"Colonel Brandt will see you now," he announced flatly, holding the door open for Woodwind. The lanky soldier, obviously interested in an explanation, remained outside as Woodwind entered the office.

Colonel Brandt sat behind an oak desk that looked new. In reality, all the furnishings were original and old as the base itself. Yet, neither scrape nor scar from years of service showed on any surface.

The middle-aged officer, grey haired and bearded, peered at his guest from behind a pair of circular spectacles. A smile spread across his ruddy face. He snickered to himself – the sound barely audible – but the action betrayed by small, rapid bounces of body fat across his chest and shoulders. He seemed curious, friendly and dangerous at the same time.

Woodwind stepped into his boot, giving a short bow as he entered the room. The tiny office, also paneled in cedar, had an eight-foot wide plaque of green and grey marble on the western wall, behind the desk. In the center of this stone display, flanked by the national flag and a regimental banner, a portrait of Tamar, the Queen of the High Land, graced the gold-trimmed tile.

"So you are the bloodthirsty miscreant from the deep south," the colonel remarked, still amused.

Woodwind extended his hand in the universal gesture of peace. "I am not a criminal," he responded, introducing himself by name. The Tamarian commander's hand felt surprisingly firm and calloused.

Picking up a sheaf of paper, the colonel commented, "That pretty little Lithian girl told me you serve her father, a warlord by the name of Velez, from the city of Shirak. I understand you are his personal captain?"

"As long as my lord lives," Woodwind replied.

The colonel discarded the paper in his hand, sat back in his leather seat, and sized up the man across his desk with an intuitive eye. "And the young soldier out there told me you've had a lethal encounter with members of the Azgar Northern Liberation Army as well?"

"I'm proud to say their blood is on my hands."

"Hmm," the colonel mused. "I find it highly irregular for the servant of a Lithian lord to wander so far north, fighting an enemy whose armies defeated your lord's people. Not only that, but you threatened a Tamarian citizen, with deadly force. Is this your personal vendetta, or are you acting under orders?"

"I've not come to wage a private war," Woodwind replied, shaking his head. "I do nothing on my own. I'm sworn to protect my lord's interests, and will continue to do so until I'm unable."

"Noble," the colonel replied, "but insufficient to account for your presence here." Then, softening his tone to assuage the uncertainty of his guest, he continued. "Captain Woodwind, I regret that my questioning may pry into your private affairs, but I am accountable to my command, and ultimately, the Tamarian people. Therefore, I must know why you've come to my country. If you want your freedom, tell me the scope of your business."

Woodwind nodded and disclosed his story, most of it, anyway. He began with the enemy invasion of Illithia, describing the cruelty of the Azgar. He spoke of Lord Velez, whose desperate attempts to evacuate his family from the doomed city of Shirak sounded both harrowing and heroic.

When the Lithian lord realized that his eldest daughter, who'd been left behind to guard the exit portals against unauthorized access, had not departed, he felt grieved and feared for her life. Lady Velez, believing that her eldest daughter might yet be alive, teleported someone she thought Brenna would trust. She sent a friend.

When Woodwind found his way back to the Velez estate, a fierce fire raged in the city, distracting enemy troops. The house had been riddled with gunfire and in it, he found several bodies strewn about, all slain with white-feathered arrows and a precision that suggested the carnage had been Brenna's doing.

Following what he believed to be her escape route through the back of the property, Woodwind tracked the young woman across town, through a subterranean passage that surfaced on a hill well beyond the city walls.

"The first few days were dreadful," he recalled. "Enemy patrols were actively searching for escapees along their perimeter, killing everyone they found fleeing from the city. I crawled through the bush on my belly, always fearing that I'd find Brenna among the piles of dead I encountered. Several days after leaving the city, I finally reached the place where I could contact Lady Velez again. That's when she opened another portal and sent my horse."

Colonel Brandt wrinkled his brow. Knowing nothing about Lady Velez, the idea of teleporting anything, especially a creature as large as a horse, seemed ridiculous. Yet the swordsman spoke with such conviction, the Tamarian officer suspended disbelief and encouraged him to continue.

"When I grew tired, I couldn't risk sleep. The Azgar release their deathwolves every evening, and I had to circle back behind the advancing enemy position in order to avoid them. For the first week, I don't think I had more than twenty-five hours of rest.

"I lost Brenna's trail after I'd doubled back, only to find one a few days later that I followed in the hope it might be hers. Trusting my instinct and knowing of her interest in your country, I moved north at a pace I could only sustain on horseback.

"After awhile, it became obvious she wasn't fleeing to the west, and I felt increasingly confident she might seek refuge here, in Tamaria. I began finding her campsites in the hill country, each one further north, until I lost all trace of her passage a few days ago. Eventually, I crossed the Tualitin and began to inquire concerning the young woman's whereabouts among your people. The cadet outside found her for me, and that's why I'm here."

Colonel Brandt found most of the foreigner's story plausible. The military policeman's report included statements that Woodwind had been cooperative with him, as well as with the local authorities, and didn't pose a specific threat against the local citizenry. The complaint filed against Woodwind had been lodged by a woman who'd made many such claims, and wouldn't have been taken seriously if had weapons not been involved.

This prompted the next question. "Alright then. You admit to killing Azgar scouts who threatened you on the road, but showed restraint when facing an armed Tamarian boy at the inn. Yet you carried your weapon into that bathroom, which implies that you perceived some kind of threat, and it's clear you possess the capability to inflict harm when you see fit. Why the sudden prudence?"

Woodwind suspected the colonel was trying to catch him telling a lie. He framed his response in terms of social context, as the boy at the inn was not a soldier bent on conquest, part of an army that had killed Woodwind's friends and members of the Velez family, whom he counted as his own. The teen possessed inferior fighting skills, and it seemed reasonable to handle the situation with restraint.

"Allfather is just. We who follow him stand before his judgment for what we do. So I am careful not to take life wantonly, and concluded that the boy at the inn posed no real threat to me."

Colonel Brandt remained skeptical. "And what of the life of your Lithian girl? Would your master be pleased to learn that your conduct landed you in jail and that by being imprisoned, you could not carry out his orders?"

"I am sworn to serve my lord in this realm with all my energy," Woodwind continued. "However, it's also true – and Lord Velez fully understands – that I must remain faithful to Allfather above all else. To dishonor the higher commission disgraces the lower one.

"I found lodging at the inn that night to avoid the cold and wind, not to indulge in luxury and create trouble for your people. The circumstances of my appearing before you are the result of misunderstanding and suspicion. These are factors beyond my personal control. Now I have faith that you are Allfather's servant here. You maintain law and order in a law-abiding land, and because of this, I'm confident you will treat me fairly. My restraint should prove my innocent intentions in this matter. Besides, I'd given my word to the young soldier that I would be staying there."

The Tamarian officer scratched his forehead. "Yours is a strange manner of thinking," he stated. "I admit that I find it difficult to fully appreciate."

"If you knew Allfather, whom I serve, you would not think so."

"So you make decisions about killing or sparing people based on a moral code?" queried the colonel.

"It's not as formulaic as you make it sound," Woodwind replied. "Moral conduct demands a disciplined mind, but it becomes habitual with practice."

The commander snickered and smiled, but whether his amusement stemmed from ridicule of Woodwind's personal philosophy or some other cause the southerner could not be certain. "Perhaps we have reached a point upon which we can both agree, although from contrasting perspectives and motives. I understand, based on your testimony, that you feel antipathy toward the Azgar."

"I do."

"Then, if you will provide me with specific information on our mutual enemy, you will serve your higher commission, and I in turn will be better equipped to carry out mine."

"What about my obligation to take the maiden home?" Woodwind asked. "If I assist you, when will you let me carry out my orders?"

Colonel Brandt laughed, exposing the motive for his humor. "First off, I don't answer for her," he replied. "In Tamaria we don't compel women to behave contrary to their wishes. This extends to obeying men with whom they're well acquainted. That choice is entirely hers to make.

"As far as your release is concerned, it is contingent on cooperation. The more accurate and valuable I find your Intel, the sooner I'll let you go."

"You're asking me to help on the basis of your word alone?" asked Woodwind. "How do I know I can trust you?"

"You say you have faith, yet you doubt my honor." Integrity resonated in the colonel's voice and radiated from his ruddy cheeks like warmth from a wood-burning stove on a cold day in winter.

"Very well," Woodwind sighed. "I'll tell you what I know. The Northern Liberation Army boasts over three hundred thousand well-equipped, disciplined soldiers who are camped within a days' ride of this place. They have excellent cannon to level your walls, cavalry to flank your maneuvers and a history of battlefield success against forces much larger than your nation can muster."

"You make them sound invincible."

Woodwind disagreed. "Allfather alone is invincible."

Colonel Brandt prompted him for specific information concerning tactics, logistics, equipment and armaments, as well as morale. Woodwind answered in surprising detail, but hearing this, the Tamarian colonel still concluded that he needed confirmation only trusted scouts could provide.

"If you fail to defeat them," the southern swordsman concluded, "they will take your land, steal your resources and enslave your entire nation."

"We'll not bend our necks to their yoke," Colonel Brandt replied. "There's more to the day of battle than the mere meeting of armies on the field. I have no doubt that their conquest will end here."

Woodwind scrunched his brow. "I don't understand why you can say that with such confidence."

The colonel arose, gesturing for Woodwind to follow. At his north-facing window, the Tamarian officer lifted the sash, allowing a swirl of cold air to sweep into the room from the howling storm in the darkness outside. "Do you hear that?" he inquired.

"I can hear nothing more than the wind," replied Woodwind, shaking his head.

Colonel Brandt patted Woodwind on the back as if he'd known him for a long time. "That, my foreign friend, is a song of victory!"

The Red Flare

Nothing in my life, much less my brief military career, could have possibly prepared me for the savage ferocity of a violent gale we experienced while camped on the Saradon, just south of the Tamarian border. Dust, propelled to bullet velocity in the screaming stream of frozen air, stung at any exposed skin like the fangs of many unseen serpents. Any object less than half the weight of a man subjected to this relentless fury was picked up and flung for hundreds, even thousands of yards.

Struggling through the canvas canyons we'd erected only days before, I did not find a single tent undamaged. Those along the fringes fared far worse than the ones near the center of our makeshift city, for in the former case, thousands of small projectiles pelted their fabric sides until seams began splitting open, rent – it seemed – by the irresistible force of unseen hands. The wind tore other tents from their tethers and tossed our shelters like cotton sheets ripped carelessly from curving clotheslines, leaving their exhausted inhabitants exposed for another freezing night.

Toward the center of the camp, piles of debris, dumped as the blunted wind slowed in its battering attack against our frail dwellings, swirled into fluttering entry flaps. Shivering soldiers repeatedly pounded new tent stakes into the rock-hard ground and repaired weary, sagging lines whose fibers, stretched and strained into fraying strings, snapped whenever they finally lost their war with the wind. Steel spires, which had earlier held our battle banners proudly aloft, fell like dying soldiers into the fragile, undulating embrace of tent tops.

In the months since our campaign began, we'd laid waste many nations. No one could stand against our massed infantry, our thundering cavalry, and the roar of ten thousand cannons delivering destruction at our command.

Now, we survived at the mercy of a force beyond our control, an emotionless, inhuman power that even the gods our priests so fervently entreated seemed unable to influence. We'd marched northward in unstoppable conquest for many weeks, only to encounter an enemy whose legions did not tremble at the sight of our camp, nor fall against the force of bullets and bayonets.

As I staggered into my tent, I sensed our doom. My men had never tasted defeat, but we could be beaten by the wind and cold as surely as we had routed every army that dared stand against us. Thus, the confidence I'd felt the day before vanished, and again, the fears of my inner soul came alive. Distracted by the savage sounds surrounding my tent, my imagination drifted and I found concentration as elusive as sleep had been the night before.

Strangely, the memory of that Lith girl from Shirak haunted me. When I closed my eyes to picture the Ice Dragon Inn, I saw her instead – crouched before me with her bow drawn tight – the passionate stare of her bright blue eyes fixed into mine. Had she loosed her arrow my life would have ended there, before I'd experienced the misery of extreme cold, before I learned to fear a winter windstorm.

As thoughts of that lovely girl blended into the sound of shrieking wind I realized I'd relinquished control over my own life. I had long believed in a fortune of my own making, yet my current situation left me feeling helpless.

Maybe I just wanted to be warm again. Whatever the reason, my work felt meaningless. Yet I planned a task set out for me by a senior officer who didn't care that I secretly wept over the loss of my beloved woman to suicide, or that I missed home, where I never worried about freezing to death in the middle of the night. In fact, the senior officers didn't care about anything other than continual conquest. Would they ever feel satisfied with our success? Or did we have to face defeat before they came to their senses?

Ah . . . the thought arose again! I'd been drafted. I had no choice when it came to military service. I carried out the orders of others, performing my duty without doubting in the rightness of our cause. Now, however, sinister, desperate sentiments filled my head. Silently I toyed with the perilous premise of deserting all I'd claimed to believe in, for if the things I cherished had their roots in the imaginings of another mind, whether of mother, minister or military man, what right had I to claim any of them as my own?

This line of thinking brought my attention back to the furious sound of wind flapping against my tent. For a moment, I entertained the thought of running away. Others had done it. Others had found no comfort in carrying out the will of an ambitious general, but these thoughts were not my own either . . . .

The opportunity vanished as a messenger arrived. He brought me Sergeant Aransen's report and told me that Legate Braegan expected a full briefing on the progress of our planned attack immediately. I wasn't ready for any detailed questioning, nor was I prepared to face a superior officer so soon after secretly committing treason. A familiar dread welled in my soul, for this particular legate had a reputation for expecting miracles, and I was no priest.

Yet I obliged the duty of my rank, and approached the legate's tent, shivering while waiting to be called inside. I heard the sounds of clinking glass and cursing wafting from his shelter. He'd been drinking again. That made everything worse. Moments later, I entered and saluted.

"Centurion Herulus reporting as ordered, sir!"

Braegan stood several inches shorter than I, but displayed a severe manner so intimidating, his persona more than made up for his lack of stature. At this moment, however, he sat at a table, conducting himself in a manner more worthy of my contempt than respect. Behavior of this kind had become more frequent as we marched north.

Muttering expletives that exceeded the brute vulgarity of an illiterate line soldier, he slurred his words like a slum-dwelling drunkard. I noticed a half-drained glass at his hand and an empty whiskey bottle on the stained, canvas floor near the table. He overflowed with explosive invective, the words lashing like a recklessly wielded saber. Volatile moods of this kind always accompanied drunkenness, and whenever he descended to this condition, I seriously feared for my life.

A desk, deeply scarred from transport, lay awash in a sea of documents awaiting his perusal. Yet he sat idle, running rough hands through thinning hair, pausing to scratch a thickening beard. In mockery of the cold, he remained dressed in the same, lightweight battle fatigues we'd worn in Shirak.

With bloodshot eyes he inspected me from head to foot, smirked to himself, then set his bottle aside to proceeded with business. "I presume you've completed your attack plans," he said in a controlled tone that belied intoxication and warned of his potential rage. This man did not like to be disappointed.

"Of course," I replied, lying, spreading my papers across his desk in order to appear as impressive as possible. "In conjunction with the artillery liaison officer, a mortar and cannon survey has been plotted. The structure is lightly defended with what appear to be young, inexperienced troops. We have supply routes planned and an estimate of the manpower required. I believe . . . ."

"I don't give a rat's anus what you believe, soldier," he glowered. "I want you to give me results." The legate brushed my papers off his desk with no more ceremony than he'd give to flicking lint from his uniform.

Relieved that he hadn't actually looked through them, but dreading that he trusted me I picked up the pile and stood at attention again. "You will have results, sir!"

"Good," he responded. "You'll attack at dawn, tomorrow. If we have to spend another night out here in this thrice-damned wind, I'll see to it that you take on these nose-picking barbarians with a wicker shield and a sharp stick! Understand?"

"Absolutely, sir!"

Without looking at me again, he barked, "Dismissed!"

I left quickly, relieved that my life and career survived that encounter. Yet I had a lot of work remaining . . . .

Before noon arrived, I'd roughed out my actual battle plan, requisitioned supplies, coordinated my attack timetable with the mess crew and deathwolf handlers, briefed my junior officers, and assembled the enlisted men. With help from Lieutenant Hicks, I distributed equipment and food among the hundred-odd soldiers who would participate in the operation. Each man carried an equal share of artillery munitions and personal gear.

Four horses, yoked in pairs, pulled two field cannon. These lightweight castings fired high explosive shells or canister. The mortar crew required two more horses to transport cast-iron mortar tubes that weighed nearly six hundred pounds each. We also brought along a seventh animal so that I could send messages quickly in battle.

I didn't feel good about this. As we marched northward, I brooded over my plans. My timetable made no allowances for setbacks. I worried that separating my forces would create trouble coordinating firepower between the mortars and cannon. These things bothered me, but not nearly as much as an intuitive sense of foreboding. I said nothing to the men about this. The only thing I heard from any of them were muttered curses about the cold.

The barbarians did not detect our approach. Several miles south of our objective, we split into small groups spaced three hundred yards apart, and moved parallel to the Saradon road, well east of the Ice Dragon Inn.

According to plan, we hunkered down in the tall grass until darkness fell, at which time my century took up three positions: one on the hilltop behind the inn for our mortar battery, the main assault force to the east of the inn, and another – out of visual range to the north along the road – that I intended to use as a screen against any possible reinforcement. This last group also provided a reserve for my frontal assault against the gate at first light.

An hour after nightfall, the wind finally began to slacken. Although protected from its fury by the hills to our west, I worried that being camped out in the open again would result in more frostbite and desertions. On the second watch, I sent the men to their respective positions, strictly prohibiting campfires because visibility on the Saradon, especially from a high point along the wall where the barbarians were sure to be watching, extended for miles. Hiding over a hundred men in the tall grass at twilight had been difficult enough, but at night, a campfire, however helpful it would have been to ward off the accursed cold, would surely clue the enemy in to our presence on the plain.

Strangely, I slept well. No premonitions of doom haunted my dreams, no deathwolf howl startled me from my slumber. Sergeant Aransen woke me up about half way through the last watch, and I felt refreshed, alert, even anxious to begin the battle. "Let's move," I ordered. "With luck, we'll take this place before the rest of the world gets out of bed."

Purpose pulsed through my veins. I supervised battle lines drawn to put the rising Daystar at our backs. When our cannon fired, the barbarians would have to stare into its brilliant light to respond. Just before daybreak I surveyed the inn's gate, seeing no movement there. Sentries on the wall remained in shelter. A scouting report from my screening force uncovered nothing unusual. We'd achieved total surprise.

My sense of hearing faded as an ear-shattering eruption of exploding gunpowder reverberated across the empty plateau, followed a moment later by the dull concussion of an artillery shell impacting against the ancient stone wall, some three-hundred yards distant. Shrouded momentarily by a stinging, sulfurous smoke cloud issuing from the cannon, I watched the methodical grace of well-trained men adjusting the angle of their gun and loading a new round into the breech.

For several minutes the barbarians did not return fire. Through my field glasses, I watched a sentry running from his post on the wall, disappearing from sight as a follow-up round from our second gun smashed into the creaky, wooden sign above the gate. Immediately after this, a mortar explosion arose from within the compound, though I was unable to hear its distinctive whistle coming in, having been deafened by the roar of bigger guns nearby.

My artillery crew bracketed the iron gate on their third shot, but it proved tougher than I'd anticipated. Since we were not receiving any return fire, I ordered infantry, arrayed line abreast, three-rows deep, to advance to the two hundred and fifty yard mark and set sights on the wall.

"Fire on my command!" I directed, subsequently motioning the cannon crew forward as well. There was no point in wasting any more ammunition if we couldn't knock a surprisingly tough gate down from this distance.

Our mortar crew had trouble dropping their rounds accurately. The trajectory of their shells arced into the influence of strong, gusty wind high above the hills, pushing some of their shells further eastward. In dismay, I watched an errant round fall well beyond its target, coming dangerously close to the infantry line I'd just moved into range. The next shot went wide, and I cursed myself for placing that mortar crew in a position where they could so easily miss and kill friendly troops.

Our infantry support cannon was a magnificent gun, accurate and fairly powerful for a weapon of its size. Although considered a light field piece in our arsenal, moving it with men instead of horses in battle wasted valuable time. Every moment our guns were silent gave the barbarians time to assemble their defenders. We lost the element of surprise because we'd begun firing too far away.

Of course, if I'd kept the horses in place, we would have had to harness them, and that might have taken even longer. What I learned from this, was that success depended on hammering the enemy quickly. Before my troops could fire again, an organized response poured over the old walls like a waterfall of death.

Instantly, I learned to hate their rockets. Steamy contrails poured from the inn, obscuring our vision and filling the air with a terrifying sound. The sheer volume of fire astonished me, for we had considered this a lightly defended structure. These barbarian anti-personnel rockets were small, fast-flying devices with canister-type warheads that instantly turned the placid plateau into a graveyard.

"Return fire!" I screamed.

The flash of individual rifles created a fleeting screen of grey rippling down our line in its wake, followed by dozens of white smoke puffs along the crenelated stone crest some seventy-odd yards distant. As my front row of men knelt to reload, the second raised their weapons to fire, exposing themselves to massed rocket attack. Five men fell, their bodies obliterated, while many others suffered horrible wounds from shrapnel and burning gas.

Once our cannon finally arrived in its new position, the gunners adjusted their angle and began hammering the gate again. Three shots later, the impact of a high explosive shell ripped the heavy portal from its hinges and sent it spinning into the cobbled courtyard beyond, where it crashed amid a cloud of dust and leaves.

Reacting rapidly, before my cannon crew had a chance to respond, barbarian soldiers rushed out from behind the wall with rifles blazing. Crouching for my own safety as large caliber bullets zipped overhead, I watched the young men form four groups on either side of the breach. With coordination that comes only from extensive training, one group fired a blistering volley while another raced forward, dropped to their bellies and discharged their weapons in turn. The third group then advanced, followed by the fourth and the process was repeated, with devastating effect.

We huddled close to the ground in disarray, near panic spreading like a brush fire among my men. Barbarian rifle shots outnumbered ours by a wide margin, while unceasing volleys from the walls showered us with hot, razor-edged shrapnel. Bullets designed to kill giants ripped through our ranks. Stricken men screamed in agony as their bodies yielded to the penetrating power of high-velocity enamel. Pinned to the cold ground, ten more of my soldiers perished within moments of the counterattack.

Whenever we knocked one of the advancing soldiers down, he seemed to get back on his feet, fully capable of pressing onward. Their body armor, whatever it was, stopped our bullets, but both types of their ammunition tore through our breastplates and unprotected extremities, killing and maiming men who fell as helplessly as dry wheat stalks before a sharp harvest sickle.

I sent a messenger on horseback ordering our screening force forward. We needed help in a hurry, and I hoped they'd arrive in time. With the battle hanging in a delicate balance, I rallied my men with words that burst from my soul like a hot geyser venting from the ground, calling for fixed bayonets before the fighting denigrated into the ancient, brutal custom of men killing men en-masse at close range.

We closed ranks to concentrate our firepower. The four enemy squads melded into a pair of separate groups, one of which continued to advance directly for us, while the other moved left to flank our position. We could soon see the details of their faces, and I stared in wide-eyed wonder when I realized how young they were . . . .

What I did next came from sheer necessity. I had to save my men. At a critical moment, I ordered my infantry to drop down, allowing the readied cannon crew to fire canister at point blank range into the advancing formations of young barbarian soldiers.

An explosion of blood and flesh erupted from within their ranks. Into the grey confusion of smoke and death I sent veteran soldiers who knew well the wicked work of bayonet and bludgeoning. Human rage mingled with the random sounds of steel on steel, the crunch of breaking bones and the cries of overwhelming affliction experienced on both sides.

In the haze I noticed an older man, an ugly commander whose presence seemed to inspire the young soldiers. Within seconds of our devastating cannon attack, his leadership reasserted control and the boys under his command renewed their courage to continue fighting. With the momentum of morale shifting in his favor, I raised my rifle and with a single shot, burst his brain like a melon dropped on concrete.

Instant panic rippled through his leaderless troops. My men seized control of the moment, their combat rage swelling until the battleground softened, soaked in the blood of its defenders.

When my reinforcements arrived, the remnant realized their battle was lost and turned to run. We shot them in the legs to prevent them from getting away, then dispatched them with the bayonet to ensure there were no survivors. Only then did I redirect my attention to the inn.

An eerie silence settled upon the scene. No further counter fire came from the battlements upon the wall. I'd lost more than 30% of my men before even reaching the gate, and knowing we'd been rendered combat ineffective in just a few minutes of intense fighting, realized that a concerted defense would easily beat us back.

It wasn't supposed to be this tough. We'd outclassed every nation we'd fought thus far, but now I worried that we'd met our match. We advanced to the wall without further incident, setting up watch positions in the towers before penetrating further.

Our cannon fired a pair of smoke rounds to the north, signaling the mortar crew to stop shelling. Disquieted by the lack of further resistance, my soldiers entered the compound in a state of hair-trigger tension, but our suspicions of ambush proved unfounded as we advanced. No further conflict ensued.

A complete inspection required several hours. During this time we came to understand that the barbarians had abandoned the inn with remarkable speed, leaving little behind but a group of empty buildings. Our search yielded only meager food supplies and a few bundles of personal effects from which we scrounged some blankets and boots. I worried that we'd be asked to account for more plunder than this.

When we checked the water tower we found its tank empty. An open valve at ground level allowed water to rush back into the well while our hosts had successfully disabled the wind pump atop its tower.

I wanted to be furious, but I'd been shocked by the brutality of the barbarian resistance and stunned by its sudden cessation. The boys we'd battled against beyond the walls were sent out to cover the retreat of others, but where had the others gone? Would they return and attack again with reinforcements?

I posted men at every lookout point along the walls and prepared to defend our newly conquered headquarters. A few hours after securing our position, I sent a squad of men to the little town north of the inn to get more food.

The distinctive hissing of a solid-fueled rocket startled me during my inspection of our firing positions. Launched by a hidden hand near the back wall, a single, red flare arced high into the cold, windy heavens.

*Junior Scout Garrick Ravenwood, Tamarian Defense Force;
Brenna Velez; Woodwind*

Trouble

The warm, sweet taste of birch sap flavored oatmeal lingered on Garrick's tongue, inspiring daydreams of languid kisses and whispered conversations in a quiet place. While he'd sat very close to the foreign woman, he'd not exchanged a single touch while talking to Brenna the night before. He'd certainly wanted his hands on her, and a fantasy arose of willingness and wonder, derived in part from recent fumbling, adolescent encounters he'd shared with an equally naive, inquisitive cousin in the hay loft of his great uncle's ranch.

But Brenna's character and charisma moderated his passion, inspiring patience. For the first time in memory, Garrick didn't pursue the dream to its usual conclusion. The amorous images of soft, scented flesh fled from his mind, replaced by recollections of endearing childhood stories exchanged in accented vulgate, of laughter shared, and of the intelligence behind Brenna's beautiful, sparkling eyes. Certainly, her lovely features piqued his interest. He desired her, but he also wanted the young woman to experience safety and contentment in his company. This feeling persisted as his ardor faded, leaving a far-away sort of smile etched upon his face.

Woodwind interrupted the young Tamarian's reverie with a barrage of social pleasantries uttered in a tone of voice that betrayed his distaste for early mornings. Careful not to spill a drop of steaming tea, the southerner set his tray down on the battered table deck long used for feeding soldiers and pulled up a chair. "Are you heading back to the inn this morning?" he inquired.

Garrick nodded. "I'll be leaving after breakfast. The sergeant wouldn't think twice about having me on dung patrol for a month if I don't show up soon."

Confused, Woodwind wrinkled his brow. "Dung patrol? You march behind the cavalry with a shovel?"

"No," Garrick explained, finding Woodwind's attempt at humor an unwelcome interruption of an arguably more pleasant meditation. "It's part of how we keep warm. Each firebase has a gas-driven system that takes heat from the ground and amplifies it using a fluid pump. We use the same gas for indoor light and hot water.

"We make the gas in a digester. By mixing plant, animal and human waste in a warm tank, we feed tiny creatures that produce combustible gas drawn off the top, similar to what happens inside your own body. Afterward, we compost the slurry and use it to fertilize our gardens.

"During the summer, when gas production is at its peak, we store extra output in a big, low-pressure tank for cooking fuel and light the rest of the year. In order to make the system work properly, someone has to shovel waste into the digester. We call it dung patrol, and it's a rather unpleasant job."

Woodwind leaned forward. "And people do this *here*?"

Garrick capitalized on his companion's queasiness, since he would have preferred eating alone anyway. "Modern forts like this one have built-in drain pipes for human waste, so unless there's a clog, we let gravity do its work. Animal dung and plant clippings still have to be shoveled into a hopper, which you might find disgusting, but it's more pleasant than freezing in the winter.

"No one really knows who designed the Ice Dragon Inn, or even when it was built, but it's a lot older than this place, so the gas system there is a retrofit. The army brought in pigs because we didn't have enough people and animals to feed the digester. Someone has to shovel pig dung into a cart and wheel it over to the hopper; that's a chore usually saved for junior scouts who slack off or don't show up for training on time."

Garrick's lecture on Tamarian technology might have interested Woodwind under different circumstances, but as he listened to further explanations regarding the correct consistency and composition of feedstock, the southerner's appetite waned. He slurped hot tea, eyeing the potatoes and green beans on his plate with suspicion. "So you put digester slurry on this food?"

"*Composted* digester slurry," Garrick corrected. "Everything you've eaten since you set foot in Tamaria came from local farms. All the old-timers know that yields decline without fertilization and crop rotation; it makes good sense to close the nutrient cycle by reusing waste. Otherwise, we can't sustain food production."

Woodwind understood how this principle worked in the natural world, but the fact that the Tamarians used human waste to fertilize their plants repulsed him. His face reflected disgust, and the tone of his voice hardened as he responded. "That's all very progressive," he began, shoving his breakfast aside. "But I have something more important than pig poop to discuss with you right now."

Garrick accepted the change in topic with a nod.

"The police told me that Colonel Brandt was a reasonable man," Woodwind continued. "Maybe he is, but he's rather suspicious of my presence in your country. So, in order for me to walk out of here with my freedom, I've been compelled to escort a scout patrol of the Azgar camp so they can file a full report. He won't let me take Brenna home until it's done.

"Now, I don't know the area. I know nothing about survival in a climate like this one, and if the worst of the weather is yet to come, I won't last long on my own. I can also imagine running into a friendly patrol that thinks I'm hostile, and wind up either dead, or back in the brig. Since I don't speak your language either, I need help. I'd like you and Brenna to come with me."

Garrick had suspected that Woodwind would make such a request, but he considered the swordsman a competitor for Brenna's affection and shook his head. "Your story wouldn't be any more credible to Colonel Brandt if it came from me. I'm just a rookie recruit, and around here, that makes me lower than the scum on a slug's belly. You're better off traveling with a regular patrol.

"And, even if I could go with you, what's to stop you from riding away with Brenna once we hit the border? You told me that Lord Velez sent you on a quest to find her, and now, with my help, you've been reunited. Why would helping me and my people take precedence over your orders? It doesn't make sense!

"Besides, last night Brenna told me that she resents how you're acting like a hero rescuing a helpless damsel when you intend to drag her off to a place she doesn't want to go. She neither wants nor needs rescuing. It sounds to me like she's in no frame of mind to go anywhere with you!"

Woodwind bristled. "What makes you think that I have to answer to a baby-faced adolescent with a phallic infatuation for a pretty girl? My business with the young lady is none of your concern, and I resent your intrusion into my affairs!"

The swordsman's hostile response stung Garrick into momentary silence. He fought back an irrational surge of terror, induced by bitter memories of brutal beatings every time he inspired his father's anger. At home, confrontations of this kind routinely resulted in merciless violence, and there, the best defense involved avoiding parental wrath at all costs. While Garrick didn't actually expect Woodwind to lash out at him, the power of deep and invisible wounds prevailed against his present experience. Garrick felt guilty for inspiring Woodwind's wrath, and his face flushed with shame. Unable to maintain eye contact, Garrick muttered, "Forgive me, sir. I meant no offense."

Having witnessed this behavior from the young Tamarian for the second time, and sensing that a dark story lay beneath this response, Woodwind reconsidered his reaction. Remembering the impulsivity of his own youth, the older man regretted allowing his anger to surface. Brenna's acceptance or rejection of Woodwind's most devoted affection remained a sensitive issue, and he'd been unwise to so readily expose the vulnerability. "No need," he replied. "I should not have been offended."

An awkward silence ensued as the two men searched their souls for words to continue. They stared absently across the mess hall, distracted by the sounds of soldiers milling in line, exchanging tidbits of personal news, their plates, cups and cutlery clinking as food service continued.

"If you'll excuse me, I have to get back to my unit," Garrick said quietly. Without another word, the cadet picked up his tray and headed for the dish room, leaving Woodwind alone with his thoughts and a plate of cold food.

***

Brenna leaned against the gelid glass of a southwest-facing window, watching deep shadows retreat from between the crags of snow-crowned mountain ridges in the distance. The base commander graciously arranged for private quarters on the top floor of this unusual fortress, but after sleeping soundly for many hours, the Lithian woman felt hemmed in by the cool, concrete walls protecting her from the dying wind outside.

A dull, dissatisfied ache crept into her soul, a feeling inspired partly by the culmination of her intense effort to reach the High Land, and having done so, of not knowing what to do next. By Allfather's grace she stood on Tamarian soil, but it had been her will, not his, to come here, and she feared that she might have made a grievous mistake.

Woodwind's post-reunion scolding echoed in her memory. "You've run away from your problems like an irresponsible child, and to claim, by virtue of your survival, that the blessing of Allfather has condoned such reprehensible behavior is little more than a rationalization to conceal the betrayal of your family! You're pursuing some demented fantasy about living up here at the emotional expense of people who love you! How could you treat your own family this way?"

"You can be such a horse's hind-end!" she thought angrily, glaring at a puff of snow driven by the wind from a distant, prominent peak. The wound inspired by her friend's accusation stung in her heart, stirring dismal feelings worse than the guilt she already felt for lying to her parents. Brenna didn't want to follow Woodwind back to Kameron. Yet, despite their disagreement, his friendship meant a lot to her, and she felt she owed the man at least a tacit attempt at conciliation for his trouble.

The first thing she didn't like about this idea centered upon the undeniable authority he would suddenly hold over her. As her father's servant Woodwind's social status fell beneath hers, and additionally, she'd lived three years longer than he. Their friendship, already suffering because he'd successfully tracked her down, would certainly deteriorate further if she returned to Kameron in his company. He would never let her hear the end of his achievement, and she hated his continual attempts to prove his worth as a suitor.

Even worse, she'd have to face her parents and admit that she'd deliberately defied their wishes. Because Brenna sincerely loved her family, the defiant act of running away rather than returning as promised filled her heart with ineffable remorse. She could not bear the fact that she'd disappointed her *Amair*, especially since nothing had changed in her unwillingness to marry Lord Fang.

"Ugh!" she hissed. The thought of breathing air in proximity to that immaculately-groomed but immoral excuse for a man disgusted her to the core. Although a powerful leader with an army of his own, wealthy and influential in the affairs of Kameron, the root of his success lay seeded in slavery and opium trade. The Lithian woman loathed his greed for power and detested his character.

She had no intention of returning to Kameron with Woodwind. "I'd rather die!" she muttered to herself.

Yet the romantic land of Tamaria had proven colder than she expected. Brenna realized she could not survive in the wilderness by herself during the winter. Living off the land had become progressively more difficult with each step northward, as her memory of hunger testified; but Garrick warned that colder, darker days lay in the near future.

"Garrick . . . ." she whispered, turning from the window. Leaning her back against the cool concrete wall, she pictured his face in her mind, imagining the strong warmth of his embrace. Brenna closed her eyes as her heart quickened, wishing that the circumstances drawing them together didn't also present obstacles to drive them apart. Her eyes opened and her lips drew into a tighter line.

During their conversation the previous evening she'd confirmed, to her dismay, that although Garrick did not repudiate her faith, he didn't see evidence of divine immanence and influence in human affairs. He believed in a universe ruled by chance and driven by natural forces, dismissing Allfather as a semantic label for things not well understood. She'd concealed her disappointment from him, but it had overflowed from her eyes and onto her pillow in the solitude and darkness after midnight.

Brenna respected his view, even though it contrasted with her own. Lithian culture encouraged tolerance in principle, so long as his position did not harm others, or damage their world. Still, she wished he shared her faith.

Overcome with exhaustion, she'd fallen into a dreamless sleep soon afterward. Brenna spent much of her early-morning prayer time trying to reconcile the undeniable attraction she felt for an unbeliever. The Lithian maiden craved his company, but the prospect of their friendship continuing seemed repulsive to people for reasons she didn't understand, or didn't want to admit.

She'd noticed how close proximity with him raised eyebrows. Touching hands – even incidentally – and speaking in the enemy's language stirred social scorn. Brenna had never experienced such disapproval before, as her musical talent, beauty and the importance of her family ensured a measure of deference from nearly everyone.

Tamarians, who knew nothing about her, judged the young woman based on her physical appearance and language – men by leering or catcalling, and women with either envy or disgust. She suspected that local people disdained racially integrated relationships, concluding that any serious affiliation with Garrick would not long be tolerated by those in authority. Nonetheless, Brenna prayed for Allfather's blessing, wistfully aware that neither the Tamarians, nor Woodwind, nor Garrick, would approve.

In the darkness before daybreak, she'd thought about staying at the base to help her Tamarian hosts in their fight against the Azgar. Brenna knew that women served in the Tamarian army, but felt too shy to directly inquire about their duties. After all, why would the Tamarians want to hire a half-breed Lithian whose best friend had landed himself in the brig for fighting with the locals?

Woodwind had seen no future for her up here, but he couldn't comprehend what she was feeling because he wasn't listening. Loyalty and selfless dedication to service, the very traits she so admired in him, clouded his judgment. In her mind, there *had* to be a spiritual reason at least partially responsible for her survival.

By extension, if Allfather had preserved her life during the perilous flight to the High Land, there must be a divine purpose for her presence here. Brenna, who'd been gifted with a healing touch, concluded that she would use Allfather's power to save lives in the upcoming conflict.

"I'm not going with you!" she told Woodwind in her mind, rehearsing for a potential verbal fray unprecedented in their friendship. The Lithian woman muttered an angry monologue while dressing to avoid both the cold and the disapproving stares of her Tamarian hosts. Then, retrieving her bow and quiver, she raced downstairs in the hope of finding Garrick before he departed.

***

Appetite prevailed over his concern for what had once fertilized the vegetables on his plate, and less than fifteen minutes after finishing the food, Woodwind retrieved his longsword and departed, accompanied by two fully-armed Tamarian soldiers.

Corporal Albrecht Fanselars had a neck the size of Woodwind's thigh, and a booming voice that seemed boundless in its ability to harass and harangue soldiers of lesser rank. Exuding an arrogance surpassed only by his mass, the soldier bullied his mule into a scamper up the steep ramp, setting a pace for the morning scout patrol that even Woodwind's gelding would sweat to maintain.

Albrecht spoke no vulgate. While this might have seemed a disadvantage to Woodwind, who could not understand him, Darrold Müller, a private soldier selected for this operation, translated calmly. "He likens you to the sticky mass of hair, mucus and semen normally found in the shower drains on base," the light-haired highlander explained. "This might not sound complimentary, but it's actually rather mild for him."

"Why is he so angry?" Woodwind inquired.

Darrold shrugged. "He said something about having real work to do and compares going you on this patrol to cleaning vomit and sickroom bedpans on a sweaty summer day. He's really not that upset."

It seemed a disconcerting statement, but Woodwind, who'd had no choice in his escort after Garrick turned him down, ignored the affront. He explained to the vulgate-speaking Tamarian where he'd last seen the Azgar camp, suggesting that they observe the enemy from the foothills west of the Saradon. Corporal Fanselars merely grunted his approval of the translation, shifting his rifle across his back for greater comfort and sliding a compact, shoulder-fired rocket launcher into a saddlebag.

Hours later, after crossing the shallow, ice-jammed waters of the Tualitin and ascending steep, rocky hillsides where a path had to be made rather than followed, Woodwind began to understand why the Tamarians rode mules instead of horses. Within the first few hundred yards of an especially severe and slippery climb, he'd fallen far behind his escorting hosts.

Corporal Fanselars sneered smugly at the summit, waiting, commenting in a tone of voice that made his contempt easy enough to comprehend, even if Woodwind couldn't understand his words. When the southerner arrived at the top, Shadow, his mount, was deeply lathered and breathing hard. The corporal shook his head, turned his mule southward and continued.

At the end of a long, hard ride, the trio arrived at an east-facing bluff. Even with the naked eye at this distance, a huge horde, armed with a vast array of artillery, appeared on the steppe below. Closer examination with a field lens brought about a sudden and serious conversation between the two Tamarians.

"Is there a problem?" Woodwind asked.

Private Müller stared into the lens for quite some time before offering a response. "They're moving," he said. "It looks like they're heading north."

Woodwind nodded. "Odds are good that they've scouted your frontier and found a suitable place to set up for a full-scale attack. I hope you can field a force big enough to hold them off."

"What idiot marches an army straight into the teeth of an oncoming winter?" the Tamarian inquired rhetorically. Then, turning to Woodwind he asked, "How many would you say they have out there?"

Woodwind beckoned for the field lens, surprised at the visual clarity afforded by Tamarian optics. Azgar banners, frayed in their struggle against the wind, flew ahead of long columns of black-uniformed soldiers. Cavalry units escorted the infantry, their horses laden with the accouterments of war. "This army took Shirak with about three-hundred thousand combat troops. The force looks about the same size to me, but maybe a few thousand less."

Darrold grunted. "How fast can that group move?"

"It depends on whether they set up a full camp or just bivouac out in the open. On average, they march about twenty miles a day," Woodwind stated. "Their field camps can be dismantled in only a few hours, and they never move without first securing a good place to bivouac."

"Incredible," the Tamarian replied, his disbelief already suspended. "That's a grueling rate of march."

Woodwind nodded. "Speed is initiative in combat."

When Corporal Fanselars heard the translation he spat on the frosty ground. If the Azgar could move that fast without trains, then their men would be exhausted if engaged before they could rest. Colonel Brandt needed time to coordinate a civilian evacuation in the immediate area, and he'd be foolish to attack an army of this size with the forces available to him at present.

Wasting no further time, the men moved northward, riding several yards below the east-facing ridge line to avoid detection from the Saradon. When they arrived at a spot overlooking the westward bend of the Tualitin River Valley, the corporal scanned the terrain ahead with his field lens, first north, then west, then east, speaking to the other Tamarian in low tones.

The private took his turn at the field lens. "We have a problem," he told Woodwind. "There's an Azgar scout party watering their horses at the river up ahead."

"Then let's go further west," Woodwind suggested.

"That'll take too long. The mountains to our northwest would be difficult to cross this time of year. We think we should wait until they move on."

"It's not a bad idea," Woodwind remarked. "But I warn you that very soon there will be many more coming."

***

A series of rude remarks and wolf-whistles alerted Garrick to Brenna's approach before he actually saw her. The young woman scurried toward the livery with her head down, rapidly descending stairs as if pursued by shame; her movement amplifying the sway of feminine flesh that attracted leering eyes and unwanted attention.

Garrick stepped out to confront the culprits and defend Brenna, despite the possibility of making the problem worse, or getting into serious trouble. He swore at a trio of ogling soldiers. "What is wrong with you?"

"Oh, you think you're tough, farm boy?" one of them mocked. "You gonna save your slutty foreigner from us?"

"You fixin' for a fight?" Garrick spat. "Try me!"

The antagonist pushed him tepidly. Garrick, who'd taken on bullies to protect his younger brother, shoved back hard, with fearlessness borne of long experience.

But he didn't get a chance to land a blow, as a sergeant came out of the livery. "What's going on here?" she demanded sternly.

Brenna held her breath as Garrick tried to explain the situation. "These men were catcalling and disrespecting my friend. Now she's a refugee, and . . . ."

"You got somewhere more important to be, son?" the woman demanded.

"Yes, sergeant," he replied.

"Then get out of here!" She appraised Brenna with a lingering eye, then gestured dismissively. "Off with you, too!"

When the sergeant returned her attention to the three guilty men, she halted their arguing for innocence with a firm voice. "I have ears, and I wasn't born yesterday," she began. "Just because you're too ugly to get a date gives you no right to show your hard-on in public whenever a pretty woman walks by.

"Now, since you have time to ogle itty-bitty big titty foreign girls, you've earned the honor of mucking out the barn. Get on it, or I'll have you working bare handed . . . ."

Garrick brought a mule out from the stable, his anger cooling, given the sergeant's favorable handling of the matter. "I'm really sorry," he said quietly, his face reflecting concern. "You don't deserve that kind of nonsense."

Her lips thinned. She glanced at Garrick, her eyes hunting for sympathy and her soul relieved to so easily find genuine empathy in his expression. "I didn't expect such rude behavior from the men in your country," she muttered, clearly frustrated. "I'd heard women were respected here."

He shrugged. "Normally that's true, but prejudice toward foreigners is widespread. The sergeant knew what was going on and gave those boys what they deserved."

Brenna's expression reflected both concern and sadness. "I didn't want you to get hurt, or wind up in trouble. I can defend myself. I don't need a champion."

"Wouldn't you stick up for me?" he asked.

That was a fair critique, and it stung her a little. "Of course I would," she admitted.

As they left the firebase on mule back, Brenna's anger rekindled. "I don't mean to belabor this, but I detest the masculine entitlement that reduces me to a stranger's sexual fantasy. My body is a gift I reserve for a man who earns my trust, my love, and my respect. May those boys suffer running sores and chronic hemorrhoids!"

The humor in her remark inspired a smile. "They should know better, but they're focused on how you look, not who you are. It's wrong and I hope their bad behavior doesn't reflect poorly on me."

"I wasn't talking about you," she replied, her indignation cooling. "I know you get aroused, but you don't act like a tomcat about it."

Embarrassed that his fervid, physical response to her proximity was both so obvious and worthy of an overt remark, Garrick fell silent.

Ahead, looming endlessly into a distant horizon, the placid Saradon seemed almost pleasant now that the wind had finally slackened. The mule plodded toward the southeast, its hooves falling heavily on the stony trail leading toward Dieter and the Ice Dragon Inn.

"What do you plan to do?" Garrick asked at length.

Brenna turned, her smiling face reflecting admiration. "About you, or your libido-crazed countrymen?"

"Neither," he replied. "I'm asking about your intentions, now that Woodwind found you. Why are you coming with me instead of going south with him today?"

The young woman turned her shoulders forward and leaned into Garrick's warm, strong body, vaguely aware of a low-pitched, concussive thunder far away. She said nothing about the sound. "By now I'm sure you realize the Azgar will attack your people and take your land."

"They may try," he said, "but we will stop them."

"May Allfather grant your wish," she replied. "I know they won't retreat without a fight, and many of your soldiers will suffer. I'd like to help by healing your wounded who fall in combat. Can you arrange that? Once Woodwind leaves I'll be alone here, and you're the only one I trust."

Garrick overlooked her spiritualizing, his quiet, unstated passion for the young woman quickening his heartbeat. The weight and warmth of her body – underscored by an inner delight that she desired his company – nearly deprived him of the ability to respond.

"I'm sure my sergeant can make arrangements with the unit commander." Although he didn't say it, Garrick longed to tell Brenna how happy she'd just made him. Instead, he gently stroked her cheek with the top side of his forefinger, barely able to contain the urge to kiss her.

Brenna sat upright. It wasn't fair to permit such contact when she felt so conflicted. Although she couldn't deny that she really liked this young man – that she actually wanted his attention and affection – desire surged through her body with such urgency, she feared its power.

"Please don't do that," she warned, momentarily making eye contact before turning her head away.

"Oh," he replied, noting the fear in her eyes, yet feeling hurt and confused by her rejection. "I read the moment wrong. I'm sorry. I didn't mean to upset you."

The Lithian woman sighed, uttering a silent prayer. "*I'm torn,*" her spirit told Allfather. "*Why does my need for physical affection and the novel desire to please that I'm feeling for Garrick chafe against my faith? You created love and you created logic. Why are these good gifts in conflict?*"

Brenna's lament ended abruptly. The swift, smoky arc of a bright red flare ascended high into the blue heaven from a cluster of hills, several miles distant. "What is that?" she inquired, pointing.

Garrick stiffened, abruptly pulling back on the reins. "Trouble," he replied nervously. "Big trouble!"

***

The list of options available to Woodwind and his companions narrowed with each passing moment as they huddled on the hilltop. "This is a common deployment tactic," the southerner explained. "Small, fast cavalry units advance, seeking contact with hostile forces. These scouting groups usually skirmish long enough to get a feel for their enemy, then retreat toward a supporting maniple.

"Any hostiles in pursuit will be drawn into battle with progressively larger units, following some distance behind, until the main army can move in."

Private Müller nodded. He felt inclined to trust Woodwind's explanation, but that meant they'd encounter a more numerous force very soon, making escape even less likely. He discussed the situation with Corporal Fanselars, then returned to Woodwind. "We think we should engage them directly," he stated. "Given your knowledge of how they operate, our odds will worsen if we wait longer."

Woodwind explained the range and power of Azgar guns. "If we move west, we conceal ourselves in taller grass. We walk the animals around, and they may not see us."

Darrold didn't like the sound of that idea. "You say they can shoot accurately to eighty yards, but our rockets have more than twice that range. If we move downhill, we can hit them first and it doesn't matter if they can see us."

Woodwind, who'd never seen Tamarian firepower in action, remained skeptical. "I'll ride down to the river and distract them," he suggested, believing that his idea represented a more prudent course of action than calling attention to their presence with fireworks that might be seen thousands of yards away.

"Maybe I can draw a few of them off, or at least, get their backs turned away from you. My horse is fast, and he's outrun them before." The southerner pointed to a prominent rock formation well to the west, across the river. "I'll meet you over there."

Albrecht Fanselars spat on the ground. "Let the idiot run off," he said. "We don't need him anymore."

As Woodwind began his descent to the valley floor, Darrold looked through his field lens, scanning the area beyond the eastern edge of the Tualitin. At a distance somewhat greater than two miles, he noticed a century-strength battle group moving northwest.

"I'm afraid the *sicklian's* lover boy is right," he observed. "There are more coming."

Although Woodwind didn't want to be seen descending the hill, Shadow, his horse, kicked up dust and protested loudly at being urged down so steep a slope. The southerner could not believe how close he was able to approach before the enemy soldiers noted his presence.

A horse, whose senses proved keener than those of the shivering men standing on the north bank of the Tualitin, raised its head and whinnied when it noticed the tall, drab-clothed civilian rider on his ebon-skinned beast. The enemy soldiers, alerted after several animals stirred, seemed confused. Their initial response remained limited to some pointing and shouting. After conferring with an officer, three men mounted up and rode out to investigate while the others watched from the far side of the river.

Woodwind halted as the enemy soldiers approached, his horse pacing, snorting and stomping the ground, anticipating a fight. Yet the swordsman did not want to engage until he sensed an advantage. "Allfather God," he prayed without closing his eyes. "Deliver your enemy into my hand!" Woodwind felt a nerve-sharpening rush surging like a spring tide through his veins.

The Azgar soldiers behaved cautiously at first. Two enlisted men, visibly uncomfortable in the cold, stopped their ponies some ten yards away and remained with muskets ready, while the third, a mackerel-faced lieutenant, approached with a drawn saber. "Clear the area!" he called in vulgate, arrogantly assuming that Woodwind understood the command.

Woodwind controlled his horse with subtle pressure on its belly with his heels. Experience had taught him patience. The southerner waited.

"Move off!" the lieutenant warned, gesticulating with his weapon the direction in which he wanted Woodwind to depart. "This is a war zone you moron! Get out of here!" The officer charged forward as if to attack, then halted, reluctant in a civilized way to needlessly shed blood.

When the lieutenant moved forward, Woodwind moved back, and when the lieutenant retreated, the southerner advanced, all the while pretending not to understand the warnings, insults and invective.

Tiring of this after a minute or two, his companions shouting for some kind of action, the officer recklessly ordered one of the men to fire a warning shot.

Feigning terror, Woodwind wheeled his horse as if struggling to control a frightened animal. This act inspired a guffaw from the other musket-bearing soldier, who fired in fun, hoping it would throw the man from his mount.

That careless action quickly proved fatal. With the moment of theater accomplishing its intended purpose, Woodwind drove Shadow forward, drawing his blade in a perfectly-timed, light speed attack that caught the unsuspecting lieutenant in the throat. Bright, very sharp Lithian steel shattered sinew and bone, severing every spinal nerve with such finality, the dying officers lips were frozen in a curse as his body slumped from the saddle and onto the unforgiving ground.

The swordsman turned his eager mount toward the two remaining soldiers, swinging his reddened blade forward with its flat edge parallel to the ground. Holding the weapon steadily, he aimed for an enemy heart as Shadow raced toward the smaller ponies.

Panic stricken, one of the Azgar tried desperately to reload, jamming his cartridge into his weapon, only to sacrifice his right forearm, trying to ward off Woodwind's thrust. The invader attempted to pull his pony away, instantly learning that his enemy was an extremely competent horseman who'd anticipated the move.

Reigning into his adversary, Woodwind withdrew his weapon, kicked his horse forward and thrust again, this time behind his opponent's bloodstained elbow. The combined mass of horse and rider forced crystal-edged steel deep into the soldier's exposed side, ending the young man's life before he could utter a scream.

Fighting in a righteous rage, venting months of pent-up antipathy, Woodwind shoved the body away and pulled back his sword just in time to execute an overhead block, deflecting a musket butt aimed at his head by the surviving soldier. But in the struggle to prevail against a Lithian blade, Azgar wood and steel were no match.

Releasing his left hand, Woodwind pulled Shadow back and turned him to the left. He stood in his stirrups, overcoming his adversary's arm strength with thigh muscle. Pushing the shattered musket overhead, Woodwind rotated his wrist to the right, forcing his blade down the side of the musket stock, aiming its tip toward the enemy's throat.

With a kick and a grunt he sprang Shadow forward, plunging the sharp longsword through the soft spot at the base of his opponent's neck, deep into his chest where damage could never be healed. His withdrawal extended into a swift, overhead circular slash, with which Woodwind decapitated his foe from the back of the neck as he rode by.

Before the falling head hit the ground, Woodwind unleashed his frenzied horse into a full westward gallop, their flight made urgent by the sound of musket fire from across the river.

***

From a distance, the only change Garrick could see at the inn were two black and red battle banners wavering lazily from flag staves set in the courtyard. The alien colors reinforced the dreadful news already weighing heavily on the young soldier's mind, but at this point, he worried more about his unit rather than which nation controlled the venerable inn. Old stone buildings could be recaptured. Friends fallen in battle were lost forever.

"What does the red flare mean?" Brenna inquired at length, reluctant to break the moody silence that had fallen over her Tamarian friend since they'd first seen the crimson streak etched across the indigo sky.

Garrick sighed, afraid of saying too much on one hand, but willing to risk a bit of vulnerability in the hope that doing so might strengthen the developing relationship with his lovely companion. "The color of a flare sends a message," he explained. "A green flare warns that someone's coming. A red flare can mean a unit is desperate, or has been overpowered. A red flare can also alert friendly forces to the reality that a base or camp has been abandoned to an attacker. If that's the case, it means we arrived too late."

Brenna caught her breath, knowing from experience that Garrick might find terrible evidence of personal loss in this place. Secretly, she wished that she could hold and comfort him, but she neither expressed, nor acted upon that desire. Instead, she closed her eyes and sent a prayer aloft in her native tongue. *"Allfather, please have mercy on Garrick. Soothe his pain and bring him peace."*

But he understood none of her words and felt no serenity from her intercession. Drawing near, he sensed malevolent violence lingering in the air. First, he noticed the tracks of something on wheels and the trampling of dry grasses trodden down by many feet. Burn marks and blackened craters marred the rock-hard, frozen ground wherever incendiary and explosive warheads had fallen.

Soon, the stench of sulfur and burnt bodies assailed the cadet's senses. Scavenging crows noisily took flight. Bits of tattered uniform and roasted flecks of flesh clung to bent, broken stalks of prairie grass, testifying to a fierce fight at this now silent place not long beforehand.

Garrick dismounted, overwhelmed by the scene unfolding before his eyes. Moving forward in disbelief, he stepped into a nightmare and found the place where his own unit had been torn apart by the savagery of Azgar cannon. He recognized what remained of Freddy Olsen, whose chest had been ripped open by grape shot. The wide-eyed expression of terror remained forever frozen on Freddy's blackened face.

Cold revulsion and an impotent sense of seething rage surged in Garrick's soul, his helplessness worsened by guilt for not having stood with his comrades in battle, even if that would have meant the loss of his own life. His entire unit lay here, some torn apart beyond recognition. Yet when he found Jan Bordmann's lifeless body, badly beaten and stabbed far more times than had been necessary to kill him, the young man gasped, fell to his knees and burst into bitter tears.

Brenna felt awful. Having personally experienced battlefield terror and knowing the heartbreak it wrought, she understood Garrick's outpouring of grief. Memories of fallen loved ones flashed through her mind. She recognized the cadet she'd walked beside, having listened to his voice, having caught his smile out of the corner of her eye.

The young woman knelt near Garrick, sliding her right arm around his broad shoulders, praying silently that Allfather would strengthen him, and give her words to encourage his wounded soul. "Your friends died bravely," she said in a soft voice, her lips nearly kissing his ear. "Honor them by stopping the ones who did this."

Garrick turned to embrace her, but did not look into her eyes. His strong arms wrapped tightly around her as she held him close. He emptied his soul of the feeling, then, afraid that she would think him weak, rubbed away his tears and raised his head, anticipating a sneer of scorn on her lips.

But she would not meet his gaze. Brenna turned her head away and shuddered. She held Garrick tightly and only after he gently turned her face toward him did the young man realize that she'd been weeping in solidarity. Seeing this strengthened him, not because he needed to be strong to offer comfort to her, but because she'd not ridiculed his sincere expression of grief.

As he looked into her eyes, noting the way her brow parted, her lower lip trembled and seeing the tension in her countenance, he began to love her. This desire had nothing to do with her attractive appearance, nor was it fueled by his appreciation of her wit. Recognizing the authenticity and deep goodness of her character in that moment sealed Garrick's heart to hers.

The Lithian woman squeezed his hand affectionately, then turned away again, her reticence returning. She wiped her frozen eyelids apart, noticing movement at the inn's gate. "They're coming," she stated, identifying a dozen uniformed soldiers on foot, leading a horse by its bridle. "We'd better get out of here."

***

Driven like an antelope fleeing from a lioness, the strong flanks of Woodwind's war horse stretched and retracted in a furious rhythm. Shadow's mane rippled in the skin-numbing wind created by his tireless stride; the labored, rushing sound of his breathing punctuated by the drum-riff clatter of swift hooves and scattering stones that sprayed upon the frozen ground.

Woodwind glanced over his right shoulder, praying that the Azgar soldiers would try to cross the shallow river. He maintained his westerly course in the hope that their pursuit would draw them across the stream. Fording the river would slow them down. But because he intended to flee north, the southern swordsman hoped they would have to traverse the water twice.

Initially, he'd been about a hundred and fifty yards south of the river and about seventy yards downstream from the enemy position. Intuitively estimating the minimum interval Shadow would need to flee in order to move beyond musket range, Woodwind aimed for a point about three hundred yards distant.

As Shadow raced forward, Woodwind realized that this course would soon put him well into Azgar range. Picturing the problem in his mind and letting the math work itself out subconsciously, he figured he needed to go westward about a thousand yards in order to outrun their ponies and effectively avoid enemy fire. At nearly two-thirds of a mile, this interval would tax Shadow's sprinting ability to its limits, and for the last two hundred yards or so he'd be at the fringe of enemy range anyway.

His only alternative involved crossing the river at a steeper angle. This would shorten the distance, but lengthen his exposure to fire. The enemy was certain to hold no quarter for anyone who had slain three soldiers in an unprovoked attack. Any option involving surrender seemed more foolish than what he'd already done.

So he pushed Shadow onward, crouching as low as possible behind the undulating head of his sprinting horse, riding in tandem with the powerful, rhythmic stretch and contraction of sweating, equine muscle.

About eight-hundred yards into the chase, Woodwind heard a sharp crack and glanced backward to witness a single puff of smoke falling behind one of the seven riders in pursuit. At this point, their respective lines of travel approached parallel, but the round fell about twenty yards short of its mark.

Two more shots followed as the distance between Woodwind and the enemy narrowed. At nine-hundred yards, the southerner heard a bullet whistle off to his left, but he dared not look back. Several seconds later the enemy fired two more rounds, and this time, the sound of racing bullets assailed Woodwind's frostbitten ears like the scream of a diving falcon.

Hammering into his flesh, a fifty-caliber musket ball slapped into Woodwind's back at the base of his shoulder blade, shattering bone, bursting blood vessels, destroying connective tissue and compressing his left lung with such force that it instantly deflated.

The swordsman dropped his weapon and coughed, feeling shock flood into his body; an instant weakness, an opaque shroud of yellow dots swirling through his field of vision. He struggled to hold on, but the trauma inflicted on his body by a bullet of this size sapped his youthful vigor and he began to slide from the saddle.

Shadow slowed as he crossed the river, but his master tumbled headlong into the icy water. The southerner landed first on his wounded shoulder, tearing its rotator cuff and assorted ligaments, then onto his face where the smooth stones in midstream crushed his nose, cheek and brow, leaving his lips badly bruised. He rolled onto his back, gazing at the sky as pain ravaged his body.

There, his blood ebbing gently into the frigid water, Woodwind felt his life slipping away. He turned his head, seeing the splash of approaching hooves, but couldn't find the strength to move again. "Merciful Allfather," he gasped. "Please, save . . . Brenna!"

Woodwind's consciousness faded until the brute pain of a cruel boot pressed into his shoulder. The southerner opened his eyes and looked into the frostbitten face of an Azgar warrior, who aimed his bayonet at the southerner's heart. Too weak to resist, Woodwind anticipated a quick end to the suffering he endured.

Just as the enemy raised his musket barrel, another shriek met Woodwind's throbbing ear. He saw the blur of something moving very fast, and as if struck from heaven, the soldier standing above him exploded into a roiling mass of burning flesh.

Woodwind blinked at the blinding light, felt the sharp sting of hot shrapnel nick his face, and as darkness enveloped his consciousness, remembered nothing more.

***

Rheanne Neergard, who typically smiled and flirted whenever she met a young man as attractive as the one standing in her doorway, instantly understood from the expression on his face that something terrible had happened. She'd never seen him before, yet the message he carried, the rifle on his shoulder, and the stridency of his appeal morphed her delight at his visit into concern.

"Vati!" she called, in an unusually serious tone. The young woman held the door open, allowing icy air to rush into the warm interior of her home. When her father did not come at once, she moved further inside and called loudly, "There's a soldier at the door. He says we've been attacked and he needs to see you!"

The teenager returned, inviting Garrick indoors and offering water – which he politely declined. Rheeanne noticed the shy, raven-haired woman hiding behind him; but after giving the foreigner a curious, lingering look-over, realized she must be Lithian, smiled without showing teeth, then completely ignored her.

Laid out in the traditional manner for a Tamarian home, the kitchen occupied a central location, surrounding a large, gas-fired oven kept warm continually during the autumn and winter. An older woman glanced up from her work and waved a greeting before returning to her task.

Fronted by a great room with an eight foot post and beam ceiling hewn from ponderosa pine timbers, the house had a spacious, airy interior that belied its ground-hunkering appearance from the street. Large, south facing windows bordered by thick, woolen curtains – pulled across the panes to prevent heat loss at nightfall – flooded even the back reaches of the structure with bright daylight. Inside stood an oak table, several chairs and a well-worn leather couch arranged in a semi-circle upon the tiled floor. On the far wall, doors led to additional rooms whose light entered through overhead clerestory windows.

A strapping, older gentleman stamped his boots to clean them of the dirty snow still lingering on the north side of his dirt-bermed home. He shooed his starry-eyed daughter out of the great room and greeted Garrick with a mixture of patronizing patience and suspicion. Many cadets had ventured under his roof in recent years, all of them interested in an evening with Rheanne.

This one, however, seemed agitated. He also had a young and very attractive foreigner in tow. A taut string held a recurve bow over her muscular shoulder. A quiver hung at her hip. She held a new broom in her hands, trying to avoid attention by saying nothing, avoiding eye contact, and standing behind her broad-shouldered companion.

Before the young soldier had fully explained the purpose of his visit, the older man dismissed the account with a shake of his head and a wave of his hand. "I've heard stories like this for months! Nothing has come of it. Winter is on its way, and no army moves north in the cold." Heinz moved closer to the kitchen stove for warmth, weary of the war rumors, wishing he'd never agreed to accept the office of civil defense liaison in the first place.

Garrick stood in disbelief. "Why would I lie about such a thing?" he said, defending his personal integrity as much as the truth of his story. "The woman who runs the general store told me that you're the man authorized to call up the militia and evacuate the town. For the sake of the people, you must do so immediately."

Heinz turned toward the cadet, irritated by his audacity. "You're nothing more than a boy, and you don't give orders to me. Now, take your pretty, little *sicklian* back to wherever she came from and be on your way, or I'll throw you out and write a formal complaint to your sergeant!"

Garrick felt stunned by the reprimand and thought for a moment to retreat, but the rage he'd felt earlier returned with sudden fervor. He stood his ground. "What is left of my sergeant is lying in a field while ravens pick at his carcass! He died defending people like you, and a whole platoon of the soldiers who killed him are marching this direction as we speak.

"I'll gladly put my life on the line for you, even if you are a tired, arrogant old man without a care for anyone or anything else. That's my duty. But you were elected to oversee civil defense, not to argue against doing your job!"

In all his years, Heinz Neergard had never heard such an outburst from a younger man, and even though he was generally quite patient, Garrick's retort aroused the elder gentleman's indignation. "You flatter yourself with impudent talk! How dare you vilify me!"

Correcting his impropriety and changing his tone of voice, Garrick continued. "I'm not intending to insult you, sir, but I must stress the urgency of the situation. There are enemy soldiers heading this direction right now. Bring a field lens and I'll show you from a rooftop."

Heinz controlled his rage, but spoke through gritted teeth to show his displeasure. "This had better not be a joke," he warned.

Mrs. Mikkels' inn happened to be the tallest building on Dieter's one and only street. The old woman was talking to herself while collecting firewood at the side of her establishment when Garrick, Brenna, and Heinz Neergard arrived. She snatched the broom out of Brenna's hand as if retrieving something precious from a thief, complaining angrily about her loss of the original item, as if it had been a priceless heirloom handed from mother to daughter for many generations.

Heinz held up his hand as a signal for her silence, which she ignored, forcing him to shout until he could be heard above her litany of laments. "Winnie, you were right!" he exclaimed. "This boy says the Azgar are coming, and we should be able to see them from your roof."

Winnie Mikkels eyed Garrick with a scowl. "I knew it!" she replied. "But you can't trust this one, *or* his slanty-eyed, top-heavy hussy. You'll have to see for yourself."

"That's why we're here," Garrick replied wearily.

The old woman rummaged through her shed for a ladder that Franz, her late husband, had used to maintain the inn's roof. Years of neglect flaked its white paint, but it allowed Garrick, Heinz, and finally Brenna, to ascend its length and stand on the roof.

While no one could see individual soldiers with the naked eye at this distance, the movement of their black fatigues contrasted sufficiently with the golden stalks of prairie grasses to catch attention.

Heinz peered through birdwatching binoculars, cautiously waiting until his view of the enemy muskets was clear enough to convince him that the advancing men represented a threat. "Old weapons," he mused. "But a bullet is a bullet." He put his left hand on Garrick's shoulder and apologized for not believing him. "I should have listened to you," he told the young soldier, "but I felt insulted instead. I ask your forgiveness."

Garrick appreciated how socially difficult it was for an older man to say this, and sincerely tried to sound gracious. "I understand, sir. And perhaps I should have been less strident and more respectful."

"I accept your apology," Heinz replied. "Come, we must rouse the militia."

***

Steamy vapor trails coalesced in the cold air, marking the paths flown by four-inch, shoulder-fired rockets. Armed with a two-pound warhead encased in steel pellets surrounded by an enamel cap, this weapon could kill armored giants at a range exceeding any projectile the large humanoids possessed. The accuracy of the Tamarian weapon depended to a great degree on the visual-spatial ability of its operator, who had but a single chance to aim the rocket carefully through an elevated rear sight, a feature lacking on Azgar muskets.

Propelled to a safe distance by a small kicker engine, the rocket's main thrust lit up well forward of its launcher, avoiding any major recoil. The resulting acceleration looked very impressive because the warhead appeared to reach its target immediately after its main engine fired. Tamarian soldiers loved this weapon because it gave an infantry team devastating firepower without the aching shoulders associated with their large caliber rifles.

Even though the rocket contrails pointed back to his position, Private Müller, well beyond the range of Azgar muskets, fired with impunity. Cavalry made an especially easy target. Horses, like giants, were large enough to compensate for the inherent inaccuracy of a single rocket, and warheads designed to penetrate the hardened, steel plate armor of mountain giants easily killed the horse and obliterated its rider.

Methodically, the Tamarian soldier rammed another weapon pack into the back of the launch tube and asked for the next target. Corporal Fanselars double-checked the eastern horizon, first with his bare eyes, then with the field lens. The only movement in evidence was a slight swaying of grasses nudged into motion by an occasional gust of gentle wind. "That's the last of them."

Woodwind's horse whinnied in the distance, pawing the ground and shaking its great head with snorts audible from over a hundred yards away.

Albrecht packed the *giant killer* and its three remaining rockets back into a saddle bag. "Let's recover lover boy's body. I'm sure the *sicklian* girl will want to cry over it."

The Tamarians found Woodwind's longsword among the rocks and weeds at the ice-hedged, southern bank of the Tualitin. Knowing Colonel Brandt needed hard intelligence, they casually stopped to collect a pair of Azgar muskets before approaching the unconscious figure lying in the shallow river. Having heard the volume of gunfire directed at him, both men assumed Woodwind had been killed in the fusillade, and were quite surprised to find him still breathing, albeit weakly.

"Well, that little long-haired maiden may lose her virginity yet," the corporal commented. "Attend to his wounds. Get him in a blanket A swordsman of his caliber doesn't deserve to die like a sick dog on the ground."

Darrold raised his eyebrows. That remark stood as the first positive comment concerning the southerner he'd heard from his countryman's lips.

The extremely cold water significantly reduced the volume of blood lost from Woodwind's wound, a factor instrumental in preserving his life. While Albrecht watched for the enemy, Darrold worked to save him. He doused the injury with sulfa powder, pulled compression dressings out of a medical kit in his saddle bag and applied these to the oozing, discolored flesh beneath Woodwind's left shoulder.

Working together, the Tamarians cut off Woodwind's clothes, wrapped him in his own bedroll to keep him warm and set him into a litter they'd fashioned by lashing muskets together. They lifted the litter carrying Woodwind's languid body sideways onto Shadow's back, securing it to the saddle straps with rope. Darrold Müller led the animal by the bridle as he rode back to base on his own mount.

The advancing enemy and Woodwind's injury compelled the men to make it back to Dead Hand Ridge in a hurry. Albrecht Fanselars urged his mule northward at a canter, leaving behind a scene of slaughter that would give pause to a shivering Azgar officer arriving less than thirty minutes later.

***

Given the mild hostility and lack of cooperation Brenna had experienced from the residents of Dieter, she felt astonished to witness their quick and efficient response to the warning toll of their temple bell. Living in a frontier town which boasted no fortifications, and an army garrison more than an hour away, rehearsing such a transition was woven into the fabric of life out here. Triad-tuned bells which normally announced the hour, or called the faithful to worship, also served as a threat warning.

In a drill, all bells tolled together. In an emergency, only the primary bell rang thrice, three times, every minute for three minutes. Men spreading frozen straw between their harvested crop rows, working forges or shoveling mash for their livestock put down their tools. Women scrubbing laundry, baking bread and repairing winter clothing stopped their chores. Old folk, whose energies typically centered on the care of young children, moved their small charges into cellars for safety. Teenage girls who had not yet signed up for national service, diligently stocking the same cellars for their families, or repairing damage from the recent windstorm, ceased their work immediately.

Two military policemen stationed in town coordinated their efforts. Many people brought their own guns. Those who didn't own one were issued weapons from a cache stocked with rifles and ammunition. Every able-bodied resident, whether man or woman, received a weapon. Well before the Azgar arrived, each citizen took up a position in key areas around the town.

Nine men, all army veterans beyond the required age for military service, formed a line across the road some ten paces back from the blacksmith's workshop, their long rifles held at parade rest. The old polish of relentless drill in their youth manifest itself in an effortless conversion from citizen to soldier.

Other people, facing the street along the roof tops, arranged in clusters of three and four upon the dirt berms behind key buildings and homes, kept their rifles at the ready. Among them, Brenna Velez flexed her bow and readied arrows for the fray.

She watched as Garrick moved among the lean-muscled, pale-skinned men who'd set up a barrier of desks, tables and wagons on the street below, her heart struggling with a desire to protect him, while understanding that this was really his battle to fight. Silently, Brenna prayed.

If any comfort for her conflicting feelings existed, Brenna felt too distracted to perceive it. As her body tensed, a fearful shiver raced up her spine and trembled through her strong shoulders. Years of dedicated training under the watchful eye of her *Relict* great aunt endowed her with great skill in the art of killing. The *Relicts* – an order of women whom the Azgar had disparagingly dubbed, *Black Widows* – devoted themselves to dispensing justice. They did not kill wantonly but trained to act in defense of the defenseless.

Brenna could hold her own while sparring with her great aunt, yet she struggled to reconcile the older woman's belief that violence harmonized with Allfather's will. It seemed out of character for the deity she worshiped – one whom she believed created all life and loved beauty – to approve of the needless killing associated with warfare.

However, Lithian warlords, like her own father, raised armies to protect their land holdings from conquest. The godly did not attack others unless seriously threatened, but they maintained constant readiness for combat and taught their children how to use weapons at an early age.

Brenna remembered those lessons well. However, Lord Velez emphasized the virtue of forbearance and mercy in his discussions with her. As a young girl she'd witnessed his restraint much more often than his wrath, and for a long time felt frustrated with her father's patience whenever he endured insult from less powerful enemies.

As her perception matured, she came to admire her *Amair's* patience. Brenna realized that Allfather possessed both the power and authority to eradicate evil, but that God also showed restraint in order to demonstrate mercy. While this satisfied her belief in a loving deity, ascribing such leniency to mere benevolence didn't answer the difficult moral issue of why the Supreme Judge permitted wickedness in the first place, and why he personally refrained from calling evildoers into account.

As a counterweight to this, Lynden Velez taught his daughters that all believers functioned in some way as agents of God's wrath. He explained that accountability did not necessarily require coercion, for there are many ways in which people are held responsible for their deeds. But when given no other option, force functioned as a necessary check to the power of evil in the world.

Brenna found it hard to think of herself as an agent in this manner. She wanted to build, not destroy, to heal and not hurt, but the purest form of this thinking created tension with her belief in social justice. Ultimately, Allfather had to destroy evil in defense of the defenseless – as the *Relicts* did – and he'd given her the means to do so. Nonetheless, she took neither pride, nor comfort in being called upon to perform this function. In her mind, it always seemed both presumptuous and a power easily abused.

Her philosophy strained Garrick's rationality to its limit. He too, believed in justice, but he defined the concept as a human construct, not a divine standard. In his view, the origin of morality lay in human psycho-biology. The need to determine right from wrong developed as a cultural construct honed by social experience. Exercising it required maturity many people never attained, few fully appreciated, and most could not recognize in him.

Preserving the ability of humanity to believe and live freely, provided that the exercise of these rights did not unreasonably encroach upon others, demanded what Garrick considered healthy respect for the diversity of thought among his people. To balance the competing extremes of law and liberty, a high degree of personal accountability and diligence in protecting the weak functioned as guiding principles for every action. This concept informed Garrick's idea of integrity. He'd carefully thought through this view and argued in its favor during Junior Scout classroom lessons on combat doctrine.

He tolerated what many considered superstitious spirituality in other people without the desire to ridicule because he could hear threads of truth in different voices. Garrick, a voracious reader, studied philosophy and found his own beliefs reinforced in slightly different forms in many different worldviews. He enjoyed listening to thoughtful people explaining their perspectives. This was, in fact, an important reason why he found Brenna so intriguing.

However, difficult moral questions arose whenever Garrick extended his ideas to their absolute conclusion. What right did the invading army have in trampling upon his nation's sovereignty? Young Tamarian soldiers – some of them closer to his heart than his own family – had been slain without mercy, an anger-inspiring, unprovoked aggression. The sight of Jan Bordman's broken body proved that Azgar had to be halted. While he understood the irrationality of his reaction seemed tangential to pure conviction, he couldn't staunch this emotional response.

Combat doctrine informed the idea that self-defense was an appropriate reason for nations to maintain armies. He rationalized that the need for national legitimacy superseded the rights of other states to pursue their policies by aggression; and by extension, that states had a right to impose their sovereignty by force of arms within their own borders. Although he knew that this nationalistic attitude also contravened his philosophy, something deep within his heart, an emotion too primitive for words, prevailed when he thought about the battle to come.

As the Tamarian cadet studied the assembled citizens of Dieter, his resolve to defend them hardened. One nation could not be allowed to sweep over another without regard for those who would be forced to endure its cruelty. His training, intelligence, strength and even his life might make a difference in his nation's ability to pursue its own destiny and make free choices.

Thus, two minds normally inclined against violence arrived at the same point, if from different directions along differing paths.

Garrick's heart beat faster as he glanced toward the blacksmith's roof and saw Brenna kneeling there, her bow in hand. From this distance, he let his eyes linger on the trim-fitting sweater that strained against every alluring curve from her shoulders to her hips. He watched her as she finished her prayer and stood to her feet. When their eyes met and lingered, he smiled.

But the happiness didn't last very long.

An enemy sergeant, his face unshaven and badly windburned, halted his twenty-five man platoon about fifty yards away and ordered them to load their weapons. The regimen of preparing muskets for battle had an intimidating effect; many of the Tamarians grew uneasy as the grim ritual unfolded.

One of the local military policemen rested his right hand on the young man's shoulder. "Son, you don't have to do this," he said solemnly. "There's no shame in taking cover. I'd be happy to stand in your place."

Garrick heard the unison chorus of rifles chambering rounds in readiness behind him, but he didn't look back. "Thank-you, sir," he responded. "But this is something I believe I must do!" The cadet did his best to restrain the pounding of his heart and trembling of his hands.

At his back, the Tamarian veterans crouched behind their barrier in preparation for battle. Rifle bearing civilians on the rooftops set their sights on the enemy and waited.

The Azgar confidently kept their muskets at parade rest, the taut, muscular response to extreme cold etched across every face. Their collective breathing steamed out into little vapor clouds, which crystallized into an iridescent haze that swirled like pipe smoke and vanished as quickly as each had formed.

A dark-eyed enemy soldier, whose physical distress in the freezing air seemed only marginally overcome by the sheer force of will and discipline, marched forward in response to his sergeant's order. In a voice loud enough for all within thirty yards to hear, he read with numb lips from a proclamation written in vulgate.

"By the authority of Lord Balinor, supreme commander of the Azgar Northern Liberation Army – for the emancipation and prosperity of free races in the north land – I hereby order you to stand down and submit to the benevolent throne of our divine emperor and his humble servant, my lord commander!"

Garrick's soul overflowed with rage and he swore venomously. "You have no authority here. We will never submit to you. Leave now, or die!"

Shocked at both Garrick's mastery of the language and the threat his words conveyed, the outraged foreigner lifted his musket to his hip. "Brave words, boy!" The soldier spat a hailstorm of profanity that linked Garrick's lineage to many common detritus organisms.

Brenna watched the unfolding scene with growing panic. What was Garrick doing out there all by himself? Why wasn't he taking cover? The Azgar sergeant ordered his troops to bring their guns up to firing position and take aim, the hammers of their muskets pulled back like shovels readied for digging graves.

"Garrick!" she screamed. "Get down!"

Brenna's bow flexed as she sighted, loosed, nocked another, found a different target and loosed again. Her first arrow pierced the left eye of the enemy messenger just before he pulled the trigger of his musket. Its sharp tip wedged its way into his brain, slicing through soft tissue until the hard arrowhead shattered the back of his skull. Death ravaged his soul before the impulse to fire reached the soldier's finger.

The second arrow found its mark in the exposed throat of the Azgar sergeant. He staggered backward, choking, gasping for breath, his life ebbing with every weakening effort to draw air into his lungs. With a curse on his lips, the foreigner slumped to the pavement, his dream of conquest ended.

Garrick heard his name, as well as the disconcerting swish of an arrow in flight, coming far closer to his own head than he would have liked. He immediately dropped to the ground and began crawling to the barricade for cover, as he had been trained to do – an action that saved his life – as only a moment later, five of the Azgar gunners fired their rounds, and the Tamarian riflemen discharged in unison.

The first fusillade of enemy musket rounds blasted the barrier erected as cover for the Tamarian veterans. A few of the large-diameter bullets found their targets, tearing through the unarmored torsos of four local men, killing two quickly, leaving another to die an agonizing death on the cold cobblestones of Dieter's single street. The fourth cursed through his pain, but worked his bolt action to chamber another round and continued the fight.

Tamarian bullets flashed toward their intended victims in response. Rifle rounds ripped through armor. Eight soldiers twitched and tumbled backward. Screams aspired above the din of battle sounds where the wounded lay, while fifteen of their unscathed countrymen bravely stood their ground in the open and once again took aim at the native defenders.

Brenna had only three arrows remaining in her quiver. Assessing the overwhelming firepower advantage enjoyed by the Tamarians, she turned her full attention to preserving Garrick's life. Noticing an Azgar soldier taking aim at her favored Tamarian cadet, Brenna sighted the soldier and proved quicker in her release than the would-be killer did in pulling his trigger.

Her arrow slammed between his neck and left shoulder, beneath the scapula where its razor-sharp head ripped muscle until it splintered on his shoulder blade. Jerking reflexively, the soldier screamed in pain, dropped his musket, and the gun discharged harmlessly into the grass nearby.

Several more Azgar bullets pounded into the Tamarian defensive line, this time killing two prosperous farmers, a recently retired engineering officer, and paralyzing a father of five children, who would never walk or work again after this day.

Just as Garrick reached the barricade, he heard someone order, "Fix bayonets!" At this he stood to aim and fire the rifle he'd taken from Jan. But as he squeezed its trigger, the cadet realized that he'd not loaded a magazine.

The surviving Azgar charged the defender's line as another volley of Tamarian fire pounded into their ranks. Two of the survivors converged on Garrick with bayonets at the ready, expecting to dispatch him as quickly as they had done to others earlier that morning.

Jamming a magazine into the weapon a little too late, Garrick put himself into a guard position at the last possible moment, grimly determined to fight for his life. The young man successfully blocked a bayonet thrust and shoved his adversary to the pavement using his rifle with both hands. When the other soldier lunged to impale him, Garrick stepped forward and rotated his body out of the way. In response, the Azgar veteran withdrew, then smacked Garrick's steel helm violently with the butt of his musket, pulled back, and beat him savagely and repeatedly.

The consecutive, concussive impacts felt disorienting, and hurt horribly, but as weakness threatened to overwhelm him, Garrick willed himself to keep fighting. He stepped sideways twice, pulled back his rifle's bolt and fired the weapon into his enemy's gut at point blank range.

Brenna witnessed his struggle in horror. Garrick fought with little apparent skill, only determination and bravery sustaining him in the engagement. Woodwind would have been appalled to see this. "Merciful God!" she exclaimed. "Save him!"

When Brenna saw the second black-uniformed soldier get up from the ground to renew his attack – intending to skewer Garrick in the back with his bayonet – she released her final arrow to fly on its swift and fatal course.

Like a sudden, crushing tide, gunfire from the villagers converged on the enemy, mercilessly killing invaders from the deep south who'd been victors of an earlier hour. From Brenna's opening shot until its conclusion, this entire battle lasted less than two minutes. As the gunfire ceased, local citizens kept their weapons at the ready. An eerie silence settled upon the scene.

Garrick, shocked that he'd survived and embarrassed to have fought so poorly, dropped to his knees and leaned against his rifle, breathing deeply to control nausea that threatened to spill onto the street.

Pallor painted his face as Brenna raced forward to steady his dizzy posture. She helped him slump into a sitting position, squatting to evaluate his condition with an experienced, medically-trained, and very concerned eye.

Unaware that she'd saved his life, he unstrapped his helmet without expressing gratitude. "My head hurts, he complained, the waning effects of fear trembling through his fingers as they rubbed across the afflicted place.

Brenna pressed her lips through Garrick's hair until she met his scalp, keenly aware of why she'd done so. Her lips touched his skin for more than healing; she'd kissed him with far greater intent in mind. She saw color return to his face and his eyes widen in wonder as a powerful, mystical, soothing warmth radiated through his head, quickly displacing the pain and nausea of his concussion.

As relief sighed through her shoulders, the Lithian woman put her hand over her heart and suggested, "Why don't you sit here and rest for awhile."

Brenna turned away to care for other casualties, hiding a rising tide of conflicted emotion as she sensed a growing loss of control over her life. She knew this meant trouble, first with Woodwind, her trusted friend whose words wounded her soul as surely as any blade could cut her flesh. She regretted her argument with him, wishing she could relive that moment and restrain words uttered in anger that could never be recalled.

And now the Azgar – having successfully advanced so far north – removed any hope of returning to Kameron and reconciling with her family. With winter on its way and the enemy army in control of all routes heading south, Brenna stood no chance of slipping through their lines.

Biting her lower lip and blinking back a tear, the Lithian maiden realized that despite wiser thoughts to the contrary, she'd chosen to love a Tamarian soldier.

Victim of Success

"Sir!" Lieutenant Rangell, my best engineer reported. "I've traced the chimneys as ordered, but my crew has found no provisions for heat in the compound, other than two cook top burners in the kitchen and a larger system in one of the out buildings."

Somewhere in the back of my mind, I felt a headache developing. As the day progressed, we realized that the Ice Dragon Inn began cooling rapidly, and we had no way of warming up its buildings. Since the primary task of my mission had been to provide a comfortable environment for the senior officer corps – a place where they could plan the systematic destruction of northern nations without freezing to death in the process – heat loss became my obsession.

"Tell me about the burners in the out building," I demanded, a depressing lack of confidence that we'd find a workable solution to this vexing dilemma any time soon hidden behind assertive words.

"I can't say much at the moment, sir. We've studied a burner located underneath something that looks like a boiler attached to a pipe. It might be some kind of heating system, but if that's so, it's like nothing we've ever seen, I don't know what they're using for fuel, and I can't figure out how it works.

"We're investigating a network of pipes that extend from that structure into the ground outside, but the soil is frozen solid, the cobblestones are difficult to remove and we don't have proper equipment for digging."

I scanned the upper floors of the old, fitted stone buildings, no longer interested in the buttresses and colored glass, noticing open windows I'd not seen before. "Get a crew to shut every outside door and window in the complex. I don't want any portal opened unnecessarily."

Lieutenant Rangell nodded. "Right away, sir."

Judging from his posture and eye contact, he seemed confident that we'd find a technical resolution to this predicament. Of course, he didn't have to face a hostile legate and answer the questions I knew were forthcoming.

First, I would be interrogated concerning the heavy casualties we'd sustained. Although I'd been briefed on barbarian weapons systems, I'd never before faced an enemy with rifles and rockets that compared favorably with our equipment, nor could I have anticipated the incredible, aggressive resistance they'd mounted against us.

I'd underestimated the manpower necessary to take the inn because I'd grown accustomed to intelligence reports that exaggerated enemy strength. Our briefings always contained a certain degree of padding, to ensure battlefield success without jeopardizing important command careers.

In truth, the giants had been accurate when assessing and reporting on the barbarians, a fact that would unequivocally deepen all doubt about my leadership ability in any upcoming combat evaluation. I felt ashamed that the soldiers who'd inflicted such unprecedented losses to my unit were, by and large, teenage boys.

My eagerness to escape the inebriated wrath of Legate Braegan and a desire to do something apart from freezing to death inspired overconfidence made worse and heightened by the urgent need to get out of the cold. I should have been more careful in scouting and planning. I would not repeat mistakes like that. I would not again be cowed into planning an assault like this in haste.

To my credit, due mostly to the bravery and skill of the soldiers under my command, I had gained control of a suitable headquarters building, but it seemed that the locals managed to hide or destroy virtually everything else. As my men completed their search of the premises, I began to worry that the compound might not meet expectations.

Where had they taken their mules and swine? Why

had we found so little food? What happened to the soldiers who'd been manning the accursed rocket launchers along the walls? How did they abandon this place so quickly?

I rubbed my forehead and stared at the gnarled branches of leafless oak, squinted at the Daystar arcing restlessly overhead, then cursed the useless wind pump on its tower. My mind searched for answers as I kicked a shattered piece of grey cobblestone, rent from its ancient position by a mortar round . . . .

"Lieutenant Hicks!" I shouted. "I want to talk to that mortar crew. Now!"

The lieutenant, a waif who looked as unimpressive in a uniform to me as I must have seemed to my own superiors, saluted with his right hand while holding his left arm across his belly for warmth.

"I'm on it, sir!" he replied, scurrying off in unfounded terror to do my bidding.

I'd sent Sergeant Aransen's squad to collect our dead from the battlefield, then ordered him to secure supplies from the town to the north. He hadn't returned, and new worry plagued me. Perhaps he'd found abundant food and supplies. Maybe his team was having trouble getting everything moved out. But this seemed out of character.

At that moment, I heard screams from one of the upstairs windows. The memory of Shirak and hidden snipers sent a chill up my spine, the gnawing, foreboding sensation I experienced the day before deepening when I realized the voice belonged to a woman . . . .

As I glanced upward, I noticed one of my soldiers reaching for an open window. I heard men's voices shouting vulgarities and salacious commentary among themselves that mingled with unintelligible, but clearly feminine cries. The terrible sounds stopped abruptly when the window slammed shut.

Visions of filtered, yellow-green light invaded my mind

like a forgotten dream suddenly remembered. An image of that beautiful Lith girl and the intelligent glare of her bright blue eyes flashed through my memory. The sound of gunfire, the sting of smoke, the terrifying sight of her drawn bow aimed at my heart inspired a strange, but powerful feeling that had haunted me during the dark hours of night when I lay alone with my thoughts. Remembering her was like seeing a vision of some avenging goddess meting judgment upon the guilty.

I had been far from innocent that day. Why had she spared me?

I don't remember charging up the steps and into the building. Vaguely can I now recall ascending three flights of stairs, my legs stiff from the cold, my lungs on fire from the exertion. I raced across parquet floors, down darkened hallways, through doors with bright brass hardware that swung open in well-oiled silence, only to slam against their stops, shudder back into their jambs and click shut as if invisible servants performed the reluctant task behind me.

Driven by the afflicted screams of a brutalized woman, not having given thought to what I'd do once I arrived, the last door burst open and I staggered, out of breath, into a crowded room permeated with the stench of sweat and sex. My men's faces turned toward me. Their voices fell silent, their eyes averted as they stared at the floor like children caught in wrongdoing.

The woman recoiled toward the wall like a discarded rag, her blonde hair draped across her body as if to hide her shame. I couldn't see her face as several men stood in the way, but her sobs cut my soul. I felt shocked and outraged. Breathing deeply, my side aching, the vision of the Lith maiden still etched in my mind, I let condemnation erupt from deep within my soul. "You disgust me!" I spat. "None of you deserves the honor of his uniform!"

"But sir," Sergeant Vitus objected in a tone suggesting

that I should understand and not react so stridently. "You must realize that the men haven't had a woman in weeks. She's just some local whore. What does it matter? We're the victors here, and we all need release!"

"What you need, sergeant," I interrupted, still breathing hard, "is castration, and that can be arranged!" I drew out my saber, pointing toward his groin to illustrate my intent.

They all trembled, afraid that I might actually emasculate them on the spot, and I might have, if I'd been more certain of support from the senior officers. Silent in their fear, I let them listen to their victim weep while I pondered what to do next.

Lieutenant Hicks breathlessly stomped upstairs and clomped into the room, breaking the tension and giving me something else to think about for a moment. "The mortar crew is waiting for you in the lobby, sir!" he reported.

I glared at him, entirely unnecessarily, for he looked even more mortified than I'd ever seen before. "You get this woman dressed and out of here," I ordered. "If anyone so much as breathes on her, I'll have your private parts sent back to Marioch in a pine box! Got it?"

"Yes, sir," he replied. Then, staring for a moment at the bruised and terrified female on the floor, he glanced back at me, clearly uncomfortable with the assignment. "Uh, what do you want me to do, sir? Where do you want me to take her?"

Irritated, I pressed the point of my saber into his chest. "As of this moment she's your problem. Deal with it!"

Directing my attention to the other men sulking in front of me, I vented the rage within me in an unbridled tide of expletive derision. "Effective immediately," I concluded, "you are on report. Wait for me at attention in the courtyard until I'm ready to deal with you. Dismissed!"

As the men filed out of the room, I noticed the

Tamarian woman had curled up against the paneled wall, clutching her uniform. To my great relief, she'd stopped her weeping. Something in her face inspired my pity, though she was my enemy and should not have expected clemency from us. I couldn't read what she was feeling by the blank expression, and since she didn't respond when I spoke to her, I figured she didn't know my language.

"Get her a bath with warm water," I ordered the trembling lieutenant at my side. "I don't care if you have to cut down every tree in the compound to do it, but I want it done right away."

"Yes, sir," he replied, meekly.

Angrily, I stormed off to meet the mortar crew, almost forgetting what I'd wanted to ask them. Clearing my mind proved impossible, as an intoxicating adrenaline rush still pumped through every cell in my body. My rage had not cooled even after I'd recovered my breath through long, unlit halls and three flights of stairs. I descended into the vaulted chamber that served as the lobby, my scowl inspiring fear among members of the mortar crew.

"Tell me what happened when the barbarians evacuated this place," I ordered no one in particular.

A brave recruit responded without lifting his eyes from the well-waxed floor. "They were already loading pack animals when you gave the signal to attack. We saw them drive mules pulling carts filled with swine toward the back wall. They got out just before you came through the gate, but we couldn't tell where they went because of the angle."

"How many?" I queried, moving for the door.

"Probably two dozen," he replied over my shoulder. "They came down from the rocket launchers on the walls and from inside the main building. It looked like most of them were young boys and women. We didn't have the heart to fire on them, sir."

Cold air slapped my face, froze my sweat and clawed

through my clothing as if it were a thing alive, trying rend my flesh with its chill. The men in my artillery detachment had only recently rotated into my century. I didn't know their names and they obviously didn't know me. "We're not here to kill women and children," I responded, trying to hide my own sense of guilt and make the men feel at ease. "Take me to the place where you saw them go."

"Right this way, sir," the young recruit motioned.

Along the western wall of the compound, hidden behind a screen of sumac and juniper, a cobbled path descended into a gated rock garden, sprinkled in a remnant robe of snow. A white gazebo stood between the overhanging branches of two huge oak trees. Behind it loomed fitted, bleached stones ascending to nearly treetop level, effectively concealing this bowl-shaped sanctum from any eyes viewing it from the hill ridges to the west.

A huge, black eagle stared from the cupola atop the gazebo, pecking at what looked like a human hand under its claw. It hissed, then flapped away noisily as I stepped up and under the slate-shingled roof.

"They came down the path, and after they got here we couldn't see anything else," the artilleryman claimed.

A hollow sound reverberated beneath my feet as I walked across the gazebo platform. Was this concealing a secret escape portal?

"Check this area thoroughly," I ordered, stamping on the floor. "Find out where the barbarians went and report back to me immediately."

I didn't bother responding to the "Yes, sir!" Moodily, I stalked back to the courtyard, trying to figure out what I was going to do with the men involved in raping the blonde-haired woman, what I was going to do with her, and how I was going to explain the whole situation to the legate when he arrived.

I didn't have to wait long.

Judging from the commotion at the gate as I approached, I sensed that someone important had just entered. Several escorting cavalry troops, their faces fixed forward in rigid attention, carbines held from the outside hip at forty-five degree angles, formed a screen to protect the officer traveling in their midst. A mottled mare tossed her head and whinnied as her rider dismounted.

Legate Braegan removed his crested helm and self-consciously combed his left hand through a stringy mass of matted hair. He'd shaven earlier, but facial hair that had grown since daybreak already darkened his complexion. Every soldier in the courtyard immediately snapped to attention, including me.

Although I didn't really want to greet him, my will didn't amount to much in the presence of a senior officer. I saluted with a vigor enhanced by the extreme cold. "Sir! I present to you the Ice Dragon Inn. Welcome!"

Braegan passed his helmet to an aide, rubbed his scruffy chin and admired the architecture, muttering profanity in astonishment. "Well, gods be blessed!" he exclaimed, though I'm sure spiritual matters were the last thing on his mind. "Our little centurion found us a church!"

My spine tensed, but I didn't respond. "Lieutenant Hicks!" I roared, amazed at the speed with which he appeared at my side. "See that our legate is given a complete tour of the facility and that his every need is met."

I could not believe how good it felt to give that order!

Braegan made some off-hand remark about how I had other duties demanding my attention and strutted up the marble staircase, muttering other obscenities as he vanished behind the massive, double hung doors and into the main building. Lieutenant Hicks followed in haste, looking like he was trying to control an imminent bowel movement with only marginal success.

I heard sighs among the men standing in the

courtyard after the latch clicked shut and the legate moved beyond earshot. Making a mental note of that reaction, I turned to face the eight soldiers I'd placed on report. Their moment of relaxation ended the instant my eyes fixed upon them, and they jerked to attention as if every spine had been pulled by a single string.

"Sergeant Vitus . . . ." I called sternly, my command punctuated by the sharp crack of a single rifle firing from the wall behind me.

"Sir!" he responded, ignoring the sound.

"You and these men will report for excavation duty at the powerhouse building with Lieutenant Rangell immediately. Afterward, you will be confined to quarters until further notice."

He offered no verbal objection, but I could see contempt welling in his eyes. I ignored the insubordinate expression and dismissed them to dig up cold cobblestones and bicker about me behind my back, as I knew most of them would. At that moment I didn't care that their laments might be heard by sympathetic ears.

Private Willancus, a moderately corpulent man with black, almond-shaped eyes and severely chapped lips, approached at a trot from his post at the main gate. "Centurion Herulus!" he called, out of breath and sweating slightly from the moderate exertion expended in three dozen strides. "Sir, it's terrible! You won't be happy, but you gotta know. Come. I'll show you."

My headache exploded with fury as the private escorted me across the cratered courtyard to the battered portal. As we approached, I could see a horse through the aperture, chewing on a mouthful of tough, Saradon grass several yards away. Behind the beast, a primitive sort of litter had been rigged, but I couldn't make out any more detail at this distance.

"Just after the legate gets here, we sees this wagon

come from up the road," the private explained between breaths. "We think it's Sergeant Aransen and his boys at first, but the wagon stops out yonder and these people begin to packing up the enemy dead we left out there. I figured maybe they was lookin' for valuables.

"We all loaded up just in case they come closer, but after they get the bodies, they go back where they come from. Then one of their men whips up that horse there, and it come towards us like a mad djinni dragging that contraption behind 'til we scared it from running more with a shot."

I began to move ahead, but the private, to my amazement, held on to my left arm. "I'm real sorry, sir," he apologized. "But I know you had lots of respect for Sergeant Aransen. What you'll be seeing out there ain't pretty."

I said nothing, insisting with my eyes that the soldier let go of my arm. Turning away from the younger man at my sleeve, I approached the horse and litter alone. With my thoughts already drifting toward the morbid, my soul prepared for the ache that comes when good men die.

Behind the skittish horse, four poles had been lashed together with hemp twine, forming a rude fan that extended like a rake from the creature's saddle. Three men had been tied to each pole, the rope looped under their arms so that their bodies dragged along the ground as the horse moved forward. Every man's arms ended in bloody, dirt-encrusted stumps at each wrist, a barbaric mutilation that showed an animalistic disregard for the dead.

I retched, my stomach responding to the macabre memory of the eagle picking at the soft parts of an amputated hand upon the gazebo rooftop. Something primitive inside me wanted to retrieve the severed appendage and return it to its rightful owner, but I was too shaken by the sight to act upon the impulse.

I wanted to weep, swept up in a tide of strong

emotions that threatened to overwhelm the levees of stoicism I'd erected in my soul. Tears would not come, however, and neither would the words to childhood prayers that – like the gods they were intended to appease – had long since vanished from my memory. Instead, I stared, cursing in whispers, letting the permanence of my separation from the finest sergeant I'd ever known fester in my consciousness.

My grief experience lingered until the extreme cold soaked through every layer of clothing I'd piled on and my body shivered involuntarily. Then, quite unexpectedly, my sorrow evolved into an altogether different feeling, one of loathing and anger, but not for the barbarians. Instead, betrayal gripped my soul like the embrace of predator, hardening into contempt for the orders that had brought us to this barren wasteland in the first place. I turned back toward the inn and spat on the ground.

I hated Lord Balinor. His leadership looked much more like lust of power and hunger for fame in my eyes. All the frustrations of rank that plagued me – the men bickering about harsh conditions, their hard work and low pay; the humiliation of taking orders from a drunkard; the unfairness of being held accountable for matters beyond my realm of control; the loneliness of sleeping on a hard, narrow cot four months' march from home – welled to the surface of my thinking like a cold spring fed from the abyss of the unconscious.

I savored wicked thoughts. I cultivated a heady sense of sanctominity over injustices done, and it thrived in the daylight of my conscious mind. This inner betrayal of my commander made me feel alive for the first time in months, and the euphoric sensation of regaining control over my own life gave me the strength I needed to analyze the dead with a clinical eye.

Blood had long since congealed from grisly bullet

wounds. Bayonet slashes, punctures and bruises from rifle butts testified to a brutal close-quarters battle, but some of these men had been slain in a far more ancient manner. Sergeant Aransen's body featured a single wound in the exact center of his throat, where a large-diameter, hardwood war arrow remained. I'd seen arrows like this in Shirak. *Black Widows* and that Lith girl I'd seen used arrows of this kind, with fletching that matched the one loosed with such precision against Sergeant Aransen.

Three other men had been similarly afflicted. One man had been hit in the eye, another in the back of the head, and the third through his shoulder, lung, and out his back. The lethality of each wound led me to conclude that at least one archer was using primitive technology with great skill. Perhaps a *Black Widow* from Shirak was now fighting alongside the barbarians? Lord General Balinor, who'd sworn to kill every living Lith, would want to know, but I had no intention of telling him . . . .

After this morning's battle, I knew that the barbarians wielded good rifles and used military rocket technology for defense. My near disaster in attacking the inn, coupled with the resounding defeat of Sergeant Aransen's squad, hinted that the advantage we'd enjoyed in firepower could be matched, or maybe even countered.

Prior to this experience, I'd presumed that our technological prowess stood above all other nations. We Azgar led our world in social, economic and military affairs. Thus, I felt shocked that these northern barbarians defied my expectations. Their modern weapons used powerful, smokeless powder cartridges and featured magazines that enabled sustained, rapid fire. If they had small rockets, did they also have bigger ones? Did they have artillery, too? And if they did, would their cannon match ours?

Who were these people?

For the Northern Liberation Campaign, our infantry

rifles had been upgraded from antiquated muzzle-loading muskets. This was how the industrialist consortiums who funded Lord Balinor's venture supplied our large, expeditionary force with cheap guns. The black powder cartridges we used left smoke trails that revealed the shooter to the enemy. Also, the ensuing smoke cloud of our rifle discharge meant that our soldiers had to wait for a clear view in order to aim and fire again.

These factors should have caused our commanders to reconsider further conquest, at least until we could be re-supplied with updated guns. I didn't think they'd believe my analysis, so I decided to keep silent. I vowed to withhold information I believed might be critical to the success of Balinor's army in its campaign. While I fully intended to use such knowledge for my own survival and to preserve the lives of the men under my command, I would limit my role in assisting the senior officer corps with their insane drive northward to carrying out direct orders.

The sound of horse hooves, clinking metal and men's voices stirred me from my secrets. From the south, long trains of marching men began arriving, and with them rode their lieutenants, centurions, centurion commanders, legates, the vice-generals and somewhere, escorted by his elite guard, Lord General Balinor himself.

I felt self-conscious about the slain men tied behind the horse and yelled toward the gate for some assistance. Private Willancus and his team brought out a broken-down wagon they'd found somewhere within the walls. I didn't stay to oversee the recovery of our dead, but walked back toward the inn with a glare on my face that reflected the pain throbbing from behind my temples.

Lieutenant Rangell seemed agitated. "I can't figure it out, sir. It's unlike any system I've seen before. There are no moving parts that we can find anywhere.

"It's got components from a gas-burning system, but

it must operate on principles that we don't understand."

"Forget it then," I ordered, annoyed that a well-schooled engineer could be so baffled by technology developed in an inferior society. "Get some heat into that main building. I don't care if you have to forge iron stoves and knock holes in the roof for smoke vents, just get it done, and get started now!"

The look in Rangell's eye betrayed his anger at being ordered to perform a herculean task with little in the way of resources, but he couldn't understand the hot water I'd be in if he didn't carry out my command in a hurry.

A messenger arrived, informing me that I'd been summoned to Legate Braegan in the main building. I wished I'd been able at that moment to take a long swig of something distilled to stir my courage, but sobriety prevailed and my feet moved involuntarily to meet the man.

"Well, here's our hero, Herulus!" he exclaimed, mispronouncing my name as if he was actually describing a bald head. "Hicks! Get your crew to stop fondling themselves long enough to throw these windows open! It looks like a crypt in here without daylight, and we're expecting Lord Balinor any minute now. Come on soldier! Stop scratching your anus and move!" Profanity trailed off his tongue like raw sewage dripping from a rusty culvert.

I could have explained the heat loss problem, but said nothing. As my men had to camp outside in the cold, I decided the senior officers should share in our misery.

Turning to me and pointing a dirty fingernail, Braegan continued his discourse with barely a breath between phrases. "We'll have a celebration to remember tonight, soldier. Arrange with the mess crew to pull out all the stops. We'll feast on mutton, ham, beef, good wine and anything else you can find. Put a smile on Lord Balinor's face and I'll see to it that your next review is a good one."

Initially, I felt too shocked to fully comprehend that he

was offering to promote me for throwing a party. The reality that we'd found very little food after taking the inn stymied my response. I didn't have the courage to admit this, so I fudged a bit. "I'll need orders for more men," I stated, trying not to cringe beneath the weight of derision I expected – the sort I'd always endured from this man in the past.

"Write it up and it's done," he replied with the sweep of his left hand, his eyes wandering up to the frescoed vaulting illuminated high above.

"Yes sir." I replied, turning on my heel, not waiting to be dismissed. The only words I heard as I departed were expletives muttered in admiration of the ceiling art.

Although the inn had been cooling down for hours, it still felt warmer within its walls than beyond them, and as soon as I returned to the courtyard, the cold assaulted me again. I cursed the name of some minor god for the discomfort I endured, and as soon as the words departed from my lips, a flash of light momentarily blinded me. Then I heard a concussive sound, much like a mortar shell impact, followed by a tremendous explosion.

Instinctively, I dropped to the frozen ground and covered my ears, a little too late.

Off to my left, in the direction of the hidden gazebo, a roiling cloud of black smoke billowed above the trees, showering the surroundings with splintered shards of flaming lumber. Brave men fled, shouting in confusion, but I stood and raced toward the scene, horrified that a repeat of the Shirak fire might ensue.

Residual heat lingered from the blast, covering an area roughly thirty yards in circumference. The warmth radiated from the ground and parts of the old stone wall, melting the thin veil of snow into wispy streams of steam that rose like resurrected ghosts and vanished into the cold, clear heavens.

Directly ahead, the scattered stones of what had been

a ten-foot section of wall lay in random heaps on the ground. I stopped a lieutenant from the mortar unit to inquire what had happened.

"It was a trap, sir," he shouted nervously. "We found a hinge in the gazebo floor. Beneath it, we uncovered an iron lid the enemy locked over the entrance to a large portal. We spent an hour trying to pry the thing open, but it had been well secured from below.

"I talked to Lieutenant Rangell about it, and he suggested we blow the lid off with a small explosive. We backed everyone away, rigged it up and fired it off, but we didn't expect the whole thing to erupt like a volcano. We're lucky no one got hurt."

Sporadic flames licked at the splintered remains of the gazebo foundation. Four men with shovels battled the fire, dousing it with dirt, and between them, a wide trench, fifteen feet deep, extended through the gap in the wall.

"Now that we know how they got out of here," I said, surveying the damage, "find out where they went. I'll expect a report from you before nightfall. Also, post a guard to secure that gap."

"Yes sir," the lieutenant replied, apparently relieved that I hadn't blamed him for the disaster.

In order to investigate the defensive needs of our northern front, I decided to scout the small town where Sergeant Aransen's men had been so decisively defeated earlier in the day. I wanted to be alone anyway, so I borrowed a horse and rode northward. Keeping my distance – so as not to be discovered and possibly attacked, killed or captured – I carefully circled the settlement from the east, staying in the tall grass, beyond unaided visual range. I found a low ridge to the north suitable for observation, which I climbed to get a better look at the town with the aid of my field lens.

I saw no fortifications. The inhabitants seemed

relatively benign, consisting mostly of unarmed old men, women, and quite a few children. The locals busily packed their worldly belongings into sturdy, four-wheeled, mule-drawn wagons. I saw no soldiers, but civilian sentries maintained watch over the evacuation from the rooftops.

Moving southwest, I passed by large grain fields furrowed at right angles to the prevailing wind, the stubble and crop roots left behind after harvest to hold the soil. On the northern and western sides, these fields were sheltered by a great swath of leafless poplar and silver aspen. Following the northern edge of this windbreak, leading my horse through the trees to lessen the possibility of being seen, I noticed movement where the ranks of trees met. There I found a family of coyotes gnawing on the remains of two dead horses. My approach frightened the skittish creatures away.

The carcasses, stiff in the cold, showed signs of a deathwolf kill. Their intestine and internal organs had been eaten right through the belly, while the muscle and bone were left to scavengers. In my solitude, the traitorous thoughts I'd earlier entertained found fruition in a scheme that would solve my banquet dilemma. I butchered the beasts as best as I could with the aid of a hatchet from my pack. I hacked away at the frozen flesh to separate meat from bone until I had a bounty.

After this, I fashioned a litter from poplar branches similar to the ones I'd seen earlier that day, then dragged the meat behind my horse as I headed back to the Ice Dragon Inn. I didn't feel very hungry, and no one else would know the origin of the evening's main course . . . .

Lieutenant Rangell demonstrated initiative and ingenuity. He fashioned a massive barrel stove out of the iron pipe his crew dug from beneath the gazebo, calculating that this makeshift device could heat the inn's hall.

Two-dozen men carried this creation on a litter hewn

from oak, setting it directly on a makeshift, cobblestone foundation laid over the parquet floor near the inn's pipe organ. He fitted a chimney above the stove that extended about six feet overhead, allowing thick, creosote-laden smoke to smother the frescoed vaulting aloft.

The lieutenant, on his own initiative, ordered several of the upper-most stained-glass windows smashed, providing an exit for the stove exhaust, making the entire building appear as if it were ablaze when viewed from a distance. When I arrived, he assured me that the inn would be warm for the festivities that night. I thought the priests would feel at home . . . .

An ever-increasing tide of soldiers and equipment surrounded the aged stone walls like a seething black sea. Islands of white canvas appeared as the infantry divisions struck camp. The immensity of three hundred thousand assembled soldiers drowned the landscape encircling the ancient inn.

Artillery troops arranged cannon around the camp's perimeter, stacking munitions behind open barrels that gaped like thousands of graves. Beyond these swarmed our patrols with gleaming bayonets and loaded rifles, hunting for barbarian blood. Our deathwolves would run free this evening, killing any living thing they found. My nation's expeditionary army exuded extreme violence, and I felt like a traitorous minnow swimming amidst a gathering of frenzied sharks.

Near the western fringe of camp I found the reserve corps. These soldiers consisted of new recruits and veterans who belonged below battle strength units. With the signed orders from Legate Braegan in hand, I requested additional manpower from the officer in charge, receiving the command of sixty men and a sergeant to replace the casualties in my own century.

My newest sergeant, a man stricken with frostbite, did

not appear physically imposing. Sergeant Hanibal hailed from a crime-ridden, prostitute-infested town called Arama, a place name meaning *cursed* in our language. The effect of growing up in such an environment became apparent within moments of meeting him, for he reduced every aspect of life to some depraved sexual act with disease-ridden strumpets barely old enough to have breasts and body hair.

I detested him immediately.

Like a slave auctioneer, the officer in charge of the reserve corps assured me that this man was fearless in battle, slapping Hanibal's service record into my frozen hand with conviction in order to prove his point. Compliments of this nature were seldom deserved, and I sneered to display a cynical, if not realistic, disbelief. Glancing through the document, however, confirmed the claim, and with him I received a squadron from the same town who seemed all too eager for another fight.

In the waning late-afternoon light, I led my unit up to the north ridge overlooking our objective. After seating the enlisted men by squadrons, I sent out a scouting team and ordered the rest to clean their weapons.

To my relief, our scouts reported the town completely deserted. One of my privates explained, "The houses are still warm and there's a stray cat roaming around. Other than that, there's no other evidence that this place had been recently inhabited."

I led the men into town, sending four-man crews into every building, but found no one home. They must have been evacuated, which spoke to an unexpected degree of social organization. Nothing made sense. We found cases of dried apples, pears and raisins; many pickled vegetable jars, a dozen casks of watered-down wine, twenty sacks of moldy flour and a sack of spiny tubers called starchines that were very difficult to peel without getting pricked.

The houses, an odd blend of the primitive and

advanced, consisted of hardened mud walls, tiled floors and pole-framed roof supports. Each home contained gas lighting and massive kitchen stoves that made them feel oppressively hot after we'd suffered so long in the cold. I ordered my men to quarter inside, giving them strict orders to remain quiet about our improved living accommodations. We were within a thirty minute march of the Ice Dragon Inn, allowing for a speedy regrouping with the main army whenever it moved. No one would know my men received special treatment.

Although Lieutenant Hicks worked out most of the planning and preparation for the evening's festivities, I took special satisfaction in watching the senior officers line up for generous cuts of "roast" at the main serving table. Lieutenant Rangell, whose ingenuity far exceeded his rank, rigged a distillation column from the back of his wood-burning stove. From this, he served hot, spiced wine distilled from the watered-down casks I'd supplied him. This wicked brew possessed as much kick as cheap whiskey, dulling the senses of the elite officer corps so that they did not realize how bad the food tasted, nor how poorly the discordant band played.

Sometime close to midnight, the mortar team leader, a capable officer, I'd discovered to my delight, arrived with a map. Although he looked exhausted, it was refreshing to see a sober face, and I excused myself from the table in order to talk to him.

"I scouted this personally, sir," he began, as if trying to impress me with his initiative. "After the natives went through that portal in the gazebo floor, they entered a tunnel that joins up with a mine shaft. It breaks out along the western side of the hill my crew was on, and there we found tracks in the snow showing they marched straight across the valley to this hill."

He pointed to a place on the map named *Dead Hand*,

a prominent peak on a long, north-easterly ridge line. "You scouted that also, I presume?"

The lieutenant nodded.

"What did you see?"

"Not much. It looks like an old star fort made out of concrete. When I brought the men close, someone shot off a green rocket. After what happened this morning, I decided it was best to back off until we could get some firepower of our own up there."

"Prudent," I replied. "Get a patrol on that hill 'round the clock. I want to know everything that goes in and out. I want an artillery survey done right away, then put every mortar, cannon and rifle you have on that fort. Be ready to engage if I so much as breathe a word to you about it."

The lieutenant saluted, promising to fulfill my command and notify me by messenger the following day.

As I turned back toward the party, Legate Braegan caught my attention. Lord General Balinor, dressed in a clean and starched uniform, stood at his side with a drink in hand. Balinor's personal body guard – twelve husky men who were portraits of sobriety painted over a broadly inebriated landscape – watched everything with suspicion.

The general lifted his glass in my direction, pursing his thin lips into a smile that sent a chill down my spine.

Legate Braegan nodded, a wide grin splayed across his face that reiterated the promised promotion. In a single day I'd become an officer with a real chance to advance rapidly through the ranks. He would see to that. He was a man of his word.

Suddenly I felt hot and the headache festering in my skull pounded with terrible fury. I stepped outside, welcoming the cold, welcoming the pain within my head, for I realized at that moment that I had become a victim of my own success.

Junior Scout Garrick Ravenwood, Tamarian Defense Force;
Brenna Velez; Woodwind; Lord Lynden and Lady Alexina Velez

Grey Clouds

An uncharacteristic look of worry flashed across Colonel Brandt's countenance. He examined the engraved metal fittings of an Azgar trapdoor carbine, admiring its fine craftsmanship, noting many scars on its mahogany stock and a burnish on its iron butt that testified to frequent contact with its former owner's shoulder.

While this weapon had seen extensive use on the battlefield, its clean condition affirmed that a well-trained soldier had cared for this gun before it came into the colonel's possession. He understood that black powder weapons require diligence to keep them in good condition, and that rigorous maintenance indicated high soldierly morale. This fact, coupled with the huge numerical advantage his enemy enjoyed, gave Colonel Brandt good reason for concern.

The Tamarian officer leaned the musket against his desk. Although a full mobilization would buy time to move civilians out of the combat zone, the colonel did not have a lot of hard evidence to justify such an extreme measure. Risking his career on a single scouting report, the testimony of two foreigners and the combat experience of a lowly junior scout, the colonel transcribed alert orders for distribution throughout the Lower Angelgate Quarter of the Southeastern Tamarian Defense Force.

With telephone lines downed during the recent storm, he encoded his orders on a machine that assigned random number values to a code representing each letter of the Tamarian alphabet. A key, punched in along the top of every page, set the code-reader on the receiving end to the correct letter-integer relationship, allowing communication between bases that could not be decoded by the enemy, should his messages wind up in hostile hands.

Opposing three-hundred thousand Azgar troops, the Tamarian Defense Force could muster only thirty-thousand, and these were scattered across a roughly rectangular zone measuring one hundred and thirty-two miles long and sixty-six miles deep. Calling that many soldiers away from their posts to do battle against a vastly superior force would leave much of Tamaria's southeastern quarter vulnerable to attack. Colonel Brandt, grateful that such concerns were beyond the scope of his responsibility, left this larger decision in the capable hands of General Ziegler, his commanding officer.

Fortunately, geography restricted possible invasion routes into Tamarian territory. High, snow-capped mountains provided a natural barrier difficult for an army to cross, especially in winter. The enemy would most likely attack through a single, low elevation pass in an attempt to overwhelm local defenses. The most likely objective of any such strike would be the regional capital of Burning Tree, an important industrial city of 200 000 inhabitants on the western shore of Broken Wing Lake.

A successful campaign to control Burning Tree and the Broken Wing Valley would split Tamaria in half, put the enemy within a three-week march of Marvic, the nation's capital, and allow the Azgar unrestrained movement through the maze of north-south valleys where most of the Tamarian population lived.

Dead Hand Ridge commanded the best access to the Broken Wing Valley from the enemy's position on the Saradon Plateau. Ultimately, Tamaria's fate lay in Colonel Brandt's ability to blunt the invasion long enough for Central Interior Command to mass its troops and counterattack. Stripping every regional defensive position of its combat soldiers would provide a force 120 000 strong, representing roughly seventy-five percent of all Tamarian troops within mustering range.

Given perfect communication, the absence of enemy attacks on the tracks or trestles, no equipment breakdowns and good weather, a mobilization of this size would typically require two weeks to complete.

With phone lines down, getting news of the invasion to General Ziegler posed a problem. Normally, rail service between Dead Hand Ridge and Burning Tree occurred weekly. But once the weather turned cold and unpredictable, the above ground portions of the electric rail network often suffered the vagaries of heavy snowfall, avalanche and frost damage. Thus, during the autumn and winter, supply trains arrived monthly at best, and the last train to Burning Tree had pulled out three days earlier.

The distance to the regional capital could be covered by a homing dove in a single day, given good weather. But the importance of the news and the ability to describe the threat required a human messenger – someone swift and strong enough to make the journey – a courier who was not essential to the local fight.

Colonel Brandt handed the stack of orders to his aide, then stared out his north-facing window where he studied his reflection against the darkness, contemplating an impending nightmare. No commander in Tamarian history had faced such an overwhelming force. No invading army had ever been equipped with heavy artillery, either. Although his outward expression remained confident, the colonel worried that his supply stocks could not sustain prolonged combat.

The colonel's aide rushed the urgent orders to a communication center, located on the windswept roof of the base. There, a corporal rolled the encoded pages into lightweight scroll cases that she clamped to the right legs of several Kitsim doves, a large, fast-flying species trained to carry military messages between nearby fire support bases in an emergency.

Within hours, combat readiness increased across the dry, southeastern region of the High Land. Local base commanders alerted military police units, who in turn, began large-scale civil evacuation procedures and reserve unit duty recall. Citizens, awakened in alarm, started moving their stockpiled food from local farming cooperative storehouses into the fire keeps to sustain the soldiers who would be defending their exodus northwest.

A staged, troop reallocation commenced according to an extensively rehearsed, pre-operational plan. Soldiers based in rear areas and at other locations further away from the impending conflict mustered and marched in the frozen darkness toward the battle zone. Their positions would be filled by reserves, usually veteran soldiers beyond the prime age for active service. Young women also responded to the call, replacing their brothers, cousins and husbands in either combat, or supporting roles.

Tamarian patrols carried heavier weaponry, departed with greater frequency, and were given more individual discretion for weapon discharge. Thus, the likelihood of a lethal engagement between the opposing sides increased with each passing moment.

***

As dawn encroached, chasing shadows across the stark, angular foothill ridges east of the Angelgate Mountains, the refugee caravan from Dieter struggled uphill toward Dead Hand Ridge. Escorted by armed militia members and a pair of military police, the rhythm of plodding hooves and squeaking axles, the steady tug of straining mules and a gentle, side-to-side swaying had long since lulled most people to sleep. Steadily, the wagons carried these newly minted refugees to safer confines, protected by soldiers and strong walls.

Garrick, who had slept fitfully in the wagon as it traveled, huddled quietly with Brenna in the freezing gloom at the rear of the caravan. Images of yesterday's events haunted his private thoughts, modified by fantasy as he willed a heroic role for himself in the unfolding drama.

Yet the reality of his best friend's death struck the cadet repeatedly, leaving him with an impotent feeling of frustration that he could not contain. He blamed himself for the demise of his unit, even though, in an intellectual way, Garrick realized that his presence alone would not have changed the outcome of battle, especially in light of his performance at the Dieter skirmish. But this only underscored the helplessness and sorrow he felt.

Brenna noticed the tension in his hands, the listlessness in Garrick's grey eyes that made him unable to look in any particular direction for longer than a moment or two. Words would just begin to form on his lips, only to vanish as he pushed them deep into the silent realm of his subconscious, where a lifetime of private pain resided in lonely, shame-shadowed solitude.

She longed to comfort him in some way, to hold him close that she might drive away the anguish, but he seemed so distant, occupied with his thoughts, that she wasn't sure he wanted her consolation. At a time when she wanted to be a good friend, willing to hear him express his true feelings, when she would have gladly let him hold her close to soothe the unspoken affliction stabbing his soul, he'd retreated into self-imposed exile.

True to her nature, compassion stirred in Brenna's heart. Braving the cold, she took off her right glove and slid her hand into his. Garrick's fingers enclosed hers, but not with the lighter touch he'd been careful to employ before. Without really thinking about what he was doing, the young man flexed his forearm muscle and squeezed her hand a bit harder than he should have.

She winced in pain and surprise. "You're hurting me," Brenna warned, not wanting to offend him and trying to keep her tone matter-of-fact.

Garrick relinquished his grip without a word, as if he'd rejected a piece of fruit at the market, and stared straight ahead.

Brenna put her glove back on, suppressing a pout, feeling hurt inside by his casual rejection of her affection. The lingering doubts about becoming emotionally involved with a godless foreigner surfaced again. Then, she chided herself for being so forward, for presuming that she could provide what he needed at the moment, when in truth, she didn't know him well enough to sense what would make him feel better anyway. She crossed her arms and wordlessly leaned back against the hard, wooden bench.

The change in Brenna's behavior brought Garrick out of his reverie, and a quick evaluation of her posture inspired concern that he'd done something irrevocably wrong. At first, he felt mildly annoyed that she'd be so selfish to ignore his obvious emotional pain and demand attention, but when he thought further, he realized that she might have been innocently trying to help. In that case, he would be the one guilty of insensitivity, and her friendship was more valuable to him than the small bit of pride expended in the minor humiliation of an apology.

"I wasn't thinking, Brenna," he admitted. "Please forgive me. I didn't mean to hurt you."

She shook her head, refusing to look at him. "It's not fair of you to treat me so coldly. I'm only trying to help." Her voice sounded sharp, brimming with emotion.

Garrick realized he'd made a serious blunder and regretted his bad manners. But the deed, once done, carried consequences in its wake, and he worried that a willful woman like Brenna might be slow to offer absolution. "You're right. I'm sorry! I know you're well-intended."

Brenna remained aloof and silent, refusing to dignify his apology with a response. An ache in her soul warned that she shouldn't play this game, but she intended to prove a point and didn't back down.

After waiting for what felt like a very long time, Garrick tapped her shoulder. "Please look at me. I'm sad because I lost my best friend, but I don't want to hurt or upset you. I wasn't thinking, and I'm sorry."

The Lithian woman finally complied, reading repentance in his aspect. She didn't understand why he couldn't express his pain, why he didn't trust her. "I can't read your mind," she told him. "If you can't articulate why you need to withdraw, at least tell me plainly what I can do to help. Your silence isn't working for either of us."

The words came easier than he'd imagined they would, and once spoken, could not be recalled. "I want to hold you," he replied, nervously.

Witnessing his endearing vulnerability, Brenna's anger melted and a smile spread across her face. "All you have to do is ask," she told him, opening her arms.

Garrick pulled her close, feeling the silky texture of her fine hair brushing against his face, the strength of her shoulders, the caress of her fingers and her yielding softness willingly pressed against him. "You don't make it easy on me," he admitted. "One minute, it seems that you want me to be near and the next, you're asking me to back away. I'm afraid to need you because I never know whether I'm going to be accepted or rejected."

Brenna held him a little tighter, biting on her lower lip, wishing she could set herself free from the restrictions imposed by fear and biological necessity. Finally, she let him go, dropping her hands into her lap. "I don't know how else to put this," she began, "so I'll be brutally honest. I've never felt this way before, and I don't know how to handle my desire for you. I'm afraid of losing control.

"My life is disciplined by faith, music and martial training. I've never met anyone whose interest genuinely transcended my beauty, and my bosom. But you've unlocked this hunger in my soul, a novel mental, spiritual and physical craving for your company. I don't know if my feelings align with Allfather's will, and while you've been very careful to respect me thus far, I still need time to build trust. This is an area where I can't afford to be wrong."

Garrick, knowing nothing about the permanence of Lithian pair bonding, presumed her fear lay rooted in violating a moral standard. But his response reassured her, nonetheless. "There's no shame in that," he replied. "Nothing worth believing in ever stands unchallenged. Words are cheap and anyone can claim to be principled. But real character is tested in the crucible of action, when doing what is right is harder than doing what is wrong."

"That's why I'm afraid," she replied, letting her gaze wander from his. "I don't know if I can."

The young man left her words unanswered for a moment, watching anticipation rising in the Lithian woman's beautiful face. "I can't speak for you, but there are two of us involved, Brenna. You're not the only one with a conscience here. As much as I want to express physical affection, as much as I want the same from you, I'm willing to set aside desire to prove my sincerity. Judging from what I know of you, I think you're worth the wait."

Brenna lifted her eyes to meet his. "That sounds great, Garrick, but how long can you resist? A few days? A few weeks? Maybe a few months? I'm not deliberately baiting you with my body, or being fickle about how I feel. I just have a lot more to lose than you do. How can I trust your integrity when you don't trust mine right now?"

This was a fair critique and Garrick knew it. He thought carefully before responding. "I need to feel more confident of my standing with you. That would be helpful."

Brenna faced forward, examining the looming outline of the Tamarian firebase, situated beyond a glacis a few hundred yards distant. A light breeze from the south played with her hair. "Would it help if I told you that I loved you?"

"Do you love Woodwind?"

"Of course I do!"

"Then no, that wouldn't matter."

Brenna sighed wearily. "It's not the same. How can I help you understand?"

"Tell me difference, Brenna. You give him lingering hugs, you kiss him on the lips and then tell me that he's like a brother to you. Well, I have an actual little sister. I love her with all my heart, but we don't go around kissing one another like you do with Woodwind."

The Lithian maiden prayed silently, rubbing her cold, unfeeling nose, wishing that Garrick would make this easier on her, but suspecting he wouldn't. Finally, she said, "Okay. I don't know how to make this reflect what I'm feeling, but I'll try. I'm comfortable and safe in your company. I want you in a physical way that's very different from the way I feel about Woodwind. Just don't ask me to compromise my faith, and don't take advantage of my trust."

Garrick agreed. "I'll respect whatever you believe in, gods and all, as long as you don't insist that I think the same way. And by now, you should feel confident that I'm willing to honor whatever physical boundaries you set."

"Then what exactly do you want from me?" she asked, afraid she might find his demands unreasonable.

Garrick's answer surprised her. "Just be consistent. If it's okay to hold me one minute, don't pull away the next. I need to know that your affection is an honest reflection of your feelings. I think that's fair."

"I can do that," she acquiesced. "And in return, I need you to uphold my virtue until I'm ready, and trust that I care. Your silence makes me feel like I'm not important."

The Tamarian cadet shook his head. "In a short time you've become very important to me. I care about you in a way I've never cared before, but I've been betrayed by people I trusted, people in my own family, and that reality makes me reluctant to drop my guard and open my heart."

Brenna reached for him, holding his face in her hands, her gaze sincere, caring and brimming with desire. "You don't ever have to be afraid of me," she said softly.

Garrick fell silent, his pounding heart quickened by Brenna's nearness, her sensuality, her intelligence, her trust. Her lovely, alluring eyes drew him closer until breathlessly, their lips met.

*****

A subtle shift in the wind before dawn brought in banks of fog, obscuring the stars overhead. On early morning walks with his wife, Lord Lynden Velez often gazed into the heavens, considering his place in God's universe. His personal wealth, power, prestige and the social and political problems he faced seemed insignificant in contrast to the incomprehensible vastness of Allfather's domain.

Lynden's faith inspired a perspective on leadership that contrasted with the attitudes held by most wealthy landowners in Kameron, who believed that their ancestral right to profit from agricultural and industrial production superseded all other concerns. Lord Velez took genuine interest in the welfare of his people, devoting his personal resources to improving the quality of the peasants' lives.

The dirt-poor vintners now under his rule had scraped a living from heavily eroded hillsides in northeastern Kameron for generations. Their suspicion and cynicism arose from the conduct of previous landlords, who cared for nothing more than collecting exorbitant rents.

Throughout the long, hot summer, Lynden worked tirelessly to win the confidence of his new constituency. He did not live an extravagant, isolated lifestyle. Rather, the Lithian lord met with local people and asked what he could do to help. He, his family, his army and his Abelscinnian friends toiled alongside them. Additionally, Lynden subdivided his property and sold the best parcels – the well-watered land along the Virgin River – to the peasants with no down payment and no interest. Lynden set up a trust from these land sales to improve local infrastructure. No previous landowner had ever behaved this way.

Lady Alexina, his exceptionally intelligent wife, traveled to Kameron City and hired a soil conservation scientist to consult on local erosion problems. In response to his report's recommendation, the warlord, with his two-thousand soldiers, bent his own back in hard labor under the late summer sky, planting native vegetation to hold the worsening gully erosion in check. He built terraces on the hillsides, dug debris dams to slow runoff, created catchment basins to store water for irrigation, excavated alluvium and hauled it back uphill so that the people he ruled would have better crops in the years to come.

After investing most of his family's wealth buying and improving land that often could not sustain its own population, Lord and Lady Velez now had little money left to pay the men under his command. This put their people in a precarious position, given that his small armed force protected these isolated holdings from roaming bandit gangs that had terrorized local citizens long before his arrival.

Xina held her husband's hand with a tenderness borne of long affection. She felt proud of him. While their present home, a run-down compound with crumbling walls, leaky roofs and gardens grown wild with weeds, lacked the comfort they'd left behind in Shirak, she fully believed in and supported her husband's mission.

There would be time enough in the future for rebuilding their estate. Their knowledge and economic ideas would create prosperity for everyone in due course, but the Lithian couple understood that the people's trust had to come first. Without local support, none of their plans would come to fruition.

Ironically, no one in the Velez household thought well of Kameron. The ancient, apathetic society bred unprincipled leadership. A thriving and illegal slave trade existed because desperate peasants, living on marginal land in the foothills or high in the mountains, sent their sons and daughters away with corrupt brokers who promised work in the big coastal cities. This industry had long prospered and profited by selling young people in clandestine prostitution and labor markets.

A small group of wealthy, land and factory-owning families systemically exploited the poor, burdening them with exorbitant interest, creating huge debts that transferred from one generation to the next. Children born into this society often worked for very low wages to pay obligations incurred by their grandparents, while creating new financial liabilities that they, in turn, passed on to their own offspring. Thus, the stratification of society continued long after surrounding nations abandoned feudalism and adopted more progressive forms of economics, social structure and governance.

Nonetheless, in the weeks following the Azgar invasion of Illithia, Lady Velez teleported Lynden, Brenna and Woodwind across enemy picket lines into Kameron, where they hoped to find refuge from the doom prophesied against their own civilization. Wild rumors of fertile land for sale in a warm climate enticed many people to flee before the enemy surrounded and destroyed Shirak. Lord Lynden found a landlord named Nemesio Fang, who offered his northern holdings for sale.

The Fang family ranked among the wealthiest and most powerful in Southern Kameron, but Lord Fang's boasting and lies quickly convinced Woodwind that the man possessed the personal integrity of a rattlesnake. "He is appropriately named," the swordsman stated, sensing that the duplicitous Lord Fang would not surrender any of his land without a fight. Woodwind, translating from Kamerese into Lithian, warned his master to break off contact and make an offer elsewhere.

As the Azgar steadily conquered Lithian cities, Lord Velez ran out of time. Lithian armies fought bravely, but could not halt the enemy's advance. Many families who fled to Kameron found themselves at the mercy of corrupt officials offering property for sale at inflated prices. Refugees, robbed of their wealth under these agreements often faced powerful armies of Kamerese warlords who ignored their contracts and evicted them.

A royal commission, established under orders from King Alejo, intervened to stop the fraudulence. The commission's report recommended relocating displaced refugees into the northern frontier, a sparsely populated region near the Tamarian border known for unpredictable weather, crop failures and banditry.

Lord Velez did not want to subject his family and the soldiers under his command to an unstable situation. Despite Woodwind's protest he negotiated with Lord Fang. The two men struck an expensive deal for a mountainous property very close to Illithia's border with Kameron.

However, when Nemesio Fang first met Brenna, nothing short of taking her as a wife would satisfy him. Lord Velez refused to comply, as Brenna was not property, but a woman with a strong will of her own. The dispute between Fang and Velez dragged on as the Azgar drove further into the beautiful, deep valley where the Sea of Tranquility lay, and the Lithian city of Shirak stood.

Somehow, stress and lack of sleep combined to create a terrible misunderstanding. One evening, while discussing the negotiations with his daughter and Woodwind, Lord Velez revealed Fang's desire to take Brenna as his wife. The impasse could trigger a clause in Kamerese law requiring court arbitration in contract disputes as a means of avoiding armed conflict. The court's decision would be binding on both parties, and could be enforced by the Kamerese National Army, if necessary.

Linking this development with the knowledge of how other Lithians had been deceived, both Brenna and Woodwind understood Lynden to mean that an additional clause in the contract, enforced by the arbitrator, obligated her to marry Lord Fang, even though Lynden hadn't signed anything. The friends returned to Shirak, explaining this idea to the horror of Lady Alexina and her other daughters.

The siege of their beloved city, compounded by the continued absence of Lord Velez and slow communication with him in Kameron perpetuated this notion among immediate family members. Xina did not tell her husband that she'd deliberately left Brenna in charge of defending the exit portal so that the young woman could flee, should she choose to exercise that option before the enemy arrived.

Once soldiers entered her house, Brenna pushed her maid, Tirra, through the magic portal, then promptly shut it down, trapping herself alone with an unknown number of hostile Azgar inside the Velez compound. The finality of her departure shocked the entire family.

Xina feared for her daughter's life and risked opening the portal again, just long enough to send Woodwind through. Later, she put Shadow, his horse, at a little-known watering hole north of town, praying he would find and save the young woman.

Two months of anxious waiting and much prayer had since transpired without any news.

Not long later, Lord Fang's intransigence derailed the contract. Eventually, Lynden found a large tract of remote land on the Tamarian border owned by a warlord named Navarro. Every detail for the property purchase transaction worked out at the last minute, convincing Lord and Lady Velez that their move served a spiritual purpose.

Nonetheless, every passing day reminded them of their eldest daughter's disappearance. Lord Velez let his imagination drift to the day of her birth as he walked with his wife. He imagined Brenna's tiny body in his arms, and recalled the wonder swelling in his heart watching the dark-haired infant nurse at her exhausted mother's breast.

Visions of Brenna laughing and running as a child, learning the piano so well she dominated every competition she entered, and watching her hone martial skills with *Malleah* Shevonne, his *Relict* aunt, threaded through his mind. Brenna could recite long passages of Lithian scripture from memory and loved singing hymns. She'd developed into a devout, athletic, and talented young woman, very much like her mother. These disparate events wove into an experiential tapestry of loving a strong-willed, intelligent soul who'd left her indelible mark upon his heart.

Lady Xina loved and missed her daughter dearly, but long hours of prayer imbued her soul with peace. The comfort had come with strange quickness. She became quietly confident in her eldest daughter's survival, no matter how grim the news of conquest from across the mountains.

Now, on a cool southwesterly wind, the winter rains finally arrived. Misty drizzle fell from the grey clouds, washing many months of dust from rust-stained, decaying plaster and rotting timber. Along the eaves of every building, droplets formed and fell on pavement, filling tiny troughs carved by centuries of dripping, creating a peaceful, soothing patter with an ephemeral romance unique to west-coast precipitation.

Alexina shut her eyes and let the moisture caress her face, acutely aware of how she'd missed rain during the long, dry weeks of summer. Far to the southeast, in the land she'd left behind, summertime convectional storms occurred nearly every afternoon, drenching the landscape in torrents of warm precipitation that fell like a waterfall from the sky. Here, the drizzle felt cold, but she savored the sensation, almost willing its cool touch to settle upon her skin.

Lynden stopped walking, watching tiny droplets adhere to his wife's fair and flawless complexion. He enjoyed the moment, admiring her, savoring the sweet scent of the grape crush, borne upon the gentle breeze, mingling with the aroma of Alexina's perfumed ebon hair.

Camille, their youngest and most fleet-footed daughter, dashed through the mist down a slippery stairwell. The maiden had raced for a very long time along the path leading to a derelict observatory, high on an eastern hill. After much searching, she finally found her parents. Drenched and shivering, her skirt hung heavily from her hips, and the pale, green blouse she wore clung to her soft shoulders, little breasts and slender belly like a second skin. "*Amair,*" she panted. "*Umma!* Aril sent me to find you. There's been heavy rain in the mountains. The runoff is washing fast through Maidenhair Canyon and it's brought down some trees that are clogging the culverts.

"We tried to move them out of the way, but the current is too strong. The upper debris dam is about to overflow and ruin all the work we did this summer."

"Is Aril safe?" Lynden queried, concerned for the well-being of his adult nephew.

Camille nodded, wiping her wet face, pushing a dangling strand of darkened hair out of her glimmering green eyes. "He's opening the gates halfway on the next three dams to let the water run through." The maiden, in Lithian fashion, had already regained her breath.

"Under those conditions it's unwise to be in the water," Lord Velez warned. "Once you've put on dry clothes, Mason will need to know what happened, and Tegene should muster the men. We'll need all hands for this. Then, bring your sisters and meet us at the upper reservoir."

"On my way," she replied with a smile. Camille squeezed her father's hand, gave her mother a kiss on the lips and darted off to do her father's bidding.

Alexina's eyes, bright as an azure blossom, met her husband's gaze. She sighed, her lovely lips wrinkled into a frown. "All that work!" Lady Xina knew that beyond her husband's confident demeanor lurked exhaustion from months of combat and endless toil. "Why don't you go up to the hot spring and let me handle this?"

Lynden Velez well understood that his wife could manage the setback without him. Nonetheless, he intended to do all he could before requesting her formidable aid. "How can I ask you and the men to work while I relax?" he queried, gently holding her chin in his hands. He kissed her lightly. "What I've done to deserve a woman like you I'll never know, but if there are sandbags that need filling, then I'll take my turn at the shovel."

Alexina smiled. "Whatever you wish, my love."

***

Silently, the hydraulic hinges controlling the gate at Dead Hand Ridge opened to admit the refugees from Dieter, and a tall lieutenant named Magruder appeared with a note pad in hand. Systematically, he organized the confused, travel-weary and often uncooperative townsfolk into groups. He ordered able-bodied men and women to separate areas for work assignments, while mothers with small children, along with the elderly, went to a holding center while they waited for evacuation plans to commence.

When he saw Brenna standing close to a soldier in uniform, the lieutenant wheeled her around by the shoulder thinking she was just another private in need of something to do. "What are you doing here?" he snapped.

Brenna's look of silent terror brought Garrick to her rescue. "She's with me, sir. She's a refugee and doesn't speak our language."

Lieutenant Magruder appraised her lovely form with a lingering eye before turning his attention to Garrick. "Why is a foreigner wearing off-base military clothing?"

"The commanding officer at the Ice Dragon Inn gave them to her because she's been caring for our wounded," Garrick replied, hoping that partial truth would suffice.

"Where's your unit, son?" he inquired, still holding on to Brenna's parka as if she were a sack of starchines in need of peeling.

Garrick pulled back on the tarpaulin covering the bed of his wagon, exposing the remains of his comrades. Choking back an outburst of emotion, he replied, "They're right here, sir."

The lieutenant's eyes widened as he let go of Brenna's coat. He drew in a slow breath, tightened his lips, and softened his tone. "Cover them," he ordered, "and contact the Mortuary Affairs Office in the basement."

"Yes sir," Garrick responded.

At that moment Corporal Fanselars, who'd ridden all night in order to get medical help for Woodwind, appeared. Exhausted, impatient and irritable, he pushed through the crowd of refugees, totally ignoring Lieutenant Magruder. "You! Scout boy!" he spat.

Garrick turned in surprise, reading the man's name tag and rank. "You're speaking to me, sir?"

"Is there another scout boy here? While you were busy fondling long-locks, her real lover took a bullet in the back. The doc thinks he'll be dead by nightfall. Tell her!"

Apprehension screamed inside Garrick's head as the corporal's harsh message stung his ears. "What happened? Where is he?" Garrick inquired.

Fanselars, annoyed with the younger man's attitude, ignored the first question entirely. "The infirmary, you idiot! You tell her now!" The corporal's tone, size and rank intimidated Garrick into immediate obedience.

Brenna's heart sank when she heard the news, inspiring tears that welled from her bright eyes. She cast her glance downward, too shy to respond.

The young Tamarian covered up his fallen comrades again, then quietly asked Brenna if she could deal with being alone for awhile. "I have to identify the remains of my unit," he stated. "We need permission for you to visit the infirmary before they'll let you in. If you don't want to wait in the hall for me, I'll head to your room I'm done."

Her response pained him. "I'll go upstairs." Sensing that he really wished she wouldn't leave him, Brenna took his right hand with both her own, guiding it to her lips. "But I'll be waiting for you," she promised, kissing his fingers.

In violation of the military code of conduct, Garrick embraced her, holding Brenna's strong and soft body close. "It won't take long," he pledged. Their affection drew some dismayed, disapproving eyes and muttered commentary as he moved through the crowd without looking back.

Brenna quickly retreated to the dark solitude of her quarters where she fell onto the bed, wept and prayed for a long time. "I've been angry at Woodwind because he confronted me with the truth of my motive for coming up here," she lamented. "This is my fault!"

Words failed, superseded by an ache in her soul that found expression in heartbroken wailing. Woodwind was more selfless and courageous than any man she'd known. True friends told the truth, and she'd become defensive because he'd been right . . . .

In the light of this personal admission, Brenna felt that she'd betrayed him and regretted her refusal to return to Kameron. Confusing and contradictory sentiments swirled within her mind. An emotional storm that ranged from rage to regret, from loss to love, overwhelmed her soul.

Then, a strange thing happened. Occasionally in prayer, when her concentration was fully focused, she could sense the exalted influence of Allfather's spirit within her. Most often, it comforted, but at times pointed out the blindness of her spiritual perception, cutting to the very core of soul until she fully understood that she was not entirely blameless in her troubles.

This time, however, Brenna experienced an instantaneous peace and felt an overwhelming desire to pray for her *Umma*. Without knowing why, she did so, and words returned with an eloquence that vanquished her earlier speechlessness.

***

Torrents of silt-laden water crashed through a steep, rocky canyon with a mightier roar than the rushing of many horses into battle. Thundering over massive boulders, the surging stream leaped into the misty air in a thousand random fountains, falling back to its roiling course, pushing rocks, broken limbs and even entire trees along its frantic, turgid path.

As Lynden and Alexina Velez watched, the rapid current undercut unstable banks – which melted into raging water like metal in a forge – exposing the tangled roots of conifer and oak that now hung tenuously from newly eroded cliffs. The debris dam, clogged with flotsam, no longer slowed the raging current. Churning water swept over the dam's rock and rammed-dirt crest with the same devastating ferocity it wielded against the stream banks.

Cynthia, whose lovely voice preceded her actual arrival, brought Mason, the chief engineer and three of Tegene's adult grandsons. "Cassie's bringing your men with shovels and sandbags," the tall, shy maiden explained to her *Amair*. "Camille is still looking for Tegene."

Sixty-two-year-old Sherman Mason – a strong, stout man whose fine physical condition probably had more to do with his profession than the minor contribution of Lithian blood in his lineage – surveyed the rapidly eroding embankment, assessing damage. "This is a great deal more water than we'd designed for," he worriedly informed Lord Velez on his return. "We stand a good chance of losing the entire system if we don't act soon."

After consulting with his crew, the bearded engineer decided to excavate a channel in order to relieve pressure on the upper dam. Soon, several hundred men, armed with pick axes and shovels, busily dug through muck and rock this crew had painstakingly built up only weeks before.

When Aril arrived, shirtless, dirty and out of breath, Mason sent him back with instructions to close the spillway gates. As soon as the water reached two-thirds the height of the dam, he was to open the gate slowly until the volume of water entering equaled the volume going out.

Alexina formed an outline with her two daughters. After she'd worked out the algorithmic sequence, Lady Velez approached her husband to explain how her plan would work. She kissed him gently, then pursed her lips. "If Allfather is willing, I'll tame the waters for you."

Camille came uphill with Tegene and his youngest adult son, Jawara, in tow. The tall, dark-skinned warrior, who'd fought at Lynden's side and earned his deepest trust decades earlier, took hold of a Lithian axe and scanned the grey clouds. "You are doubly blessed, my friend," he told Lynden. "The Holy One sends you rain and firewood at the same time!"

Tegene always found something positive to say, and Lynden had long appreciated the good humor of his lifelong friend. The warlord glanced at the line of men standing behind him, waiting for their role in the drama, then accepted an axe and a coil of rope from Mason. Turning back to his wife, Lynden said, "We're ready now. My prayers and blessings go with you."

Alexina retreated to a quiet spot several dozen yards away from the excavation, where she and her daughters would not disturb the work progressing behind them. Standing close together, the three sisters joined hands, taking turns in asking for Allfather's favor on behalf of their mother, for all power that she exerted derived from him.

Having learned water polymerization as a child, Alexina knew how to put her mind into a dimension where molecular bonds could form with dissolved minerals. She could do nothing on her own in that intersection, but Alexina *believed* that Allfather would reveal his power and work through her to tame the raging waters.

Never before had she attempted anything on such a massive scale, and complicating her effort, controlling the rapid rise of runoff required continuous growth in the polymer chain equal to the cube of speed times volume in the water stream. This required intense focus, and an ability to solve problems quickly.

Lady Alexina inhaled sharply as power and warmth surged through her body. Concentrating on her complex task, the Lithian woman took command of the raging waters in Maidenhair Creek.

Subtle shifts in subatomic material relationships controlled the transfer of minute bits of matter into energy, providing the force by which hydrogen bonds came apart. With its molecular structure disrupted, new bonds formed with broken mineral molecules, linking with hydrogen and oxygen into rapidly evolving, continuous chains.

This change in form thickened the volatile semi-liquid like gelatin, squeezing out silt that dropped, dry as desert sand, into the rocky stream bed. Once the water achieved this state, Alexina Velez lifted her hands and *believed* that the stream would obey her command to rise.

A strange quiet descended. Like a great, liquid serpent, the water polymer reared silently out of its course, arced over the disintegrating debris dam, then returned on the far end to its natural state where it cascaded loudly into the rising lake below.

Racing onto the dry ground created by Allfather's power, Lynden and Tegene scrambled toward the knot of trunks and debris clogging the spillway culvert. Reaching the topmost tree, the Lithian warlord wrapped the rope around its bulk, secured a slipknot, then gave a shout to the crew waiting up on the bank.

Groaning, the men strained against the weight of the snag, whose entangled branches embraced other derelict companions in a mass of twisted limbs. Tegene attacked the snarled boughs from one side while Lynden hacked through thick stems of green wood on the other. Their Lithian axes, boasting extremely sharp and durable crystalloid polymer edges, enabled the men to cut through thick timber with heavy strokes, until the tree trunk slipped from the grasp of its fellows and slid uphill.

Sherman Mason flung another coil of rope from the south bank that landed in the warlord's outstretched left hand. Lynden wrapped another tree trunk and set to work on cutting it free. Tegene soon dripped with sweat, but he sang while working, the other men joined him, and the regular rhythm of two axes chopping steadily through snarled branches provided a percussion accompaniment to their raised voices. With tireless tugging from the men on the bank above, the fallen fir finally dislodged from its resting place.

Five jammed logs came out this way, clearing the concrete culvert of blocking debris. The two men bolted uphill after nearly forty minutes of hard labor, aching from the strain, but pleased to find the additional spillway engineered by Sherman Mason ready to fulfill its purpose.

With a weary word of thanks to Allfather, Alexina let go of control. A mighty crash reverberated through the canyon as water, reverting to its rightful state, collapsed back into the stream bed, sending up showers of muddy froth, returning to the untamed snarl of swirls, eddies and rapids preceding her work.

As the water level rose, it coursed into the newly dug spillway instead of wearing down the dam, allowing the soldiers to repair damage to the structure with sandbags.

Cynthia Velez arose and grasped her exhausted mother's arms in wide-eyed astonishment. *"Umma!"* she cried. "I saw Brenna. She's married!"

***

Garrick bade farewell to the silent members of his junior scout class in the cold light of the morgue. This experience left him feeling numb disbelief, as if he expected cadets blown apart by Azgar canister, bludgeoned by rifle butts, bullet-ridden or bayoneted, to meet him at the barracks later in the evening. The permanence of their demise brought a surge of strong emotion to the surface.

"That's Jan Bordmann," the young man concluded, barely able to contain himself. "He was my best friend."

Captain Mullenhardt, the officer responsible for burial preparations at the firebase, peered over his spectacles. "I understand how difficult this has been for you," he replied, pulling a blanket over the dead teenager's face. "Take comfort in the fact that he and the others died bravely in defense of our people. Thank-you for your help."

Garrick saluted and left, a sense of uselessness deepening the depression already haunting his soul. As a soldier with no unit, no mission and no purpose in the midst of an impending invasion, his loss felt overwhelming.

Walking listlessly through the hallway, Garrick's mind meandered toward musings of Brenna. As he thought about how much he wanted her comfort at that moment, his pace quickened. Brenna would understand. She would listen and her soothing hands would make him forget the ache he felt inside. She would be the friend he needed.

Pulled abruptly out of his private world by the appearance of the base commander, Garrick stepped to the side of the hallway and snapped to attention.

Colonel Brandt and a cluster of other officers were returning from a trip to the officer's mess. Having heard how the enemy wiped out Garrick's unit, the colonel returned the junior scout's salute, then paused.

"Yesterday morning I ordered you to alert your sergeant and the civilians in Dieter concerning the Azgar invasion," Colonel Brandt stated.

"That's correct, sir."

"And you were unable to contact your unit in time?"

"No sir, I was not. I went to the Ice Dragon Inn first, but saw the red flare while I was about a mile away."

Colonel Brandt nodded, knowing from personal experience that losing friends in combat is difficult to accept. This young man needed something to do, and Colonel Brandt needed something done. "I have new orders for you, Junior Scout Ravenwood. If you complete this for me, I'll assign you to a regular unit with full pay."

"That would be an honor, sir." Garrick said this, thinking that the colonel had some minor function for him to fulfill. He had no idea that the actual mission would task his strength, stamina, and risk his life.

"Follow me. I'll fill you in on the details."

Long after she'd retreated to her room, gazing from a window overlooking the hexagonal, inner courtyard, Brenna watched several soldiers erect something that looked like a drilling rig. The men set up a metal truss that gleamed in the daylight, directly in the midst of a circle painted on the cobblestones. The circle appeared to be the focal point of all activity in the courtyard.

An officer checked everything, and when satisfied, motioned toward a set of double-hung doors that opened at his bidding. The soldiers removed sections of steel plate, uncovering a single track, set beneath the cobblestones. A rail cart emerged, gliding forward as four men strained behind its mass. The cart stopped just as Brenna heard a knock and Garrick's voice from behind the door.

She let him in, but didn't extend the affection he desired. Instead, she pulled him toward her window, her eyes brimming with excitement. "What are those men in the courtyard putting together?" she inquired, her grip on his forearm surprisingly strong for such a small woman.

He wanted her touch more desperately than he had the courage to admit, but honoring her curiosity, he set aside his desire for the moment. "Oh, that's a launch tower for one of our liquid fueled rockets," Garrick explained. "They have longer range than the smaller, solid-fueled ones and carry a hefty payload. I hear they're really expensive, so we don't deploy them unless we want to hit something big and important."

Figuring she'd been looking at some kind of weapon, her next question followed naturally. "How far can they fly?"

"From what I understand, if we have reliable spotters in the field and the math is done right, they can easily hit a base camp on the Saradon from here. They're gyro-stabilized and accurate to at least fifty miles."

Brenna raised her brows disbelievingly. "Really? That seems awfully far for a rocket."

Garrick shrugged. "They're the largest in our inventory. That crew will spend two hours just getting one of the pair ready to launch, and when something that big lands, even the giants wet their pants."

The Lithian woman remembered the unbearable pounding of Azgar artillery deployed against Shirak and wondered how the weapon being readied beneath her would compare. Uncomfortable with the memory and uncertain how Garrick would respond to the need she felt in her soul, she nervously changed the subject and asked in a timid voice, "Can you please take me to see Woodwind?"

Garrick, though he longed for Brenna's affection and wished he could spend more time alone with her, led the maiden through a maze of hallways, where the echoes of many other footfalls mingled with their own. They arrived at a door guarded by a husky soldier who wouldn't take his eyes off of Brenna, no matter how uncomfortable his leering made her feel. After showing him the written authorization from Colonel Brandt that Garrick had secured earlier, they entered the facility.

The pungency of pus, urine and dried sweat mingled with the antiseptic odors of rubbing alcohol and bleach inside the infirmary. Clean cots, covered in stiff, white linen sheets with wool blankets folded neatly at the near end, awaited occupancy in silent rows arranged at right angles, with precisely the same space between each rail frame.

In Tamaria, as in most cultures, care of the sick and wounded fell primarily to females. Nurses and young volunteers clad in blue uniforms, rolled bandages, recounted medicines and prepared polished trays of ghastly cutting instruments. They paced their work amid a stream of consonantal chatter that ceased quickly when Garrick led Brenna into their domain. She felt their disapproving gazes rest on her, realizing that her entrance caused the conversational disruption.

The young cadet acted unconcerned, despite the sudden quiet. Yet even his confident demeanor couldn't mask tension hanging in the air. Most Tamarians regarded foreigners in general – and Lithians in particular – with suspicion. To his great frustration, Garrick found that close proximity with Brenna stirred indignation and disgust – even when they weren't touching.

The Lithian woman realized this problem had grown steadily worse as she and Garrick spent more time together. Not knowing what to say to the infirmary workers, she kept her eyes averted, enduring their contempt and disapproval in silence.

Behind the empty cots, several women attending patients returned to their work as the young couple approached. With her eyes widened in concern and fear flooding her expression, Brenna darted along a row occupied by sick and wounded soldiers, where she saw her dying friend, Woodwind.

The southerner lay on his belly, his skin pallid as light from the twin moons, his shoulder swathed in a blood-drenched dressing that needed immediate attention. Sweat gleamed on his bare back and forehead. Brenna interpreted these symptoms as indicators of serious infection. She had to work quickly if she intended to save him, but given the contempt projected on her, didn't want to offend her hosts. "Have you any idea who's in charge here?" she queried.

Garrick pointed to a tall, slender woman who turned her head as he gestured. She approached, her stride exuding self-confidence, her countenance appraising Brenna with condescension. The doctor, certain that Lithians lacked intelligence, stared at Brenna's bosom with disgust before appraising Garrick. The maiden's shapely form confirmed an inaccurate presupposition about the young soldier's interest in this foreigner that informed Dr. Meine's scoffing. She didn't bother introducing herself.

Brenna ignored her, letting Garrick deflect the physician's disfavor. Instead, she conducted her own diagnosis, listening to Woodwind's labored breathing, putting her ear to his back to hear his weak heartbeat, then examining the bruises and lacerations on his face and shoulders with a clinical eye. Silently, Brenna bowed her head, praying earnestly until she felt power surging through her flesh and tingling in her lips.

"This is no place for superstition," the doctor spat. "I will not have this . . . this . . . bathycolpian wood nymph witch disrupting the care of my patients!"

Garrick staunchly defended Brenna with confidence that belied his youth. "How can you say that if you've never seen what she can do? Besides, you told Corporal Fanselars that you think the man will be dead before the day is done. What does it hurt if she takes care of him?"

One of Woodwind's lungs had collapsed. Brenna suspected that his blood volume had declined dangerously and worried that her friend had suffered massive internal bleeding. The fever – a natural response to infection that often resulted from bullet trauma – seemed out of control, and if Woodwind's body didn't cool down soon, he'd likely develop brain damage.

Dr. Meine demanded that Garrick leave with the young woman immediately. She threatened to call the guard if they didn't comply.

He produced the order from Colonel Brandt, which the irritated Tamarian woman read with increasing impatience. "The colonel is not a medical professional," she complained. "He doesn't understand the implications . . . ."

Brenna's worry for Woodwind soon overwhelmed her fear of conflict with strangers. Angrily, she stopped the escalating argument. "My friend is dying! I need a basin, new dressings and cold, wet towels right now!" she commanded, *believing* she would be obeyed.

Dr. Meine stopped in mid-sentence, called a nurse and ordered the requested supplies. Strangely unable to control her own will at that moment, the Tamarian physician watched as the raven-haired foreigner cut Woodwind's bandages with her hyper-sharp boot knife.

"Did you remove the bullet?" Brenna inquired, examining the crusted, blackened entry hole.

"Yes. It had flattened, but didn't fragment and came out easily. I cauterized the wound to prevent infection and blood loss."

Brenna shook her head in despair at such ignorance. "Injuries like this heal better if you stick to pressure dressings and ice. Cauterizing bullet wounds only increases tissue trauma." She continued discussing battlefield medicine with Dr. Meine as if the Tamarian woman had treated her as a kindly colleague with whom she might casually debate the proper care regimen for a hypothetical patient. Without a sideways glance, Brenna pulled her hair back and bent down to kiss Woodwind's injured shoulder.

Garrick watched wonder and fear evolve on Dr. Meine's face. Wherever Brenna's lips touched Woodwind's injuries, inflamed flesh instantly lost its swollen redness. Small cuts vanished as she kissed damaged skin. His misshapen shoulder melded into place at her touch. Woodwind's torn rotator cuff would take more time to heal, but the immediate change in his wounds astonished and terrified the curious Tamarian care givers.

"Can you please hold him down for me?" Brenna asked. "He'll cough violently when I pull the fluid from his lung, and he'll keep coughing until everything's out."

Garrick, Dr. Meine and a nurse positioned themselves around the prone southerner, then rolled him onto his side. Brenna held a metal basin in her left hand, healed all the damage to Woodwind's bruised, swollen face, then closed his nostrils and gently placed her lips over his mouth.

Garrick tensed insecurely. Something inside him did not want the young woman kissing any lips aside from his own, even though he realized that this was not the same kind of kiss she had given him while they rode on the wagon. He watched nervously, trying to control irrational jealousy as Brenna took in a deep breath and slowly blew it into Woodwind's mouth.

The southerner jolted as if struck by lightning, his youthful strength rippling through every muscle. Brenna backed away, holding the basin up to Woodwind's lips as he coughed and spat out a bloody, yellowish, foul-smelling fluid. The sticky liquid splashed all over Brenna's hands, arms and sweater, inspiring the nearest thing to a curse Garrick had ever heard from her.

"Possum slop!" she moaned, appraising herself.

Woodwind cleared his throat and quieted. The Lithian woman sighed, frowned, and after washing her hands, began mopping his mouth with a wet towel, her hands moving gently, even lovingly as she worked.

"You're a foreign witch! This is the work of demons!" the physician exclaimed.

Brenna stiffened and glared at the doctor. "Don't call the light darkness," she replied sternly, her eyes gleaming. "I have no power of my own, and Allfather is not evil."

Dr. Meine, intimidated by Brenna's forceful response, averted her gaze. The doctor's hands trembled. Her lips tightened. In her years of medical practice, she'd never witnessed healing power like this. Its shock and impact etched into her memory, shaking her entire belief system to its core, leaving a profound and lingering impact.

Garrick smiled in triumph at Brenna's vindication. He knew about her medical qualifications, but her healing skill defied logic. He'd theorized that a yet unknown natural process explained everything, as it made no sense that this deity of her imagination could impact the material realm.

In his mind, her mysterious healing skill served as another indicator of Brenna's good character. However, he couldn't deny the strange power flowing through the young woman, nor could he rationalize it beyond his theorizing. Of all the experiences in life he didn't fully understand, this ability of hers ranked as the most unsettling example.

Distressed by the mess on her garments, Brenna asked the nurse to keep Woodwind's skin cool with damp towels until she could clean her clothing and return.

"Dextrose and saline drips will speed his recovery," the Lithian woman stated, wiping her hands with a towel.

Dr. Meine held on to Brenna's arm before she departed. "I owe you an apology," she began awkwardly, "At first, I presumed you were a stupid little tart who ran naked through the forest looking for sex. I'm ashamed of how wrongly I misjudged you, and I'm sorry."

Why would this woman think such a wicked thing? Yet Brenna's heart softened, acknowledging the doctor's maturity and courage with a brief, "I forgive you."

When Dr. Meine returned to her other patients, Brenna finished cleaning the worst of the mess from her sweater, whispered something in Woodwind's ear, and afterward let Garrick lead her out of the infirmary. "The stink on these clothes is unbearable," she remarked.

"Let's get you something less form-fitting to wear," he suggested, somewhat nervously. "The way you look in that sweater works for me, but other people get the wrong idea when they see you."

The cadet asked the lecherous infirmary guard for directions, then took Brenna upstairs. He wanted to talk, but didn't know how to broach the subject.

Brenna sensed his restlessness. "Are you upset at me for what happened in there?"

He shook his head. "No. That was impressive. There's just something I have to tell you that I don't want to say."

Brenna tensed, expecting an argument, her imploring eyes expressing sadness. "Is it about Woodwind?"

"It ain't," Garrick affirmed. "I'm happy that you saved him, and judging from all the social tension in there, I suspect you'll need that doctor on your side." He hedged, struggling to avoid blurting out words he shouldn't say. "I have to leave, Brenna. Colonel Brandt gave me new orders."

The young woman stopped in shock. As she paused in the midst of the hall, the outstretched fingers of a passing soldier found a soft spot on her backside where his hand wasn't welcome. She slapped it away with a speed, strength and dexterity that drew lecherous, mocking laughter from one of his companions.

Garrick exchanged harsh words in Tamarian with the soldier, who shrugged and replied in vulgate, "Yeah, like your little slut is good for anything else."

Pulling her companion away from the escalating conflict, not wanting Garrick to fight over such stupidity, Brenna's irritation at the rude behavior quickly faded as worry washed across her face. "Where are you going?"

Garrick picked up his pace to avoid more unwelcome attention. "I can't say," he replied quietly. "If I could tell anyone, you'd be the first to know."

"You don't have to tell me anything," she responded. "Just take me with you. I don't care where it is, as long as I can stay in your company."

His gaze remained locked on hers, with admiration constrained by growing devotion he still lacked the courage to express. The young soldier dismissed the daydream that sprung to mind with a shake of his head. "I'd love that, but I can't. I have orders, and I have to do this alone."

"Garrick," she responded, her desperation rising. "Please don't leave me here by myself. I can't even walk down a hallway smothered to my neck like a widow without some lewd soldier trying to fondle me. I don't feel safe."

The Tamarian cadet sighed in frustration. "Are we speaking the same language? You told me early this morning that you're afraid of losing control when you're alone with me, but now you want me to sneak you out into the wild land where we won't meet another soul for days? I don't get it! Besides, wouldn't you be better off staying here with Woodwind? Isn't he supposed to be protecting you?"

"That's not it," she replied, annoyed. "You're oversimplifying the issue. From what I've seen, I fight far better than you do, but I don't understand your culture. I don't speak your language. I don't know why people stare at me. I don't know anyone else around here, and other than you, nobody seems interested in respecting me.

"You've proven your integrity, and being left behind will be much worse for me than being alone with you. Besides, what if you get hurt? Who's going to help you?"

Garrick, a little stunned by Brenna's testimony, found her blend of worry and anger compelling. "I don't deny you have legitimate concerns, but do you honestly think that I want you less than anyone else around here?"

The Lithian woman dropped his hand. "What I think is that love is a choice, not a knee-jerk reaction to what you desire. I know about masculine arousal. I've seen and felt yours several times, but you don't salivate and try to paw my soft parts like I'm a cheap whore whenever you look at me." Brenna's brow narrowed and her eyes burned angrily.

"You'd have me risk a court martial over this?"

"No," she sighed in resignation. "Do what you must. Just don't ask me to be happy about it."

Garrick toyed with the idea of taking Brenna with him, but that would contravene his mission. If anything went wrong with Brenna in his company, she'd share in whatever punishment he'd be certain to face. "There's no getting around this," he said, weakly. "I'm a soldier. I have orders. I obey them. The future of my nation is at stake."

Brenna took his hand again and held it tighter than before. "You really are a warrior, Garrick. Your people should be proud of you." She looked down, suppressing the anxiety that had ripped a ragged edge across her voice and continued walking with him in moody silence.

They arrived at the commissary, a cavernous room where stored supplies stacked on metal shelves reached for the ceiling. There, an attractive, blonde-haired female clerk in a red beret seemed far more eager to assist Garrick than Brenna found appropriate under the circumstances. The other woman smiled as Brenna glared at her, then sauntered seductively toward a filing cabinet in an adjoining room with his papers in hand.

"How soon before Woodwind can travel?" Garrick asked, apparently changing the subject.

"That depends on how fast he can fight the infection," Brenna replied. "It might be as early as tomorrow; it might be a month from now. The timing is in Allfather's hands. Why do you ask?"

"Colonel Brandt wants to evacuate the two of you with the civilians when they go north. It's likely that you'll be safer there than here."

Brenna felt helpless. "Evacuate? What happens if Woodwind hasn't recovered? I feel obligated to stay here and care for him."

Garrick shrugged. "In Tamaria, we generally don't compel people to do anything against their will, but military necessity demands that civilians move to safety before we conduct combat operations. From what you and Woodwind say about the size of this invading army, it's going to get ugly in a hurry."

"Where will they send us?" Brenna asked, annoyed that a swordsman of Woodwind's caliber and she, a warlord's daughter who'd fought against the Azgar in full view of the locals, would need anyone's protection.

"Burning Tree to start," he replied. "We have a big army base on the lakeshore, but then likely to Marvic, our capital city. It's the most secure place in the country, and we have regular, all-season rail service running up there."

Brenna crossed her arms and scowled when the clerk returned with Garrick's papers, her mild aggravation blending with envy as the other woman continued her flirting. Stricken by uncertainty and her desperate fear of strangers, Brenna smoldered with many frustrations.

Garrick's grey eyes expressed sympathy. He slid his hand around her back and patted her shoulder affectionately, hoping that no one else noticed. Brenna's countenance and body language revealed enough distress to inspire his empathy, but in the presence of the clerk, who smiled coquettishly, he kept his counsel to himself.

Several socially uncomfortable minutes and a few silver coins later, the flirting commissary clerk stacked two packages labeled, *Medical / Female / Petite* on the counter. To these, she added broadhead arrows measured to Brenna's draw length and several items Garrick requested for himself, including a compass, camera, field lens, light sticks, rations, flint and a tin cookstove for preparing food.

"I asked Colonel Brandt to authorize you for work in the infirmary until you have to leave," Garrick told Brenna. "I'll give the orders to you before I go. I wish I could do more, but this is the best I can offer."

The young couple left the commissary and returned to her upstairs room. Behind the shut door, Brenna permitted a lingering kiss and didn't stop the young man's hands from wandering down her back with rising urgency.

Although she longed for the wonder his touch inspired, the Lithian maiden felt self-conscious about the stink on her sweater and wanted to change. Wistfully, he let her go, noting the desire in her dilated eyes as he turned away to watch the impending rocket launch.

Brenna distracted herself by opening the garment packages with the ordinary interest of a young woman trying on a new outfit. She innocently began to change, not intending to test Garrick's honor, but doing so anyway.

"When do you have to leave?" she asked, drawing his attention away from the rocket assembly as she slipped out of her skirt.

He watched her shed the soiled sweater in silent disbelief. Brenna paused, standing in her filmy Lithian camisole, waiting for him to respond. While Garrick had seen her wearing this garment when they first met, he couldn't believe how she trusted him at a moment when he wanted her badly and didn't feel particularly trustworthy.

The young soldier had always been careful not to stare, but she looked so lovely, even though the fabric of her maiden blouse revealed far less of her now than it had when freeze-dried to her form. Garrick turned away, tempering the passion that surged through his flesh. In a very short time Brenna had risen to a place of significant honor in his life. He restrained his longing for her sake, verifying, in a moment where a less worthy suitor would have proven weak, the true mettle of the young man's character.

Brenna recalled Warrant Officer Rand's reaction when she'd stood outside the shower, and realized she'd just committed another social blunder. Like Woodwind, the Lithian maiden didn't consider the ordinary act of discarding apparel concupiscent, but observing Garrick's widened eyes and quick turning away, realized that he and the other Tamarians thought it so. Not knowing what to say, she continued dressing as if she'd done nothing wrong.

Below, the launch tower now sported a pair of large rockets, their sleek, dark forms already aimed into the heart of the sky. Two more awaited final assembly and fueling on a cart several paces away. "We need to eat, and then I have to go," he responded, finally answering her question.

Brenna pulled another chair to the window. "My heart and my prayers will be with you," she soothed.

"I'd like to see them launch the rocket from here before we head to the mess hall," he said. "Do you mind?"

"You can stay as long as you like," she replied. Her tone whispered an invitation, a hope that he would linger.

Garrick watched a soldier secure battery cables to the breakoff leads and flip a switch, activating motors that spun the rockets' oxidizer and ethanol fuel pumps. A high-pitched whine aspired from the courtyard, the final warning for all personnel to take cover.

The young woman leaned across Garrick's back, her strong, sculpted arms encircling his broad shoulders, her hands caressing his chest. Her thick hair draped like a silken scarf over his neck that slid smoothly as her lips found a bit of exposed skin to kiss. Her body felt soft, and her strength reassuring.

Sounds of fury resonated throughout the courtyard as the oxidizer reacted violently with the ethanol / water mix in the rocket engines, producing a progressively brighter blue flame at their bases. With an intense burst of white-hot light and an ear-numbing scream, one of the rockets leaped into the overcast heavens, rattling windows in its fleet, ecstatic flight.

Before human senses could recover, the second joined its mate in shrieking toward the distant Saradon, etching forever upon the mind of an awe-stuck Lithian maiden the sensational memory of its brief and brilliant birth, and leaving behind a lingering, pillared pair of grey clouds in the stormy sky.

Sudden Death

Struggling to stay alert in the overcast darkness before dawn, Lieutenant Hicks and I watched the bright torches of deathwolf handlers approaching from the east. We shivered inside the shattered remains of a Tamarian watchtower, comparing predictions of our next assignment against the staccato, background clatter of awakened soldiers coughing. Living in close quarters spread tuberculosis and pneumonia rapidly among those of us not previously exposed to illness, and this, coupled with the extreme cold we'd experienced in the high altitude this far north, heightened our susceptibility to sickness.

The lieutenant yawned, rubbing frostbitten fingers that our gauntlets could not protect from the cold, complaining more effectively about his discomfort with body language than any words he expressed. Our half-hour march from Dieter managed to draw sweat from our frozen pores, but the warmth didn't last long.

"How can we be sure the giants will muster as promised?" he inquired. "I worry that we'll have to retreat if the barbarians put up much of a fight. The men are grousing that we've gone too far."

I shrugged, struggling to contain my true feelings. "I'd rather die in battle than freeze to death!"

Distant, finger-like vapor clouds trailing bright lights fell through the frigid sky from the west, growing larger as the seconds passed. Given their soundless approach, I felt the dread of being targeted by incoming artillery.

Suddenly, we realized our lives were in danger and we dove to the floor. At the last moment I heard a shrieking overhead that chilled my soul, arcing rapidly eastward as the moments passed. My face contacted cold stone and I laced my hands over the back of my head for protection.

A huge explosion shattered the early morning air, followed by a tremendous concussion that shook the ground, jolting rafters already weakened by mortar impacts. Debris rained painfully on my shoulders. Silence washed mercifully over my deafened ears and I heard nothing more for a long time. Choking in the suffocating dust, my back throbbing from welts and bruises, I called in vain for Lieutenant Hicks.

One of the massive, pine joists lay across his back while his legs had been buried in debris from the roof. I tried to move the timber, but slipped on a dark slick near the young lieutenant's head, falling to my hands and knees amid a spreading pool of blood. Then I noticed the unnatural twist to his neck and his flattened skull, crushed by the very beam I'd been trying to relocate. Lieutenant Hicks would never draw breath again.

Overcome with nausea, I retched violently. With bile stinging my throat and my teeth etched with stomach acid, I scrambled down the ladder in disoriented haste, not knowing what to do.

Other men ran hither and thither. I witnessed wide-eyed terror in their expressions, saw their lips moving, but I could hear nothing other than a strange, hollow echo in my ears. The moment seemed surreal, filled with images and sensations so removed from the normal reality of my military experience, it felt like a nightmare.

My perceptions, heightened by strong emotion, absorbed every detail. I watched as another fiery, cylindrical shape plunged into the upper floor of the Ice Dragon Inn. A brilliant burst of light flashed through every portal, followed by a multi-hued shower of erupting glass and belches of black smoke. The ensuing concussion toppled graceful stone buttresses in tandem, and with them whole sections of slate-shingled roof collapsed.

The destruction astounded me!

Dead men littered the courtyard. Others, maimed by the blast and its fiery aftermath lay in pathetic, twisted heaps, their burned faces distorted in agony. I began moving them away from the wall and building, mercifully unable to hear their cries of pain.

A long delay ensued before our medics arrived. During that interval, several men helped me gather up the bodies of our dead in preparation for burial. Working together, we dislodged the remains of Lieutenant Hicks by dismantling the ruined watchtower.

Untrained in medical care, the only thing I could do was to make the injured as comfortable as possible. A nameless centurion died as I watched. He'd been muttering for a woman repeatedly, and though I could not hear his words, the motion of his lips and tongue formed the name *Bella* as clearly to my mind as if he'd shouted the syllables in my ear.

Two or three hours passed before I could hear anything clearly. At an emergency officer's meeting, held in the cramped confines of what we called the powerhouse building – the only one that remained undamaged – I learned that similar rocket attacks had been hurled against our sprawling camp for most of the night. This explained why the medical staff had been so slow to respond to the strike on the inn. My ignorance of this development, along with the losses we incurred went unnoticed, for when queried, my account of the most recent attack proved sufficiently vivid to deflect any suspicion regarding my whereabouts during the evening.

We argued while waiting for the senior commanders to arrive. One group wanted to withdraw until we could fully consolidate our supply lines and rearm. These men did not speak as cowards. Their counsel, realistic and prudent, couldn't overcome the persistent, majority belief in our cultural superiority that defied their better judgment.

Others argued for immediate retaliation in the hope that our guns could silence the enemy's terror from the sky. Many officers insisted we would enjoy better odds of success if we acted immediately and attacked with overwhelming force before the barbarians could mobilize and reinforce their defenses. I stood among them.

Confusion reigned within the officer corps. We'd been surprised and frightened by the firepower hurled against us. Fear fueled outbursts of insult and invective usually reserved for the ears of the enlisted.

All clamor ceased, however, the moment Lord Balinor entered the room. His presence commanded our attention. Every eye fixated on a man who appraised us with a mixture of pride and patronage, much like a doting uncle might lavish on a favored nephew. Lord Balinor strode to a table, motioned for a map and spread it out for us to see.

"We will respond to these attacks in kind," he began. "Combined Arms Units numbered seventeen to thirty will march northwest before turning south at Kicking Horse Gap, the nexus of the Saradon and Broken Wing Valley. These units will crush enemy opposition in the northern Dead Hand and Copperhead Ridge formations.

"Combined Arms Units numbered one through sixteen will prepare fortified positions on reverse slopes in the Dead Hand formation as directed by their commanders.

"Units thirty-one to eighty will constitute the main assault body at the appropriate time. These forces will bivouac on the steppe as a reserve until battle preparations are complete. From there, we will drive westward, overwhelm the enemy army and secure our objective at Burning Tree.

"Your vice-generals will explain the details and individual unit assignments. That is all, gentlemen." Lord General Balinor arose to a unison chorus of salutes, then strode through the door without looking back.

My century belonged to Combined Arms Unit Seventeen, part of the group charged with an encirclement maneuver in the hills to the northwest. When Vice-general Diabilos outlined the orders, I objected, explaining that my mortar crew could begin pounding the enemy right away. "Can we be reassigned? My men have completed short range artillery surveys for Dead Hand Ridge and I can have shells falling on that fortification before nightfall."

What I didn't say, was that the rest of my century was comfortably quartered, apparently beyond rocket range. I had no interest in moving them. Also, Lieutenant Hicks had hidden our Tamarian prisoner in a small, basement room. If anyone discovered her, I believed she'd suffer more of the same brutality that had so enraged me after we had captured the inn. At some point – after interrogation – I thought she'd serve as a hostage to exchange with the enemy, but I couldn't protect her while marching around in the deplorable cold.

Vocalizing a desire to attack right away screened all suspicion about my motives. Nonetheless, I felt impotent, angry enough to take the vice-general to task over the issue of delaying immediate retaliation by moving north.

Legate Braegan, fighting off the effects of yet another hangover, dismissed my argument. "Shut your mouth, Herulus," he spat, making an example of me in front of the nine other centurions he commanded. "You're running on the ragged edge of a court-martial with that kind of talk. Take your orders and do what you're told."

Outside, I cursed the cold smudge outlining the feeble Daystar, hidden shamefully behind thick clouds. I cursed the accursed rockets, then, once beyond earshot of the powerhouse building, savored several linguistically complex expletives for two particular members of the senior officers' corps, whose callous unwillingness to listen would result in casualties they cared nothing to prevent.

Knowing that my men could have pounded that Tamarian fortress with mortar fire until our bigger guns came forward made me even angrier. This, coupled with a sense of social humiliation, hardened my resolve to somehow regain control over my own destiny.

The half-hour walk to Dieter took me five minutes less than it should have. Once there, I sent a messenger on horseback to the mortar unit, ordering them to pack up immediately and move north to a rendezvous point at the north end of Dead Hand Ridge, roughly forty-five miles from their present location.

Lieutenant Rangell did not express dismay when I ordered him to replace Hicks as squad commander, overseeing Sergeants Hanibal and Vitus, in addition to the burden of combat engineering he was currently and so capably fulfilling.

Even though my unit had been designated a century, it did not consist of 100 men. With the development of cannon and mortars, most Azgar infantry units in private armies like ours incorporated specialists trained in the use of such weapons, as well as the traditional number of foot soldiers, medics and a small contingent of engineers.

At full strength my command included 100 infantry, five sergeants, four lieutenants, twenty gunners, two engineers and three medics, a total of 135 soldiers. The designation preserved an organizational structure dating back nearly a thousand years, long before the widespread use of gunpowder.

In the months since my promotion to centurion, I'd never had a complete century to command. Of the three combat disciplines allocated to me, the gunners were most frequently reassigned. During the infrequent periods when my personnel requests were approved, I never received more than ten of the twenty artillery soldiers typically assigned to a unit like mine.

Until now, this hadn't mattered. Our rifles and steel armor were more than a match for flintlocks and muskets fired by teeming masses of undisciplined hordes. My experience fighting against these northern barbarians revealed that our current threat differed significantly. I'd become convinced that we needed to engage with our heaviest weapons and fight bravely to defeat them.

My unit left Dieter with a full complement of infantry, thanks to the addition of the detestable Sergeant Hanibal and his rabble from Arama, but we still needed a lieutenant and twelve gunners. Each of us carried sixty-five pounds of kit, including food, ammunition, and camping gear, a burden that soon had us sweating despite the cold. We marched through frozen grassland for two days, skirting the rugged, eastern edge of the tree-crowned Dead Hand Ridge formation, camping in the open beneath the grey sky.

In the distance, heavy snow crept beneath the lingering cloud mantle that enveloped mountainous ridge lines known locally as the Copperhead Range. Hoar frost coated evergreens, the leafless oak and poplar on the rocky hillsides, demarcating an elevation line where winter already held sway, and the region beneath, still under the less severe authority of autumn.

Signs of civilization appeared in the early morning of the second day. Abandoned farmhouses dotted the landscape between intersecting dirt roads. We tramped through hay stubble turning west near Sutherlind, a town world famous for its annual apple festival.

My unit reached the rendezvous point by noon, well before the cavalry arrived. The men felt tired and sullen from our long march. Their constant complaining about hardship irritated me. Disquieted by our surroundings, I felt ill-at-ease, sensing the barbarians were watching from the hills as we set up a temporary camp in the shadows of the ridge line.

Later that afternoon, Centurion Cavelli, a scout troop commander, approached with his mounted soldiers. He asked where Legate Braegan had set up his command center. Knowing Braegan's penchant for arriving after hostilities had commenced, I informed Cavelli, within earshot of the other centurions under his command, that I was willing to assume leadership of the maniple and coordinate infantry support until the legate arrived. But I also made it clear that I intended to wait until artillery and infantry support arrived before advancing.

"We passed half a dozen centuries about a mile back," the deep-voiced centurion said. "The rest of your infantry maniple is two or three miles behind them. Since you're senior centurion, I'll report to you as soon as we make contact with the enemy."

Generally, relations between infantry and cavalry remained cordial and we coordinated operations well. Yet Cavelli seemed eager to engage the enemy, probably thinking – as I had previously – that his troops would easily overrun any resistance.

Evidence of evacuated civilians hinted that the Tamarians knew we were operating in the area. My combat experience prevailed against bravado, and I counseled caution. "It will take less than an hour for support to arrive. You should wait until then before moving off."

Cavelli paid no attention to my advice. In fact, he treated me as though I'd actually agreed with him. "Very well," he replied. "I'll send word to you when we encounter the barbarians."

My subsequent protests were articulated to the hind-end of a horse. I heard the Arama boys snicker at my impotence, as Cavelli and his equestrian troops trotted westward in double file, their carbines held outward from their hips, a pair of black and red battle banners snapping smartly northward at the head of their advancing column.

The wind had just begun to pick up again, and with it came tiny flakes of snow. I'd never seen falling snow before and wanted to savor the moment, but command responsibilities distracted me.

As additional infantry and light artillery arrived, I ordered their units formed up in standard maniple configuration: a checkerboard arrangement two rows deep and twenty-five men wide, with light cannon and mortars set in every other square. I placed five gunnery crews on each flank, with two centuries of infantry held in reserve to reinforce where necessary.

Before we'd finished setting up our deployment, the sound of gunfire and small explosions echoed through a narrow canyon to our southwest. I told the men to leave their camp gear, load weapons and prepare to support the cavalry. As was standard practice in field deployments, I ordered a modest contingent to guard our equipment and prevent theft, hoping that any engagement we encountered would be small enough for a single maniple to handle.

Suddenly, the surrounding hills erupted with rifle and rocket fire. Bright flashes of light peppered the ridge line and steamy contrails crisscrossed through the cold sky until the collective fog of their vapor trails obscured the enemy positions. Whenever the wind momentarily swept the air clear, hundreds of additional rounds screamed from the ridge line, their exhaust blotting out my view.

Endless bullet impacts and explosions rippled through our startled ranks. Arrayed on the fringe of the Saradon, we stood without cover, barely within range of our guns, could not see the enemy and did not know where our cavalry troops had gone. Most of us had never seen such heavy fire. The coordination between enemy units spread for several hundred yards along the hills shocked our soldiers and astounded proud officers under my command who'd not expected these angry barbarians to put up such a fight.

The air thickened with lead, hot shards of razor-sharp shrapnel, the blinding radiance of detonating artillery shells, the stench of burning flesh and the terrified cries of afflicted men. Though the roar of their cannon tubes echoed across the plain, their rockets inspired sheer terror. These were larger than those my unit faced at the Ice Dragon Inn, and their noise was nothing like we'd ever heard. Every launch sounded like ripping glass, and as waves of their warheads burst through our formations, entire squadrons vanished in roiling vapor. Fearing for my life, yet feeling strangely in control of the moment – despite the chaos swirling around me – I screamed orders above the din.

I saw nothing valorous in the enemy's conduct. Theirs was an industrial approach to war, a massive expenditure of ordnance that hurled naked fury at us in unending waves. The uncaring brutality of it felt shocking.

Thankfully, my centurions kept their heads cool and prevented the infantry from discharging weapons prematurely. Our cannon and mortars erupted in response, pounding the hillsides with the same fury their high-explosive shells had once wielded against the stone walls of Shirak. Tall conifers trembled and shattered beneath their thunder, a foretaste of the punishment wrought by bigger guns yet to be brought into battle.

I ordered the men forward at quick pace, trying to get them on the hill and among the trees where they could return fire and suffer less from the weight of enemy attack. That aggressive move likely prevented disaster. I believed that once we wrested control of the hilltop from the barbarians, we'd command a prominent piece of high ground, allowing us to protect the additional troops scheduled to arrive by nightfall. This was my first attempt at large scale leadership, and the last fully coordinated movement my maniple made before the battle disintegrated into confusion.

We advanced despite heavy losses. Many brave men fell, their blood staining white snow like spilled wine on a wedding dress. I spread out my troops to reduce the effectiveness of enemy fire, but the smoke and noise prevented many other centurions from following my lead. Some unit commanders sent reports claiming thirty to forty percent casualties before we covered the hundred-odd yards to the base of the foothills.

By the time we were in range to return fire, my front ranks looked ragged. They released their first volley and stopped to reload while the second line moved ahead, but our trapdoor rifles seemed pitiful once their machine cannon opened up and we faced an endless, deadly rain of death dumped on our heads from above.

A messenger from Centurion Vivanus, operating on my right flank, found me when my unit reached the snow-skirted base of the foothill ridge. "Our cannon is breaking them, sir. The centurion says the enemy troops above our position have started moving their artillery further south. The barbarians are shooting at us with only rifles and machine cannon now."

"Pass the word down the line," I ordered. "Tell the others to push straight ahead. My boys will join up with your unit and we'll push the enemy off the top of this hill."

"Yes sir!"

The young soldier dashed off to my left while I grabbed a private from the last rank of my own century. "Go back and tell the mortar and cannon teams to hit this northern section hard for five minutes."

I ordered Lieutenants Rangell and Pellas, the officers in my own century, to start moving their men uphill as soon as the artillery bombardment ceased. "Once you get into the trees, file the soldiers to the right until you meet up with Vivanus and his troops, then wheel left. Make it work and we'll make 'em run!"

My idea was to wrap around the retreating enemy from the flank while pressuring them head on with the remains of my maniple on the left. If successful, the barbarians would be caught in a cross-fire with only further retreat south as a means of escape.

Smoke shells from the mortar teams signaled the end of the artillery barrage. Racing uphill against a torrent of machine cannon and rifle fire, fighting deep mounds of loose gravel covered in slippery snow, we met up with men from Lieutenant Mariden's unit and pushed forward with them. I never saw Vivanus, but Lieutenant Mariden told me that he was making progress on the far, right flank.

Resistance stiffened. We encountered prepared kill zones featuring their infernal machine cannon. Their soldiers, protected behind barricades of fallen timber set at right angles to our advance, fired at us with impunity. They made us pay a very high price for every inch of ground. Only raw courage, grenades and the sheer weight of our superior numbers kept the battle moving forward.

I watched Sergeant Hanibal live up to his reputation for fearlessness as he dashed through a hailstorm of rifle rounds and crouched at the base of a derelict, ponderosa pine. The boys from Arama followed him, though nearly half of their number didn't survive the merciless fire. As soon as my men had moved into position, I gave the order to charge across open ground. My words sent many fine men to their deaths as a swarm of black uniformed soldiers surged uphill, their voices raised in an angry chorus.

The barbarians refused retreat and would not surrender. I saw glistening bayonets arc forward, resting upon the barricades in deadly, defensive bristles, their steel tips reddened as brave, Azgar warriors tried climbing over the obstacles. The bodies of fallen soldiers soon piled up so high, the men who followed climbed on the dead, stood and fired their guns into the enemy at point blank range.

This horrible scene inspired nightmares for months afterward. The fighting denigrated into a wild fray of hand-to-hand combat. Brutal, violent deeds were exchanged between men who'd never before met, between men who might have shared a beer and traded dirty jokes, had their encounters occurred under different circumstances.

Of course, I'd been in combat before. The difference this time was that I felt struck by the senselessness of our attack. These barbarians defended their homeland against our intrusion with tenacity, while we aggressively fought against them, trying to deny these men sovereignty over their own land.

Why?

I was only following orders, but what man had the right to decide that other men should die this way? By whose authority had death in a foreign land on this scale been decreed? In the midst of battle I thought about this and realized that our men were following *my* orders . . . .

My responsibility for the carnage occurring on this isolated hilltop hit me hard and made me pause. Could I have somehow prevented this from happening? What recourse did I have? Disobeying a direct order from a senior officer would earn me a date with a firing squad, but my refusal to disobey what now appeared to be an immoral command was responsible for an even greater loss of life.

But my men successfully breached the barbarian barricade and swarmed forward, their shouts of triumph aspiring above the crackling din of carbine fire.

Just then, Private Willancus knocked me to the cold, hard ground. "Get down, sir!" he screamed.

A volley of enemy rocket warheads slammed into my immediate vicinity. I felt hot shrapnel pelt my neck and heard it ping off my helmet. The private shuddered, then moaned as he fell across my chest. Willancus had bravely sustained the damage intended for me.

I squirmed from beneath his body, shocked by the grisly mass of bloody flesh that had once been his back. His eyes were frozen in terror, and despite my best effort, I could not find a pulse in his neck. I screamed for a medic, partly in rage and partly in fear for having so narrowly escaped sudden death.

Junior Scout Garrick Ravenwood, Tamarian Defense Force;
Brenna Velez; Woodwind

Unspoken Secrets

Sullen masses of thick, dark cloud settled oppressively between the steep, parallel ridge lines that bordered the Broken Wing Valley. Harsh wind screamed beneath the overcast canopy, painfully driving dry lumps of snow into Garrick's squinting eyes. Riding on muleback, he battled forward against the storm, his determination taxed, but not overcome.

Remembering Brenna's teary farewell, her soft lips kissing his own, and her belief in his promise to reunite after she'd evacuated soothed away insecurity that had long tormented his soul. Garrick meditated on many comforting memories of her. Yet knowing that the fate of his nation lay in his ability to reach Burning Tree before the Azgar advanced too far to be stopped, he urged the mule onward.

Crossing windswept pastureland on the valley floor, reckoning his path from memory to make the distance as short as possible, Garrick skirted Sharp Talon Ridge. This formation – the remnant of a huge, ancient moraine – had blocked a more recent lava flow. Over the centuries, volcanic ash and windblown loess built up to form a thick bed of fertile soil in which apple, pear and cherry trees flourished. Hot, dry summers that featured long daylight hours encouraged fruit trees to yield abundant harvests that enriched the fortunate families owning property here.

Farmers who lived further north dealt with thinner soil and colder temperatures at higher elevations, which shortened their growing season. Cyrus Ravenwood, Garrick's father, always cursed Sharp Talon Ridge on his annual, autumn journey to a famous apple festival held in a town called Sutherlind on the Saradon. There, farmers from all over Tamaria, and the Peran Confederation marketed produce to buyers from as far south as Marioch.

Cyrus Ravenwood's fruit fared poorly against the lovely, delicious varieties from Sharp Talon Ridge because his trees were not as strong and his trip to market took longer, resulting in lower quality fruit from early picking and bruising from a rough ride south. Even in a good year, the Ravenwood crop barely earned enough to sustain the family for a single season.

Soon after Garrick turned ten, his father decided to juice and ferment part of his harvest. This, he reasoned, would make it easier to transport. The cider sold well, earning Cyrus Ravenwood more money than he'd made in the previous three seasons, but he didn't manage his sudden prosperity well, and the wealth didn't last through the ensuing winter.

Facing marital problems and determined to get rich quickly, Cyrus fermented every apple from his orchard the following season. But other farmers, including those from Sharp Talon Ridge, brought their own cider to the apple festival that autumn, significantly reducing its price.

Cyrus returned home with a lot of unsold product, and barely enough money to survive the winter. Depressed, he began drinking too much and soon became a stranger to the children who loved him. In that year, an affectionate father fell into the abyss of violence and a reign of terror prevailed in his household. In that year, his wife and three children learned the meaning of fear.

Sylvia Ravenwood shielded her daughter and eldest son from the rage erupting more frequently from her husband, but their relationship had been precarious from its outset, and her marital indiscretions worsened the situation. Cyrus despised her pleading, and her shed tears increased his anger. Rejected by her lovers and unable to change a domestic dynamic that already suffered many strains, Sylvia wore disgrace like a fading garment and retreated into the traditional Tamarian religion for comfort.

Household management declined. Floors and windows went unwashed. Garments remained un-mended and flower beds that had once graced the vegetable garden grew wild with weeds. Neighbors discussed the Ravenwoods in whispers, with heads shaking.

Garrick assumed increasing responsibility in the orchard. He pruned his father's trees, chased away birds, thinned every heavily laden branch to avoid breakage and carried water upon his own broad shoulders to keep the trees alive in the heat of summer. In payment for his labor, he received scorn, ridicule and a collection of bruises and black eyes that inspired so much shame, he created elaborate lies to conceal the truth.

Garrick's younger brother, Algernon, resented the behavior of both parents. Sylvia openly favored Kira, his twin sister, while she loathed Algernon. The boy grew angry, often provoked his father and deplored his mother's many weaknesses. The year before Garrick joined the Junior Scouts, Algernon and Kira conspired to set the alcohol still on fire. In order to protect his younger siblings from their father's wrath, Garrick smuggled the twins onto a northbound train.

After the young Ravenwoods arrived in Marvic, Tamaria's capital city, Garrick pleaded with the leadership at the sacred Temple Elsbireth to adopt and educate his younger siblings. Believing he'd placed them where they would be safe from harm, Garrick returned home to help his father manage the orchard.

When Cyrus heard of his eldest son's deed, he beat Garrick so severely, the young man nearly died and spent more than a month recovering from his injuries. Fearing for her eldest son's life, Sylvia made arrangements with her mother and sent Garrick on a journey to his Great Uncle Werner's ranch on the Saradon, north of Sutherlind, warning him to never return home again.

Life at the ranch, though filled with hard work, had been graced by the presence of Gudrun, a lovely, nubile second cousin whose curiosity about the opposite sex found an object of study in Garrick. The two of them spent a lot of time alone in the hayloft after his arrival, but her interest faded when he grew to expect more from her than she cared to offer.

Garrick wanted, more than anything else, to love unselfishly and be loved in return. In his mind, he associated the physical contact exchanged between he and his cousin with a true, committed love. The young man expected that his devotion be requited in kind, but Gudrun wanted only to experience pleasure, and Garrick was nothing more than a means to an end for her. She began to increasingly despise his affection and sought other lovers, but this only made him want her more fervently.

Annoyed, Gudrun told him that she hated him.

Several months later, however, the teenaged girl became pregnant. When she approached her cousin and begged that he marry her and take responsibility for the child, Garrick found himself torn between love for the young woman who'd awakened his sexuality, and distrust in her sincerity. If she couldn't be faithful to him outside of marriage, how could he believe in her fidelity as a wife?

Knowing of his mother's frequent indiscretions, Garrick refused to comply with her wish. Gudrun told Uncle Werner that Garrick was the father of her unborn child, and enraged by this news – feeling betrayed after he'd trustingly opened his home to relative in need – Uncle Werner sent Garrick off to join the Junior Scouts. "They'll make a man out of you," he'd said.

Those memories and the heartache Garrick felt when he thought about them blurred into the stormy landscape. He didn't like to cry, but there was no one around to laugh at him now and he felt better afterward.

Becoming a Junior Scout solved many problems. The rigorous regimen kept Garrick too busy to think about the circumstances that had sent him to the enlistment center. Training hard gave him a goal to strive toward, his comrades had become a second family, and the honor of defending his country filled him with healthy self-respect. Junior Scout life had a predictable rhythm, and earning money enabled him to regularly support his siblings.

But the Azgar invasion destroyed everything. Stung by the harsh reality of combat, where death shattered the bonds of friendship and failure to defeat the enemy meant slavery for his people, Garrick's idealistic mind wrestled with its belief that justice, in its purest form, should always prevail against evil. His philosophical view raged against an unyielding problem: Who decided what was right and wrong? On whose authority did the definition of justice come into being? If these words existed merely as labels for abstract concepts, then the concepts themselves were subject to the interpretation of human minds and could not be absolute.

This line of reasoning led him to understand that the Azgar probably considered their invasion justifiable, while he and his countrymen viewed the incursion as evil. Garrick had listened to Brenna explain that without an external, universal standard of right and wrong, confrontation between opposing national wills invariably occurred on the business end of a bullet, at the tip of a bayonet or the edge of a sword.

Although he accepted the logic of her claim, Garrick knew enough about history to understand that religious people fought wars, too. He couldn't embrace the existence of a God, finding materialist explanations more compelling. While Brenna's intelligence pleased him, and he found that her mind sharpened his, he wouldn't abandon his worldview just because it didn't easily answer every question.

Sharp Talon Ridge loomed to his left. Garrick stopped to dismount in its wind shadow before leading the mule uphill, concerned that the snowy path through the wild sumac and juniper growing on its flanks might be too slippery to ascend while mounted. He didn't realize he was being watched, nor did he think about the faithful trail of footprints he'd left behind in the falling snow.

***

Brenna trimmed Woodwind's beard with a comb and a straight-edged razor. "You didn't have to be brave to impress me," she said in her native tongue. With swift and confident strokes, she quickly restored Woodwind's characteristically well-groomed appearance.

He smiled wistfully, glancing at Brenna's blood-smeared smock. All the nurses wore the same outfit: a loose-fitting, short-sleeved blouse and baggy pants. While these garments were comfortable, they concealed a woman's figure. Woodwind didn't care what the other nurses looked like; he found the opacity distressing on Brenna. As long as she wore her diaphanous maiden garments, he held some hope that they might reconcile their differences. Looking at her in this outfit, he felt as though she had suddenly married when their relationship had not been given the proper time for closure. And that thought saddened him.

Woodwind's gaze wandered across the room, noting that many beds were now occupied. Half a dozen overworked nurses scurried from patient to patient, attending to their comfort, offering water, checking and changing bandages on soldiers who'd stood bravely against their enemy, only to find courage insufficient to blunt the overwhelming Azgar advance. New casualties arrived through the open doors on the far wall, creating a sudden increase in noise and activity.

Brenna turned when she heard her name called by a nurse across the room. Understanding nothing more the Tamarian woman said to her, Brenna nodded in acknowledgment, knowing she was needed. In a short time, the native care givers abandoned their prejudices. Having grown dependent on her skills, they recognized the Lithian woman's value, and Brenna thrived where her natural benevolence found appreciation. This change enabled her to serve with grace and gratitude. Woodwind had long recognized and appreciated the goodness radiating from her soul. In his mind, Brenna represented an ideal woman, the beautiful personification of feminine virtue that always felt tantalizingly out of reach.

He longed for her now, partly afraid that the morphine he'd been given for pain would allow the secret words to tumble from his lips. Believing that she would never requite his clandestine admiration, Woodwind controlled his yearning, dreaming privately that she might change her mind. "Allfather will bless you for every soul you snatch from the grave in this place."

Brenna raised her eyebrows, removing the bib she'd used to collect his facial hair. "I'm convinced that Allfather brought me here for this reason," she replied. The Lithian woman reached for a warm, wet towel to wipe down his face. "I'm sorry," she continued, "but they need me right now. I'll come back as soon as I can. Meanwhile, get some rest." Brenna squeezed his hand as she stood.

Woodwind nodded, admiring the grace in her stride as she walked away. He'd watched Brenna create her own role in the infirmary with skilled volunteer work. Yet she was more than a mystical healer. Sliding his fingers through his neatly trimmed beard, Woodwind recalled that Brenna had shaven him for years without ever letting the razor cut his flesh. Others, who'd not respected her virtue, or skill with bladed weapons, had not been as fortunate.

The Lithian maiden took in a deep breath to quell her fear of curious Tamarian officers, who'd brought in their wounded and stared at her – ostensibly to verify accounts of her healing skill. She'd resorted to hiding, or trying to look busy until after Dr. Meine finished triage, attending to the most serious cases behind a surgical screen where none of the healthy soldiers could see what she was doing.

Brenna felt no anxiety among the wounded. These men often lay unconscious or in morphine-induced apathy when she ministered to them. Not a single soldier perished under Brenna's watch, though many who might have been saved never survived the journey from the battlefield to benefit from her prayers. To the ongoing astonishment of the medical staff, some of the most critical cases improved dramatically within moments of her intervention. Allfather blessed Brenna and saved many lives through her as the day blended into evening, and evening into night.

The constant arrival of new casualties kept the Lithian woman too busy to eat, take a break, or worry about anything other than the soldiers under her care. Their agony, evident in labored breathing, on dirt-blackened faces, and in glassy eyes that might never again see full use of their extremities moved her heart. As the night wore on, the infirmary filled up and a long line of wounded men wound into the hallway, around corners and into other rooms.

Absorbed in her task, Brenna lost track of time. Many hours later, long after Woodwind had fallen asleep, a private who introduced himself as Darrold Müller found Brenna attending to a dying soldier in the hallway and ordered her to collect her belongings. "The Azgar have taken a lot of ground in battle just north of here. Colonel Brandt wants all civilians evacuated at daybreak, before the enemy gets into artillery range and prevents your escape."

The Lithian woman wiped her sweating forehead on her right sleeve. "When will that be?" she inquired.

"Within the hour," the Tamarian soldier replied.

Brenna shuddered. "I'm working hard here. Is there no way I can stay to help?"

Darrold shrugged, his bloodshot eyes attesting to a serious lack of sleep. "I'm sorry, miss. The colonel sent me to find you in particular. I'm responsible for seeing that you're in that caravan. Those were his orders." The soldier's tone of voice demonstrated unyielding resolve.

The anticipated dread of seeing unfamiliar people in strange surroundings flooded Brenna's heart, as it had when Garrick warned her that this would happen. "Your nurses are already overworked," she responded. "That will worsen if I can't stay. Besides, my friend is too weak to travel and I'll worry myself sick if I can't care for him."

Private Müller shook his head. "It's not my call."

Flustered, but understanding that she could not persuade the soldier to disobey an order, Brenna meekly slid past him and returned to Woodwind's bedside. She awakened her friend with a kiss, then explained the predicament in her native tongue.

Woodwind nodded to Darrold Müller before returning his attention to Brenna. "He's a good man," the southerner replied, clasping her fingers with genuine affection. "Take my sword to defend yourself, and the coins in my pouch to pay for your needs when you go. When this is all over, I'll find you again, as Allfather wills."

Brenna bit her lower lip, genuinely worried that she might never see him again. "I feel like I'm deserting you. If you die here I'll mourn you to my grave!"

Woodwind blinked back a tear, knowing she meant to comfort, not realizing her words had the opposite effect. "I swore to your *Umma* that I'd find and look after you, but in truth, you've always been in Allfather's care. Honor me and your loved ones by staying alive. The Tamarians will protect you. Go with them, my beloved friend."

Brenna sensed that Woodwind had already resigned himself to being left behind, as though he'd expected all along that she would leave him. Trying to assuage her own guilt, Brenna held his hand like she would never let go and prayed until Private Müller urged her to say farewell. The Lithian woman took Woodwind's prized longsword, but left all the money in his pouch, tearfully kissed her friend, then turned away without looking back.

Woodwind sadly watched her go, realizing with great clarity, in spite of the morphine, that their lips would never meet again.

***

Windfall apples, partially hidden beneath snowdrifts and frozen solid until spring, lay in neat piles around the smooth trunks of dormant trees. Most farmers in the Broken Wing Valley fermented and distilled bruised or fallen apples into ethanol to fuel their machines, lights or heat their homes during winter. But this orchard owner, unwilling to collect and store the damaged fruit on the fringes of his land, decided to let it rot on the ground rather than give it away.

Garrick, leading his mule by the reins, caught his breath on the summit of Sharp Talon Ridge after a long, slippery climb. He spat on the snow, disgusted by the wasted fruit. Dead Hand Ridge now lay beyond sight, obscured by many miles of atmospheric haze, steadily falling snow, and fading daylight.

A gravel road connected each farm to Sharp Talon Village, where a station stood on the rail line to Burning Tree, far to the north. This route, the most direct way of reaching the regional capital, would lead Garrick to the military headquarters on mule back within three days. That seemed like a long time to deliver an important message.

The mule tensed, nickered, and pawed the ground, swishing its tail nervously. Garrick patted the animal and spoke soothingly, noting its widened eyes and snorting. That's when he heard the horrifying growl of a slavering monster, and turned to see a huge wolf crest the ridge. The massive, crimson-eyed beast paused, as if startled to find its prey so close, so alone, so vulnerable . . . .

With its black mane bristling, spotted with pure white, dry snow, the predator's powerful shoulder muscles twitched in anticipation of an easy kill. Garrick's mind matched Brenna's detailed description of an Azgar deathwolf with the creature standing before him, and the horror that he could not outrun it seized him like the embrace of an angry bear. Frozen in terror, he didn't reach for his rifle fast enough to save his life.

The mule bolted, retreating rapidly up the road. But the huge predator chose the easier prey that stood transfixed in dread. The beast charged forward – its muscular body airborne in a leap that bent its flexible spine like a massive spring. As the deathwolf crashed into the young soldier, sharp, powerful claws ripped through his parka and its jaw clamped painfully onto his left shoulder.

Garrick's feet slid from beneath him. He slammed into the ground as if he'd been pummeled by a giant, landing hard on his back. Pain, panic and disorientation flooded the young soldier's mind. He'd not been trained to fight monsters like this.

The deathwolf tore at his midsection with its powerful paws. Typically, this killed a victim quickly, but Garrick was wearing armor that its trenchant claws could not shred.

Struggling to breathe against his attacker's crushing weight, the cadet pushed and kicked in a vain attempt to force the monster away. Terrified by the crunching of canine teeth chewing into his armor, screaming as sharp pain stabbed his shoulder, he felt like he was being eaten alive.

Fighting against the incredible strength of a savage beast five times his own weight, Garrick wiggled his left arm free and clawed at the deathwolf's eyes and ears, enraging the slavering brute. The monster turned its hideous head, snapped at Garrick's hand, caught leather in its teeth, then twisted its great neck and began to gnaw, pinching flesh in an excruciating vise.

Garrick gasped for air. He smelled decay in its hot breath and felt sickly, warm saliva dripping all over his face and sliding down his neck. The petrified cadet held his hand in a tight fist, grunting as he pushed the deathwolf's jaws away, valiantly battling to preserve his life while he struggled to reach the combat knife on his belt with his right hand. His sense of duty and desperate longing to survive quickened his will to live, and thus, he did not give in to the natural urge to let the deathwolf prevail, and he refused to stop struggling.

The padded glove limited his ability to feel, but Garrick soon wrapped his fingers around the knife hilt. With herculean effort, he pulled the weapon from its sheath, and with a clumsy, right-handed stab, shoved the blade sideways, into the back of the deathwolf's jaw, where he twisted the weapon and cut into the creature's throat.

The monster retreated from the attack with blood gushing from its wound. It thrashed at Garrick's right arm with its powerful left claw, trying to pin his hand, or bat the blade away. Garrick switched the weapon to his now freed left hand, stabbing and cutting with all his might.

Infuriated with its inability to kill quickly, the deathwolf fruitlessly tore at its victim's belly. The beast retreated and lunged repeatedly, only to meet the sharp sting of the soldier's knife blade in response. Its rage intensified, but its anger could not prevail against the determined young Tamarian's strength, stamina and fighting instinct.

As the deathwolf backed away for another lunge, Garrick's shoulders met an apple tree trunk. Desperate hope flooded his mind. When the monster pounced again, the cadet twisted to the right and plunged his knife deep into the deathwolf's neck as its deadly jaw met the tree instead of his body. Garrick tried reaching for his rifle, but the weapon lay beyond his grasp.

When the creature turned in its attack, Garrick's right hand instinctively picked up an apple. Frozen solid, it was hard as granite. He used it as a weapon, whacking the deathwolf's snout with desperate, adrenaline-fueled fury.

The creature retreated, hissed and snarled, opened wide its blooded jaw, then lunged for Garrick's throat. But instead of finding soft flesh, the beast encountered something cold, hard and unyielding. Choking and raging, it bit down forcefully, breaking back teeth until the apple eventually softened and shattered.

Garrick jabbed his blade deep into the deathwolf's neck and crammed another apple into its mouth. He grabbed a fistful of its thick, spiny mane with his right hand, slammed his head forward and hammered the deathwolf's nose with his helmet for all he was worth until the creature batted him aside and began thrashing its head back and forth to rid its mouth of cold, hard fruit.

Garrick groaned from the heavy blow. With coordination fueled by fear, the Tamarian cadet rolled through the snow, and reached for his rifle. He staggered to his feet, chambered a round, and took aim.

The deathwolf cleared its bleeding mouth, growling, circling its prey warily before uttering its distinctive scream. The loud, terrifying sound shook snow from tree limbs.

Garrick fired four shots at point blank range into the creature's chest. Each powerful, .70 caliber round knocked the deathwolf further and further back before it finally slumped into the snow, unable to threaten its prey again.

Inserting his spare magazine, Garrick chambered another round before retrieving his knife. He kept a wary eye on the still heaving mane of his adversary before standing back to regain his breath.

Not even a giant could take that kind of punishment! Garrick shuddered. Tiny little Brenna had faced eight of them all by herself . . . .

Checking the extent of his wounds, Garrick felt grateful that strong armor had preserved his life. While the monster's teeth and claws mangled his parka and uniform, the deathwolf's bite didn't penetrate the armor straps over his shoulder, but he'd been badly bitten where his vest offered no protection. Further, his body felt like he'd been mercilessly beaten with a stout stick, resulting in nausea and a dizzy sensation that dropped him to his knees.

Garrick struggled to calm his intense, fearful breathing. Serious pain ravaged his entire left arm from the shoulder to the fingertips he used for eating and writing. Weakness and shock motivated him to find a place to care for his wounds in a hurry.

Just then, the horrific screaming of a wolf-pack in the valley below alerted Garrick to an even greater danger. He could see five dark shapes running at top speed through the hay fields he'd crossed before climbing onto the ridge, and he knew intuitively that they were after him.

Garrick's heart sank. If four rounds from his rifle couldn't finish off an already wounded deathwolf, there was no way he could take on five healthy ones all by himself. He didn't have enough ammunition. And now on foot, he'd make much slower progress than he could on the mule. Fearfully, Garrick shouldered his backpack with a painful grunt, then staggered into the orchard toward a steep, rocky hillside several hundred yards to the west.

***

Colonel Brandt read the latest battle reports, distracted by disappointment. This, his first major command action, resulted in little more than loss and retreat. The hastily prepared defenses set up to stop the Azgar at Kicking Horse Gap had not stemmed the enemy tide, and casualties inflicted on the Tamarian defenders were rapidly swamping medical facilities at every operating firebase within a sixty-mile radius.

Scout troops observed the Azgar moving heavy artillery and many wagon loads of ammunition into the hill country just east of Dead Hand Ridge, a sure sign that the invaders were not cowed by the long-range rocket attacks Colonel Brandt had ordered against them three days earlier. Scouts spotted infantry units, previously camped on the Saradon, marching westward in preparation for their invasion of the Broken Wing Valley.

Based on these reports, Colonel Brandt believed the enemy fighting its way down from Kicking Horse Gap would hit Dead Hand Ridge on the flank while a larger force made a simultaneous frontal assault from the east. Although he could expect fire support from base commanders in the Copperhead Hills to his west, he'd not expected the Azgar to deploy and attack so quickly.

Woodwind, that lovesick southerner, had been right. The astonishing speed of the Northern Liberation Army's deployment seized the tactical initiative, forcing the colonel to react to whatever move they made. This fact, coupled with their numerical superiority, explained how they'd conquered so much territory in so little time.

The colonel believed he had neither the necessary manpower, nor sufficient munitions to hold back the Azgar horde for long. Complicating his command situation, under standing orders his forces had to protect civilians, but the evacuation of women and children necessarily delayed full-scale military action.

The citizens of Sutherlind, a town to the north of Kicking Horse Gap, should have been evacuated through the Copperhead Hills to avoid conflict with combat operations. The Azgar offensive, however, overwhelmed that area before its people departed, forcing friendly units to restrain counter force attacks while the civilians moved further south to find safety.

The firebase at Dead Hand Ridge accepted an exhausted group of refugees from Sutherlind sometime after midnight on their second day of travel, but because the Azgar were so decisively overwhelming all Tamarian opposition, Colonel Brandt had to order them, as well as the citizens from Dieter, to evacuate westward at daybreak. He could not accept their request for the customary military escort, either. He had no soldiers to spare.

Polishing off his second cup of tea in a single hour, the colonel appraised his empty briefing room and cursed, torn between his instinct to command aggressively and his need to delay the invaders until reinforcements arrived. Colonel Brandt ordered his subordinates to withdraw from their positions as soon as unit losses exceeded fifteen percent, hoping to maintain a credible force in the face of overwhelming odds.

The colonel studied a local map with the most current unit positions on both sides indicated with colored pins, and cursed for a different reason. However fierce and quick the enemy might be, their ability to maneuver would soon be limited by rough terrain. Their big guns might be terrible, but they'd be difficult to move before being triangulated by heavy rocket fire from nearby bases. Their troops might be numerous and well trained, but none had experienced a Tamarian winter. Their morale would likely plummet after freezing for many bitter days and long, northern nights. This was the most pleasant thought he'd had since first hearing from Woodwind.

The humiliating Tamarian retreat – a temporary necessity for the sake of protecting civilians – would end. At a time of his choosing, the colonel would send thousands of brave men to meet the enemy with a ruthlessness characteristic of Tamarian commanders for many generations. He believed that each soldier under his command possessed the skill, courage and tenacity to stand fast against the oncoming horde, in spite of their dreadful weapons and fearsome reputation. He would not cower from fighting the Azgar, as they couldn't choose their ground and had yet to face the unrestrained might of Tamarian fury.

But could his small and beleaguered army hold out long enough to be reinforced?

Calling his aide from beyond the portal, Colonel Brandt collected his papers. When the skinny warrant officer appeared, the colonel paused. "I want a report on the progress of the civilian evacuation. Tell the officers in charge that I need those people out of here within the hour."

***

Private Darrold Müller lingered casually at Brenna's side, trying desperately to sustain her attention while Lieutenant Magruder patiently organized an irritable swarm of weary civilians who'd assembled in the slush-covered, central courtyard of the firebase. The dark-eyed soldier, wrongly believing that his charge found these proceedings remotely interesting, dutifully translated the lieutenant's shouted instructions. "He's calling for able-bodied men to serve as caravan defenders, since there will be no military escort on the trip to Burning Tree. The men queuing up are getting orders that allow them to sign out weapons.

"It's an unusual move. We're supposed to have reserves and older veterans beyond the age for service filling those rolls. But I guess everyone's fighting at the front."

Brenna scanned the crowd nervously, her tension heightened by the sheer number of strange faces. They spoke a nonsensical clatter of consonant sounds, formed by lips cracked with cold and edged with fatigue. Older folk, she noticed, listened the most carefully, while a small knot of teenaged toughs too young for military service and too proud to join the Junior Scouts postured boorishly among themselves and broke into hysterical laughter for reasons that the apprehensive maiden didn't understand.

Runny-nosed little children in rumpled clothing chased one another in unending games of tag, or clung to the tattered skirts of their mothers, while older siblings inched heavy packs forward in the line designated for wagon loading. Baby screams mingled with shouted commands, laughter and hundreds of other voices engaged in incomprehensible conversation. Diluted by human sounds, the impatient neighing, snorting and hoof-stomping of mule teams echoed off the inner concrete walls, thickening the freezing air of early morning into a kind of mad roar above which Brenna felt, rather than heard, the uncontrolled quickening of her heartbeat.

"Where do I go?" she asked, anxious to get away from the clamor, wishing she could just run away, find Garrick, hold him close and be held close in return. "Where did all these people come from?" Then, thinking out loud, she muttered, "I think I'd be safer traveling by myself."

Darrold let his eyes wander slowly over the beautiful maiden, appreciating how her clean, damp sweater clung to her curves. She had a strung bow around her backpack, and carried a sword that looked too large for a small woman to handle. "You can hardly move in all that gear," he remarked. "How do you expect to stay out of harm's way?"

"Allfather protects me," she replied. "Please, just let me go. Tell your commanding officer I wouldn't cooperate. Tell him whatever you like!"

The Tamarian private shook his head, insisting that it wasn't a good idea for a woman to travel alone in a war zone, even though he'd heard that she'd eluded the Azgar for weeks on her long journey north. Her attractiveness, however, soon softened his resolve and he agreed to look for a spare mule. "Wait for me here," he said, anxious to do something – anything – that might please her.

Pfc. Müller had not been away long when Brenna felt a strong tug on her hair. She nearly fell backwards as a burly, good-looking boy pulled her close from behind. Encouraged by his companions, the teenager forcefully squeezed her breasts with both hands – which *really* hurt – while banging his hips into her backside. The Lithian maiden willed her camisole to harden like armor and twisted away. Shock and pain washed over her reddened face.

Far quicker than her attacker could react, Brenna unsheathed her sword and swung the blade in a graceful, overhead arc, stopping its sharp, crystalline point dangerously near her attacker's throat. "Mind your manners!" she warned in vulgate.

A collective gasp, widened eyes and whispers spread through the crowd in the immediate area. Helder Haas, who'd presumed Brenna was too small and weak to wield such a big weapon, didn't want to lose face in front of his friends, and refused to back down. The young man uttered an expletive. "I swear, she's got iron tits!" he announced, strutting forward, risking serious injury by reaching to fondle her again. "Let me warm you up, darling. It's cold enough to freeze them big ole' titties solid!"

Brenna stepped back, keeping the blade straight and level, knowing that a simple thrust would create a far bigger problem than the one it solved, but also afraid that her more powerful adversary would hurt and humiliate her again. "My body is none of your concern," she replied angrily. "Just leave me alone and I won't hurt you."

Helder mocked her, swaggering in a semi-circle. "A tiny waif like you, threatening me? Come on!" he taunted loudly, clutching his crotch. "I know you want it. Let me pull out my sword and make you howl like a she-wolf in heat!"

No one found that remark amusing. Men shouldered through the crowd, moving forward to intervene if the woman needed help, glowering at the boy threatening her.

"I'm sure you spend many hours all alone polishing that little thing," she retorted. "But if you're fool enough to fondle yourself in front of me, I'll quickly make you fit to defend virgins for the rest of your miserable life! Now back off, or you'll find that this blade is sharper than your wit!"

Brenna's humiliated foe foolishly assumed that she wasn't serious, and also that his glove offered protection from her weapon. But her threat rang true. As he attacked, she stepped leftward and the Lithian blade's hyper-sharp edge easily sliced through Helder's leather glove. As he cursed, clutching his bleeding hand, a man moved forward to protect Brenna, angrily berating the boy and insisting that he'd earned his due reward for disrespecting a woman.

That's when Corporal Fanselars burst through the ranks, preceded by a storm of angry invective. He ignored Brenna and her defender, shoving the antagonist with such force, the young man landed among his terrified friends, and three of them tumbled wetly into the slush.

A hacking tirade of profanity, punctuated by a hard slap in the head amused the bystanders, who approved with cheering and applause. After terrorizing the assailant, the corporal calmed himself and turned to address Brenna, but she'd slipped away through the crowd.

Darrold Müller found her near the livery. "I'm sorry about the harassment," he began. "I shouldn't have left you alone. The kid who bugged you comes from a rich family. He's a well-known troublemaker with a bad attitude, and everyone knows he deserved much worse than he got."

"I shouldn't have to draw a weapon in my defense among your people," Brenna remarked acidly, afraid that she'd have to face someone's wrath for threatening the boy.

"He won't bother you anymore," Darrold assured. "Corporal Fanselars hauled him off to the brig and he'll face charges for assaulting a woman. You can ride with the nursing mothers. They need privacy, and since you're handy with a weapon, they'll be safer in your company."

Brenna considered the widespread prejudice she'd experienced thus far, and wrinkled her brow. *Ugogo* Penda had never said anything about this. "I don't think they'll want me riding with them. They'll call me a whore."

Darrold laughed and shook his head. "I don't think so. These girls are all . . . young and unmarried. You're a saint compared to them."

Brenna resented the comparison, but said nothing.

Private Müller led the way to the back of the caravan. Three blonde-haired women with infants sat on their baggage, cuddling their swaddled, sleeping children against the cold, while a fourth fiddled with a cushion, trying to find a comfortable sitting position in her seventh month of pregnancy. These women shouldered the responsibility of motherhood while enduring social ostracism imposed on unwed teenagers with babies. Unspoken rejection traced its shadow across faces that should have been lit with the first flushing of real, committed love.

The Lithian maiden felt sorry for them, but at the same time, sensed that they instantly regarded her with the same kind of disdain and patronage commonly projected upon women of questionable moral standing. Subtle expressions of contempt flashed across their chapped lips, knowing glances flickered between their tired eyes, and a smirk conveyed near unanimous conviction.

Brenna, the only virgin among them, endured their unjust judgment in silence.

Several uncomfortable minutes later, overworked soldiers began loading the last wagon. Heinz Neergard, whom Brenna recognized as the civil defense liaison from Dieter, approached their wagon and took his place on the driver's seat. He greeted Brenna warmly in vulgate, much to the surprise of the other women, and asked her about Garrick as the women climbed aboard.

"There's a war going on and he has a job to do," she replied with a matter-of-fact but ambiguous shrug. Brenna thought herself clever for deflecting scrutiny away from his secret mission.

Yet at the mention of Garrick's name, one of the mothers burst, rather rudely, into the conversation. "You know Garrick Ravenwood?" she asked in astonishment, nearly allowing her abruptly awakened infant son to tumble from her quivering grasp.

Brenna, leery of the sudden inquiry responded, "I do. Why do you ask?"

The young mother moved forward in haste, discarding her haughty attitude in less time than it took her to sit comfortably beside Brenna at the front of the wagon. This disruption further upset her son, who began fussing until his mother bounced him on her knee and patted his back to settle him down. "I take it you've seen him 'round here, somewhere?" she asked.

Brenna smiled at the infant, a strong, healthy lad whom she guessed was between six and seven months old, judging from his size and behavior. In the boy's face Brenna could see a similar rugged handsomeness that she found irresistible in Garrick. "You have a beautiful child," she replied. Since the young mother had ignored her question, Brenna did the same.

The Tamarian teenager, who looked like she could have been Garrick's sister, shrugged. "I can't take credit for that," she stated. "He looks like his father."

Brenna studied the woman's features, noting her attractive, rounded nose and fawn-shaped, gray-green eyes. The child shared those attributes most strikingly, though his mouth and chin seem to have come from another family. "May he grow up healthy and strong. May his character and conduct always make you proud."

Brushing a stray lock of blonde hair out of her eyes, the young mother turned her wind-burned face toward Brenna. She noted that this foreign woman in a red sweater was too slender to warrant riding in this particular wagon on account of an obvious pregnancy. Having heard whispered rumors that Lithians were insatiable lovers, she wondered if this shapely foreign thing had been caught in an act of intimacy with the young man. "Tell me about Garrick," she said, her inflection suggesting she expected a moist morsel of explicit gossip.

Brenna focused on the child, letting him hold her little finger with his tiny hand, watching vaguely familiar expressions flash across his face. "Garrick is gentle, intelligent and brave from what I have seen, but I haven't known him long." The Lithian maiden pulled her finger away from the baby's grasp, put her glove back on and reiterated her question. "Why do you ask?"

"Hasn't he told you about me?" the young mother inquired, trying to soothe her child as he renewed and amplified his fussing.

Brenna scrunched her brow, puzzled. "No, but I haven't asked, either. Who are you to him?"

"Just a minute," the teenaged mother interrupted, unzipping her coat and opening her blouse to nurse. In Illithia, this wouldn't have merited a second glance, yet when Heinz asked her to seek privacy in the covered part of the wagon, the mother snapped at him with shocking venom. While Brenna didn't understand the angry words, she found the tone of this response disrespectful and rude.

The teenager scowled at the attention she'd drawn. Her little one had stopped his squalling and nuzzled into his mother contentedly, gazing at her in innocent, wide-eyed gratitude. Only then did she drape a blanket over her shoulder for warmth. When she turned toward Brenna, she finally answered the question in a sad voice.

"Last year Garrick came to stay at my father's ranch and I fell in love with him. He cornered me in the barn and had his way. When I got pregnant, I begged him to marry me, but he refused and ran off to the Junior Scouts. My name's Gudrun, and this is Harold, Garrick's baby."

***

Many hours earlier, Garrick had raced in near panic through the orchard, heading for a steep escarpment arising on its western edge. His lead on the dreadful, pursuing deathwolves narrowed until their frenzied voices closed on his heels and he could hear their breath heaving rhythmically in the cold air. Garrick, who'd never been a strong runner, dashed through the last row of dormant apple trees and scrambled uphill.

Cold, slippery snow coated a deep bed of sharp rocks, whose angular shapes blended in the darkness like an arsenal of giant arrowheads strewn across an ancient battlefield. Although his rubber-soled military boots were far better suited for climbing than the soft pads of deathwolf feet, Garrick lost his footing, slammed his knee against a stone and slid several disconcerting feet before reaching in desperation for a light stick.

Sharp pain stabbed his wounded hands as Garrick twisted the chemical lamp, activating its luminescence. The cadet squinted as his eyes adjusted to its radiance, stumbling clumsily until he could see clearly in the artificial light. He held the stick between his teeth as he climbed.

In his urgency to escape, Garrick did not realize for several minutes that the deathwolves were falling behind. As his endurance waned and muscles ached from exertion, the young Tamarian grimly readied himself to stand his ground and fight for his life.

But the deathwolves, bred to run over open ground, could not climb the rocks very well. As they laboriously ascended the steep slope, Garrick waited nervously, his rifle loaded, aimed and ready. Just as they came into the bright influence of his light, the creatures stopped in their tracks. They screamed, howled and pawed the ground in frustration, but would not step any closer.

"Ha!" the Tamarian soldier taunted, stepping down slope, watching the fearsome beasts retreat. He remembered Brenna telling him that deathwolves were not active during the day, and he'd wondered how the Azgar managed to get such bloodthirsty creatures into pens without risking attack. Now, seeing firsthand their terrified reaction to bright light, Garrick theorized that the enemy used something like magnesium torches to make the deathwolves docile. The idea made sense, given their behavior, and Garrick felt wise for having solved the mystery.

Rather than forcing the deathwolves downhill, where they might abandon their pursuit of him in order to hunt easier prey, Garrick turned westward, ascending very rough terrain, hoping the evil beasts would follow. Ever faithful to his calling, he led them away from Sharp Talon Village to preserve lives and property. Still afraid and prudently cautious, Garrick didn't want to risk another confrontation.

As he climbed higher, the snowfall intensified, his footing felt less certain, the air even colder and the wind more swift and fierce. Exertion kept him warm, but he was growing tired. Eventually, declining temperatures dimmed his light stick until he felt certain that its output would no longer keep the pursuing creatures at bay.

Determined to survive, Garrick battled his fatigue, fear and hypothermia, as debilitating pain wracked his body with every movement. He set small goals for himself, rewarding his aching body with rest when he reached a certain outcropping, or the low, deformed shape of an isolated tree struggling for survival in the bitter niche where its hapless seed had long ago fallen.

Weary and winded, Garrick crawled to his goal – the rail bed connecting Sharp Talon Village with Burning Tree, before stopping to catch his breath. As he panted there, Brenna's beautiful face appeared in his imagination, and he heard her soft, soprano voice calling his name. The exhausted cadet checked his compass to make sure he was going the right way, and struggled northward.

Keeping his head down against the brutal wind and swirling snow, Garrick followed the contour of the spur line that guided him toward a steep gorge several miles away. Although nearly blinded by white out conditions, this carefully-graded path lead toward a canyon where Garrick had hiked as a boy. There, he knew he could find shelter in a mountain hut. He hoped to arrive before his lightstick went out, if the deathwolves didn't catch and kill him first.

Several times he heard their petrifying voices screaming at him from behind, but each time he stopped, they did not enter the dying circle of light surrounding him. For hours he plodded along in deep snow until his legs felt like iron rods, his nose and lips – even beneath a woolen scarf – lost all sensation.

Sometime well after midnight, the landscape narrowed and slid toward the long-anticipated canyon. Birch and conifer trees closed in on the rail bed, offering shelter from the wind, while to his left, the mountainside encroached in an abrupt slope, smothered in deep snow. Huge boulders beneath the white blanket, formed fearsome and grotesque shapes against the dark terrain.

In the waning glow of his light stick, Garrick stumbled across a path cutting through an otherwise seamless drift of dry snow. There he saw deep, steep-sided boot prints. Many heavy feet had trodden here, creating a trail leading from the train trestle and up the mountainside. Far too large and deep for human feet, these tracks testified that several giants had passed this way within the past hour.

Garrick shuddered.

Suddenly, his light stick dimmed to a single candle's output, and he heard one of the deathwolves bounding toward him through the deep snow, her labored breathing audible over a lull in the sound of the wind. Garrick turned eastward, found the narrow stairs descending into the canyon, and climbed down as quickly as he could. Trembling as his boots searched for secure footing, the weary soldier followed a slender trail about thirty feet above the frozen current of Hecate Creek.

The deathwolf, having long pursued her prey, saw his warm, glowing mass vanish into a background of cold and darkness. Enraged, she screamed angrily, then leaped toward the place she'd last seen him. The massive predator dove gracefully over Garrick's head and into the icy abyss, where the sounds of her dying yelp and crushing bones sang a pitiful, attenuated song amidst a deep drift of snow.

Shaking in terror, Garrick crept along the path, hardly breathing for fear that a misstep might cause him to fall to his death as well. He knew this trail but had never come this way in the snow, and never in severe pain. Grimly determined, the Tamarian cadet forged onward.

Several feet above his head, the four remaining creatures arrived, snarling in frustration. They raced along the ledge, screeching in demonesque harmony while they searched in vain for the trail that would allow them to pursue their prey and close for a kill. But they could only see his warmth inching away, not the path he traced.

Screaming hideously when they realized their quarry had eluded them, the deathwolves retreated into the darkness, the memory of their pursuit lingering with the young Tamarian like a long-remembered nightmare.

Nearing exhaustion, Garrick finally reached the mountain cabin. This tiny log structure, set on a rocky outcropping overlooking both the creek and the Broken Wing Valley to the east, served travelers who needed shelter from the frequent storms that arose in this region.

In the feeble glow of his dying light stick, Garrick found its door unlocked and the cabin unoccupied. He shuffled into a small room containing a cot with a moth-eaten blanket, a multrum toilet and a wood burning stove. An old pair of skis and a rusty spear stood like tired sentries in a corner, guarding a dozen pieces of split birch and a pile of hardwood shavings.

Garrick shut the door and pulled down its latch. With fingers trembling from lingering fear and the bitter cold, he gathered the birch and kindling to build a fire. Once he and the cabin felt warm, the cadet struggled out of his parka, armor and uniform to inspect his injuries. In places were teeth and claws had found flesh, he applied bandages from his kit. Utterly depleted, he collapsed on the cot, wrapped in the blanket, and fell into a troubled sleep.

***

Copperhead Ridge loomed as an impregnable, granite stronghold; its steep and stony flanks lay veiled in a thin coat of snow that reflected a silvery sheen. Jagged, deeply eroded cliffs crowned heights swathed in the mysterious, metallic gleam of snowy rock rising above long skirts of accumulated alluvium. A brooding cloud canopy brushed the rugged peaks, shrinking, it seemed, from the prick of sharp stone.

A huge terminal moraine marked the southernmost advance of an ancient glacier, and beyond it, the Broken Wing Valley slung from the overcast heaven in a classic U-shape, its stony, mountainous walls scoured smooth by the agency of ice long since returned to the sea. The glacial washout field showed the scars of dead riverbanks, while the land beyond the moraine lay littered in drumlins and kettle lakes, its rich soil supporting lush stands of wild grasses and cultivated hay now dormant beneath drifts of blowing snow.

This land supported large herds of cattle and horses with abundant food and water, but every tree that dared raise its limbs more than twenty feet above the valley floor suffered in an incessant wind that severely deformed foliage as it swept southeast from its birthplace, a little over two hundred miles to the north.

Making steady progress, the convoy plodded forward. Conversations had long since died down, and sheer boredom prevailed among the refugees.

Brenna awakened on the hard bench behind Heinz Neergard after a fitful sleep. Glare from the bright landscape hurt her eyes – a problem she'd never experienced, as snow didn't fall in her homeland – so she picked up Woodwind's longword and focused on its thin, transparent edge.

Like other priceless Lithian weapons, this one blended the extreme sharpness of advanced, ceramo-ferric metallurgy with a hammered, lightweight alloy body. Microscopic spaces between the metal layers in this weapon contained a specialized polymer fluid that exerted hydraulic pressure on its edge, instantly filling any defects created in combat with a crystalloid solution that hardened instantly in air, repairing damage to its brittle cutting surface. Balanced to perfection, the weapon felt nearly weightless in battle, and in Woodwind's powerful grasp, could sever limbs as thick as a human thigh.

This blade – crafted in a specialized factory called a light forge from thin sheets of metals and other materials – had been carefully fabricated into the deadly, killing tool in Brenna's hands. Its forging required many steps and several months to complete. A flourish of craftsmanship, manifest in elaborate engraving upon the bluish, alloy blade and intricate, geometric settings for silver-framed turquoise and blood quartz tiles on its tapered blade brace, displayed an attention to detail that transcended mere function. Fine leather, wrapped over a gel pack that covered its strong, carbon core, allowed the handle to conform to the grip of its user. Lithian blades blended fine art with a technology few humans understood or appreciated.

Brenna, however, knew the worth of the weapon she held, and as she reflected on its value, Woodwind's generosity in offering it to her inspired lengthy moments of moody contemplation. She had long known of Woodwind's love for her. He was a decent and moral man, whose virtue and integrity had won her father's trust. Few could challenge his wisdom, or boast beyond his skill as a warrior. These characteristics inspired many people to comment that he and she would make the perfect couple. Her long struggle to find a decent suitor added urgency to these messages.

But every time Brenna let such a thought creep into her mind, it filled her with a kind of dread she couldn't explain. Courteous, well-mannered Woodwind could be quite condescending. While unquestionably loyal, she always found a personal agenda at the root of his actions. Further, his mind analyzed every situation and relationship with a kind of logic that constantly sought an advantage.

This hyper-awareness made him a dangerous adversary, and even though Brenna loved him as a friend and trusted him with her life, their relationship always teetered on the edge of outright competition. The constant tension wearied her.

Handsome Garrick, whose behavior favorably impressed the Lithian maiden, always listened with the intent of understanding. The Tamarian soldier eloquently explained his views on issues in a way that never insulted Brenna's intellect, or made her feel uncomfortable if she disagreed with what he said – even though he *was* godless. Garrick praised her thoughts as meritorious, without ever insisting that she accommodate his views. His consistent lack of need to dominate their relationship freed Brenna to be herself for the first time with any man outside her family.

He'd also stirred her nascent, innocent sexuality. Whenever thoughts of Garrick breezed into her consciousness, her body reacted in ways she'd never before experienced, and most distressing for a woman of her spiritual caliber, she *wanted* this unbeliever to overwhelm her with these novel and wonderful feelings.

But after hearing Gudrun's story, Brenna felt heartbroken. She'd wanted to believe in Garrick's sexual innocence. She wanted their eventual nuptial bliss to be a secret shared only between the two of them. It frightened her to realize that this fantasy already existed in her mind after knowing him for so short a time. The impact of Gudrun's revelation deflated that dream so rapidly, the realization that Garrick might not be a decent young man after all, nearly brought tears to Brenna's eyes.

But she'd refused to cry. The Lithian woman let anger take root in her heart, not because she wanted to hurt Garrick, but because she felt she never should have let him draw out the feelings of desire that so willingly flowed toward him from within her soul.

Brenna sheathed the sword, struggling with the concept of loving someone whose fidelity could be questioned. She then reasoned that trustworthiness in the ultimate sense belonged only to Allfather. Garrick was just a man, after all, and also much younger than she.

Nonetheless, would he really abuse Gudrun in the manner she claimed? Brenna remembered moments alone with him, times when Garrick had been perfectly willing to restrain his desire for her sake. Long experience with amorous young men fueled gratitude and appreciation for his consistent self-control. No one had ever treated her so respectfully. Why then would Garrick behave with such temper toward her, when he'd supposedly overpowered and discarded his cousin only months before?

Brenna could not attribute a change of heart to some deep, spiritual awakening, for Garrick certainly could not be accused of even a remote belief in the spirit realm. Also, he suffered from the Tamarian cultural stigma regarding modesty to such an extent, she found it difficult to believe that a common brute who'd recently forced himself on a helpless girl could blush to see another one standing before him wearing her underwear.

Nothing made sense. A flood of contradictory feelings raging in her soul stopped cold in the chilling reality of a baby boy who looked remarkably similar to Garrick. Did he gain Gudrun's trust, only to break it when she was vulnerable? If so, could Brenna believe in his gentle manner and comforting words? Or was Gudrun lying?

Brenna returned to the present when the caravan abruptly halted. Heinz Neergard stood up to see over the preceding wagon, noting that the head of the train had stopped at some kind of a roadblock, just in front of the mound that marked the terminal moraine. Confusion and anxiety began spreading among the civilians.

His vision had been much better in his youth, and now, even with glasses on he could not tell what the problem was from this distance. Worried that some kind of conflict might begin, he turned to Brenna and spoke in a calm tone. "I'll find out what the trouble is. Can you please take the reins?"

Brenna put the longsword underneath the driver's bench and complied with his request as he departed. When the mules began nervously pawing the ground, the Lithian woman scanned her surroundings for danger. Squinting, as falling snow uncomfortably reflected UV light like many little mirrors, the dark-haired maiden couldn't see the head of the caravan clearly.

But turning around, Brenna froze in fear. Black uniformed cavalry troops advanced up the road, their carbines held from the hip at forty-five-degree angles. The last of their number joined ranks from behind a boulder-strewn mound several dozen yards distant from where they had quietly watched the caravan pass.

Swiftly, Brenna climbed over the bench, brusquely shooing the young mothers into the covered part of the wagon. "Stay down!" she warned. "We're being attacked!"

Sensing fear in his mother's heart, Harold, Gudrun's baby, began screaming. His cry awakened the other infants, who followed suit as their mothers labored through the narrow center aisle and into the covered section at the rear of the wagon.

Brenna reached for her quiver and quickly strung her bow. "Merciful God," she prayed aloud. "I can barely see! Please, deliver your enemy into my hands!"

Gunfire erupted near the front of the caravan. Screams and shouts radiated from the confused scene. Glancing backward, she noticed the front rank of mounted enemy soldiers raising their rifles to return fire, so she kept her head low and urged the mothers to do the same.

Brenna slapped the reins, urging the mule team forward as a bullet splintered a side board of her wagon. She heard another round whistle off to her left and prayed desperately for her life, knowing that the enemy would quickly catch the slower mule team and she'd soon be forced to fight in earnest.

Heinz Neergard waved frantically from the side of the road. Brenna slowed the mules to a near stop in order to let him climb aboard. The old man took her hand and pulled himself into the driver's seat once more, wasting no further time in urging the mules into a dead run.

The first cavalry soldier who dared close on the last wagon felt the hot kiss of a steel-tipped arrow slam into his lips. His partner, approaching on the opposite side, faced a similar fate through the center of his neck a moment later. He tumbled backward from the saddle and bounced into the legs of a trailing horse. The hapless beast crumpled forward and shed its rider, who slammed into the ground headfirst, breaking his neck.

Six cavalrymen dashed past Brenna's wagon, attempting to drive the slower mules off the road and subdue several wagons at once. Tamarians with rifles fired back, demanding that the enemy honor their threat, which permitted the Lithian woman a chance to wield her bow.

Brenna loosed twice to her right, crouched behind a bench to grab more arrows without looking, then turned the other way and sent two more on their terminal flight. She hit the two riders on her right in the back, one through the right kidney and the other just left of his spine, through the lung and out his chest. On the opposite side, she loosed as enemy soldiers turned toward her, hitting the first in the chest. His companion, presenting a better target, fell clutching an arrow shaft through his neck.

Two more arrows slipped into the southern woman's cold fingers as a rifle round shattered the back of the bench in front of her. Once again, she pushed forward on her bow, her arms aching from the intense exertion, and found a target in the heart of a cavalry officer charging his mount toward her from the right. Swift and true, her arrow found its mark, but as his body crashed to the ground, it rolled beneath the wagon's back wheels.

A great bump lifted Brenna from her crouch, forcing her next shot high. Four screams and the intense wailing of young children emanated from the covered section just as another pursuing enemy soldier fired his gun. Brenna dropped to the wagon's floor and heard the bullet whistle as it closed. Searching frantically for her quiver as gunfire erupted all around her, the young woman scrambled beneath the front passenger bench, found her arrows and grabbed another handful.

The lull in her defending gave an Azgar soldier an opportunity to turn his horse, ride alongside the wagon and attempt to board. If he could kill the archer, his companions could seize the caravan for its food. His unit, cut off from its supplies by Tamarian infantry, had not eaten a meal in four days. All of them were very hungry.

Stepping into the wagon proved more difficult than he'd thought it would be, for the road surface, though frozen hard in the cold, had grown slick with ice. Heinz deliberately moved the wagon side to side and it bounced with a random frequency the cavalry soldier found impossible to anticipate. Just as he stepped in, reaching for a bench to stabilize his balance and clearing his back leg over his horse, the archer suddenly reappeared.

Brenna popped up from behind the second passenger bench and let an arrow fly at point-blank range. This time, she didn't miss.

At that instant, Serena, the pregnant teenager, appeared from the covered section. Tears streamed down her cheeks, and a look of dread evolving into dozens of horrified expressions stung Brenna's compassionate heart. An Azgar soldier stood behind her, his left hand clutching her quivering jaw, his right hand holding a bayonet to the young woman's swollen belly. "Drop the bow, little Lith cow!" he demanded angrily. "No god in heaven can save this whoring wench from my hand!"

In one fast, fluid motion – before his reflexes could respond to her movement – Brenna loosed an arrow that slammed through the blasphemer's left eye.

"Say that to Allfather's face!" she snapped as his lifeless form fell.

Brenna retrieved Woodwind's sword from its hiding place. Guiding Serena, who was sobbing and shaking, to a safer place on the floor, the Lithian woman stepped over the dead soldier and plunged into the canvas canopy where the other women were screaming for help.

"Light!" she commanded, her *belief* manifest in an instant, ultraviolet radiance that flooded the canopy and made her eyes glow like a star on a clear, winter night. Brenna could see perfectly in bright light too blue for humans, and inside, she faced no glare from the snow. Two cavalrymen were trying to subdue the women, while a third was just climbing into the back of the wagon.

Placing her booted foot on the shoulder of the first enemy soldier, Brenna shoved hard, the force of her muscular leg turning him toward her while his back slammed against a bench. Before he could react, she'd thrust the sword into his chest and rotated her entire body to the left, leaning forward so heavily that her extended right knee nearly touched the floor. This motion twisted the blade quickly, snapping her victim's ribs as the retreating steel wedged them apart.

In the confined space beneath the canopy, Brenna's small size gave her a distinct advantage. Her tiger stance allowed her to withdraw the weapon and arc it overhead to attack again in a single, smooth motion. Woodwind's blade found the neck of the second soldier and sliced a deep gash through his flesh until Brenna stopped her downward stroke and lunged forward, driving the blade up, into her adversary's lower abdomen with two powerful strides that shoved the weapon through him to its hilt.

Gasping in the horrible realization that his life had suddenly ended, the invader fell backward while Brenna twisted in a reversal to the right. He knocked his head against Gudrun's soft thigh when Brenna stepped forward and the blade slithered away, leaving him to die with a huge hole in his belly as she turned her attention to the back of the wagon.

She swept the Lithian blade high to the right, its tip just touching the canopy roof as the young woman danced forward. Many years of intensive sword training endowed her with strength that belied her petite stature. She attacked with great force, executing a cross-cut on the third soldier that severed his left arm at the shoulder. One quick step forward put her in the perfect position for a two-fisted thrust through the soft flesh in the middle of his mandible. When the sword tip stopped on the hard surface of his inner skull, Brenna used momentum to push him out of the back flap through which he'd entered moments before.

Other Azgar horsemen declined to board the back of the wagon after seeing their dead comrade ejected in such a quick and gruesome way. One of them fired a shot through the canopy out of sheer frustration, but the bullet sailed high, shattered the tip of Woodwind's sword, then ricocheted through the floor without touching a living soul.

Instantly, the blade repaired itself. Its internal, crystalloid polymer hardened into a perfect point as if by magic. Before Brenna had taken a single step, its deadly edge had been flawlessly restored.

Heinz Neergard drove the mule team with a skill that stemmed from long experience. His ability to keep the wagon under control strained against his personal comfort as Azgar horsemen tried to board. They wasted ammunition trying to hit him, but he returned fire using an old revolver he'd hidden in a box beneath the bench. Heinz reined back the team and kept his head low.

One cavalryman, who tried using his horse to push the mule team off the road, became the elderly Mr. Neergard's first kill. He fired at the left rear flank of the Azgar pony, which subsequently tumbled to the valley floor and shed its rider.

Brenna stepped out of the canopy just in time to hear frightened Serena scream about a soldier who'd successfully boarded the wagon. The tall, dark-eyed southerner drew his saber and slashed an angry, outward sweep aimed at Brenna's pretty head that she countered with an effortless, outward parry.

The Lithian woman executed a hard, downward cut that sliced through his clavicle, followed by a deep thrust into his chest with another half-turn exit. Facing left with her blade at chin level, Brenna stepped into a side kick, the force of which not only freed the impaled soldier from her sword, but also sent his body tumbling toward the frozen ground, never to rise. After seeing 15 of their comrades easily dispatched, no one else dared attack the last wagon.

Ahead, Heinz could see other members of the convoy slowing and turning off into a defensive circle. Dozens of readied rifles, wielded by veterans, fired in defense of their families, quickly and decisively ending the enemy's attack.

Heinz pulled the wagon in at the back of the formation and dismounted to lock the wheels. A handful of teenaged boys dashed over to unhitch the mule team while a few older women arrived to help the young mothers and their children move to the center of the circle for safety.

Brenna prayed in gratitude, praising Allfather while she regained her breath. Squinting in headache-inducing discomfort, she swiped Woodwind's sword on the shirt of the blasphemer, struck by the irony of his last utterance, then recovered her bow, quiver and slipped into the covered part of the wagon to get out of the blinding snow. She curled up alone, praying tearfully for the pain in her heart to go away.

***

A mottled Kitsim Dove, speckled with dry snow and shivering from the extreme cold at high elevation, found the rooftop aviary at Dead Hand Ridge and hopped down into the sheltered warmth of a receiving pen where food and water awaited. After the bird descended through a one-way door, a spring mechanism rang a bell to alert the communications clerk that a message had finally arrived. Anticipating the bird's return, the clerk hastened to remove its report.

When Colonel Brandt read the news from the Copperhead Hills, he nodded gravely. Colonel Taylor, another commander, had written coordinate positions his scouts had fixed on Azgar artillery positions. These Colonel Brandt gave to his aide for cross-checking with his own data, though he fully expected a close match.

In terse language the report stated that bad weather and the unexpected presence of enemy troop reserves near Kicking Horse Gap interfered with reassignments from further north, preventing a full-scale reinforcement of Dead Hand Ridge from his sector. This news made the prospect of halting the enemy advance doubtful in the near term.

Thus far, every Tamarian unit had yielded ground to the invaders. What had started out as a coordinated withdrawal was becoming, in some places, a hasty and humiliating rout. Though the rate of effective weapons discharge remained high, the Tamarian Self-Defense Force crumbled under the weight of superior numbers, crushing artillery, effective maneuver and dwindling supplies. Judging from the combat reports littering the colonel's desk, infantry morale had been deteriorating rapidly, especially over the past day. Some units had done a lot more running than fighting.

Colonel Brandt hoped he would see the last of his retreating troops by nightfall. At that time, he could let the fortress defenders and rocket corps deal with massed enemy concentrations while his field troops received a much-deserved rest. Several infantry companies had been fighting and falling back for well over thirty-six hours to permit the civilian evacuation, time for which they'd paid dearly in spilled blood.

Though deteriorating weather would interfere with long-range rocket support, the Azgar would face winter's fury to a much greater degree, given that their troops and artillery were deployed outdoors, without shelter. Woodwind, the lovesick southerner, had volunteered for duty after recovering – rather quickly – from his injuries. He believed the Azgar couldn't cope with a bitter winter.

"Let them bask in it!" the colonel snapped. "Let them eat, sleep and die in the snow!"

***

Vivid visions, pain and night terrors startled Garrick from his sleep many times during the lonely hours before dawn. Dreams of death and dismemberment chased him into consciousness, frightening him awake for what felt like forever. When grey light finally filled his small, warm room from its tiny eastern window, the young Tamarian felt too tired to stay awake and could not motivate himself to move out of bed.

A full three hours after daybreak, only marginally rested, Garrick set wood on the stove coals and began preparing to move on. He made oat cakes slathered with peanut butter and dried apples, drank tea with breakfast, washed his face, cleaned his wounds, then made a feeble attempt to split fresh firewood and kindling for the next cabin occupant.

After extinguishing the fire with snow, Garrick decided to take the cross-country skis along. Traditional Tamarian religious practice demanded that a gift of equal or greater value be left to replace the item taken, so that the spirit of the place would not be offended and wreak vengeance upon the disrespecting thief.

Garrick would have obliged the custom, but only because he believed it was wrong to steal, not because he feared the vengeful wrath of some minor deity. With nothing superfluous to offer, he knew that using skis would enable him to cover ground much more rapidly than he could on foot. He left a quarter sterling coin, worth a day's wage – the extent of his money at the moment – knowing that this meager gift would not cover the cost of the skis he'd taken. Garrick reasoned that saving the Republic was more important, anyway . . . .

"I wonder what Brenna would think," he mused aloud, curious that ethical questions so consistently brought thoughts of her to mind. "Would she frown on me for taking a pair old skis like this?"

Garrick didn't want to admit how much it mattered to him that she might, or that if she didn't, that her explanation would entail some fascinating, well-thought moral precept in an unexpected light. Her opinion had risen to a kind of second standard by which Garrick judged himself, and Brenna didn't have to threaten or cajole in order to wield such influence. Her integrity commanded that kind of respect.

This acceptance of her spiritual philosophy demonstrated conclusively that Garrick already loved Brenna, for he would not have bent his will toward hers so willingly if it hadn't been his delight to do so. As the young man climbed out of the canyon with the stolen skis and poles strapped to his back, he made up his mind to tell her that he loved her when he had the chance.

He hoped she wouldn't scorn his devotion as Gudrun and other girls had done. Garrick made the vow with confidence in the Lithian woman's excellent character.

Hard climbing brought Garrick back up to the rail bed, where he'd earlier seen the giant tracks. During the intervening hours, tiny snowflakes, falling endlessly from the overcast heavens, substantially filled in the boot marks. Thus, to his great relief, the young soldier concluded that no giants had recently been in the area. He recorded the surroundings and prints in photos as evidence.

After carefully crossing the trestle bridge on foot, he stopped to put on the old skis. They featured an adjustable leather toe binding that Garrick snugged securely around his rubber-soled boots.

As he stood, the young soldier noted two crucial things he'd not seen during the night. The first, was that the poles holding up telephone lines had been cloven with only one or two strokes of an axe. The lines themselves lay severed on the snow, proving that sabotage, rather than the wind, had cut communications with Dead Hand Ridge. He took out his camera again to document the damage.

Shovel marks in the nearby snow proved that a broad section of the rail bed just in front of the trestle had been deliberately buried. Curious, Garrick dug through a shallow spot using gloved hands, where he found that the tracks had been torn apart. A derailment at this point would almost certainly result in the train plunging into the steep chasm cut by Hecate Creek.

Anger burned in his heart. He'd uncovered evidence that the treacherous giants had secretly allied with the Azgar. Cutting communication and preventing resupply by wrecking the rail line aided only the invaders. Had he not tangled with the deathwolves during the previous night, he wouldn't have come this way, and no one would have known about the ruined rails until disaster struck.

Garrick carefully documented everything with his camera, cursing the Azgar for their invasion, and cursing the giants for colluding with them. After opening the vents on his shredded overcoat, the Tamarian cadet resumed his northward journey. Pain, his ever malevolent companion, protested at the slightest movement of his arms, abdomen and chest. All he could do was endure.

Determined to warn General Ziegler quickly, Garrick traveled in a distance-eating rhythm made easier by the gentle slope of the rail bed. While the Tamarian cadet felt grateful that it didn't take much skill to ski here, a sense of urgency pushed him past his pain. Garrick brooded about the secret until nightfall and his aching body forced him to find shelter.

***

Four days after leaving Dead Hand Ridge, the civilian refugee caravan lumbered into the snow-blanketed city of Burning Tree. Steam clouds rose from industrial complexes powered by geothermal vents, where the raw materials of Southern Tamaria were forged, cast, cut or spun into a bewildering variety of products destined for distant markets on the swift current of the Desolation River.

Sprawling on the stormy banks of Broken Wing Lake, Burning Tree looked beautiful from a distance. Its gas-lit streets bustled with business, even as winter settled over its dormant orchards and vineyards. Panting locomotives whistled into massive, vaulted stations with frescoed walls and gleaming metal roofs while graceful, steam-powered stern-wheelers sheltered in protected quays. Their cargoes of cloth, timber, processed ore and passengers vanished into networks of narrow roads lined with factories and finishing plants, hotels, sweat shops, casinos, whorehouses, beer halls and every human venture and amusement imaginable.

Brenna shivered wearily, trying to ignore the excited chatter of young mothers who brimmed with wonder as the caravan passed many thousands of buildings, each venting steam as if on fire. In their enthusiasm, the mothers didn't notice urine-stained alleys heaped with rotting trash, the strong scent of burning opium and hashish, nor did they see the pimps, teenaged prostitutes and hungry street urchins lurking in the shadows. The Lithian woman saw what the others would not see, and it made her sad to realize that the fantasy of this free land included so many kinds of slavery.

Ugogo Penda, whose stories painted a positive picture of her father's homeland in Brenna's impressionable mind, never mentioned the scenes she witnessed while riding past reeking fountains of hot, factory effluent. Burning Tree revealed its dark secrets to her soul, melting away every illusion she'd long cherished as surely as its venting spouts of sulfurous mist turned bright, blinding snowflakes into dirty puddles of stagnant water that reflected the darkness of human settlement, rather than glorious light.

The Lithian maiden tried to pray, but the novel ugliness of the city distracted her thoughts. She searched for something beautiful, only to find her eyes fixed on a retching drunkard, her ears assaulted by the shriek of spinning wheels and grinding metal, or the reek of cooking fish overcoming the sense-numbing cold.

Ordinarily, it might have been possible for the young woman to accept the stark reality of a human city up close, but Brenna found that the ugliness she witnessed somehow exposed and magnified the ache she felt for Garrick. Brenna honestly loved him, but the thought that he'd been hiding a terrible secret stabbed her heart with sorrow, just as the scenes unfolding before her unbelieving eyes destroyed the myth of perfection she'd once believed as a naive little girl and replaced those happy stories with shame and regret.

As the caravan descended into the military compound on the western fringe of the city, it left the squalor, passing through a large gate, and moved into an area of austere, plastered straw housing units, open fields and clusters of angular, concrete buildings. The military compound, though far cleaner than its surroundings, appeared depressingly symmetrical, as if its architects put on a good front to mask the lie beyond its borders.

Brenna considered what she would say when she saw Garrick again, but words failed to express the tension she experienced between devotion and disgust. Did she know the true Garrick, or did she love a fraud? Had she blinded herself to his faults? Were her feelings for him merely the common, physical and fleeting varieties associated with passion and often mistaken for the transcendent love she longed to experience?

Like the transformation of the city from a distance, the Lithian woman wondered if her affiliation with Garrick would survive when investigated under the perfect standard of Allfather's judgment. Could she honestly claim that this relationship was true and pure in God's sight?

Brenna examined her own motives and found no fault, but she wondered silently what other unspoken secrets lay lurking within Garrick's troubled soul.

*Centurion Commander Dathan Herulus, Azgar Northern
Liberation Army*

The Crucible of Honor

I'd learned how to calculate the distance from a rocket impact to my position by counting the elapsed time between the bright flash of its blast and the low thunder that rumbled beneath my tired and swollen feet. This time I'd forgotten to count and I could feel the strange solace of warmth sweep across my face. Its sweet, deathly caress tantalized me as I longed for its final comfort. Something struck me on the cheek, and thinking I'd been hit by a scrap of hot enamel, I wiped my wind-burned face with a numb finger and found a lump of burning flesh.

It belonged to someone else.

Shouts and the sound of a gunfight reached my ears from our left flank. Two more explosions followed, each one closer and more terrifying, and after these I heard the distinctive whir of a machine cannon firing.

The shadowy forms of running men appeared in the wind-driven snow, expressions of panic painted across their faces. Lines of dread blended with a myriad of cracks, broken blood vessels and flesh chapped raw by the cold. When the enemy bullets impacted, they riddled many bodies with seventy caliber rounds from behind, and those men unlucky enough to survive fell to the snow-swept soil and waited in agony for their lives to end.

Others fled blindly onward, some of them dropping rifles, munitions and backpacks in order to flee faster. The shock of seeing my own men retreating filled me with panic I'd not known since I'd first taken command in Shirak. I screamed curses with an eloquence that bordered on the poetic, and with the help of Sergeant Hanibal's threats, rallied twenty men to defend our position. With grim faces and determination, we loaded our weapons and waited for the barbarian attack.

This time, however, we never fired a single shot. The enemy infantry, rather than attacking us, wheeled eastward and slammed into a reserve unit protecting a munitions dump. Several minutes later, after an intense firefight, a spectacular eruption of fire and billowing smoke announced another barbarian success.

I should have ordered a supporting attack and pinned the enemy against our bigger guns, but truthfully, my feet had become so badly bloated I could barely walk and many of my men suffered misery exceeding my own. After eight days of heavy fighting, exhaustion, interminable cold and lingering hunger sapped our will to resist the enemy beyond honoring an immediate threat.

I'd not seen Sergeant Vitus in two days. Desertions began outnumbering battlefield losses, but my imagination strained to comprehend how anyone could survive the unholy cold or escape from the long arm of starvation. I figured that anyone who managed to avoid our patrol pickets and subsequent firing squads would quickly succumb to the ravages of winter, or become prey for roaming deathwolves.

Legate Braegan promised that blankets would arrive soon, but I didn't believe him. Every morning as the tally of exposure deaths climbed, my troops gathered to divide belongings from the dead among the living. Several days after our breakout at Kicking Horse Gap, this task evolved into a morbid ritual that fueled violent outbursts with increasing frequency.

Our desperate condition dulled all civilized polish, until the macabre inheritance of a dead man's possessions became disproportionally vital in maintaining morale. I'd broken up three fights in as many days and worried that I could not long maintain the control to keep my soldiers from killing each other. Our survival seemed so tenuous, we'd become more savage than our barbarian enemies.

Turning away from another skirmish lost, I stared at the object of my deepest loathing, memorizing its every nuance. From a distance of twelve hundred yards, the fortress at Dead Hand Ridge peered over its desolate peak with menacing angularity. The ugly thing loomed like a massive, pagan idol. Its defenders ceaselessly ministered in a fruitless effort to sate its unending thirst for blood.

Our first attack faltered against the devastating effect of massive, coordinated defensive fire. Lord Balinor opened the strike with an artillery bombardment. He intended to sustain the shelling for twelve hours, but not long after our cannon opened up, a responding rain of counterbattery fire silenced every large weapon we'd brought to bear. Not only did the barbarians destroy some of our best gun tubes, we learned that intense cold and snow made moving in replacement cannon very difficult.

Then, lacking artillery support, my maniple, along with five thousand other troops, launched our second attack in neat columns. We marched at 108 paces per minute across the fire glacis, intending to form a double line once we moved into rifle range. A swarm of small arms, machine cannon and rocket fire, aimed in crossing patterns from inside the fortress, ripped into our infantry with such force, a collective, audible moan reached my ears from over three hundred yards away.

I witnessed incredible slaughter. Huge blocks of men collapsed in great waves, as if mown down by an invisible machine. Before we managed a retreat, nearly three thousand men lay dead or dying, with another thousand suffering non-critical wounds.

The remaining artillery that we'd brought forward for this attack, mostly small pieces that could be moved with relative ease, pounded the fortress through the night. At daybreak, after we'd regrouped, Lord Balinor ordered yet another attack.

Fifteen thousand fresh troops advanced under the cover of falling snow. This time my men were deployed in defensive positions rearward, and because of the reduced visibility, we could only listen to the shriek of rockets, the crack of gunfire and the screams of dying men as our comrades pressed forward.

We knew nothing of their fate until the enemy launched a thunderous heavy rocket and artillery barrage, followed by a sudden counterattack. Barbarian soldiers poured onto the battlefield, appearing as if by magic. Their units slammed into our flanks with such ferocity the cream of our infantry melted in the heat of their precision fire. On the cold, confused battlefield, enemy troops pursued our fleeing foot soldiers in what initially looked like a rout, but exhausted reserves stood firm and turned the enemy back.

In brief, brutal engagements with entrenched troops like mine, the barbarians fought with fanatical ferocity. They succeeded in clearing our forces from the hilltop, then melted back into the fog and snow, only to reappear with mortifying suddenness in vulnerable places where we least expected an attack.

My day had been full of violent, small-scale skirmishes that sapped all courage from my men and left me trembling at the sound of enemy artillery. I'd been ordered to hold my position until more troops came forward. We'd waited for many hours because the tedious process of dragging heavy gun tubes uphill was compounded by human lethargy in the cold, and lengthened further by rough terrain.

Because my unit strength had fallen to below thirty-percent, I believed we could not hold out against another concerted attack and sent word to Legate Braegan to this effect. Roughly an hour later, he sent fresh troops to replace my soldiers, relieving me of my position and ordering my soldiers back to the Ice Dragon Inn to rest.

We straggled toward the southeast through rugged hill country, following a snowy road with the accursed wind at our backs. Hampered by frostbitten feet, exhaustion and hunger, our column stirred the sympathy of a passing sergeant responsible for driving empty ammo caissons back to the inn. We hobbled onto the two-wheeled carts with battle worn weariness, wordlessly grateful for the kindness, knowing it would never be repaid.

Brush fires, ignited by long-range incendiary warheads, smoldered smokily on the distant Saradon. Dull-orange flames fed on tons of dry grasses and fanned across the steppe like the fabled Place of Burning. It seemed strange that fire could spread in a place so cold, but evidence of snowfall vanished as we descended toward the plain, and I could see that beyond the hills, little, if any, moisture had reached the ground during my absence.

My conscious mind considered the scene and longed to luxuriate in a fraction of its warmth, while the betrayer deep within mocked the fate of our many horses, whose forage, consumed by the insatiable fire, turned into heat and smoke before my tearless eyes.

I knew we would soon have meat in our stew again.

Long after nightfall, we pulled into the protection of the crumbling walls surrounding the Ice Dragon Inn. Deep shadows from smoky torches flickered against the shattered remains of ancient masonry, forming ghostly shapes that danced a dirge for what had once stood as a proud and handsome complex. Bonfires burned in the courtyard, surrounded by grim-faced, shivering men struggling to stay alive in the cold.

Most of the millennial oaks that had grown in manicured groves remained only as hazy memories in my mind. The places where their gnarled branches once reached now lay open to the overcast sky. This compound now stood as a skeletal shadow of its former glory.

I rationalized that the lives of men were of greater importance than the existence of old trees, but when the traitor in my soul accused me of responsibility for destroying this lovely place, of belonging to the power-mad group seeking glory and personal wealth, I thought of nothing in my own defense.

When I tried to find an officer in charge of the courtyard area, the responses ranged from vague to abusive. Worse, whenever we sought warmth near one of the bonfire pits, the threat of readied bayonets promptly discouraged us from coming closer. I grew angry. My colleagues should have permitted us the basic human need for warmth, but they also feared freezing to death, and in an environment where everyone worried for their own welfare, no one offered assistance to us.

I knew that the inn's main hall had been reserved for senior officers. I knew that they would take a dim view of a mere centurion commander with lowly infantrymen taking up residence in their comfortable sanctum, but I also knew that most of these officers were at the front, and my men had been cold too long.

A fallen buttress and disheveled slabs of slate from the collapsed roof lay in great heaps upon the gritty marble surrounding the inn's grand entrance. Broken bits of pottery from shattered planters and tiny shards of colored glass gleamed prettily in the harsh light of a magnesium torch. The debris offered a bit of shelter from the wind for the solitary pair of guards standing watch at the door.

Something of the fear that chained other junior officers to blind obedience melted from my mind, supplanted by a rare, personal rage that made me courageous at that moment. These men, my men, whose bravery on the battlefield could not be questioned, deserved a better bed than the dog's rest we were afforded out in the open cold. I moved my soldiers up the stair.

"Hold up, sir," one of the two guards warned. "These premises are off limits to junior officers and the enlisted."

I ordered my men to fix bayonets. "The way I see it, you have a choice," I responded, shifting my gaze between the guards, giving them ample time to think. "You either step aside and let us in, or we'll step over your bodies when we walk through the door."

The second guard reached for his whistle, but Sergeant Hanibal's bayonet warned against further action. My men peacefully disarmed the sentries, gagged and bound them, then brought them inside with us.

An eerie silence prevailed inside the cavernous gloom of the inn's main hall. Great hunks of fallen ceiling and broken stone littered the scarred, parquet floor. Aside from the hissing furnace, still belching black smoke, the huge hall remained quiet, filled with wonderful warmth and the pleasant smell of wood smoke. I settled my men around the iron stove and drifted into a deep sleep.

The awareness of dull, persistent pain and noise outside awakened me very early the next morning. My feet throbbed, and every bruise and aching muscle clamored for attention. A strange, muscular weakness and the constant gnaw of hunger testified that I'd gone far too long without enough food.

Hobbling toward a broken window, my face felt the familiar sting of extreme cold as I looked into the courtyard. Horse-drawn carts, piled with canvas-covered battlefield casualties, clogged the outer gate, and a shouting match between two junior officers began to escalate rapidly.

I understood something about orders to bring bodies back to the inn for identification, but the other junior officer, obviously a man with troops occupying the courtyard, refused to allow the carts inside. He screamed about disease killing the rest of his men and didn't care who had given the accursed order.

In the midst of this quarrel, the crested helm of a legate moved forward among the ranks, silencing the argument immediately. My eyes widened and my throat went dry. It was Braegan . . . .

"Get up!" I barked. "All of you! Now!" The terror of looming retribution lurched my aching body into action and utterly vanquished the bravery I'd felt the night before. "Out the back and be quick!"

Sergeant Hanibal, ever anxious to shed blood, asked, "Want me to kill the guards?"

I glared at him, but he didn't flinch. "Don't do anything stupid! Find a room to throw them into." It didn't occur to me at the moment that my option, while merciful, was equally asinine.

We scurried through a broken wall on the south side of the inn, assembling near a disintegrating tower in the dark. Moving westward, we made our way toward the deserted gazebo ruins, enduring the penetrating blast of freezing wind rush into the courtyard from a great gap in the western wall.

I sent Sergeant Hanibal and six line soldiers off to find us some food. They returned about twenty minutes later with a cold stack of griddle cakes and a basket full of boiled eggs. This amount of food could have fed fifty men. Though it represented meager rations for a full century, the vestigial group of survivors under my command ate well that morning. When Hanibal boasted of how they'd swindled the quartermaster into believing he was feeding a full century, I actually felt proud of him for the first time.

During our meal, word came by messenger of orders demanding unit commanders assemble outside the gate to identify casualties. I sent Sergeant Hanibal and my troops north to Dieter, the town where we'd quartered before, promising I'd come as soon as I'd finished my grisly task.

I didn't realize I would never see them again.

Armed with a pen from my pack and a notepad, I followed other centurions and lieutenants in a silent procession through a ghastly maze of carts laden with bodies in various stages of dismemberment and decay. A necessary detachment prevailed among those of us who'd seen a soldier's fair share of fighting. We moved stoically through the line, stifling emotions for the sake of our personal sanity. Even so, the incredible number of casualties seemed overwhelming.

I spent over five hours examining the carnage, jotting down notes on the soldiers I recognized. Surviving families would at least hear the fate of their loved ones, however sorrowful the news. Bodies that had been too badly damaged for identification would not be pardoned by a priest – for the clerics needed names to perform extreme unction, and we'd suffered so many desertions we didn't know whether a missing man was dead or AWOL – nor would those dead be mourned back home as our customs dictated. Traditional rites of lamentation for those killed in action had not yet caught up with advances in warfare.

I'd written thirty-two names on my list by the time I found Lieutenant Rangell and his squadron. Many puncture wounds, lacerations, bruises and heavy blood stains on their stiffly frozen uniforms attested to a fierce, hand-to-hand fight, probably in the late stages of battle near the firebase when enemy resistance had been most intense. Overcome by the sudden enormity of my loss and barely able to control the flow of tears, I left the line and wandered, emotionally shaken, toward the inn.

As I neared the main steps, Legate Braegan staggered from inside the building and nearly slipped on the gritty, marble surface. A gleam flashed in his eye, several days' growth of beard remained on his reddened, wind-burned face, and the strong, blended odor of alcohol and dried sweat permeated the cold air around him.

"Hairless! You devil!" he slurred with a wicked smile. "You been hidin' honey on the sly!" The inflection of his voice chilled me like the wind and died in a fit of smug, drunken laughter.

"Sir," I responded, trying not to take offense at his consistently careless pronunciation of my name. "I have no idea what you're talking about."

"Oh-ho-ho, you know!" he retorted, wide-eyed. The legate put his arm around my neck, half strangling me in an attempt to balance himself as he pushed me upstairs. His riding crop dangled near my face. "Don't give me that holy act, you sly dog! You had me thinkin' you were a homo, but now I know better . . . ." His speech slumped into an ocean of obscenity, with wave after expletive wave foaming from the shore of his chapped, swollen lips.

Truthfully, I felt terrified. Although the man seemed to live in a perpetual state of inebria, his behavior on the extreme end of the drunkenness scale had always been unpredictably violent, and I had no idea what he intended to do with me.

All the courage that had served me in battle strained impotently against the iron chain of indoctrinated obedience, the whip of intimidation and welts of humiliation accumulated throughout every degrading experience in my career. With the meekness of a timid, guilt-ridden child I let the legate lead me, trying to ignore the growing cries of an afflicted woman assailing my ears.

Braegan thrust me into a banquet room on the extreme south end of the building. I saw many senior officers present, their faces ablaze with drink, rage and degrading laughter. I also saw the agonized countenance of the blonde-haired Tamarian woman whom I'd rescued many days before, her hair spread upon the tiled floor, her back arched painfully over a chair as two men stood on her bruised and battered arms.

She endured this public agony and humiliation with afflicted cries as Vice-General Diabilos committed rape.

"So hairless, you thought you'd keep this one all to yourself? Little secrets like this make for bad morale! You have to share your honey with the rest of us too!" Braegan tensed, gripping my neck with a single hand as if he were trying to crush my spine.

I said nothing. I felt sick and dirty standing in the room, and when I tried to leave, Braegan grabbed me by the ear and screamed at me to stand at attention and wait my turn. I knew exactly what he meant, but nothing about the depravity I witnessed there aroused me.

After Diabilos finished, he stepped over the stricken woman's legs and a junior officer moved in to take his place. Braegan, however, had a different idea. "Get out of there," he slurred. "Give the little centurion a chance to have some fun!" With that, he shoved me into the center of all attention and many high-ranking eyes fell upon me.

I did nothing. I felt shocked, disbelieving. When Braegan urged me on, I didn't comply. "Are you proud of this?" I asked.

Braegan and the others roared with laughter. "What's the matter, hairless? Can't get it up?" The legate made motions with his riding crop that vaguely resembled a crane straining under a heavy load, much to the amusement of his fellow officers. "Or maybe you're a homo after all! Come on, soldier! Show the girl a good time, and that's an order!"

I felt intense pressure to obey the command. Six months earlier, I would have given in, done the deed, and justified my behavior with arrogant words. We were the great nation who had a right to the spoils, and this girl would have meant nothing to me. No moral authority could rightfully restrain our actions, and we were accountable to no one. I'd once thought that way.

But I had changed.

I don't know where the courage to utter the words came from, but as they left my lips I felt an overwhelming surge of peace flood through my soul. "No sir!" I replied. "I will not!"

Braegan laughed at first, but soon his expression changed dangerously. "I said that's an order, soldier. Drop your pants and do as you're told!"

"Your order is illegal, sir, and I will not obey it."

The room grew quiet, save for the sobbing of the stricken woman. Braegan approached me with narrowed eyes and a menacing tone of voice. "An order is an order, centurion commander. There is no legality involved. You either obey it, or face the consequences."

This time, I returned the glare, and barely controlling my own anger, replied, "I will do no such thing . . . sir!"

Naked fury brimmed in the legate's eyes. With the speed of a striking viper, he lashed out at my face, striking me hard on the cheek with his riding crop. Although I'd made a reflexive attempt to ward off the blow with my hands, I didn't move in time and felt hot pain hammer my left cheek and sting in my eye. Adrenaline poured through my body, but I controlled the urge to fight back and wordlessly stood tall.

Just as Braegan was about to hit me again, Vice-General Diabilos restrained him with an upheld hand. "Don't make a fool of yourself, Braegan," he spat. "Get this man out of here."

The vice-general called for the two guards who'd been stationed beyond the doorway. They took my rifle from its harness on my back, my saber and bayonet, then bound my wrists. Acting on the orders of Diabilos, they also cut the woman free.

My eyes never met hers, but the woman said weakly, "The spirits will bless you!" in perfect vulgate as the guards pushed me beyond the door.

Braegan, contemptuously retorted, "May you burn forever, hairless!"

His words echoed in my mind as I walked down the dark hallway. I knew I'd just condemned myself to death, and that I would not have long to consider the consequences of my deed. But Braegan was wrong – I wasn't like him and he couldn't mold me into his own image. He would never have the honor of walking into the crucible I had just chosen to enter.

The Weak Link

Traditional hospitality in Kameron, even among the peasant farmers of the far northeast, called for celebration whenever a dignitary or wealthy merchant arrived in town. The timing of such visits in rural areas most often coincided with harvest season, when food stocks reached their peak, so that the rich could exploit the limited resources of the poor without having to provide rations for their servants out of their personal wealth.

Lynden Velez received a telegram from Fair Haven Fortress, informing him that a dozen heavily laden barges had departed that town, intending to dock in Helena the next morning. Although technically a river port, the tiny village of Helena, huddled on the rocky, northern bank of the rain-swollen Virgin River, never received more than a single barge in a month. Helena lay at the navigable end of the river, and no market existed eastward of the freehold over which Lord Velez presided.

Most of the river traffic in Northern Kameron ignored the Tualitin system and dutifully proceeded up and down the massive Angry Bear River, splitting east toward Burning Tree at the nexus of the Desolation, or continuing northward to the railhead at Fallen Moon Bay, beneath the famed citadel of Marvic. Tamaria, small but mighty as an industrial nation, Vathera to the far north and the Peran Confederation on Tamaria's northeastern border, made up a vast trading block over which Kameron, by virtue of her privileged geography, served as bread basket, trading partner and gateway to the western sea.

The timing of this mercantile traffic aroused Lynden's suspicion. He quietly put his army on alert and set out to visit to Alonso Meta, Helena's mayor, for advice on how to best respond to the merchant's unwelcome arrival and avoid offending local sensibilities.

Wisps of thick fog swirled up from the river, flooding the gently undulating landscape with a grey veil that concealed all background references and diffused the mid-morning light. As Lynden walked along, retreating mist revealed tangled, overgrown mustard that threatened to overwhelm neglected rows of naked vines linked by long strands of rusting wire. The cool, musty aroma of leaf mold and damp soil smelled of slow decay, augmented by the ruin of abandoned buildings leaning toward collapse upon crumbling stone foundations that had not seen repair in many decades.

Prosperity, once the hope of Helena and its surrounding vineyards, eluded the little town like a shadow on a cloudy day. Given a fair chance, the region might have known some vitality, but its previous landowners had been quick to move profits elsewhere, and the majority of peasants who worked in the vineyards never had a chance to even complete their tiny, stone and mortar homes.

Many local residents lived in dilapidated bungalows with shabby metal roofs streaked orange-brown with rust. Those who'd been able to afford glass for their windows could not prevent the vandalism wrought by bandits and jobless ruffians who considered the shattering of windowpanes a particularly sporting distraction.

Most young people did not stay in this place, and for that reason, the dwindling population of Helena and its surrounding area consisted mainly of grandparents who'd seen their children move far away, widows, and older bachelors whose lack of personal hygiene was at least partially responsible for their solitary lifestyle.

Lord Velez worked hard to win the confidence of his new constituency, and began to witness a restoration of hope among them. Many, whose skepticism shone brazenly on their faces when he first arrived, now regarded the warlord as an honest man.

These conservative, tradition-bound people now accepted the Velez family whole-heartedly – even though their language and customs were foreign to them – and the change in their regard for the Lithians transformed the town itself. People greeted Lynden Velez with genuine admiration, and in return, he remembered their names and spoke kindly to them while he walked the muddy streets.

Alonso Meta lived in a modest, but well-maintained home along a sheltered lane at the northern edge of town. Flanked by a boarded-up school on one side and a reputable winery on the other, the mayor's house seemed ideally suited to represent the solid respectability that should have been the hallmark of Helena's citizenry.

Lynden spoke briefly with Ricardo, the mayor's polio-stricken son, whose condition confined him to a wheelchair usually occupying a sheltered place on the front porch. Ricardo retained full control over his upper-body, but pain prevented him from spending much time at his work.

At age forty-two, the younger Meta earned his living carving wooden trinkets and toys from trees native to this region. He had an artistic gift that Lynden hoped would blossom into a more prosperous business once the little community achieved its goal of economic growth.

"My father is working on the accounts," Ricardo stated. "I'm sure he'll be pleased to see you. The front door is open."

Lord Velez thanked the woodcarver, stomped the mud off his boots and entered the Meta house. The peculiar odor of burning kerosene mingled with the lingering scents of unwashed linen and a combination of wood smoke and dust that, while not altogether unpleasant, testified that the mayor and his son did not spend much time cleaning. Alonso Meta had lost his wife to tuberculosis three years earlier, and a general clutter in the living room suggested that the rest of the house probably looked equally untidy.

Alonso, a friendly man whose white-bearded face wore the hardships he'd endured with serenity and grace, greeted Lynden warmly as the warlord removed his coat in the living room. "Please, sit down," the mayor invited. "Let me get you a nice glass of wine."

The local field blend possessed a pleasant flavor, just sweet enough, Lynden thought, and would likely fetch a fair price in the large cities down river. After the usual exchange of pleasantries, Lord Velez broached the subject of his current concern. "What do you know of the Maridom Trading Company?" he asked, referring to the business that owned the approaching boats.

The mayor cut a small slice of white cheese, chewed it thoughtfully, sipped his wine, then set the glass down on a serving table layered in months of dust. "Maridom Trading is a diversified textile wholesale company," he began. "Last year, they brought us a shipment of tapestries and rugs. These were well made and beautiful, but their prices were beyond our means. They know we are not wealthy, but the merchant master is a friend of our former landlord, Lord Navarro, and most of us felt pressure to spend money we really didn't have.

"They shouldn't have expected much from us, but they left expressing disgust and called curses upon our ancestors. Incidents like this create a reputation that's hard to live down. Merchants talk among themselves . . . .

"We suffered some minor vandalism, and two or three young ladies were socially compromised during their visit. The merchant master offered us nothing by way of compensation for the actions of his crew, either. Like many of our problems, we were victims of poverty, and they haven't come back."

"I see," Lord Velez replied. "You say they're a textile company. Have they ever brought anything other than expensive floor coverings?"

Alonso Meta nodded, finished his wine and poured another glass, offering his guest a refill, which Lynden politely refused. "Yes," he replied. "Navarro typically bought our work clothes from them and deducted the cost from our profit shares. Of course, he added his own mark-up . . . ." Mayor Meta smiled, shrugged and tilted his head to the side as if resigned to fate. The transaction he'd just described was one of many ways that Kamerese landlords perpetuated debt among the peasants.

That comment inspired Lynden's indignation. His brow narrowed, but he didn't elaborate. "How many barges have they usually sent here?"

The mayor grunted, his smile transforming into a frown. "A small one and it came in the spring. They intended to buy wine for the return trip, but since their hold remained full, they departed with only a cask or two. It's unfortunate. Our market here is small, but without the ability to sell our goods downstream, we will never grow."

Lord Velez sipped his wine, savoring the delicate flavors on the back of his tongue. He had an idea for taking care of the marketing problems and made a mental note to invite a longtime friend as a guest for dinner. "Considering their last experience here, do you find anything unusual about their return? Do other Kamerese merchants behave this way?"

The question required more thought than the Lithian warlord expected in response, but it confirmed his own suspicion. "Two things trouble me about the news," Alonso began. "The first is that they're coming back at a time of year when our winter food supply must be preserved. They know this, yet custom dictates that we must entertain them.

"None of us would object to a reasonable visit, but I hear they're bringing a dozen full-size barges, which means we will be feeding well over a hundred men for as long as they stay. This I find much too insolent to be an oversight.

"That many crew members wandering through town with nothing to do will be trouble. You, my friend, had better hide those pretty girls of yours, or at least, put them in long dresses and give them a sober escort with loaded rifles the whole time those hooligans are here."

Lynden Velez scowled at the thought of his daughters being mistreated. "Is there any protocol that would permit us to politely turn the merchant away?" he asked, hopefully.

"I'm afraid there is no other way," Alonso replied. "We survive on the strength of our social reputation, and if we don't entertain the salesmen, word will get around and soon no one will call at the dock."

Lord Velez didn't like hearing this, but he'd learned what he'd needed to know, and the rest of the conversation drifted slowly into topics of a more benign nature.

***

Terrifying shell impacts rumbled through the dark halls of the fortress at Dead Hand Ridge. Faced with the genuine danger of a methane leak and possible explosion, base personnel had dutifully closed every gas valve, depriving their countrymen of whatever aid and comfort the light could afford them. Swirling concrete dust, barely visible in the gloom, created a suffocating atmosphere indoors that lined every mouth, clung to sweaty flesh and irritated the lungs of each man and woman before it settled out into a gritty film over the once-polished floor tiles.

The mortars, with their high angles of attack, were the worst, Woodwind thought. Since the beginning of the artillery barrage, Woodwind noticed the fortress disintegrating from the top down. Cannon shells, initially ineffective because the base walls deflected them, now often brought down huge chunks of concrete from the upper levels weakened by previous mortar impacts.

With thanks to Brenna, he'd fully recovered from his injuries. Yet rather than trying to escape through enemy lines at night, Woodwind chose to stand with the base defenders. Ordinarily, the addition of a single man might not have made much difference, but he *believed* in Allfather, whose power and active influence the Tamarians would neither recognize, nor appreciate.

For the first few days, Woodwind worked on a team calculating ballistic attack solutions against known Azgar artillery positions for the rocket crews. Counter-battery fire, coordinated with nearby Tamarian bases, initially stunned the enemy and prevented large-scale bombardment of the fortress at Dead Hand Ridge. This allowed its defenders to repel several direct assaults.

But the Azgar responded by bringing more guns forward. Their commanders, evaluating Tamarian fire tactics, spread the cannon and mortar batteries apart so that a single rocket warhead could not destroy more than one gun crew. When possible, they also began moving their guns to different positions after firing several rounds. In this way, their weapons became much more difficult to destroy. Within a few days, the Tamarian supply of heavy rockets dwindled, then depleted. Equipped with relatively small, three inch howitzers, the fortress at Dead Hand Ridge lost the only effective response to long-range enemy artillery they could muster.

As unchallenged mortar shells screeched overhead, gradually pounding the proud concrete fortress into rubble, Woodwind feared for his life, praying almost continually. Many combined stresses, ranging from his inability to directly understand his Tamarian hosts to lack of sleep and the horrifying reality that unless they were relieved and re-supplied soon, the base would certainly fall, made his prayers uncharacteristically desperate, and as intimate as Brenna's had ever been.

From a firing port one floor above ground level, Woodwind's view of the unfolding battle stretched eastward toward the horizon. Aided by borrowed binoculars, the southerner observed long lines of enemy infantry marching purposely toward the front. Thousands of horses, supply carts, caissons and cannon tubes converged, delivering the crushing might of the invader's army into a massive, overwhelming locus against this tiny, crumbling firebase. It seemed only a matter of time before its intrepid defenders lost their struggle to stop the enemy.

Although he could not comprehend their speech, Woodwind well understood the universal language of fear. He sensed in their nervous tension, their harsh voices and petty conflicts a genuine anxiety that all men experience whenever they anticipate an imminent, violent death. Memories of friends and acquaintances, resurrected in facial expressions that had also infected the Lithian defenders of Shirak, underscored the gravity of the circumstance every Tamarian soldier in Woodwind's vicinity faced. Surrounded by the enemy on all sides – with no hope of escape – each man contemplated death in his individual manner, and though their reactions to it ranged from serenity to near-insanity and terror, each response reflected an intelligent effort to come to terms with the grim consequence of combat. Everyone felt exhausted. Constant explosions jarred every nerve and prevented rest.

Covered under this crush of artillery fire, the next enemy charge commenced. Woodwind watched the adversary line up beyond the glacis, spread out until each man stood six paces from his neighbor. The Tamarians prepared to repel, opening ammunition crates and chambering rounds; aiming their weapons at discreet points on the killing ground. All a defender needed to do was fire his gun directly ahead at anything entering his limited field of vision. It had worked well in the past.

This time, however, the Azgar did not merely mass their troops and send them headlong to their slaughter. In between the advancing ranks of infantry charged long streams of fleet-footed cavalry, dashing forward to blunt the Tamarian defense.

Woodwind set the binoculars down, realizing after a few moments of watching that the daring equine attack would reach the fortress walls. Many thousands of hooves thundered across the glacis as the final artillery shells slammed into the concrete overhead. Then, as if announcing the demise of all resistance, a large section of the third floor, along with the exterior of the second, gave way and slid into the defensive trench that circled the stronghold, killing every soldier within ten feet on the third level and burying many more below.

Dust swirled in the incessant wind. The sudden appearance of daylight and exposure to extreme cold announced, as the rubble settled, that the troops in Woodwind's area would face the enemy unprotected. Further, the debris from the stricken wall created a crude sort of ramp leading up to the second floor.

No matter how quickly they fired, the Tamarians could not stop the cavalry charge. Thousands upon thousands of horses flooded across the battlefield, and where many hundreds of their stricken bodies fell victim to rifle and machine cannon fire, others followed and pressed onward in an unstoppable, equine tide.

The officer who'd been standing next to Woodwind snapped backward in an explosion of blood. He'd been struck in the face by a bullet and died instantly. With his demise, genuine panic rippled through the young soldiers nearby. Woodwind witnessed an instant, deadly shift in morale, and knowing the danger this wrought, muttered the most sincere prayer of his life. "Merciful Allfather!" he breathed. "Help us! We can't stop them!"

***

When Lynden returned to his villa, a subtle downcast to his gaze caught his wife's attention. Lady Alexina noticed that he addressed and dismissed one of their servants with less cordiality than was his custom. He seemed distracted and unable to focus until his worried eyes found her watching from the balcony. She smiled, his expression softened, and as she strode gracefully toward the stairway, the Lithian woman reached for her husband's hand.

Lynden ascended with quick steps, admiring his wife as he approached. He felt captivated as ever by loveliness that transcended the physical perfection of her beauty. They shared a spiritual bond, a likeness of mind whose strength had grown in many years together. In addition, undiminished by the passage of time, a powerful sensuality prevailed between them that emerged wordlessly in a glance, a slight change in posture, a glisten in their eyes and a flush across their faces.

Their daughter Acacia, whom they called Cassie, had been transposing a favorite piano composition on her lute. She stopped playing when her father entered, noticed the way he looked at her mother, and sensed that her parents needed time alone. Cassie gently put her instrument down, and scurried to close the double doors leading to her parents' wing of the house, saying "I love you" to them as the latch caught.

Alexina pressed her warm lips against her husband's mouth, exchanging delicate, moist caresses with his tongue. Lynden's strong left hand pulled her body close while his right hand brushed gently through her long, black and white hair. She pulled away slowly, put her hands on his shoulders and spoke quietly, "Talk to me first, my love. Tell me what's on your mind."

He nodded. "We have a serious problem . . . ."

Safely away from any listening ears, they lounged on their bed and discussed the approaching merchant convoy. Lynden expressed his worries candidly while his wife listened, and she, rubbing his shoulders while they spoke, assured him that he had good reason to be concerned.

Their conversation gradually drifted into silence, words replaced by the tender, imploring insistence of fingers caressing flesh. A gentle escalation of tension, a comforting exchange of pleasant, familiar, physical sensations and the resulting release of energies merged husband and wife into a singular, sensual experience uniquely and exclusively their own.

After regaining their breath, they remained together in a languid embrace, smiling at one another as they always did, exchanging whispered comments in praise of each other, and occasionally venturing a caress that suggested they should continue. In this case, however, a knock from the door altered the mood. Alexina picked up her gown and slipped away while her husband dressed.

Lithian culture jealously respected the privacy of married couples, and it was considered discourteous to disturb the intimacy of lovers behind closed doors. A knock under these circumstances implied a serious problem in need of immediate attention.

Cynthia Velez apologized for the interruption. The maiden, who stood nearly as tall as her father, had inherited more human traits from him than had her sisters. Heavier than both Alexina and Brenna, Thea developed an hourglass figure that very few Lithian women attained. The physical differences that contrasted Cynthia from her prettier, more delicate sisters made the young woman unpopular with Lithian men, very sensitive, and extremely shy.

Xina evaluated her daughter's facial expression, and opened her arms for a loving embrace. "My darling Thea! What's wrong, honey?" she inquired. "Are you hurt?"

Cynthia shook her head while holding onto her mother for comfort, then stepped back as Lynden approached and threw her arms around him as well. "I just woke up from a nap. I've had another dream."

The look exchanged between husband and wife expressed genuine concern. Cynthia Velez had a long history of dreaming about events that invariably came to pass, and she seemed to know the difference between an ordinary nightmare and a premonition, even though she couldn't explain how this was so. In every instance where she recalled frightening details, her parents had learned to take warning.

"Come and sit with us," Alexina offered. "Tell us everything you remember."

Lynden encouraged their daughter to sit on the bed, then called for one of the servants and requested a pot of tea. Tirra, an older woman who'd served as Brenna's maid, rushed off to do the warlord's bidding.

Thea sat with her hands folded on the pretty, lace-patterned fabric of her gown. "I don't remember how it started," she began. Her eyes, lacking much of the Lithian sparkle in low light, grew wide as she spoke. "But I saw the same army that drove us from home fighting in a cold place. They were freezing to death.

"Then I saw Brenna, traveling with strangers on a wagon. She was alone. I didn't see her husband. Enemy horsemen came after her." At the mention of her sister's name, Cynthia's eyes brimmed wetly. "It was bright and blinding as they tried to kill her. She bravely fought them all by herself, and no one came to help . . . ."

Thea paused to regain her composure. "Woodwind came to mind after this. He was in a fortress with pale-eyed men who were fighting a long battle. The enemy kept attacking over and over again. His guardian told me to *break the chain,* but I don't understand what that meant.

"The last part of the dream made no sense at all. I saw twelve boats coming up the river. They stopped in town and men with guns got out and forced everyone to carry huge boxes over the mountains." Cynthia stopped and turned toward her father. "*Amair*, you have to stop them. If you don't, the enemy will kill both Blynn and Woodwind." Thea used the blended form of her sister's first and middle names, a common practice in the Velez family used as a term of endearment.

Lord Velez bowed his head for a prayerful moment and stared at his hands. When he looked up again, Thea's lovely face appeared expressionless, but Alexina's eyes, illuminated by worry, pleaded for him to affirm their daughter's testimony.

"Allfather sent you this dream?" he asked.

Cynthia nodded slowly. "I have no doubt. I've already prayed for them. You should too . . . ."

"Of course," the warlord replied, solemnly. "We will do whatever Allfather wills." They held hands and interceded for Brenna and Woodwind. Afterward, Lynden kissed Thea on the forehead, his wife on the lips and promised to return after retrieving a map from the library.

Cartography had been practiced in Kameron for nearly fifteen hundred years. Most of the original land surveys west of the Angelgate Mountains, while very old, were extremely accurate and useful.

Like much of the dilapidated villa, its library suffered from broken windows and a leaky roof. Much of the literary treasure once preserved here had fallen into decay. Bird nests lined some of the higher book cases, whose shelves had been whitewashed by droppings. Mice and rats destroyed many leather bindings of a book collection written in three languages, one of which was no longer spoken. Tika, Cassie's feline, had grown fat on the dining fare of this room alone.

Its stench could overwhelm the senses on a warm day, but it didn't smell as bad in cool weather, provided anyone brave enough to enter breathed through their mouth. Tika earned a gentle scratching behind her ears by greeting the father of her mistress as he opened the map case. After several minutes of searching, the warlord found a local land survey, frayed at the edges, but still legible.

Returning to his bed chamber, Lynden opened a curtain to let more light into the room, then spread the delicate vellum on the bed for his wife and daughter to examine while they sipped their tea. The Angelgate Mountains formed a high wall on the eastern boundary of his land, descending into the steep-sided foothills that followed the curve of the Virgin River and eventually smoothed out as the tributary emptied into the Tualitin, the river that comprised his northern boundary.

"I've received a telegram about a merchant convoy en route to Helena," Lynden stated. "The timing of its arrival and the size of the flotilla give me the impression that this is more than a merchant coming here to sell wares." Lynden's expression reflected concern as he pieced together a scenario that made sense of his daughter's dream. "From Helena, you can see that there's really nowhere for them to go, other than through Maidenhair Pass.

"Tamaria, the only sizable market in this region, lies north of the Tualitin River. There's no way to access markets further east, unless they unload their cargo at Suicide Cataract, right on the border. You can see from the contours that the Tualitin flows through a steep canyon for many miles as it falls from the Saradon. There are no roads there, only a military railway, so that's not a good route."

"But if they're really heading for Tamaria, they should be traveling up this river," Alexina offered, pointing to the Desolation. "They'd be backtracking by coming here first, so Tamaria can't be their destination."

"Well," Lynden cautioned, "if they're trying to get their goods out to the Saradon – on the other side of the Angelgate Mountains – and they don't want the Tamarians to know about it, shipping from here makes sense."

Cynthia nodded, her mind grasping her father's analysis. "You're thinking their cargo is actually intended for the Azgar army?" She measured the distance on the map and divided figures in her head. "They could easily be near Tamaria by now. The Saradon gets cold in the winter. Since we're closer to the sea, the seasons change there before our winter comes. This rain we're having here is likely turning to snow on the other side of the mountains."

Lord Velez agreed. "Our eastern boundary runs along the Angelgate ridge line. Maidenhair Gap is the only mountain pass within fifty miles that is low enough in elevation not to get snowed in during the winter. The shortest practical distance between the navigable part of the Virgin River and the Saradon follows Maidenhair Canyon, where we built the debris dams this summer. The only port anywhere near that canyon is Helena, so I think it's more than coincidental that these Maridom Trading barges are heading here. They're not coming to sell their wares to the locals; they're coming here to avoid the Tamarians."

"What are they transporting?" Xina asked.

"This morning's telegram gave no details of their manifest. It could be anything from guns and ammunition to some other kind of contraband. Mayor Meta says this company sells high quality textiles."

"Then it's likely warm clothing and blankets," Alexina concluded. "Thea saw the Azgar freezing in the snow. I'll bet that company has a contract to supply winter clothing. The reason they've brought twelve barges all the way out here is because they're outfitting an army." The Lithian woman narrowed her eyes, determined to protect her eldest daughter. "We can't let them get away with this."

The task sounded easier than Lord Velez knew it would be to carry out. "Indeed, but I have only two thousand soldiers, none of whom I can afford to pay. Mayor Meta insists we must entertain merchant convoy, while Thea says I must stop them. What do you propose?"

Lady Alexina smiled mischievously. "That's a simple matter, my love." She leaned over to kiss her husband's lips and told him, "I will sink their boats . . . ."

***

As a freezing wind swept away the stinging cloud of concrete dust, three lines of Azgar cavalry formed just beyond the defensive ditch. Their horses remained several yards apart so that the Tamarians could not effectively mass fire against them. After the first line fired, the second line moved up to discharge weapons while the first retreated to reload. By the time the third line engaged, the soldiers of the first line were ready to shoot again, creating steady pressure on the fortress defenders.

Woodwind grudgingly admired both the intelligence of his enemy, and the courage they demonstrated by exposing themselves to short-range defensive fire. Despite very heavy losses, the Azgar kept coming. Human nature demanded dealing with the immediate threat, in this case, the cavalry attack. Doing this, however, enabled the infantry to advance across the glacis with minimal losses, a feat they'd never before managed, despite facing repeated and decisive defeat after several attempts.

The foot soldiers soon arrived in sufficient force to attack every breach in the walls. Crackling small arms fire, bullet impacts, whirring machine cannon and the screams of dying beasts and men merged with the merciless laughter of winter wind as the Azgar's Northern Liberation Army flexed its formidable muscle.

Strangely, inexplicably, Woodwind suddenly became more aware of the sounds around him. In this heightened sensory state, he felt a tremble race through his spine and realized that he could now understand every terrified word uttered by the Tamarian soldiers surrounding him. The sounds and structure of their language now carried meaning to his ears.

Wasting no time in thinking about the enigma of this mysterious ability, Woodwind circulated among the young men and women, laying his hand on their shoulders to give them courage. "Be strong. Allfather will fight with us, and if we have faith, we can defeat them."

Despite their distress, the young Tamarians sensed something powerful in the soul of this mercenary southerner. Woodwind's brave words, confidence and calm demeanor replaced terror with just enough courage to enable frightened soldiers to stand and fight. This was all Woodwind could really ask them to do, but he *believed* that it would be enough.

Following Woodwind's orders, surviving soldiers in his area formed two groups of six on either side of the twenty-foot-wide breach. Three volunteers climbed up to handle a machine cannon on the third floor. Woodwind warned them to pick their targets carefully and fire only at close range. He took the short sword from a fallen officer and moved into a position in the exact center of the breach. "This is where we stand!" he told them. "Let no Azgar foot touch the floor here, and we'll live to see another day!"

In a spot where the remaining wall extended roughly three feet above the second floor, Woodwind crouched for protection against a heavy volley of enemy fire that pelted the wall behind him. Glancing to either side, he realized that the mortal fear his hosts had just overcome began to return as a swarm of black-uniformed infantry began climbing up the rubble heap toward them.

Tamarian resistance stiffened. A steady stream of rifle fire ripped through wave after wave of attacking troopers until their bloodstained bodies lay in tangled heaps on the killing field. Still, the invaders pressed relentlessly forward, the sheer weight of their numbers carrying the battle. The first group to survive the climb to the second level arrived, out-of-breath, to face an expert swordsman.

Woodwind stood tall, entering a kind of altered state in which no thought prevailed against the holy warrior within. He personified God's vengeance, executing a swift outward block that deflected a bayonet aimed at his heart. Riding the carbine barrel upward on the hand guard, Woodwind pushed the gun aside, pressed down and lunged into the chest of its owner.

Kicking the impaled victim of his attack away, the southerner lashed to his right, cut the throat of another enemy soldier, then followed this lethal move with a left-side circle block that caught the gun barrel of a third soldier and rode it up toward the sky. A reptile-quick retraction and thrust found its deadly mark and departed before the dying adversary tumbled backward.

The swordsman had very little room to move, but the men he faced had to climb over debris to reach him. Simple blocks and parries transitioned effortlessly into powerful cuts and thrusts, dismembering hands, piercing hearts and disemboweling any Azgar soldier who dared attack him. Woodwind's blade sang to the right in a strong, downward arc that evolved quickly into an attack as his weapon slipped above a parried rifle. Woodwind slashed swiftly to the left with such brutal force, the sword cut as cleanly through his enemy's neck as an executioner's guillotine.

Watching the foreign man stand in the breach, the terrified Tamarians grew more confident. Woodwind's raw courage, his great strength and tremendous skill, along with his utter ruthlessness gave them hope.

Woodwind flicked the blade leftward and lunged with a mighty grunt, dropping his right hand free to thrust his sword tip into the left shoulder of his next victim. A quick withdrawal, another thrust and forward step plunged the Tamarian sword hilt deep into his enemy's abdomen.

With merciless brutality, Woodwind dispatched any enemy soldier who dared stand against him. Aggressive, swift and pitiless, the southerner inspired terror among his attackers. The tenacity of this defense did not diminish as the afternoon wore on, and as the battle denigrated into general hand-to-hand melee around the breach, exhausted Tamarians, inspired by Woodwind's example, somehow found the strength to keep fighting.

The Azgar infantry, having come so close to overwhelming the defenders, swarmed ahead, absorbing all the point-blank firepower the Tamarians could hurl against them. Because of the steep angle and continued pressure from protected firing ports, they could not level their carbines at Woodwind and his allies and shoot. After discharging their weapons at the defenders on the wall, the black-uniformed soldiers had neither the room nor the time to reload, so they engaged with bayonets or sabers, counting on the press of numbers to assure their success.

Gradually, an increase in the volume of rifle and machine cannon fire being delivered from the base began blunting the enemy assault. The momentum of battle shifted, and along with it, the defenders' morale strengthened. Azgar troops waiting beyond the defensive ditch for their turn to move ahead fell like autumn leaves shaken in a great wind, with progressively fewer of them remaining alive to press the attack.

Woodwind blocked a bayonet thrust, but had no chance to attack as his enemy withdrew fearfully. He heard a gunshot behind him take down an Azgar officer with a pistol, then another, which killed his retreating opponent.

After this, no surviving enemy rose up to meet him. Panting in exertion, spattered in blood and drenched with sweat, Woodwind retreated behind the shattered wall and watched the surviving enemy infantry withdraw in disarray, leaving the glacis stained with many thousands of casualties. No army could sustain losses of this magnitude for long, and in celebration, a great shout went up among the weary native defenders.

Woodwind raised his right hand into a triumphant fist, but then bowed his head and quietly, in the alliterative, Lithian tongue, thanked Allfather for deliverance.

After this, he examined the dead enemy in his vicinity and noticed that most of their fingers shared a sickening, mottled blackness. Woodwind saw faces and lips chapped raw, with scabs overlaying the windburned flesh. Nearly every corpse lay swaddled in two or three layers of summer clothing, but even this could not protect them from the fury of winter in the northern hill country, or worse, out on the open Saradon.

The madness that drove the Azgar high command to continue senseless frontal attacks against Dead Hand Ridge, rather than laying siege and waiting until spring, became clear to Woodwind. The enemy could not bypass the fortress without exposing their staging areas to long range rocket fire, but neither could they remain in the field, enduring harsh wind and freezing temperatures. Woodwind realized that the enemy wouldn't stop until either they'd prevailed, or had been decisively defeated.

How then, had the Tamarians managed to overcome what looked like certain loss? Glancing backward, Woodwind noticed many friendly soldiers clad in clean uniforms. Where had they come from? He watched men stack new ammunition boxes along the back side of the hallway. Work crews with shovels and pick axes moved forward to clean up the mess.

Somehow, Dead Hand Ridge had been reinforced. Woodwind's ignorance of Tamarian logistical resupply capabilities through their underground rail network made him believe that a Tamarian force had successfully broken through enemy lines. He could not begin to appreciate the frustration of Azgar commanders, who knew better.

Exhausted from hours of fighting, Woodwind watched a Tamarian officer approach. The man saluted and began to speak, but to Woodwind, the words once again consisted of a meaningless jumble of guttural, consonant sounds, and he understood nothing.

***

Alexina meditated alone in a private spot overlooking her estate. Far below, as the rain-swollen Virgin River raced northward toward the Tamarian border she thought about rocks hidden beneath its current. Cold rain, accelerated by an occasional gust of wind, matted her thick black and white hair, gradually darkening the costly indigo gown that graced her perfect shoulders.

An officer's meeting would begin as soon as light faded from the sky, and though she normally didn't concern herself with the conduct of her husband's small army, Alexina knew that Lynden would appreciate her presence, even if she merely sat at the back and reserved her comments until they were alone. But she also felt curious about how her husband's officers would react to her plan.

Voices, laughter and the sloshing sound of wet feet tramping through puddles aspired above the patter of rain on foliage. Alexina quietly backed into the shadows of a cedar grove until members of her husband's army finished filing to their seats. Though the men would have politely stopped and allowed her forward in deference to her position, Xina savored her moments of solitude.

This preference for seclusion often caused people who didn't know Lady Velez to accuse her of snobbery, but reticence remained an integral part of her character, and she rarely sought the company of anyone beyond the circle of her immediate family. In addition, Xina's high intelligence intimidated less capable minds, and because she'd descended from a very wealthy family, it had always been hard for her to find true friends.

Peering through foliage, the Lithian mother suppressed laughter as she watched her daughters, dressed in the ugliest, least form-fitting attire available in Helena, stomping along the trail under the alert watch of Kimoni, Xola and Jawara – three of Tegene's youngest adult sons – who often served as their armed escorts.

Camille, her youngest, lamented loudly, "I hate wearing this thing! I feel like an absolute cow!"

Thea held her sister's hand as they walked. "Then you'd better ask *Umma* to adjust our dinner menu," she replied, smiling. "A big salad may better match that ugly gown, but remember that it's unladylike to chew your cud!"

Camille showed her displeasure by bumping hips with older, much larger, Thea. Separated in age by at least five years, Alexina's daughters enjoyed camaraderie without rivalry common among siblings closer in age.

Acacia followed several yards behind with her boyfriend, a handsome young attorney named Jared who'd been living with the Velez family for three years. As was her custom, the taciturn maiden listened to her sisters banter back and forth without responding.

Everyone loved Jared. His mother, a retired concert pianist, had initially wanted him to court Brenna, but he preferred her slimmer, quieter sister. Jared adored Cassie, and their relationship had become quite serious, but the couple would wait patiently for Brenna to find her partner first, before Cassie moved away to live with his family.

Yet if Cynthia's clairvoyance could be trusted, Brenna had already found and married her partner. That seemed unreasonably quick for a Lithian courtship, but Lady Xina's eldest daughter had a well-earned reputation for willfully defying conventions . . . .

Despite feeling proud of her daughters' transitions into womanhood, Lady Velez occasionally entertained half-hearted wishes that they'd forever remain carefree children, when their lives were not burdened by social pressure.

As soon as the gentle patter of raindrops prevailed on the forest floor and the rush of wind returned like a lover's whispered words through the towering treetops, Lady Xina scurried onto the trail and soundlessly took a seat on the soft, damp sphagnum moss three rows behind Sherman Mason, the stocky engineer. An exchange of eye contact and the briefest hint of a smile across her husband's handsome face assured Xina that he acknowledged her presence.

Tegene, though he sat in the place of honor at Lynden's side, would listen to the proceedings without comment. Like Alexina, the elderly Abelscinnian gentleman preferred to voice his views in private, after everyone else had the opportunity to speak.

Lord Velez opened with an invocation. He explained the various social problems created by the merchant convoy's arrival the following day. When he outlined his daughter's Azgar resupply theory, murmurs swept through the assembled men. Everyone present had suffered personal loss at the enemy's hands, and their emotional wounds remained raw.

Loran, commander of a scout unit, arose. "Although we have no quarrel with the people of Kameron, any cooperation with the Azgar will likely result in ongoing extortion. They have a long history of this behavior. If you turn the convoy back by force of arms, as socially difficult as this may be, you will prevent a larger problem later."

Lynden acknowledged the point. "I agree, but we need to be careful. We live among people who don't understand us, and though we've worked hard to demonstrate our trustworthiness, anything we do that creates hardship for them endangers us. Our position requires local support. Their trust is a gift offered with conditions, and for that reason, I prefer we act with wit rather than force."

The discussion following these remarks gave the officers an opportunity to express support for decisive military action, or to offer alternatives. In this case, these ranged from quarantine and bureaucratic inspection that would delay unloading, all the way to arresting the merchant for treason. This manner of leadership suited Lithian culture, with its high regard for individualism and free expression. Every man who rose to speak respected the view of dissenting colleagues without passing judgment on the merits of any proposed action. They remained unanimous, however, in stating their willingness to defend the Velez family at all costs.

Alexina waited until every officer who chose to speak had the opportunity to do so, even though she'd come to the meeting prepared to outline her plan. While she had a right to command their compliance, Lady Xina preferred to persuade. When she arose to speak, the impact of her beauty in the indigo light, coupled with surprise on the part of the men who had not seen her arrival, highlighted the impact of her words.

"Gentle warriors, your willingness to fight for our cause transcends courage. But I don't wish that any of you should perish. If we can do what must be done with minimal bloodshed, surely Allfather will bless our plans."

Lord Velez listened to his wife explain the details of her idea and marveled that he'd been blessed by such a lovely and intelligent partner. Her proposal solved every problem that he and the people under his rule faced.

"In this way, the destruction of their ships and cargo will appear entirely accidental, and neither they nor local residents can hold us accountable for losses in a natural disaster," Xina concluded.

Loran stood again, and after being acknowledged, expressed his support for Alexina's innovative concept. "My lady," he remarked in closing. "Given the previous behavior of this outfit's crew while visiting Helena, I recommend evacuating your household as a precaution. Should the merchants become enraged and wish to harm you after their ships and cargo have been destroyed, it would be easier for us to assure your safety in a secure place."

Alexina appreciated his input. Lynden seemed to have something to add, but he deferred for the moment and let his wife conclude. She smiled as she spoke. "As always, we leave ourselves in your competent care."

Next, Lord Velez created specific tasks and a time sequence for each event in the plan. Refined by further discussion, these duties evolved into an organized, operational strategy, in which every unit of his small army played an important role. This iterative process established personal ownership among the officers, who appreciated how Lynden listened to and respected their expertise.

Lord Velez dismissed the meeting with a benediction, confident that his men would begin their work immediately. The warlord kissed and embraced each of his three daughters before sending them off to perform tasks better accomplished by charisma and wit, than muscle.

"Your intellect continually astounds me," Lynden told his bride when they were alone. "If I had married you a decade earlier, my fortunes would be multiplied tenfold."

Alexina's eyes widened, feigning wonder. "If you're so easily impressed, perhaps you're right!" She drew near, laced her fingers behind her lover's back and snuggled her hips into his.

Her sensuality quickened his pulse. "No doubt," he replied, kissing and caressing her gently, "we would also have many more children!"

***

Coordinated, counter-battery attacks began at dusk. All three Tamarian forts in range of Azgar artillery positions commenced massive fire missions in response to resupply, and new orders issued by General Ziegler at Central Command Headquarters in Burning Tree. Soon, the enemy cannon fell silent.

Colonel Brandt sensed a lift in morale among his troops as soon as the big guns began firing. Ordinary line soldiers, who could do nothing other than cower in terror whenever enemy artillery exploded overhead, stood taller now that Tamarian guns were again reciprocating. Their rockets would soon follow, and then the enemy would tremble in terror once again.

Emergency underground resupply, the combat variable whose influence enemy commanders could not control, created problems of its own for Colonel Brandt. Tamarian fire keeps normally housed only 400 soldiers. In war time, using every bit of available space, hot bunking troops not on duty and speedily evacuating the wounded, the fortresses could accommodate as many as 1 200 men.

Yet this strained the mess crew, water supply and waste disposal systems. Long lines for food, water and the toilet tested every soldier's patience to its limits. Hallways, narrowed by stacks of war provisions ranging from ammunition to latrine paper, suddenly became crowded and difficult to traverse. Furthermore, finding necessary supplies among hundreds of crates scattered throughout all five floors of the base required nothing less than inventory control bordering on the miraculous, especially in the dark.

Enemy mortars created an additional problem. Every previous emergency situation faced by the Tamarian army permitted overflow sleeping accommodations in the central courtyard, but with Azgar shells arcing over the base walls and impacting inside, this area resembled a rail yard after a boiler explosion. Tamarian engineering crews worked through the night to clear the area, so they could subsequently erect and launch rockets from the courtyard.

Underground munitions magazines became new sleeping areas out of sheer necessity. The labyrinth of secret, subterranean passageways that usually served as a means for defending soldiers to unexpectedly appear on the battlefield now overflowed with troops awaiting a command to engage the enemy.

Those orders, signed by General Ziegler, now lay in Colonel Brandt's pocket. Very soon, that slip of paper would set in motion an incredible effort to provide the men, the material, and firepower necessary to crush the enemy and drive them beyond the Tamarian border.

Their first task, however, involved holding out for five more days. During this time, resupply trains would arrive every six hours, worsening the overcrowding problem. Colonel Brandt surmised that this waiting period allowed infantry units to deploy in the field, where they would participate in a coordinated counterattack.

The timely resupply of his plucky little firebase and the subsequent campaign to rid Tamaria of its invader, Colonel Brandt reflected, had been assured by the arrival of the teenaged Junior Scout he'd sent to command headquarters at Burning Tree. The Tamarian colonel believed that no other singular deed had as much bearing on the outcome of the imminent battle.

He would never know the real truth.

***

Heavy rainfall poured from the dark grey, afternoon sky as twelve stern-wheeled steamboats leased by the Maridom Trading Company labored upstream toward the tiny dock in Helena. Unable to accommodate such large vessels at its rickety pier, Alonso Meta, who served as the local port master in addition to his duty as mayor, instructed the boat pilots to drop anchor and moor their vessels in midstream.

Standing in the dry comfort of a second-floor hotel window, Lord Velez watched Mayor Meta greet the merchant master, imagining that Alonso would probably offer effusive apologies for the rain, as if the weather was behaving like some wayward child having a tantrum. Shifting a pair of binoculars to study the face of the merchant master, Lynden Velez felt his pulse quicken.

"Tirra!" he called, a sudden anxiety sharpening his voice far beyond its normal tone when addressing servants.

The Lithian woman quickly entered from beyond the door, worried that the stress in her master's voice revealed some unforseen issue that might ruin their carefully crafted plan. "Yes, my lord," she replied.

Lynden beckoned her to approach the window, then returned his gaze to the scene below. "The situation is urgent. My daughters are in peril."

Evacuation had been planned only the face of an immediate threat. "Why, my lord? What's the danger?"

Lord Velez took a step back and offered the Lithian woman a view through his binoculars. "The man who would force Brenna to marry against her will is traveling among the merchantmen."

Tirra, who'd served as Brenna's maid for as long as Lord Lynden's eldest daughter had been alive, uttered an invocation as she twirled for the door and dashed down the stairs. The light patter of her swift feet on the street faded as the hotel door banged against its latch.

Using his binoculars again, Lynden checked the river's water level against a small mark painted on a stick stuck into the far bank several yards upstream. This unobtrusive gauge recorded that the flow had been falling for hours. Now that the boats were in port, the time had come for the river to rise again.

He sent a message to Sherman Mason, ordering all work under the engineer's supervision to begin. Every unit in Lynden's personal army went on alert, especially those deployed near the river. Another command went to Aril at the debris dam locks, followed by a report to Alexina that he'd started the clock on her operation.

Down at the dock, he could see a problem developing. Steamship crew members started unloading cargo, much to the dismay of Alonso Meta, who argued helplessly, but couldn't stop the work. As the crates piled up on the shore, Lynden took his rifle, called for Tegene and a company of elite troops, who followed on horseback as they marched to the riverbank.

The warlord did not dismount when the merchant master approached, nor did he return the feigned delight of Fang's greeting. "What do you think you're doing?" Lynden replied tersely, speaking through a translator, as Lord Fang and the locals did not understand Lithian. "Who gave you the authority to unload here?"

"This little venture is another of my many mercantile subsidiaries," Nemesio explained, gesturing broadly toward the heavily laden steamships in the river. "We have important business with the Tamarians over the mountains, so the unloading must begin immediately."

Calling for his troops to chamber rounds in their rifles, Lynden put an immediate halt to the unloading. "The locals tell me that you must be entertained, so I'll tolerate your unwelcome arrival until your men have had their fill and rest, but not a moment longer.

"Tomorrow morning, you will go back the way you came. If you have any commerce to conduct with the Tamarians, do it on their soil, not mine!"

Lord Fang, taken aback by the threat, needed a moment to regain his lost composure. He noticed movement on the nearest barge deck as the men on watch prepared to fire their own guns in his defense. Their actions calmed him, but he held up his hand to prevent the outbreak of a fight. This venture was too valuable to run afoul because of a minor insult from a petty warlord.

The merchant master narrowed his eyes and spoke in a menacing tone. "I've graciously overlooked your baseless attacks on my honor. I did not contest the court ruling that cheated me out of your daughter's hand! But I will conduct business if I must do so by force of arms, and I will not take orders from you!"

Lynden wheeled his horse around, glancing at the assembled villagers, who'd discreetly moved away from the scene for their own safety. "My daughter's hand is neither mine to give nor yours to possess, and you don't need another wife. You speak of honor, yet you have none. I believe nothing you say, and we are done negotiating.

"You didn't come here to fight. You're outnumbered, outgunned, and I will not hesitate to defend my rights on this land. Don't insult the hospitality of my people. Take your food and drink, then go back from whence you came."

Lynden urged his mottled gelding onward and rode off, trusting that his armor – along with sniper teams he'd hidden along the shore and among the rooftops – would protect his back from any foolishness Fang might order. In doing so, he gave the merchant an opportunity to save face by explaining the confrontation to the mayor and the villagers in Kamerese. Any misunderstanding that might develop could be explained later. At the moment, Lynden had more important matters pressing on his mind.

Three hundred yards downstream, at a place where the river narrowed as it cut through high, rocky banks on either side of the shore, Sherman Mason and his crew labored relentlessly in the cold current. Five corrugated culverts, placed upright so that the water could flow around them, lay in a straight line from the near to far bank. From a temporary pontoon bridge equipped with portable cranes, squads of soldiers lowered large buckets into the culverts, then dumped the drawn water back into the river.

Sandbags, placed around the inside edge of each cylinder when the water inside was only knee deep, held the pipe in place while the work crew gently placed felled timbers on the upstream side of the culvert line and sunk them to the river bottom with tied-on weights. Additional sandbags, lowered into place over every row of timber, formed a crib dam that served to hold back some of the water flowing downstream.

The water level behind the dam began slowly rising. Sherman Mason estimated that the river needed to swell no less than three feet above flood stage for Alexina's plan to work. By measuring the water flow with a weir, he calculated a time interval of roughly six hours before the river would reach its recommended height – perhaps a little less, depending on rainfall. In that interval, Mason's crew had to work hard to finish their task, but he felt confident that they'd complete the dam on schedule.

"I'm still concerned about the explosives," Sherman explained, his worry illustrating that he didn't fully trust the power that Allfather could wield through Lady Alexina. "If they get wet and don't blow, this thing is going to be a whole lot harder to tear apart than it was to build."

Lynden nodded, understanding. "There is risk in every undertaking, my friend. I think the enchantment sequence will dry the charges, but if not, the river current itself will work in our favor."

After visiting the crews on the pontoon bridge, Lynden felt satisfied that their work was progressing as planned. Riding along a narrow path across an abandoned vineyard and through the forest, the warlord checked the troops on picket duty, and confident they were alert, rode on to survey the banquet preparations.

One of the local wineries kept its seasoning casks deep inside a series of caves cut into a hillside, so that the wine ageing process might benefit from the cool, even temperatures prevailing underground. Among many connected chambers, two large rooms often served as an exclusive dinner club for the landlord.

Normally, kerosene lanterns and oil torches lit the facility, but on this occasion, Lady Alexina provided candles that cast much of their light in the ultraviolet spectrum, creating gentler shadows on the rough-hewn rock. White linen tapestries woven in subtle, shaded mosaic patterns, hung from hooks on the walls. The artwork added elegance to the cavernous area, and reflected enough candlelight to make the rooms bright. It also meant that Lithian eyes would see better in here than those of their human guests.

This evening's menu consisted of curried salmon, rice pilaf, a spicy vegetable medley, green salad, bread, and a cheese platter served with local wine, all prepared by the Velez family kitchen staff. Chamber music accompanied the food service to keep the mood calm. Lynden also assigned selected soldiers to conspicuous posts within the two rooms to ensure that the proceedings did not become rowdy.

With everything in order and meal preparations well underway, Lynden thanked everyone for their efforts.

Just before leaving the winery, Lynden received a message that Lord Kerry Halvord, an old friend who'd evacuated Illithia before the invasion, had arrived at a downstream checkpoint. Lynden ordered the messenger to send Lord Halvord to the school gymnasium immediately.

Helena's large high school lay unused and had fallen into such disrepair, the roof of one building had already collapsed. Its gymnasium, however, functioned as a town hall and storage facility, and as such, the effort to keep it in good repair showed. Throughout much of the day, the relocation of warehoused goods and diligent cleaning turned the dusty building into an emergency shelter, a role it could retain for years to come.

Lord Velez checked to make sure that cots, blankets and pillows were properly stowed, so that it didn't look like advance preparations had been made for a large number of men to billet overnight. The guests would set up their own accommodations later in the evening.

When Dr. Halvord arrived, Lynden greeted him with an affection that spoke of long friendship. The Lithian physician now owned a steep, rocky plot of land to the west with few residents and little hope of growing good crops. During his search for an appropriate land purchase, the doctor specifically sought inexpensive, river front property and promptly built a dock to moor his small fleet of sail and steam-powered barges. Since farming in this region yielded erratic profits, Kerry hoped to prosper transporting trade goods along the windy river canyons.

No one, other than Lord Lynden, knew why he'd been invited to the banquet. The evening's planned activities provided Lynden with a means to change the shipping habits of Helena's port authority, while simultaneously helping a friend establish his business in the northern frontier. This change would give local products access to markets that Dr. Halvord had already established.

Furthermore, Lynden could do this out of necessity, without being accused of patronage. When he explained his intentions to Lord Halvord, his longtime friend expressed enthusiasm for the idea and delight at the thought of helping to bring Fang to ruin.

"That man is a menace to every living female under heaven!" Kerry observed. "The virgin daughters of Kameron will honor you for ridding the world of him."

Lynden put a servant in charge of Kerry's comfort, urging his friend to relax until the time arrived for the banquet. When he returned to the hotel, Lynden checked in with Tirra and retired to the solitude of his room to wait until the river reached its appointed mark, hours later.

During this idle period, the possibility that his mission might fail for reasons beyond his personal control haunted Lynden's mind. Knowing that worry would handicap his ability to think clearly, he left the operational details in the capable hands of his subordinates, and invested his time privately seeking Allfather's blessing in prayer and meditation.

His thoughts drifted back many years, to his first encounter with Alexina. Their respective collegiate teams had faced one another in a very rough game of lacrosse one hot afternoon. She ran with such speed and agility no one could stop her, but during a daring move to snatch a high pass, the two collided, fell, and he landed on top of her. She remained so focused on the game that she pushed him off, sprang to her feet and didn't remember the incident.

He, however, could not forget . . . .

Lynden thereafter obtained permission to court the beautiful maiden, dreaming that she would one day become his bride. Alexina proved to be a gracious, faithful companion despite strife, sickness, and sorrow. She divided disappointment and celebrated his every success. Lynden thanked Allfather for blessing him with a good wife.

The warlord prayed a blessing on her, asking for strengthened faith so that she could accomplish the work she alone could do that evening. He also prayed for the safety of the soldiers serving under his command, and the citizens of Helena, who would endure the plan's aftermath.

When thoughts of Brenna came to mind, a heartfelt ache spilled into a wordless, solitary tear that coursed down Lynden's cheek. He wanted to embrace his eldest daughter and tell her that he loved her more than words could express. The heartfelt affliction that Brenna might not feel assured of his acceptance and affection lingered like a festering wound. He prayed for her, longing to see his firstborn daughter again.

Allfather, he *believed*, understood this pain. After interceding for Brenna, Lynden asked for a blessing on Cassie, Thea and Camille, and felt a comforting peace settle on his soul. Only then, could the warlord find the willingness and courage to pray for his enemy.

As daylight fled from the stormy sky, the marker on the far bank finally vanished underwater and Helena's dock lay awash in the swollen current of the Virgin River. Only a handful of sentries remained at their posts on board the river barges, struggling to keep dry under the walkways against a heavy, driving downpour. They appeared more bored than vigilant.

The time had come. Lynden dispatched Tirra to the place where Alexina waited, then headed to the winery to take his seat at the banquet. He greeted the locals warmly, but said nothing to Nemesio Fang and his entourage.

Hard rain driven by gusting winds formed thousands of tiny ripples on the turgid current, ceaselessly pattering its swirling surface in ranks that seemed to randomly retreat and advance across the muddy water. Alexina had spent the night working out the math she'd use to accomplish her task. She felt tired, but confident.

Once started, she could not alter the sequence without starting again. That process would quickly exhaust her. So, the Lithian woman rehearsed her plan, then knelt at the bank of the river and entreated Allfather's favor, as three of her daughters were also doing at the observatory.

Lady Alexina began by drawing energy from the clouds, pulling it down in flickering sheets of heat, running from the lower flood control gate all the way to Sherman Mason's crib dam. This undertaking required her to control energy evenly, over the entire distance of the enchantment. Too little, and the effect she desired would not happen. Too much, and she'd set everything around her on fire.

As the Virgin River warmed, vapor began rising above its surface. At that point Alexina called lightning from the storm overhead, creating an intense sheet of blinding light that crashed into the river from where she stood, spreading between Sherman Mason's dam and Maidenhair Creek. The subsequent thunder shook the ground, rattled windows in Helena and terrified the men on watch aboard the cargo barges. It also signaled every Lithian sniper to run for cover. In the darkness, not a single human eye noticed their flight.

Her calculations of the required energy to accomplish phase-change had been correct. Instantly, all the water in the Virgin River boiled into wet steam and billowed from the banks with the wind, exposing naked rock below.

Deprived of buoyancy, each of the heavily laden barges instantly fell nearly seven feet into the empty stream bed, shattering keels, cracking hulls, and throwing neatly stacked crates of cargo into a splintering chaos of wood fiber and cloth. As the mass of the river boats settled, their merchandise flattened under the crushing weight overhead.

Inside the idling boilers on board, the absence of liquid water vaulted temperatures, creating a sudden, exponential pressure increase that ripped the containers apart. Expanding, dry steam propelled shredded steel like twelve huge bombs exploding at one moment. This destruction cast hunks of boiler plate, chunks of hull and engine assembly into the sky, knocking down trees on the riverbank and flinging debris nearly eighty yards in every direction. No one on the barges survived.

Alexina commanded the mist to collect upstream, where she released its remaining energy. Vapor condensed into liquid again. A deep rumble resonated across the landscape as many tons of water poured back into the riverbed and gushed forward furiously. Lady Xina raced for safety uphill with athletic speed. The noise also signaled Aril to open all the gates on the Maidenhair Creek dams.

The Virgin River thundered in her banks, roaring downstream in a ground-shaking torrent like the rage of a vengeful, primordial beast. When the current swept over the remains of the Maridom convoy, it churned the broken vessels into twisted scrap and rapidly thrust their derelict remains northward.

Sherman Mason watched all this with his evacuated crew. It took several minutes for the turgid flood to reach his position, allowing plenty of time for him to detonate the explosives that destroyed the dam they'd labored to build. Just as Lynden predicted, all of the charges were dry, and when they blew, the corrugated culverts tipped over, parallel to the riverbank, as planned.

When the raging river struck the weakened crib dam, the flotsam at its leading edge plowed through the carefully weighted timbers like a massive battering ram, ripping the assembly apart. Angry waters coursed through the culverts and raced downstream, unhindered.

A messenger arrived at the banquet hall, announcing, to the stunned surprise of Lord Fang and his crew, that a flash flood had just destroyed their boats and cargo. Lord Velez raised his eyes to the ceiling and offered silent thanks to Allfather for Cynthia's warning dream, Alexina's clever plan, and the divine mercy to use his family in breaking the weak link in the Azgar supply chain.

Second Thoughts

All of the earlier resolve that Brenna believed she could sustain in Garrick's presence melted away as she prayed over his wounded body in the infirmary. After using her ID from Dead Hand Ridge to gain entry, she'd healed many festering wounds, falling into desperate intercession that he'd survive a serious fever, until exhaustion swept her to sleep. His delirium faded overnight, and when she awakened, the young woman thanked Allfather and prayed for the desire to forgive him of anything he'd done wrong.

The nurse in charge, a slender woman with greying hair and good manners who spoke passable vulgate, arrived for her rounds and told Brenna that the cadet had staggered into General Ziegler's office, delivered his message from Dead Hand Ridge – along with a roll of film – then collapsed on the floor from exhaustion, pain, and blood loss.

"He'd been muttering something about a wolf," the nurse told her as she set out fresh clothing, a new uniform and parka for him. "But he was incoherent. We think he stumbled into a bear's den for shelter during a storm, aroused the creature, but managed to get away because it was groggy from hibernation. He's lucky to be alive."

Brenna, having examined bone-crushing bite marks on his left shoulder, deep gashes on his arms and upper thighs that evidenced powerful claws – wounds that nearly grazed his genitals – along a badly mangled left hand, knew the monster he'd faced. Few people endured the fury of a deathwolf and survived, let alone travel for two days before reaching help. Tough torso armor and a loin guard had saved his life until she arrived. Garrick's courage and determination inspired her admiration, overruling conflicting emotions to the extent that she found herself blinking back tears when he finally stirred from his sleep.

His smile disarmed her doubts, while the strength in his grasp reassured her of his recovery. His expression revealed an endearingly boyish infatuation that gradually melded into something much more serious. "Brenna," he said, summoning a different kind of courage, sitting upright and taking her right hand in both of his, "I love you."

She had known this long before he'd found the fortitude to utter the words, and sensed that speaking them revealed more about the extent of his trust in her than she felt comfortable admitting to herself. For a moment, she considered saying nothing about her knowledge of his past, fighting against a more rational belief that revealing truth now – bitter as that might be to him – would wisely end their relationship before it developed into something serious and more difficult to discontinue in the future.

Brenna held her breath, uttering a silent prayer, searching for words to explain her doubts in a way that might not hurt, if that were possible. "Did you say that to Gudrun?" she asked, regretting the question immediately.

Garrick's face froze for a moment, indicating he'd been caught off guard, but he didn't betray any guilt by quickly looking away. He let out a deep sigh, closed his eyes and muttered an expletive in his native tongue. When he opened them again, Brenna's expression had turned cold. "Yes," he replied, "I've told Gudrun that I love her."

Although she didn't intend to sound harsh or condemn, Brenna had no idea how quickly her interrogation eroded the young man's confidence in her sincerity. "And how did she react?"

The young soldier dropped her hand and flopped back against his pillow. "No better than you are," he complained, successfully fighting tears and covering deep hurt by venting a bit of anger. "The only difference was that she laughed about it. I suppose your age and wealth has endowed you with better manners than she can muster."

Stung by the acid remark, never having heard such words from Garrick's lips, Brenna struggled against the urge to retaliate. She refrained, partly in shock, but mostly because she loved him and didn't want to see him hurt. "That's not fair, Garrick," she replied in a strong whisper. "You've said absolutely nothing about her. How do you expect me to react when she tells me her baby belongs to you, and that you forced yourself on her? The thought of anyone acting so coldly and irresponsibly is reprehensible!"

Garrick shook his head and crossed his strong arms. "Why should I have said anything to you about her? What happened between the two of us has nothing to do with you. No one gives me any credit for self-control. Everyone assumes that her story is absolute truth, and that I'm a rabid sex freak who foams at the mouth when I'm alone with a girl. You, of all people, know me better than that!"

The truth of his testimony clamored for recognition in her mind, but the momentum of her argument brought out the one bit of evidence that worried her the most. "Yes, you've always been careful with me. But Garrick, the boy looks just like you, and that makes her story compelling."

An expression of incredulity washed over Garrick's face, his grey eyes rolling in disbelief. "Did you look at her? She's my cousin, Brenna! People who don't know that often mistake us for siblings. Her boy looks like me because *she* looks like me. If you had any confidence in my integrity, family resemblance wouldn't be an issue.

"What really hurts is that in spite of all the time you and I have spent alone together, you're quick to blame me for her promiscuity. I didn't get her pregnant!"

Brenna, not knowing Gudrun and feeling insecure about her own feelings for the young man, failed to appreciate that Garrick might have also exhibited self-control with someone else. After all, she well understood that such restraint did not come easily to most men.

But her personal fear of losing control in his company drove her to impose an unrealistic expectation on him. She'd convinced herself that Garrick should never have put himself into a position where any such accusation had potential merit. That wasn't reasonable, and she should have known better, given the many hours she'd spent traveling in his company, or alone with him, behind a closed door. Yet Brenna – caught up in the emotion of the moment – didn't realize how irrational her argument had become.

"How do you know that the baby isn't yours?" she retorted. "Family resemblance aside, Gudrun says it's true. What does she gain by claiming you're the father of her child? Why would she lie about such a thing?"

Garrick reached for the clothes the nurse had left for him, modestly sliding into undergarments beneath his hospital gown. "There's no point in defending myself when you presume that I'm guilty. I'll admit I have a lot to learn about women, but give me credit for knowing how children come into the world! That baby is not mine!

"And what do you know about Gudrun that makes her accusation so believable? Did she somehow transcend humanity in your presence and prove herself incapable of fabricating a sad story? I don't claim to comprehend her pathology, so if you can enlighten me, I'd gladly learn the lesson. Then maybe next time I'll be wise enough to avoid anyone with soft body, a pretty face and a lying tongue!"

Angrily, Garrick grumbled in guttural words Brenna didn't understand. He stood, slipped into pants and a new shirt with his broad back turned so she wouldn't see the tears he restrained, not fully appreciating how his posture filled Brenna with remorse for discussing the issue at all.

After putting on his boots, Garrick's wet gaze met hers. He saw hurt in her expression, but feeling hurt himself, refused to offer comfort. "I should never have trusted you," he said, then stalked away in silence.

The young soldier ignored Brenna's pleading as he left the infirmary, putting on a parka and gloves as he scurried to find an exit door. Unfamiliar with his surroundings, he picked a roundabout path to the outside, emerging to face a fierce wind blowing small flakes of lake-effect snow. He trotted to the stony shore of Broken Wing Lake, gazing for a long time at its frozen shallows and the long fracture lines running in jagged patterns across the ice. There, confident that no one could see him, Garrick wept bitterly.

***

The base at Burning Tree ranked as the largest military installation in Tamaria. Boasting several thousand acres of expensive lake-front property, its premises served as a training and administrative center for the Southern Defense Command, whose rail and dock facilities rivaled those of many large cities.

Troops had been arriving by steamship for three days. All rail traffic on the western shore of Broken Wing Lake had been re-routed to avoid the Angelgate Mountains, with most of the troops and equipment moving across the lake by stern wheeled boats and then through the secured electric rail tunnels in the Copperhead Range.

Some ten thousand soldiers waited at Burning Tree, scheduled for deployment yet to be announced. Among these, a second lieutenant named Oskar Kohler checked his unit register, noticing a pair of unfamiliar names. "Sergeant Krebes!" he called. "Who are these two new parasites on my unit list?"

Krebes, a career master sergeant who'd been serving longer than his young lieutenant had been alive, knew exactly who the younger man was talking about and responded without looking at the paper. "Velez and Ravenwood, sir?"

When the lieutenant grunted in response, the sergeant continued. "Velez is a medical specialist, a mercenary, and Ravenwood is a scout graduate. They were cleared through General Ziegler's office this morning."

Lieutenant Kohler cursed. With his unit heading into combat for the first time, he had no patience for green recruits who probably didn't know the difference between a rifle and the back end of a pruning hook. The lieutenant, suspicious of the senior officer corps to begin with, believed this foretold bad luck stemming from the disfavor of the spirits. "When they report, put them on latrine patrol and dish duty right away."

"I'm afraid that's not a good idea, sir."

The young officer placed his hands on his hips and glared at the older man, annoyed at the sergeant's casual impertinence. "What do you mean?"

Krebes realized his lieutenant had a lot to learn. "I put their files in your box this morning, sir. The woman is a refugee with exceptional combat medic skills. Having her in our platoon is a bonus. Her dossier practically glows with the good deeds she did down at Dead Hand Ridge. She's also got a written commendation for her role in saving a refugee caravan with just a bow and sword. This is not someone you'd want cleaning toilets. Scuttlebutt has it that she's a *sicklian*, and quite a looker too."

Lieutenant Kohler tried unsuccessfully to hide a sudden burst of interest. "I've been busy. I had no time to read this morning." That wasn't true – and the lieutenant knew it was part of his job to familiarize himself with the soldiers under his command. "What about the other one?"

"He's fresh out of the junior scouts with some combat experience and a recommendation from the general. He's also fluent in vulgate and translates for the young woman."

"Very well. Assign them quarters and notify me as soon as they report. I'll be in my office."

Sergeant Krebes saluted. "Yes sir!"

***

The rapid, polyphonic exchange of counterpointed melodies played over an ostinato bass line drifted through the military chapel, resonating across lovely, hardwood floors to mingle sweetly in the vaulted rafters. There, the notes exchanged overtones as pleasing to the ear as warm kisses delight the lips.

Gudrun Averil could tell – though she could not claim to be a musician – that the composition required a great deal of skill and a lot of practice to play. The Lithian woman excelled at everything she did, it seemed. As Gudrun approached, she noticed that the organist could barely reach the foot pedals and stretched rather awkwardly to ascend scales on the huge organ's second register.

As her slender fingers danced over the keys in triplet patterns, Brenna's concentration temporarily distracted her from the hurt she felt after her argument with Garrick. Brenna heard every error that went unnoticed by the sole member of her audience, grimacing whenever she played a single wrong note or faltered even slightly in her timing.

While the organ produced powerful tones that resonated majestically through its massive pipes, Brenna strained to keep her toes on the right pedals without sliding off the seat cushion. She felt annoyed because she was too small to play the full-sized instrument really well, but also, her lack of practice showed. Still, it felt good to play again after many weeks away from any kind of keyboard.

Gudrun listened for several minutes, her initial admiration of Brenna's skill fading into boredom as she grew accustomed to the complex interaction of melody and rhythm. She'd not come to listen to the woman play, but it would have been rude to interrupt – so Gudrun waited.

Finding Brenna had taken more time than she expected, and the uncomfortable tingle and tight heaviness that signaled she needed to nurse made the young mother anxious to return to her apartment quickly. Her son, Harold, would likely awaken from his nap within the next thirty minutes. Although Gudrun's friend Liese had agreed to care for the boy if he cried, Gudrun wanted relief from her own discomfort soon.

Brenna's heart skipped a beat when she noticed the Tamarian teenager standing near the organ. Stopping abruptly, the Lithian woman turned toward the young mother, not really knowing what to say, and further, not realizing that her silence increased Gudrun's apprehension.

"I'm sorry to bother you," the Tamarian mother began. "But I heard that you're leaving and I need to talk to you."

Noting the young woman's discomfort filled Brenna's heart with dread, as she sensed that what she was about to hear would crush her soul. Careful to conceal her concern, Brenna managed a brief smile. "What about?"

"I've been thinking lately . . . . We all know the spirits are with you. We've never seen anyone fight like you did. You were very brave, and everyone's afraid because the spirits heard us whispering about you."

Brenna remembered the disgust and disdain of the Tamarian mothers, letting the returning hurt she felt dissipate in silence before responding. "Allfather has always preserved and sustained my life. Saving us was his work, not really mine."

"I reckoned you'd say something like that," Gudrun continued, leaning against the organ console. "Maybe the spirits brought you to Garrick because he lives what he believes, just like you do. I admit that when I first saw you I felt a little jealous because part of me didn't ever want him to find a woman he could love, and I didn't want him to ever find someone prettier than me."

"What gives you the idea that he loves me?" Brenna inquired, wishing she could be confident that he did.

The Tamarian mother let out a knowing smirk. "Garrick needs someone to love. He comes from a broken family and can't help it. Besides, you have a beautiful face, a body I'd kill to have, and when I listen to the way you talk, I know he couldn't resist you for long."

Barely able to control a surge of grief welling in her soul over the argument she'd had with him, Brenna bit her lower lip and shook her head. "I don't want to talk about this," she murmured.

When Gudrun noticed the difficulty Brenna was having in controlling her emotions, a blend of fear and guilt made it impossible look the Lithian woman in the eye. Avoiding Brenna's countenance, Gudrun glanced at the organ pipes and the ceiling vaults instead. "That's not really what I came here to tell you anyway," she admitted, letting her guilty gaze drop to the windows and then the floor. She paused for a moment to control the trembling in her fingers, gathering courage before continuing.

"I've been having second thoughts about something I've said that might have hurt you. My Harold's been sick, so I went to a priest, who he told me that the spirits will take my son away to punish me if I don't make it right."

The remorse in Brenna's heart could no longer be restrained. As emotion rose in her misty eyes, the Lithian woman wished she could be alone to let the feeling wash away in a flood of tears. Gudrun didn't have to continue. Brenna knew in her heart what the treacherous teenager was going to say before she uttered another word.

"I lied to you about Garrick, and not just you, I've lied to everyone . . . ." Once she began speaking, Gudrun bared her soul, but not in a way that expressed regret for what she'd done. Her voice remained steady and never faltered while she told the truth for the first time.

"He's always been sweet. And after he arrived on the ranch, he paid attention to me and really listened. I'll admit it was flattering for awhile, but then he kept saying that he loved me, over and over again. I guess I got sick of hearing about it. I wanted him for more than just words, but he was always so reluctant to touch me and love me – you know – like a man touches the woman he loves. I wanted real passion, not some reluctant, juvenile obsession.

"So I ripped up all the poems he wrote and threw away every present he gave me. I made fun of him behind his back and avoided him to the point of being rude, but he kept following me like a puppy dog. Every time I turned around, he was there. All of my friends started laughing because he was so obviously crazy about me.

"It was really embarrassing. Even my *Mutti* tried talking him out of acting so foolishly, but he persisted with his crush until he finally wore her down. A few months later, she actually wanted me to make things right with him, which is kind of like the kiss of death, you know?

"I played the game and started telling her that I was going somewhere with Garrick when I was really spending time with some of the boys in town. He would cover for me. He would lie so I wouldn't get in trouble. In fact, one night I stayed out kind of late and when my *Vati* didn't find me in bed the next morning, he was furious. So I said I'd gone looking at farmland with Garrick, and *Vati* gave him the strap. Garrick took the beating and never said a word! Even after that, he promised he'd never betray me.

"Everything was fine until I started missing my period, and I had to do something before it started to show. I thought *Vati* wouldn't be angry if he believed that Garrick and I just made a mistake and I got pregnant. It was the perfect plan because everyone else thought we were spending all this time together, and I figured he'd go along with it because he said that he loved me.

"But I never counted on him saying no. He told me he was tired of being used and gave me this big lecture about how love is supposed to be pure and work both ways. Well, what does he know about real passion? It made me mad. I wanted to hurt him, so when *Vati* wanted to know who was responsible for the baby, I told him it was Garrick."

Brenna, who had grown up in a family with strong personal bonds and high moral standards, seethed at the injustice of Gudrun's deception. Wiping her eyes dry, the Lithian woman erupted with contempt when she spoke. "You wicked, vain and loathsome girl! You don't realize the damage you've done! You've destroyed Garrick's reputation, and crushed his trust in the higher virtues of love. Worse, you've done this in a cold-hearted way that transcends cruelty. He struggles with trust because of your duplicity.

"I don't know how you can sleep at night, let alone talk about this like you're describing a family picnic. Have you no remorse at all? Didn't you imagine your story would hurt other people?"

Taken aback by Brenna's stridency, and rightly fearful of her wrath, Gudrun felt flustered and held her arms across her trembling body as if trying to protect herself from attack. "I didn't mean it to go this far! I guess I got so used to telling the lie, it almost seemed like the truth to me. It sounded more real to other people after I dressed the story up a bit, they believed me, and besides, what does it matter to Garrick? He hates me anyway!"

"It's not like you didn't give him reason!" Brenna retorted. "He did nothing to deserve this from you."

"Not true!" Gudrun spat. "I told him to back off. I told him that didn't love him, but he didn't listen!"

"That doesn't justify your contemptible behavior. He was at your mercy while you systematically destroyed his honor. The least you could do is tell your family the truth and apologize to him."

Gudrun backed away. "Look, I don't care to hear a sermon from the likes of you! I've said what I had to say, and I don't need your advice about what's right and wrong." Angry, because she knew in her heart that Brenna was justified in this conclusion, Gudrun lashed out before scurrying away. "What's done is done, and at least people won't wonder why he's interested in a *sicklian* slut like you!"

The insult paled compared to the hurt Brenna felt inside for doubting Garrick's character. "You don't deserve him," she whispered at the fleeing figure, wondering in her own heart whether she did, herself.

***

An hour after Garrick reported for duty, Sergeant Krebes marched into the latrine, not bothering to stomp the dirty snow off his boots before entering and thus, ruining the spotless appearance of floor tile the young man had labored to achieve. "The lieutenant has summoned you," the sergeant said, inspecting Garrick's work with satisfaction but offering no word of appreciation. "Secure the scrub gear and report immediately."

"Yes, sergeant! May I have permission to wash up?"

The older man appraised the new recruit, noting his sweat-drenched undershirt, that his pants were now spattered with soap stains and smears of rust from the oxidized bolts that held neat rows of multrum toilets in place on the tile. Few soldiers bothered to get on their knees to clean the floor around the toilets, but this one had done so without being told he had to do it. Such evidence of personal initiative and pride in completing a menial job well impressed the sergeant favorably.

"I'll give you ten minutes, son," he replied. "Don't keep the lieutenant waiting."

"Count on me, sergeant. Thank-you."

After showering and changing, Garrick stepped into Lieutenant Kohler's small office, grateful that he'd cleaned up before meeting his new commanding officer. Heated by a clanging, geothermal steam radiator, the insulating properties of its straw bale walls retained warmth that soon felt uncomfortable, even with a single, east-facing window open to the blustery chill outside.

Garrick's heart fluttered uncontrollably when his eyes rested on Brenna's lovely face, catching there a curious glimpse of expression that blended sadness with fear. He noticed that some fool had dressed her in a winter combat uniform whose bodice buttons strained to hold the fabric in place, forming wide gaps that revealed the lacy, Lithian camisole she wore as an undergarment. This seemed too conspicuous to have been accidental.

Who would do such a discourteous thing to her? She'd removed her parka to deal with the heat in Kohler's office, offering the lieutenant an opportunity to let his eyes linger lecherously upon her ample bosom.

Annoyed, Garrick clicked his heels and saluted smartly. "Private Ravenwood reporting as ordered, sir!"

Lieutenant Kohler moved his gaze from its pleasant fixation and brought it to rest on a file folder whose contents Garrick could not read from where he stood. "At ease, soldier. I hear you speak Southern Vulgate."

"That's correct, sir."

Kohler appraised Garrick with a smirk. "Never bothered learning it, seeing as there was no point at the time." He smiled, leering in Brenna's direction again.

"But since this pretty little thing will be staying with us for awhile, I just might change my mind. She marched in here and wrote your name down. I sent her to get kitted out, and we've been having a real party for a good thirty minutes waiting for you to get your backside down here. Translate for me. What does she want?"

Garrick faced Brenna, afraid to find anger in her eyes; not sure what to think when he didn't see any. "Uh . . . why did you call me in here?" he asked, trying to speak without stumbling over every word and not attaining the level of success he wished to achieve.

"We need to talk," she replied. "Gudrun admitted that she lied about you. I should have felt confident in your integrity, given your conduct with me, and I'm sorry I questioned your honor. Please, forgive me for doubting you."

A quick glance in the lieutenant's direction inspired a racing heart. "Do you understand you've just put me in a difficult situation?" he asked in the most straightforward, matter-of-fact tone of voice he could muster. "This is the first time I've met my new commanding officer, and he thinks you need me to translate for him."

"Can't you think of something to say?" she pleaded.

Garrick paused for a moment before he came up with a suitable lie, then tried not to smile as he uttered it. "It's the ill-fitting combat uniform, sir," he began. "She says it violates every tenant of decency and modesty she learned from her saintly mother. Also, she respectfully requests that you stop staring at her soft parts . . . sir!"

Embarrassment raced across the young lieutenant's face, and he stammered like a child caught stealing. Kohler fumbled through the papers on his desk and reached for a pen. "Get over to the commissary and set her up. Make it quick. We're moving out before nightfall!"

Garrick saluted, then motioned for Brenna to precede him out of the office. "I could get in big trouble for telling tales like that," he warned, quietly. "No officer cares about my personal problems. The army's my only future."

Brenna slid into her parka, chiding herself for making matters worse, rather than narrowing the gulf between them. "I'm sorry," she replied meekly, falling into a silence that she worried would forever prevail between them.

The young man seethed when he learned that it *was* his lieutenant who'd arranged to stuff Brenna into such tight clothing. That casual disregard for her dignity reflected badly on the armed services, but during their perfunctory return to the commissary, Garrick lied again to cover up his commander's actions. He explained that the language barrier had interfered with his lieutenant's understanding of Brenna's true size. That story seemed plausible enough to deflect suspicion, allowing the Lithian woman to exchange her uniform for a larger, looser-fitting one.

The new outfit attracted fewer leering eyes, allowing Brenna to blend more seamlessly into the military environment. She felt grateful that Garrick cared about her comfort and reputation, wistfully wishing they could talk and make things right; but she said nothing because he seemed preoccupied, and was perhaps, too angry to speak.

Trudging through drifts of blown snow, wishing he could find words that would restore his relationship with the beautiful maiden, Garrick searched half-heartedly for Sergeant Krebes. He noticed Brenna squinting and shielding her eyes – behavior he'd not seen before – but felt too afraid to ask why she seemed so uncomfortable outside. His nearness to the lovely woman, coupled with the knowledge that he had to serve as her translator, would have filled his heart with delight before their argument in the infirmary.

Now, however, he struggled with the conflicting need to protect his self-esteem, and his longing to forgive and reconcile, the latter motivated by genuine admiration and the powerful, physical attraction he felt for her. Acting in harmony with his ethics, Garrick had once believed that denying self formed the essence of love. Yet behaving that way with Gudrun resulted in heartache and a ruined reputation. Only stupid people made the same mistake twice, but was it wise to discard a virtuous and beautiful maiden because of a previous woman's misconduct?

Even though Brenna once told him that she appreciated his definition of love, he suspected that her odd obsession to preserve her virginity – and her quick belief in Gudrun's story – fueled irrational fears about his intentions. Garrick decided it wouldn't be fair to criticize Brenna using the same standard he now applied to his pleasure-loving cousin, but he couldn't deny the hurt he'd felt when she so stridently believed Gudrun's story.

To her credit, Brenna recognized her mistake and apologized. This reality revealed maturity and honorable intentions on her part. Yet knowledge of her imperfection didn't soothe Garrick's pain, nor did it calm the clamoring voices of second thoughts echoing within the dark, shame-filled corridors of his young mind.

***

Huge, steel cylinders filled with ethanol stood in deep snow drifts beside the tracks of the military railway station. Distilled from tons of ammonia-processed, pressure treated straw, gravity fed the fuel into a pair of tank cars directly behind a massive, workhorse machine. Frequent, violent bursts of wet vapor streamed from vents near its wheels, its cyclic discharge like the breath of a slumbering monster.

The Model 17 steam-electric locomotive burned ethanol in a turbo-compounding boiler to generate steam. Hot exhaust from fuel combustion turned a hydraulic motor, providing power for its gear system, while superheated steam drove a rotary-valved, radial steam expansion engine at a constant rate. Coupled to a flywheel driving a giant generator and several electric motors, the Model 17 was far stingier on precious fuel than its predecessors. With the help of auxiliary battery power, this locomotive could climb grades that stalled older, less efficient engines in the midst of their ascent.

The Republic of Tamaria had many miles of nightmare hills, though most of the lines through these were being converted to pure electric service as quickly as the national railway could raise capital for the project.

Complex and temperamental, the Model 17 required maintenance and tinkering that bordered on the mystical in order to perform at its peak, so the engineering crews who worked on these machines lavished meticulous attention on the fickle power train system whenever one of them paused at a station to take on fuel and water. Thus, a swarm of skilled crew members fluttered over the locomotive like pest-eating birds on a bison's back.

Brenna cut and folded compress bandages into four-inch squares from rolls of gauze in her medical kit. She and Garrick sat on the platform as he absent-mindedly oiled his rifle and sharpened his bayonet. He kept an ear alert for the order from Sergeant Krebes to board the train, but he and Brenna did not speak during a long delay at the station. Thousands of listless soldiers boarded train after train, departing into the winter darkness while the Fourth Platoon, Epsilon Company of the Fifth Infantry Division, the unit to which Garrick had been assigned, waited.

Their platoon boarded last. Lieutenant Kohler, overtly avoiding eye contact with Brenna to an extent Garrick found amusing, admonished his soldiers to sleep on their train ride. "We have three days of hard marching ahead of us, and I want all of you well rested before we start."

Garrick climbed aboard the final troop car, slowly forging his way through its narrow aisle toward the back. Humid vapor from human breath condensed on windows inside the unheated cabin, enclosing the raw reek of stale air stained with sweat, bad breath and mildew. Through the dark chaos, Garrick felt Brenna's hand grasp his arm, as if seeking comfort, and though he didn't respond, the young man let her touch linger.

Several minutes after sitting on the hard, wooden bench next to Garrick, Brenna heard the high-pitched whine of powerful electric motors above the dull roar of male voices and felt the train's torque push her against the back rest. The tug of its acceleration continued well after the giant machine pulled past the military station and headed west along the southern bank of the Desolation River.

The decision to avoid the Angelgate Mountains and move troops along commercial lines to the west had been prompted by Garrick's discovery and photographs of giants vandalizing the more direct route. Rather than risk the loss of an expensive locomotive and many valuable soldiers, General Ziegler opted for this alternate approach. Although this move required a fifty-five-mile march northwest, following their arrival at Suicide Cataract on the Tualitin, the Seventh Infantry would attack from the southwest, where they'd been ordered to "*Sever supply lines and cut the head off the enemy.*"

General Ziegler's plan called for two divisions to move through the Copperhead Range, march south and attack from its north, relieving the defenders of Dead Hand Ridge. Once the Azgar turned to face their new threat, the Fifth Infantry's assault on their southern – and if all went as planned, rear and lightly defended flank – would recapture the enemy's command center at the Ice Dragon Inn.

The giants, waiting to loot derailed supply trains crossing the Angelgate Mountains, would have nothing to fight. Keeping them out of the battle permitted Tamarian commanders to focus on the invading enemy. The giants would be dealt with at another time.

Garrick knew nothing about the operational details of his mission. Unable to see anything in the overcast blackness outside, boredom and the gentle, side-to-side sway of the train as it rumbled toward its destination, lulled him into sleep.

He awoke nearly five hours later, aware of the amorous sensation of Brenna laying asleep with her head on his left shoulder. An occasional gap in the cloud cover let light from the twin moons, reflected off the snow, illuminate the cabin just enough for Garrick to watch her as she slept.

Brenna believed that Allfather loved beauty. In her flawless feminine form the young man caught a glimpse of her creator's handiwork, a blessing given to please the eye and reverently quiet the soul of anyone who might pause to appreciate God's goodness. Trustingly, innocently she slumbered, her face reflecting the serene peace of a saint in the arms of an angel guardian.

Garrick wanted to take hold of her lovely hands and kiss her gently. He wanted to pretend that nothing had ever happened to disrupt the love he felt for this incredible, intelligent woman and wished with wistful, personal remonstrance that he could re-live their dispute in the infirmary and handle it differently.

The fantasy, however, ended when Brenna woke up and eased away from his shoulder. "I'm sorry," she whispered. "I didn't mean to lean on you."

Something in her posture and tone of voice expressed enough regret to inspire a glimmer of courage in Garrick's heart that matched the mysterious gleam of her bright eyes in the darkness. "I wish you wouldn't be," he replied, holding his breath and bracing for an acerbic remark he hoped would not come. "I wish you'd trust that I love you."

Brenna turned toward him, noting the apprehension in his expression and the endearing vulnerability of a soul willing to believe that she wouldn't hurt him again.

"Garrick, I've prayed about this, and I feel terrible. I've been acting out of fear, not faith. I have no reason to believe that you'd ever take advantage of me. It was wrong to believe you would ever want to hurt me. I'm sorry, Garrick. I should never have doubted you."

Garrick gazed longingly into the soft radiance of her beautiful, bright blue eyes. "I'm sorry for reacting angrily. I regret my impatience and the hurtful words I've spoken in haste. But I can't take any of that back. What can I do to prove to you that I'm sincere?"

Brenna took his left hand in hers, holding it firmly as if she never intended to let him go. "The truth is, I've always been able to trust you. From the moment I noticed you climbing down the hill to help me, in every attitude, in every word and every action, your integrity has been obvious. It's not you. I should have known. I'm sorry that I didn't.

"I love you, Garrick. I hope you can find room in your heart to love me more than you've ever loved anyone in your life. That's what I want from you. That's what I need."

Garrick drew her close, desperately grateful to hold her again, soothed and relieved at the strength of her reciprocal embrace. "I forgive you, Brenna. All I ask is that you trust me and love me back. I'll be gentle with you. I'll always be good to you. I promise."

A warm smile spread across Brenna's face, reflecting contentment. She'd done the right thing and peace filled her soul. Their lips met and lingered – softly and persistently, gently rising in mutual passion. In that moment, she believed that she'd never again fail to trust him, and would never again have second thoughts about choosing to love her brave and handsome Tamarian soldier.

Justice Without Mercy

"You're an absolute idiot! What did you think you were doing defying my authority like that? When did you become so high and holy that you can pass judgment on the rest of us like some vengeful god incarnate?

"Well you're not a god, hairless! I don't even think you're really a man. You're a blithering, blundering, accidental orgasm of two morons too excited to know when to stop fondling each other for the higher good of humanity! You're the progeny of proto-brains who should have been shot for defiling the race. Fortunately you, the vaginal vomit of their unforgivable union, won't live to defile the world with more of your kind."

Legate Braegan spat on the dungeon floor and ground a bit of dry straw into the cold stone with his boot. He ranted scornfully, flinging disgusting epithets and disparaging my character, claiming that I'd betrayed him after he'd taken me under his care.

I didn't fear him anymore, knowing that his insults would soon fall silent, drowned out by the last crack of rifle fire I would ever hear. He no longer held power over me. Braegan's ranting pattered on my ear as harmlessly as rain falls on a rooftop. Though he shouted foolishly, the absurdity of his threats were clarified by a heart beating restlessly closer to its destiny with death.

Every claim of greater glory for the empire sounded like the empty promises of corrupt priests, who for a little gold, offered to spare my soul from everlasting torment. But I was already experiencing an anguish for which their platitudes provided no sanctum, and their prayers no absolution. Glory, whether made of mutable material or of the fine perfection of eternity, could not be a thing bought at the expense of the powerless and still be an asset worthy of my striving to attain.

I'd now set my sights on loftier ideals. In the fine focus of a mind contemplating its end, the grand extortions imposed by the mighty on the meek could not be justified by proud words. My new perception laid bare the avaricious motive of our conquest, exposing its cruelty as brutal and violent. Nothing I'd done in this war had been an act worthy of human pride.

I mused on the fact that nations build armies to defend themselves against the aggression of others, or to project their own to meet whatever ends are justified by political leaders as worthy of the expense. While national interest is collective by definition, personal ambition distorts the pure idea of a population's welfare. The consequences of corrupt leadership decisions directly impact individual soldiers, who must deny themselves and carry out the orders of commanding officers – even if those orders result in the loss of his life.

At one time I revered this kind of loyalty. It appealed to me because a willingness to die for the precepts of a nation-state seems – on the surface – a selfless and noble attribute of the soul. I'd longed for my role to harmonize with the twin paradigms of courage and honor, believing that Azgar society was both morally and intellectually advanced. I found it perfectly natural to presume that our interests were also in the best interest of other nations. I believed in the fundamental goodness of my empire and its people. In retrospect, I learned that we behaved no better than the despots we displaced.

This issue ultimately led to my insubordination. As a citizen soldier, my right to make moral choices had been taken away. I had to obey, or die at the hands of my own people, even though I found the raping repugnant and the slaughter senseless. Our culture had convinced us of our right to conquer and commit atrocities. We'd become angry little gods whose wrath, like a wildfire, couldn't be sated.

My soul searched for an impartial standard by which to judge behavior and condemn the cruelties I'd witnessed, but found only my own mind at work. Do victors create moral authority whenever they triumph on the battlefield, or must everyone answer to a higher power in the end? Does the victory in war belong, as our priests so fervently proclaim, to the nation whose actions most closely approximate the ideal of godliness? If so, why must the gods be appeased with endless blood sacrifice in battle?

Listening to Legate Braegan bring up arguments of this nature felt like listening to an adulterer boast of great love for his forsaken wife. I realized that we could not claim the moral high ground over any of the people whose land we had taken, even though I'd once believed that the morally corrupt and technologically-backward Lithians of Shirak deserved the destruction of their city.

I thought about that Lithian maiden, recalling how her bright eyes glistened in the yellow light. I'd disdained her people and judged her as immoral, but now I finally recognized that she'd not wanted to hurt anyone, even men who'd invaded her home. She hadn't killed me when given the opportunity. With profound clarity, I thought back on that day and realized that every soldier she'd slain had tried to kill her first. Now I understood why she'd been waiting for me to pull the trigger. Now I understood why she hadn't released the arrow she'd drawn for me.

If preserving life is moral, why does a soldier who chooses that path face condemnation? The act of defying a corrupt and senseless authority is far more noble than the mindless conformity for which he would be otherwise lauded when following orders. I concluded that the moral conduct of that breathtaking Lithian girl exceeded my own. The comfort I'd found in justifying the cruelty of our conquest – simply because I was carrying out orders – seemed cowardly in the closer scrutiny to which I now subjected myself.

If my impending death meant anything, it served as justice for my failure to do the right thing sooner. I determined that while the guilty would sit in smug judgment and condemn me for refusing to conform to their most recent act of evil conduct, the cumulative weight of responsibility for my earlier transgressions would be the real reason for my execution.

Driven relentlessly into an abysmal and severe depression by the hopelessness I felt, my slumping sense of personal esteem found a strange comfort in the cold starkness of my prison surroundings. Deprived of food and given only dirty snow for water, my mind felt unfettered of its need for nourishment. In this transcendent austerity, I contemplated my every secret with such focus, I barely noticed the legate's leaving and found cold, dark days drifting into long, wintry nights until my mind dulled and I found myself listening to the screaming wind for hours.

By the time a guard finally brought me some food, I nearly felt too weak to eat. A little while longer, and I might have expired from starvation and exposure to the extreme cold inside my lonely cell. I'm sure this method of execution would have delighted some of our more frugal logisticians.

To my dismay, eating only fueled my despair. Shortly after my second meal, the guards washed me down with water so hot it felt like I was being burned alive, ordered me to shave, then threw me a clean uniform. They told me I had to look presentable for the proceedings.

The senior officers conducted my court martial in the room where I had committed my act of insubordination. Vice-general Diabilos, seated at the head of a long table, presided over a panel of two other vice-generals and three legates, all of whom had been present during the rape. After hearing the case against me, these men would decide my fate by a majority vote, something they could have easily done without the formality of these proceedings.

Legate Braegan acted as the prosecuting officer, looking tired and pale, but sober – for a change. His presentation of evidence, substantiated by my military record and often the testimony of my own men as witnesses, astonished me in its detail.

The legate established me as a renegade officer who resented taking orders. Beginning with my getting lost in Shirak, he portrayed every small error of my brief career as if each incident deliberately undermined his authority, squandered resources, or gave comfort to the enemy.

He reported that I'd underestimated the manpower necessary to take the Ice Dragon Inn, and further, that I'd blundered in a senseless, diversionary attack against Dieter, which resulted in the loss of Sergeant Aransen and his squadron. The inn, he claimed, did not prove satisfactory during his initial tour of the facility because it lacked a source of water and a functional heating plant. He told Diabilos that he'd pointed these problems out to me, but that I'd done nothing to correct them.

What a liar!

Excessively frequent and harsh discipline – meted senselessly and without mercy upon my men – constituted the next theme of prosecution. Sergeant Vitus testified that I'd threatened to emasculate him and pressed my saber against the chest of Lieutenant Hicks for what he called *minor offenses*. The sergeant gracefully omitted what I'd caught his men doing, suggesting, as he verbally danced around the topic, that his squadron had been engaged in releasing pent-up energy, as young line soldiers are inclined to do.

My order to Lieutenant Hicks to care for the female Tamarian soldier underwent a miraculous transformation during the proceedings. Braegan claimed in one part of his argument, that in providing food and shelter for her, I was giving aid to the enemy.

Later in the afternoon, he attested that after the woman had been heard screaming for food and water, my "callous neglect" of her needs constituted cruelty toward a prisoner. The death of Lieutenant Hicks, whom I'd charged with her care, coupled with the fact that I'd been fighting in the foothills for a week under his orders conveniently escaped the legate's recall of facts.

Similarly, my "needless" attack on Dieter became a sinister plot to reward my men with superior living accommodations in exchange for their silence regarding my renegade conduct. Because the messenger never arrived to tell them, my mortar crew didn't receive the orders to move north with the rest of us. Braegan interpreted this as favoritism toward my infantry and engineering troops, as well as a snub against his authority because my mortar unit remained in place, contrary to his orders.

Of course, several officers present at the court martial recalled the legate's anger at me when I had argued for my mortar crew to remain in their position. This incident appeared to establish Braegan's contention that he'd been too long tolerant of my personal disrespect and refusal to follow orders.

Then, he talked about the incident with Centurion Cavelli, the cavalry officer, claiming that I'd ordered the men – who had not been seen since – to advance and engage the enemy without infantry support. Braegan suggested that I did this to gain favor as an aggressive centurion commander in the eyes of the senior officers.

When Vice-general Diabilos requested the written record of this incident, Braegan's signature appeared on the bottom of the document. He'd not been there, so I was not surprised that my own report, as senior officer present, did not make it into the court record. Further, acting as my own counsel with no advance preparation and no ability to call witnesses, I could not rebut the accusation.

Extending his argument, Braegan contended that I engaged the enemy before an adequate number of troops and artillery had come up to support the attack, resulting in heavy losses. He stated that I had no authority to initiate hostilities, which was quite true and understood by everyone present, even though I did have the right to respond in defense of an enemy attack.

Of course that's what I had done, but without the ability to call witnesses, I had only my word to rely on. In this court, that wasn't enough.

My battle actions faced constant criticism, despite the fact that my men successfully forced the Tamarians out of their prepared positions and into a headlong retreat. Braegan claimed that my request for relief was a ruse to cover command incompetence because it came after my failure to support an artillery unit in a heated fire fight.

When the pair of guards I had ordered Sergeant Hanibal to lock in a room stepped forward to offer their testimony, the smirk of triumph on Braegan's face nearly burst into open laughter. The credibility of their story, coupled with their objectivity magnified the only real mistake I'd made in my career, and after this, I gave up any hope of defending myself.

Interestingly, the deed for which I had been arrested never came up for discussion. The court's silence on this issue, the one time I had openly defied a direct order, illustrated the injustice of these proceedings.

Following a contemptuous summary of my behavior as an officer, Vice-general Diabilos read formal charges of insubordination, incompetence and treason. He had me stand and asked me if I had anything to say in my defense, as if my most eloquent words might serve to exonerate my name against overwhelming evidence.

"No," I replied, drawing knowing nods and murmurs from those in attendance.

A brief exchange of whispers among the officer's panel pronounced my sentence with greater effect than a scream. In a stately manner, Diabilos stood and cleared his throat. "This high court of the Northern Liberation Army finds Centurion Commander Dathan Herulus guilty on all counts," he stated. "We hereby impose the sanction of execution by firing squad, to be carried out at noon tomorrow. This court is dismissed."

Although the verdict seemed as predictable as daybreak, its official announcement chilled my soul and left me feeling a deeper despair than words can describe. A desperate desire to survive surged through my mind. I felt like a drowning man gasping for air at the surface of a whirlpool, fighting constant tension between every conclusion my reason had drawn and the intense despondency of a soul wanting to stay alive.

While being led back to my cell, I passed by a window and noticed that the courtyard, which had been crowded with enlisted men and junior officers, now lay deserted. I overheard talk among senior commanders about a flanking maneuver and troop redeployment, but I didn't realize the significance of this discussion.

Unable to sleep that night, I saw flashes of light against the far wall of my cell and listened to a low rumble spread across the Saradon. Hours later, the awesome, unmistakable roar of six inch artillery mingled with the fearful shriek that preceded heavy rocket impacts.

I don't remember falling asleep, but I rested fitfully. My slumber, haunted by vivid visions of impending death, wrought despair throughout the cold, lonely darkness like night terrors stalking a frightened child. My imagination conjured narrow escapes from the firing squad, only to continually confront the dreadful event in its chilling finality. There would be neither rescue nor redemption for me. I'd been condemned, and no one cared.

A sudden, terrifying explosion jolted me from slumber in the weak light of daybreak. Somehow, I'd been aware of the artillery sounds drawing closer, but the direction of the sound had changed and I could tell that lighter guns were now firing. Mortar tubes within the compound opened up several minutes later, followed by rifles fired from within the inn's old walls.

When I heard the sound of keys beyond my door, I knew the dreaded hour had come early. The guard told me that he'd just received orders to take me upstairs without breakfast. When I asked him what was going on in the courtyard, he laughed and shook his head.

Bitter cold and harsh wind bit through my skin as I preceded my escort outside. The thought of going to a place of eternal burning and never having to suffer through another moment of winter seemed mildly comforting as I waited in line for my date with death.

Most of the men being shot were deserters who'd not made it through our picket lines. The blonde-haired barbarian woman whom I'd rescued stared at me until the execution crew put a black hood over her head. She stood motionless while the firing squad readied its rifles, then she squirmed wildly when the rounds impacted her body.

I stepped over her discarded corpse, disgusted by the impotent futility of my attempt to save her from harm. An expression of shock remained frozen on her face. This was the last thing I saw before the hood that had just covered her head came down over mine.

The distinctive sound like shredding glass and the screams of dying men assailed my ears. I heard the loud, rippled cracking of rifle fire and braced myself for an impact that never came. Hundreds of small explosions burst in a frenzied swarm of sound accompanied by the sharp sting of shrapnel pelting my skin. I stood, blinded, for an interminable time.

Screams of rage and agony, the clash of metal, small arms fire and the crunching of many boots filled the courtyard. Commands shouted in a tongue I could not understand became clear as the din of a brief but intense battle died down. Off to my right I heard a female voice speaking my language.

Confused, not grasping the significance of what was happening; I didn't initially comprehend the meaning of the words and didn't think to respond. Someone forcefully removed the executioner's hood, twisting my head downward with such power I thought my neck would break. For a moment, the light hurt, but as my vision cleared, astonishment overwhelmed my soul and stopped my heart for a moment.

The Lithian girl who'd spared my life in Shirak stood in front of me . . . .

Dressed in a barbarian uniform spattered with blood, the lines of her lovely face and abundant form were unmistakable. Stunned to find me beneath the executioner's hood, she stood back and gasped, covering her mouth.

Next to her stood a broad-shouldered soldier, young as the original defenders of the Ice Dragon Inn. His eyes glared vengefully as he dropped the mask in his right hand. In his left hand he held a large caliber rifle with a blood-smeared bayonet that he pointed toward my heart.

"Wait!" the girl entreated, pushing his weapon away. "Please Garrick, don't kill him!"

The young man shook his head. "He deserves to die."

She moved between us, holding her hands outward, like a frail shield protecting me from his wrath. "Yes," she replied. "He's our enemy, but when will the killing stop?"

His eyes flashed between hers and mine. I could sense the struggle between his instinct and the restraint inspired by the young woman's intercession. I could tell he felt eager to finish me off, but she didn't back down.

"If you take his life, how are your actions different from his and those of his people?" she asked, her voice almost pleading. "Right now he's powerless. He can do nothing to harm you, or anyone else. But you have the power to choose between justice and mercy. Allfather alone is righteous in judgment. He alone is right to condemn, but Allfather loves mercy. Justice without mercy is tyranny!"

To my great relief, he *believed* she was right.

Epilogue: My Farewell to the Empire

The verdicts of history depend on the biases of whoever records the events. I found Tamarian military records surprisingly honest in assessing the impact of my nation's invasion. Their assessments described the conflict in a factual manner, avoiding the self-congratulatory language employed by analysts on the opposing side.

General Ziegler's bold flanking maneuver succeeded in recapturing the Ice Dragon Inn. As the two armies battled through the deepening winter, vastly outnumbered Tamarian forces retreated to high ground in the hill country. A long series of attritional clashes ensued, until combat losses and mass desertions forced Lord General Balinor across the Tualitin River. Artillery and rocket barrages reduced the Ice Dragon Inn to heaps of smoldering rubble.

Its ruins were left as a memorial to the fallen.

Operations against the giants began in the spring, with Tamarian forces conducting a crushing campaign to rid the southern mountains of all giants. By late summer, every clan south of Burning Tree had been destroyed.

The Tamarians declined to boast of their eventual triumph because their senior officers realized that extreme cold, disease, starvation and desertion played significant roles in driving back the invader. As small-scale skirmishes and artillery duels continued across the Tualitin for many weeks, the Tamarian political leadership renewed its mutual defense treaty with King Alejo in Kameron.

Lord General Balinor established fortified frontier outposts within a few miles of the Tamarian border and consolidated his hold on lands already conquered, further south. When an envoy from the giant king arrived, he ordered the messenger stripped of his clothes and sent north. Diplomatic relations between the Azgar and the giant clans were never reestablished.

Legate Braegan survived in battle against the Tamarian Seventh Infantry. He earned a promotion after Vice-general Diabilos fell during a heavy rocket attack and returned to Marioch the following spring. His military experience brought notoriety, and the Emperor subsequently appointed him as a regional governor over an area once controlled by Brenna's *Amair,* Lord Velez.

Nemesio Fang lost a fortune when his fleet sank in the Virgin River. He refused transport on Lord Kerry's boats and led his surviving crew on an overland journey home. Fang's extensive land holdings provided a cushion against the disaster. When expanding markets in the profitable opium trade caught his attention, he enlarged his personal army and equipped his men with modern firearms. As Southern Kameron slid into civil war, Lord Fang used the conflict to plot revenge against the Velez family.

Woodwind took the underground rail to Burning Tree shortly after the Tamarian army lifted the siege of Dead Hand Ridge. He spent much of the winter in a frustrating search for Brenna, finding her just before spring arrived, when the Tamarian Seventh Infantry rotated out of the fight and returned to base at Burning Tree. Colonel Brandt recommended Woodwind for an Iron Star, and he became the first foreigner decorated for military service in defense of the Republic.

During breaks in the battle, Brenna composed many long letters to her family, describing her experience and expressing regret that she might have hurt anyone by not returning home as planned. She outlined the terrifying tale of her experience following the demise of Shirak and expressed gratitude that Woodwind had found her.

She also described how she met Garrick, and how deeply she'd grown to love him. Brenna remained in Tamaria, serving with Fourth Platoon – despite suffering a severe bout of snow blindness – until the war ended.

Garrick never received public recognition for his perilous journey to Burning Tree. The event served as a minor footnote in his dossier. However, he attracted attention from senior offficers because of his relationship with Brenna, and the importance of her family in the upcoming Kamerese Civil War. Lieutenant Kohler recommended Garrick for officer training and sent him to Marvic, Tamaria's capital city. There he intended to reunite with his siblings and introduce them to the Lithian woman he loved. Yet nothing turned out as well as he'd hoped.

Once the Azgar war ended, Helder Haas, who'd assaulted Brenna at Dead Hand Ridge, was convicted of his crime in a military court – since the offense occurred in a firebase – and faced a sentence of three years in prison.

In mid-spring, Woodwind carried Brenna's letters across the Tualitin into Kameron, following the Virgin River to Helena. His wartime experience, and the end of his hope for marrying the maiden he loved, left him feeling listless. Woodwind found a new mission working with elite Tamarian forces operating secretly in the wilds of Northern Kameron, but remained part of Lynden's army.

Growing political unrest forced Lord Velez to fortify his land holdings. Though he did not desire foreign funding for his planned economic revitalization, he desperately needed investment, creating a web of interests that extended north, into Tamaria. Some local residents felt betrayed by this foreign influence, but without these connections, increasing turmoil brewing in the south would have quickly ended their dreams of property ownership.

I, Dathan Herulus, spent the winter in a Tamarian prison camp. Four months after my court martial, I faced another trial, this one for crimes against the Tamarian people. Again, I did not contest my guilt. I was sentenced to thirty months of forced labor and a long parole, rather than death. I also had to report my activities with local police.

While my nation raised a new army that lay poised to pounce on Kameron, I remained in Tamaria, where I learned the language and found work as a library historian. In my own quiet way, I had forever bidden farewell to all ambitions of empire.

****

Thank you for reading the Anniversary Edition of ***The Edge of Justice***. I sincerely hope you've enjoyed the story, the first installment of the Deveran Conflict Series.

Other titles include:

The Long Journey
Crisis
Ceremonies and Celebrations
Dreams and Missions
The Inquest
Secrets and Whispers
Blood on the Warpath

Novellas in the same milieu include:

The Girl in the Game
The Hollow Solitude
Four Days to Freedom

More information on the Deveran milieu and characters can be found at the Newadventure web site:

www.newadventure.ca

www.ingramcontent.com/pod-product-compliance
Lightning Source LLC
Chambersburg PA
CBHW020347220726
48290CB00014B/1305